Glass Houses

Glass Houses

Sandra Howard

POCKET
BOOKS

London · Sydney · New York · Toronto
A CBS COMPANY

First published in Great Britain by Simon & Schuster UK Ltd, 2006
First published by Pocket Books, 2007
An imprint of Simon & Schuster UK Ltd
A CBS COMPANY

1 3 5 7 9 10 8 6 4 2

Simon & Schuster UK Ltd
Africa House
64-78 Kingsway
London WC2B 6AH

www.simonsays.co.uk

Simon & Schuster Australia
Sydney

A CIP catalogue record for this book is available from the British Library

ISBN-13: 978-1-4165-2198-3
ISBN-10: 1-4165-2198-4

Typeset by Palimpsest Book Production Limited,
Grangemouth, Stirlingshire
Printed and bound in Great Britain by
Cox & Wyman Ltd, Reading, Berkshire

For Michael, my inspiration and my guide.

Acknowledgements

I owe many thanks to a wide circle of people. To Vivienne Schuster who originally pressed me to have a go at a book and to Hilary Johnson for her invaluable help and guidance in how to write one. I am enormously grateful to Jonathan Holborow for all his colourful and informative tips about the newspaper world – any mistakes and misunderstandings are entirely my own. My thanks to John Wolfe and Malcolm Stewart for their considerable medical expertise; to my accountant, Tony Sullivan for his insights; to Belinda Boraston who, as an experienced carpenter, so helpfully explained the risks from wood-dust and board; and to Paul Tory who also helped with this. My heartfelt thanks go to my agent, Michael Sissons, and to my wonderful editor, Suzanne Baboneau, so unfailingly inspirational and encouraging, and all the team at Simon & Schuster. Finally, I must thank many long-suffering friends and my family: Michael, who found new, and previously undetected, reserves of patience, and my three children, Sholto, Nick and Larissa, who showed me the light in so many ways.

'Of all forms of caution, caution in love is perhaps most fatal to true happiness.'

Bertrand Russell

CHAPTER 1

'I'll go for them,' Barney offered. He was good in the mornings, even after a heavy night's drinking. Victoria found it irritating, though she wasn't entirely sure why.

'No I will. I feel like it – I want to,' she said rather desperately, knowing he would have pottered and been ages, wandered up to the King's Road for croissants, probably, and chatted up a girl over a quick espresso. She had to see the papers: they'd been tipping her for a job in Government and it was three days after a General Election, the moment of truth, the weekend when MPs were tensely waiting for calls.

She left, feeling a sense of release at being out of the house. It was a dewy October Sunday morning, pale-gold, as though the sun were behind gauze, and the air was still, with no noise of traffic. She was so on edge. Downing Street wouldn't call, she wanted it too badly; it was like waiting and hoping for a lover to propose.

Looking back at the yellowish-brick Victorian house with its holly-green front door, she thought it had been a lucky buy, years ago, just before a property boom. They were small terraced houses and aside from the elderly couple next door, Hartley Street was popular with rich divorcées and young City couples with a first child. The front gardens had bay trees, camellias, solanum, and clipped box: typically chic Chelsea. Theirs let the side down a bit, though the Penelope roses were still flowering and a stout hydrangea was turning a glorious autumnal red.

The corner shop was in a parallel street and run by the Vhadi family. Victoria went in under the blue awning sheltering the fruit and veg and gathered up five Sunday papers, resting their weight on the tall counter.

'A lot of reading there, Mrs James,' Mr Vhadi said, smiling, half-eying a youth swinging open the cooler-cabinet door. 'Congratulations on the Election result, by the way.'

'Thanks very much. I'm glad it's all over.'

'I read they might be making you a Minister.' He sounded curious.

'You shouldn't believe all this stuff in the press,' she laughed feeling the strain. He was methodically easing the papers into a flimsy carrier and she burst out, 'Don't bother, I don't need the bag,' but he carried on and handed it over with blandly friendly eyes.

Turning back into Hartley Street, she had to negotiate a lumpy old woman with long straggly grey hair like a wizard's, whose two muscular mongrels were pulling on leads. Her black matted sweater was covered in stains and it was easy to imagine a lonely life in some squalid block of flats with drunken neighbours and dropped needles on the stairs.

But she had her dogs. And her life might be just as she chose, Victoria thought, giving the woman a brief flutter of a smile then carrying on, feeling an inarticulate anger welling up in her that the same couldn't be said of her own.

If the call from Number Ten actually came, it would be bitter-sweet, a thrilling chance, a whole new artery of opportunity, but Barney would react badly. Every breakthrough, every threshold reached, it was always the same. Even in her barrister days he'd been resentful: it was so wearying and debilitating. He liked having an achieving wife and talked proudly, almost as he would about the size of a fish he'd caught or a new car. He wanted it both ways, she thought despairingly. Politics, for some reason, particularly rubbed him up. Winning Southampton East so unexpectedly five years ago had been a bad night, certainly no warm words or celebrating.

The press had got wind she might be knocking out a Junior Minister and had turned up in their droves. Barney had been all smiles and kisses at the count – 'my wife the MP!' – but later, at home, he'd shown his darker side. His worst eruptions could be counted on her fingers; she understood them but they were indelibly etched and not something to share.

Would the call come? 'Downing Street here, Mrs James.' Her adrenaline fired up with fresh coals. Barney was so perverse. He would mind almost as much if it didn't come; he cared in his own way, and after all the press build-up he'd hate facing his grey-suit solicitor colleagues at Simmonds & Key with no news.

She thought about loss of privacy. Ministers were shielded by the Private Office but also glaringly exposed. Barney liked the lime-light though and her long hours, that so suited his lifestyle, would be even longer. There would be compensations. Her constituents made a big fuss of him, too. 'You're such a tease,' old ladies would say. 'Such a one!' They all adored him.

People did. His hair was the butter-yellow of a young child's and always sexily in his eyes; he was constantly throwing it back. He should never have been born blond, Victoria thought irritably, going in at the gate of number sixteen, her stomach taut as a drum.

She was greeted by tempting smells of sizzling bacon and freshly brewed coffee. She felt grateful that Barney loved cooking – he was a natural – and he took wonderful photographs too, beautifully composed like paintings. But any list of his talents, she thought sarcastically, had to include his women – he had a particular gift there. It was a fundamental problem; their relationship lacked constancy and a sense of completeness, that Plimsoll Line of trust. It had done since the very beginning, sixteen years ago, even before their daughter Nattie was born.

Victoria went down the flight of stairs that led straight into the big knocked-through kitchen, a good space where they did all their living. There was the television, bookshelves and an old blue-check sofa at one end, glass doors to a patio with a vigorous fig tree at the other, and on the wall opposite the stairs, set into a chimney breast, was the small wine-red Aga – Barney's most successful extravagance. All his herbs, oils, cookbooks and copper pots were on alcove shelves and the kitchen was always snug. When Nattie was home for Sunday lunch or school holidays she would sit on the Aga's sturdy silver rail with her feet on a chair and phone all her friends.

Barney put the bacon in to keep warm and came to take the papers. He thumped them down on the kitchen table. 'God, you've bought an entire tree! No nice fresh croissants – or did you forget?' He knew the shop never had any.

'Don't be so loud, I want to hear the radio,' Victoria said crossly. They were talking about Chris Hartstone and Cabinet jobs. Chris had been Shadow Health Secretary in Opposition and she his junior.

She stood listening. 'Hartstone will get Health, that's a no-brainer,' a political commentator was saying. 'And Victoria James will probably go there too, I'd say. They worked well together in Opposition. She's relatively inexperienced, but has just the media-friendly image they're keen to promote.'

Barney was propped on his arms reading a football report but taking it all in, she was sure. He straightened up and grinned, slightly edgily. 'There you are – home and dry.'

'Don't do this to me, just don't!'

He kissed her lightly on the lips. 'You'll get in on looks alone,' he murmured, getting more into the kiss then, when all she wanted to do was read the papers.

'We should call and see if Nattie's coming out.'

'I just did; she's not. She's having lunch with Maudie and her parents at that new place in Newbury, the one written up for its amazing crèche – her parents have that afterthought, remember?' His teasing grin was back; he'd looked a bit piqued at her unresponsiveness. 'Couldn't we have one? Ministers can have babies in office, can't they?'

Victoria ignored that. 'You might have waited till I was here,' she complained. 'I wanted to say hello.' Nattie was home from school most Sundays though, and perhaps it wasn't the perfect day for a relaxed family lunch. God, the waiting was awful.

Barney kissed her again, pressing hard on the seat of her jeans. She brought his hands round and held on to them. 'Not now, love, let's have breakfast. I'm starving!'

'Lucky you never put on weight,' he threw back, going to the Aga. 'Just think of all those lunches and dinners you'll soon be eating . . .'

'Are you being deliberately cruel?'

He produced the food and she could finally look at the papers. All the political pundits had her down for a job in Health or Culture.

Her life would be so changed. She thought of the long slog, the speeches to handfuls of people in cold village halls, late sittings, occasional praise; was it all about to be worth it?

Her father, a doctor, had been found guilty of euthanasia in the distant past, but far from a brake on her progress, it had given her curiosity value, a slight notoriety. John Winchwood had had a keen interest in politics and shared it; as children, she and her older brother Robert had argued hotly about issues such as Greenham Common and Star Wars. Excited by the idea of advocacy, she'd been set on the Bar; politics as a career simply hadn't entered the frame. That had happened accidentally, one of those capricious fancies of fate – a nerdish boyfriend taking her to an Oxford Union debate, a thought-provoking speaker and the seeds of interest sown.

She remembered the Union Chamber seeming like a smaller, slightly moth-eaten House of Commons, and being surprisingly seductive, with its old brown-leather benches, not the green of the Commons or the Lords' red, although the President's chair could have rivalled the Speaker's. The pimply little incumbent of the day had looked quite lost in it.

An Ethical Politician is a Contradiction in Terms had been the motion and invited grandees had taken part: a journalist who had wittily mined the rich seam, and a politician – one of those called the best Prime Minister the country never had – who'd defended with passion. Political decisions taken for the greater good, he'd said, but perhaps causing loss of jobs, for instance, might seem harshly uncompromising but it was ethical, the moral thing to do. He was dismissed as an apologist yet in Victoria he had aroused some hidden spark. That evening, her life had swung like a weather-vane and suddenly pointed in a new direction.

The call came at two. Victoria shot upstairs, ripped off her jeans and flung on the carefully considered taupe skirt and tweedy jacket. It looked dreary as cold tea. She pulled on high-heeled chocolate leather boots and felt better.

'For God's sake!' Barney called upstairs. 'They don't want you till four – come and finish your lunch. I'll drive you there if it'll calm your nerves.'

She raced down to the kitchen again. 'Would you?'

'Sure. And I'll wait – it won't take long, will it? I can read the papers.'

'What's this all about?' She was suspicious of such untypical accommodation.

'Love of my wife,' he said, with another of his maddening grins.

'I want you to be Minister of State for Housing and Planning at the Department of the Environment. Ned Markham will be your Secretary of State.' The Prime Minister was smiling.

Victoria stared, astounded. The job was so unexpected. Straight to the middle ranks; he must surely hear her heart thudding. Apart from a Private Secretary taking notes they were alone in the Cabinet room. A commanding portrait of Sir Robert Walpole hung over the mantelpiece behind the PM, who was seated halfway down the vast table.

He took off his glasses and looked at her expectantly. He had pleasing looks, brown hair, a quiet manner but well-expressed convictions; people admired him for being both sincere and practical. He had won them over against the odds and injected real excitement. They thought he would get things done.

'I'll do my very best, Prime Minister,' she said, the words coming tumbling out.

He half-rose. 'And one day, I hope you'll be sitting where I am!' She got up on cue, taken aback by the flattering remark, and thanked him with a glowing smile. Leaving, she decided he probably said the same thing to everyone he appointed.

She hung on to her smile for the matronly woman minding the Cabinet Room, for Private Secretaries, and outside on the steps of Downing Street she offered it shyly to the huge mass of media.

'Over here, Victoria. This way, there's a love!'

'What you got? Health, Culture, Education?'

She walked down to the fortress gates feeling eyes and cameras on her back and worrying futilely about the high-heeled boots. Her insides were fluttering like a trapped bird. To have had five minutes in Downing Street and come out a Minister was a wonder and unreal, but the job was going to take guts of steel. It would be so very easy to fail.

Barney had parked his white BMW off Parliament Square a few minutes' walk away. Victoria flung herself in and couldn't help bubbling over with her news. He chucked a newspaper on to the back seat and flicked on the ignition. 'Well done. You know fuck-all about housing, though – it's hardly your area is it?'

It *was* his, she thought; he had property clients and a big new one, too. And she'd dismally failed to play things down. 'You know it's not about areas,' she said meekly.

Driving away, he turned and glared accusingly. 'They can't have put Markham in the Cabinet! He's a fossil, a throwback. When did Ned Markham ever get on a number eight bus?'

'He probably came here on the twenty-four, as he lives in Pimlico.'

'Don't give me Pimlico. He owns half bloody Staffordshire, for God's sake!'

'So? He's well qualified to look after the environment then, isn't he?' She felt angrier for knowing Barney had a point – Ned was actually quite sharp but he did hide it well.

Stopping at a traffic light, Barney tucked her hair behind her ear and brought his hand to her cheek. His hazel eyes were conciliatory. 'Thinking about Nattie?'

'Yes – it's how she'll cope at school. I'm going to be so under fire from the media in this job – really in the eye of the storm. I get to do Downsland, Barney. It's for me to recommend giving it the go-ahead or not, and that's a hellish responsibility. There's nothing more controversial at the moment.'

He seemed unsurprised. With his quick mind he must have got there already. Downsland was a proposal for a whole new town to be built in lovely countryside south of Dorking. To the residents it was an unparalleled disaster, to conservationists an ecological one – nightingales were scarce in Britain and they nested in the local thorn thickets – and to glamorous young protestor Sam Swayne, camped at the site with his supporters, it was a chance and a challenge to slay the Goliaths of Government and the developers.

There could be Downsland locals at Nattie's boarding school, Victoria thought wearily, and it was a cause the Sixth form would care about. 'Natalia's mother only wants to bulldoze the whole Green Belt!' How would she take it? How would her parents ever know, with that barbed-wire cordon of teenage stroppiness?

Barney parked untidily as though he didn't intend being long. Even before they were indoors he said, 'You haven't forgotten I was seeing Dick for a quick drink?'

It was news to Victoria and she felt winded. 'I thought we had something to celebrate.'

'Of course we have, silly, but I must go. It is a potential client, hon, and you know how Dick needs his hand held.'

Dick's hand? On a Sunday early evening? Her unspoken objection tasted sour on her tongue; it was her moment, her day, after all. Barney would come home later, and be all sweetness and light and obliging. He was never going to change.

She made calls. Telling her parents was heartening but Nattie could have sounded a bit more thrilled. 'That's really cool, Mum, wonderful. Got to rush, see you!'

Dinah would cheer her up, Victoria thought. They went back a long way, she and Di; they'd shared a room at university. Di had terrific style: leonine looks, streaky blonde hair, a handsome big nose and warm eyes, green as malachite. She was a talented artist specializing in painting façades and interiors, and was never short of clients. It was an uncomplicated friendship; they led different lives and had never felt a need to compete.

'Can you take me through it,' Di said, 'where a Minister of State fits in?'

'The most junior Ministers are Parliamentary Under Secretaries of State – they get called pussies – then it's Minister of State and then you're a Secretary of State and in the Cabinet!'

'So you're jammy, you've skipped being a pussy and you're in line for the rotten eggs!'

Barney was at the door and Victoria ended the call.

He came in, all energy and exuberant chat, with flowers and champagne. 'Dick was gobsmacked and sends huge congrats! I didn't say what job,' he added hurriedly, 'I know that's still under wraps. These are for you.' He thrust the bunch of white chrysanthemums at her.

'But you knew we had champagne here,' she couldn't help saying, trying to banish the thought that the flowers had come from some girl's flat; they had a slightly room-wilted look.

'I got us a nice chilled bottle. I had to go, darling. Dick couldn't pull in new business if his life depended on it – although,' Barney said, taking off the foil. 'This guy was into brewing a special beer for Indian restaurants and I think we're too staid for him!'

She felt somewhat mollified, though Barney was a master of believable yarns. Dick, another partner in the firm, was his great golfing mate and so boring he could send people to sleep before the soup. He had a wiry wife, June, who had close-cropped hair like a scrubbing-brush and some hard-to-fathom appeal for Barney. Time on her hands for extended lunches, probably. There were no children. June and Dick were a rather sad couple, Victoria thought.

They had the champagne and watched the news. The first Cabinet appointments were announced and there were flashes of the later comings and goings. She saw herself leaving Downing Street. The commentator seemed impressed. The junior positions weren't to be decided till the following day.

Barney gave her a dig. 'You can't have that frightened wimpish smile any more. You're in the driving seat now, hands on the levers of power!' He was sounding cheery but she knew it was cloaking jealous sensitivities.

'Hardly,' she said lightly. 'Certainly not if I make a hash of things. And the downside starts right away, darling, with no more proper privacy. I know it's a lot to ask.'

He took that as a putdown. She felt his body go tense and longed not to have said so stupid a thing. 'I'll do something about supper,' he muttered, getting up without a backward look.

Victoria was thinking about her new boss, Ned Markham, as they sat down to eat. She liked him but he was hardly Modern Man. Could you really have a Cabinet Minister who strode his estates while the world moved on and transsexuals could change their birth certificates? And Ned, with his passionate love of the countryside, would be temperamentally opposed to Downsland, she thought – but perhaps that was being unfair.

The following night, they were due to have dinner with Barney's senior partner, Hugh Simmonds, his wife, Mandy, and the big property client Barney looked after.

'What are you thinking about so hard?' he demanded suddenly.

'Just that I shouldn't really come tomorrow evening,' she said slowly. 'It's best I don't meet Roland Chalfern now I'm doing Housing. He might even be involved in Downsland.'

'For God's sake! Chalfern's into buying failed factories, building on the land, that sort of thing. You must come. He'll know you have to be punctilious. It would be letting down Hugh – and fucking up Mandy's seating plan.' Mandy Simmonds was a humourless pain; neither of them could stand her and regularly picked her to bits.

Barney could be very endearing, but he tried too hard with his Harrow- and Cambridge-educated senior partner, Victoria thought. He had some ridiculous inferiority complex, but it was such nonsense. Hugh was mild-mannered, dull; completely harmless.

Barney's lack of confidence was hard to understand. He was a diplomat's son; he'd gone to a West Country boarding school and got a first at Exeter. Had he missed out on proper family life? His mother had died from breast cancer when he was fifteen and his father retired early to Cornwall where he lived on gin and grew orchids. There was a much older brother out in Japan. Victoria knew that with all his insecurities, Barney leaned on her and needed to be emotionally propped up. She understood that and accepted it, but there were limits to holding back with her own career.

He was looking cajoling, 'Chalfern's been asking to meet you, hon, and think of Hugh's surprise, the Housing Minister coming to dinner!' She knew she had to go.

It was another sunny day. When Victoria went out at eight o'clock, the appointed time, a silver ministerial Prius was waiting outside. The driver got out to meet her. 'I'm Bob,' he said with a chubby, avuncular smile. He was solidly packed and had a reassuring air of calm about him. He wouldn't make needless chat, she guessed as he opened the rear passenger door.

Returning the smile, she said, 'I'd really rather sit in the front. I find it easier to read.'

Cynthia, their nosy elderly neighbour who missed nothing, was glued to the window. She had a distracting habit of flaring her nostrils. Barney called her 'My Little Pony'.

In the car, chauffeured, released from traffic battles, Victoria stared down at the papers. Her picture was on the front of the *Post*

— a tabloid with a serious edge. The caption read *The glamorous new face of government*. She found it hard to concentrate.

Bob said, 'Two minutes,' into the car-phone and then they were outside the revolving doors of a towering modern building. Victoria clambered out feeling humble.

A tall bony man with a prominent Adam's apple stepped forward. 'Welcome to Environment, Minister! I am Martin Whiting, your Principal Private Secretary. Please call me Marty, everyone does.'

'Thanks. I'm glad to meet you.' Marty was about her age, nearly forty, and his gingery well-arched eyebrows gave him a look of constant astonishment.

He took her through some security paraphernalia and then to the lifts. 'We're on the fifth floor. Tim and Sue are the other two Private Secretaries. I'll explain how we divide it up. We'll go in the outer office — they're all very keen to say hello.'

They walked down a deserted corridor until Marty opened one of many identical doors. Would she ever find her way on her own?

There were four people seated at desks, mostly looking friendly. 'Welcome!' Tim said, appraising her coolly with light-blue eyes. 'We'll make it all as smooth as we can.'

To Victoria, that sounded subtly belittling; he didn't rate her, she was there for her media appeal, not a serious player. 'I'll try to learn fast,' she said, put out and determined to prove him wrong.

His desk looked clinically tidy beside its chaotic neighbour, belonging to Sue, the other Private Secretary. 'No excuse,' she confessed, noticing the look. 'It really offends Tim — he felt vindicated when I knocked over my busy Lizzie and got earth all over the keyboard.' She smiled happily in his direction.

'I've never seen one such a size – it's a little tree,' Victoria said. Sue nodded vigorously, which set her wavy chestnut hair bouncing with a life of its own. 'Yes, you just have to keep dead-heading them and they go on and on!' She looked more like a cheery chalet girl than a highly-qualified civil servant. She reached for an empty yoghurt pot and popped it in the bin with a little grimace.

'And this is Wayne, who'll be doing the diary,' Marty said.

Wayne answered questions looking down and away like a gauche footballer interviewed on television. He was very young and had rather dramatic sideburns.

Marty smiled. 'I'll show you your new office now.' It was huge: spacious and functional, with dreadful bombproof net curtains, uninviting as drab underwear. There was a large oval conference table with a high-gloss patina; gloomy battle-scene paintings and two armchairs covered in pleasingly faded blue chintz. 'You'll let us know if there's anything you need, Minister?' His manner was gentle and anticipating, a reassuring counter to Tim's cool.

'Everything's great, thanks,' Victoria said, wondering if the paintings could be changed. 'I like the chintz chairs. Shall we go and work over there?'

'Your predecessor thought they belonged more in *Fawlty Towers*,' Marty murmured. The light aside was a comfort. They sat down and he rested files on his knee.

'What's top of the agenda?' she asked, knowing the answer.

'Downsland's a bubbling cauldron, I'm afraid,' he said anxiously. 'Tempers on the boil.'

'You can say that again. Anything else?'

'The construction union has been stepping up demands for a

ban on MDF board. It's universally used, competitively priced and quite a serious problem. DIY enthusiasts and the construction industry love it, but it contains urea formaldehyde – which the union says is carcinogenic. Cutting fibreboard creates particularly fine dust particles apparently, that their workers are breathing in all day.'

'Mark Doherty's the union leader, isn't he? I'd like to set up an early meeting.'

At that moment, the Permanent Secretary, Sir Henry Weekes, the senior civil servant in the Department, looked in. He was renowned for his formidable intellect. 'Welcome, welcome. So glad you've joined us,' he beamed.

Victoria got up and took his outstretched hand. 'It's good to be here.'

They talked about the busy legislative programme ahead. As he left he said with a twinkle, 'Now, not to take this amiss, but it is delightful to have so becoming a Housing Minister.'

She smiled wanly.

It was a long, intense, structured day. Victoria was beginning to worry about being late for Barney's dinner when Marty told her the Secretary of State wanted her up for a chat. 'Sue will show you the way,' he said.

Ned Markham's office was as vast as a Hollywood mogul's; it had huge windows but only rooftops, no great London landmarks were to be seen through them. Armed with a glass of mineral water, Victoria went to sit on a stiff leather sofa. Ned sat opposite, and when he crossed his long elegant legs, pale-yellow socks came into view. He was good-looking in a silver-haired, square-jawed sort of a way. In his sixties, he seemed out of kilter in a new, unusually young Cabinet.

He sipped whisky and regarded her warmly. 'Delighted you're here, my dear girl. You're in for a torrid time. Downsland's a bugger, it won't win us any friends.'

'The press will be stirring it for all they're worth, I'm sure,' she said.

'Angie Newton, our Chief Press Officer, is good, though. She's as tough as they come – could see off any Sergeant Major!' Ned talked on sociably and Victoria finally had to explain about the dinner. He smiled indulgently. 'You'd better run then. Mustn't incur Barney's wrath this early in the day.'

Hurrying back to her office, Victoria found Angie Newton waiting for her. Marty, too, his eyebrows forming anxious arcs. 'Angie would like a very quick word, if you can manage it,' he said. 'We're getting so many press requests for you.'

Angie was big-framed, platform-bosomed, dressed all in black: every bit as formidable as Ned had described. She and Marty pulled up chairs. 'I'm ex-Fleet Street,' she declared. 'I know where the bodies are buried, but I suggest going easy on interviews till we can chuck 'em red meat.'

Victoria agreed and was told of the requests they would be turning down.

'The *Post* want the Minister in for an editorial lunch on Thursday,' Marty ventured.

'Better do that,' Angie barked. 'Good paper to have on-side. You know William Osborne, the Editor?' Victoria had seen him at functions and Party conferences but they'd never actually met. 'He's a big cheese now, with that *Firing Line* programme he does on television,' Angie went on, 'but he's still Bill to his mates. He lives near Downsland, so he could start making things difficult.'

'But wouldn't other papers love accusing him of nimbyism?'

'Oh, it'll be very subtle stuff. He's extremely persuasive, so you must be on your guard.'

Victoria felt annoyed: it was something she didn't need to be told. Her private line suddenly rang though, and distracted her. It was Barney. He said – very audibly – that he would have to go on ahead, that it was too bad of her and she had just better get her act together and get a fucking move-on. Angie grinned while Marty bustled about looking flustered and finding a few last papers for the red ministerial box.

He carried it down and handed it to Bob who was waiting in the car. He then said, standing with his arms limp at his sides like someone in an identity parade, 'If you ever have any problems, or worries, if I can ever help in any way . . .'

She was touched. 'Thanks – and for everything else today, Marty.'

She felt bitter. Her first red box had seemed symbolic, an achievement: almost like a medal. Taking possession of it should have been a moment of pride but Barney's call had denied her that small thrill.

CHAPTER 2

Hugh and Mandy Simmonds lived in a crescent of lofty houses in Notting Hill. Victoria parked her Mini Cooper between two hefty gas-guzzlers, unnerved to see it was well after nine. She went up the path and banged down a shining lion's-head doorknocker, feeling hard-done-by and tired.

A Filipino maid took her up to an all-beige first-floor drawing room that cried out for colour, strong paintings, anything uplifting. 'What excitements!' Hugh exclaimed, offering warm congratulations. 'So good of you to make it.' It sounded like a little dig.

People were standing in two groups, drinking. 'I'm dreadfully sorry,' Victoria said, looking round anxiously. 'I'd hoped you'd have started.' There was a palpable air of relief in the room that dinner might at last be about to happen.

'We'll go straight down then,' Mandy said crabbily. 'Just do the introductions, Hugh.' She patted hair that Barney likened to a hennaed judge's wig, gathered up her kaftan and swept out of the room.

Victoria met the Chalferns who had a considerable height

imbalance. Gloria was a tall blonde in a turquoise sequinned jacket; Roland was small and sallow with bluish lips. His sparse black hair combed sideways made his pate look charcoal-grilled.

'Housing Minister and beautiful with it,' he said, leering.

'It's good to meet you,' Victoria lied. Dick and June were there – inevitably, since he was one of the partners in the firm. She decided on balance that nothing was to be gained by mentioning the Sunday drink.

'And this is Angus and Jane Weatherill,' Hugh said, moving her on.

Angus had to be a banker. He was bull-necked, his head set forward, making him look as though he might suddenly charge.

'The City's not too sure about your lot yet,' he said with a flirty grin. 'We had a few jitters today.'

'I had them, too – first day in the job.' She laughed. 'But the City's got no worries.' His wife, who had a neat cap of fair hair and pearls, stayed silent at his side.

Barney was with them. He gave Victoria a peck. 'Long first day then, hon?' he enquired. She felt the chill behind his jovial smile.

Chucking back his wayward hair, he did a neat pirouette that landed him in the Chalfern group. June gave a snort of laughter at some interjection of his.

At dinner Hugh asked blandly about the Election and Victoria struggled against boredom. She said brightly, 'Did you see that piece in today's *Post* about why they lost? It was called The Missing Vertebrae. We'll need to keep very straight backs or they'll be after us!'

The editorial lunch invitation had come from Jim Wimple, the

Political Editor. If William Osborne were there too, she thought, she would definitely need all her vertebrae in place. He was a power-house, witty and punchy too, as anchor panellist on his television programme, *The Firing Line*. She felt renewed annoyance towards Angie for her patronizing warning about being on guard.

The main course, duck, was dry and overcooked. Feeling guilty, Victoria turned to Roland Chalfern and, determined to steer clear of politics, she asked tamely, 'Do you have children? We have a daughter of sixteen. She boards and I do miss her.'

'Two lads at Harrow,' he said. 'Our Chris is in with Hugh's boy.' He ran his arm along her chair-back. 'Now Vicky, me dear, a quick word of business. We're not going to start playing silly buggers over green-belt land, are we?'

'We do need to strike a careful balance,' she said glacially.

He let his fingers trail her shoulder. 'Beautiful women never give much away.'

'And Ministers can't,' she snapped, hardly believing his awful-ness. To her horror she felt his foot out of its shoe rubbing suggestively on her calf. She pointedly shifted her legs and tried to catch Barney's eye. He was chatting up Gloria Chalfern though, and looking and sounding quite drunk. The evening got worse and worse.

'Coffee upstairs, everyone,' Mandy announced.

Victoria went up and bravely made her excuses. 'It's been terrific fun, Mandy, but I'm really sorry — I do have to go now. I've still got a red box to do at home.' Barney turned bleary venomous eyes on her but she didn't care; it was such sweet relief getting away.

Working at her desk at home, her skin was still crawling with revulsion at Chalfern. He had invited them to his place on the Costa del Sol, his finger making little circles on her arm as he spoke.

When Barney finally got home she braced herself for a tirade. He was stinking of whisky; she could smell it as he walked in the room. 'You don't give a shit,' he began immediately. 'Turning up so fucking late, the first to leave by hours.'

He had come behind her chair and started fingering her neck. When his hands slid down inside her shirt, she elbowed him away in a fury. 'Don't, just don't! I am trying to get on.'

'You fucked up on the dinner, couldn't you at least come to bed now?'

He suddenly sounded so forlorn and plaintive; she turned in her chair feeling guilty after all. 'Sorry about being late, darling – there was a last-minute meeting and it was hard to say no. But God, that Chalfern's a shit and a slime-bag. How on earth can you stand having him as a client?'

She said it unthinkingly. It was tiredness. A shadow crossed Barney's face; he drunkenly jabbed at her chest. 'What's it to you? What's my job ever meant to you? You just wanted to get back to that fucking red box of yours, didn't you? You couldn't bloody well wait.'

He set an uncertain course for the door. She turned back to her desk, upset. The grandfather clock in the hall struck one; the lateness of night felt silky and soothing, but exhaustion was sucking her in like a bog. Her work finally finished, she sighed and locked up her box. She went upstairs, thinking it was too much to hope that Barney would have gone to sleep.

He was lying naked on the bed and watched her come in. As she was moving about the room he got up and stumbled over, grabbing hold of her, trying to give her a kiss. His breath was bad; she couldn't help feeling repelled and pushing him away, let fly.

'It's late, I'm exhausted; I've had a nerve-racking first day. I came to the dinner, I did that for you, I had Chalfern all over me like I was some kind of easy-lay lap-dancer – he nearly got my wine in his face – and now you! Leave me alone for once, can't you, for Christ's sake! Just let me get some sleep.'

Something snapped and he hit her. His arm lashed up like a striking snake, knocking her sideways and catching the side of her head with force. The shock of it: the sound and then the silence, the pain – it was a sickening moment. She felt a scream rising inside her. He hadn't hit her in a long while. Her head was throbbing, the room beginning to spin. She sank down on the bed and lay curled in a ball. No scream came, just quiet tears.

Barney started getting dressed. He would have sobered up, and be feeling bad; he never said so but he had ways of letting her know. She wanted him gone and felt even more wretched. When the front door slammed, her tears became loud sobs.

'Don't marry him,' her father had said. 'We're always here for you; we'll help – you know that.' Sixteen years later and she was still trying to prove to him that her marriage could work.

She felt unutterably low. A drumming headache was pounding her thoughts to a powder. Where was Barney? Why didn't he come? She got aspirin out of the cabinet and took three. In bed the pain was constant, but gradually, mercifully, sleep gathered her in and her mind began to drift.

* * *

Barney woke her at seven with tea. He looked freshly shaved and spruce as if he'd had a good night's sleep and was off for a game of golf. 'I wasn't sure whether to wake you,' he said, 'you were sleeping so sweetly. I slept in Nattie's room so as not to disturb you.'

She took the tea. Her head felt tender and sore. 'Thanks, I'd have been late,' she said tonelessly. He stared down at her, looking solicitous. It was making her feel quite desperate to be alone. 'You go now, love,' she urged, trying not to sound hysterical. 'I'm OK, I'm fine.'

There was an area of shadowy bruising on her forehead but she thought her hair would mostly cover it. Nattie was home on Thursday evening for the start of half-term. That was in three days. There was a Downsland briefing and the *Post* lunch that day, too.

She got dressed and went down to the kitchen. Barney poured coffee and put bread in the toaster. 'I don't want any,' she muttered.

'I'll do supper,' he said contritely. 'You'll be back around eight?'

'Should be. Thanks. I must go now.' Her red box was in the hall and bending to pick it up she let out a long despairing sigh. It was late; Bob was waiting. 'Bye,' she called down to Barney as a small olive branch. Her sense of his dependence made it hard to harbour bitterness. There was no meanness in him, just a frustrated lack of control. Besides, life had to get back on an even keel.

Marty slipped her little glances during the morning but it was probably just her pallor.

Wayne came in for a diary session. 'I'd like to fit in a hairdresser's appointment,' she said a bit awkwardly. 'Possibly early Thursday, before the Downsland briefing?'

'We could push that back a bit,' he suggested. He had the suspicion of a grin and Marty was looking admonishing; was it some sort of in-joke about Ministers getting their hair done? Well, tough. She needed to be feeling good for the *Post* lunch. The prospect was unnerving; Angie Newton or her deputy from the Press Office would be coming, and it was possible William Osborne would be there.

Osborne would put himself about with Cabinet Ministers, she thought, but she was new and junior. He also mightn't show because of Downsland – not wanting his own staff thinking he was lobbying and trying to make his mark with her.

But he might come; he must desperately want to stop a new town sprouting up with the speed of mushrooms, close to his home. He was sophisticated, ruthless: attractive, too. Wayne was talking diary matters; she had to pay attention and not worry about dealing with the *Post* Editor. But if it turned out she had to, she would need all her wits and vertebrae – a very straight back.

CHAPTER 3

William Osbourne looked out of his bathroom window; it was a beautiful Thursday morning. The sliver of Thames he could see between the backs of office blocks was glimmering like satin. His tiny flat might be near Charing Cross and have no outlook, but it was somewhere to sleep and at work he had a fabulous view. The *Post* building on the South Bank was tall, tight to the river. He loved seeing the vastness of London, the church spires, the giant cranes like Eiffel Towers.

He finished shaving and called his driver. 'I'm going to walk it, Dave. Check with Margie but I think I'm in for the day.'

'Will do,' Dave said. 'Shout if you need me.'

The Embankment was solid with traffic. William crossed the road to be close to the river and strode out. He thought he might buy a caffè latte and a croissant at the good place near the office. Proper breakfasts happened at weekends when Ursula cooked him eggs and made wonderful porridge on icy winter mornings.

The air, even with its shimmer of exhaust fumes, felt good. He had needed the walk, time to think through whether to use the Skeat photographs. He would chew it over and listen to arguments in the morning conference but knew his mind was made up. He would publish the photographs. William loathed Ivor Skeat. Not particularly because he hadn't a moral, scruple or care under his skin, he just did.

Skeat's newspaper group was a canker, a boil on the media scene. His papers were redtop without exception and base as they come, but they raked in the punters. The *Courier*, the group's big circulation daily, overlapped with the *Post* in the struggle for sales. Ivor Skeat had once tried to poach him but William had resisted all the lavish inducements. He liked working for a quirky individual like his South African proprietor, Oscar Bluemont, who looked like and was as loud and extravagant as Mr Toad. Oscar seemed remarkably free of aggrandizing ambitions, content with his one highly successful, cause-espousing tabloid – always assuming it kept on an upward trajectory.

William knew he risked joining the *Courier* in the sewer, going for Skeat's wife and his top female columnist, but the pair had been seen canoodling in a public place and that column was so piously hypocritical, they deserved all the *Post* could throw at them. And those pictures would shift papers; that certainly came into the equation.

Oscar was the problem, William thought, crossing over Blackfriars Bridge. These magnates stuck together and Oscar would close ranks with Ivor Skeat, no question.

Proprietors had too much bloody power, ringfencing themselves, expecting the kid-glove treatment. He though, wasn't greatly looking forward to Oscar's inevitable post-publication call.

Queuing at the café for his breakfast, he began thinking about Victoria James. She'd been all over the papers with hack headlines about the best of the new Government bunch. In one, much used photograph her almost shoulder-length brown hair was partly covering her face. She had a hesitant smile and looked vulnerable, almost fragile, but there must be some toughness, too. He kept seeing her wide eyes and feeling their gaze; he found himself almost smiling back.

Apart from absorbing a few remarks from lusting journalists, he'd been little aware of her in Opposition. As Hartstone's junior she'd kept a low profile; she wouldn't be able to do that now.

He quite wanted to meet her. She would assume he'd only showed at today's lunch to lobby her, William thought, and Jim would too. Jim Wimple was a good Political Editor, with good antennae, but the chemistry between them was lousy. The whole issue of Downsland needed careful handling.

He went in to the *Post* building feeling the usual burn of excitement from just being there. It was like a shot of neat brandy. People greeted him and he grinned back at a few. In the lift, seeing him loaded up with his briefcase and cup of hot coffee, eager staff sprang to press the lift button for him. His was the tenth floor.

'Hi, Margie!' he called cheerfully, routinely, going in through her outer office.

She was on the phone. 'Cape Town,' she mouthed. 'Oscar. Put him through?'

William grimaced but he hurried to his desk. Oscar calling was ill-timed. When he saw the Skeat pictures he'd be in a blasting rage, get straight back on the phone, yelling down the line: 'And I phoned and you still didn't tell me!' His accent was like an excess of tannin in wine, very rough on the senses.

He was in thundering voice. 'Hey, Bill! How goes it back there?

So how do you rate this new buncha politicos, then – any darned good? Fucking useless as the rest?'

William held the phone at a distance. 'Bit soon to tell. There's a couple of old wankers in the Cabinet and the rest are wet round the ears. Some good new blood in the middle ranks. We've got the best looker coming in for lunch today, Victoria James. Jim thinks she's one to watch. Hartstone at Health is possibly bad news, too loose a cannon, but for all the inexperience I'd say this lot have the right idea.'

'But no free ride, don't ease up on 'em. And do some digging. Sex sells.'

'You saw we had a go at Hartstone this morning?' They faxed Oscar the paper daily; it gave him the look and feel of it, better than online. 'They'll soon know where we're coming from, but a new Government does need time to bed down.'

'Balls to that! Get the gloves off now and let's have a bit of action and a few fireworks.'

Happy to oblige, William thought, putting down the receiver, but he felt a slight tightening of the gut. No one played a dirtier game than Ivor Skeat.

His senior team filed into his office for the morning conference. They settled down in tubular-leather chairs round the low table by the window. William's desk was a lone bastion of traditionalism; solid, red-leather tooled, he liked it – it helped him preserve his distance.

People spoke in order. The Deputy Editor, George, was silent, ruminatively picking his nose. William found George a flair-free zone, a no-brainer deputy but he knew it was partly a façade. George had his own agenda, they all did.

The Assistant Editor, whom he hadn't much time for either, cleared his throat.

'Yes, Jack?' William said impatiently. George mollycoddled Jack, possibly cunningly to point up his wetness.

'Oscar is on his fourth wife, Bill – and there are all his little shenanigans. It's just—'

'Not done? Well, it is by me. So I'm cocking a finger at Ivor Skeat? Time someone did, for God's sake.'

Jack stared down at the table, looking discomfited.

'You're dismissing proprietor solidarity then, not worried about Oscar sounding off?' He removed his glasses and got out the wretched hankie.

'Sure. He'll yell it's aiming low, that we're being too rough on the poor bugger, but that's just too bad.'

'Filthy-rich bugger, you mean,' Charlie on the news desk snorted. 'I wouldn't shed any tears.' He grinned. 'They'll call you a lesbo-phobe, Bill.'

'You'll have a nice new bunch of enemies,' Jim said with ill-concealed satisfaction. 'Skeat will really be out for blood.' He scraped back his chair. 'Got to go: Treasury press briefing. You're coming to lunch – Victoria James? Early marker for Downsland, perhaps?'

'It's tight, I'll check it out with Margie,' William muttered, seething. Jim had gone a step too far; he had just better watch it.

The morning conference ran its course and with William's irritated mood pinned to him like a rosette no one was prolonging things. They were hardened hacks but showing uncharacteristic caution; it was probably the prospect of some wearying internecine warfare in the newspaper world. They had more than enough problems with their rivals already.

The leader writers came in; the day took off. William's anger at his Political Editor slowly receded. Now that Jim had fed in the myth that William's problems with Downsland meant lobbying was the name of the game, there seemed little point, he thought, in not going to the lunch. He wanted to meet Victoria. It was that picture; something in him had stirred.

Jim had been keen to get her in early. He said the Whips had thought her a reliable pair of hands in Opposition, good solid performances, but Jim believed her to be better than that. She'd been elected as MP for Southampton East against the odds, seeing off a Junior Minister, and her maiden speech – on children in care – had been the best of her intake, Jim said. She could turn out to be a real high-flyer.

Canny of the PM too, William thought, putting a looker in charge of Downsland. If she was going places it gave her a chance to shine. But politicians were all the same. No doubt she was yet another ambitious, humourless MP – but she did have haunting eyes.

It was after one. 'I've taken Mrs James and her Press Officer to the dining room, Bill. You're running a bit late.'

'I know, I was just trying to find her cuttings. I've looked every-where.'

'I gave them to you only yesterday.' Margie rolled her eyes. 'I'll get you another set.' She thrust a few letters under his nose and he felt in an inside pocket for his pen.

Following Margie out he thought casually how much he depended on her. She was a leggy redhead, in love with a travelling flute-player and desperate to get married. Having met the flautist though, William thought the signs weren't good.

He was halfway out of her office when he stopped and turned. 'You'll get those cuttings right away, Margie? Something's bound to crop up that I'll want to check while it's fresh.'

She nodded and vigorously pointed at the watch on her outstretched arm. William rolled his eyes, mimicking her, then grinned and hurried out of the door.

*

The *Post*'s dining room was small and panelled in light pine. Victoria stood by the window, admiring the stunning view. 'A match for the London Eye,' she enthused, turning back to Jim with a slightly forced smile. He was rather a struggle to talk to, the sort of pallid man in rimless glasses whose lack of animation was catching.

They were standing around having drinks. Angie had filled her in on the two other people there. Accurate descriptions: Mike, the Housing Editor, was certainly a sweaty old hack and the leader-writer, Crispin, did look 'a toff egghead' with his well-cultivated stare.

A wavy-haired waiter topped up her mineral water. Jim eyed the door. 'We'll give Bill a few more minutes,' he said a bit uncertainly. 'I'm pretty sure he's coming.'

It would be less sticky when they sat down, Victoria thought, and she tried to make an effort. 'You were so unfair to my old boss Chris Hartstone this morning, Jim, really harsh.'

He replied that Chris was too radical, trying to do too much, too soon. As he droned on Victoria glanced at Angie who was all in black again – even her hair was black, short and spiky. She had put on some amber beads for the occasion though, and a scarlet slash of lipstick.

In the car on the way over she had briefed Victoria about the

Post. 'You know Jim Wimple, of course. He's easy to pass by in the street in spite of the ad-man black shirts but he's astute. A bit rigidly authoritarian. Osborne's the libertine. Sports pages are good and the Fashion Editor Beverly Leander's quite a star; she's always on some chat show or other.

'Osborne's a family man, there's an English-rose wife somewhere out in the Downsland sticks; we never used to see her when I was on the same paper. Three children, I think. Circulation's up, bucking the trend. He gets the results. There's no one more ruthless, but I think he's got a speck of conscience buried deep.'

Jim was still on about health. Victoria chipped in a word or two but her thoughts soon drifted again – this time to Marc, her hairdresser of the Daniel Day-Lewis looks. With the Downsland meeting only able to be put back half an hour, Marc had come in especially early for her. His remarks though, chatting into the mirror in his easy way, had been unsettling. She'd been too taken up with the briefing meeting all morning, too peeved at her officials' opaqueness when she'd asked how crucial housing provision at Downsland was to meeting new targets, to think much about Marc until now.

He had talked on while cutting her hair. 'Like the shirt! Lovely soft tone, that apricot.' She had been keen to avoid an interview-suit look. 'You've got quite a bruise here – what have you been doing to yourself? I'll try not to hurt.' He hadn't expected an answer, trendy friendly hairdressers never did. But they absorbed it all, she felt sure, and arrived at their own conclusions.

Just then, William Osborne came in. He was tall, with untidy straight dark hair and expressive brown eyes. Late forties, possibly: hard to tell. 'Sorry if I've held things up,' he said, looking round with a sheepish grin. His eyes landed on her and he smiled more positively, immediately coming up and shaking her hand. 'Hello, Victoria – the lady in the news!'

'Hardly,' she laughed. He had firm hold of her hand and for a fleeting second their eyes locked. It just happened, his smile fell away and his look became completely compelling. She felt her face redden like a schoolgirl's. 'After reading how much importance you attach to vertebrae I've been trying to keep a very straight back,' she said over-brightly.

'You look beautifully upright,' he said, smiling again, 'but we're kind to new governments, so I think you can relax. The roughing up comes later.'

Jim suggested they sat down. William walked her to the table with his hand under her elbow but directionally, just barely touching. Jim seated her between himself and William and the other three sat opposite.

Sweaty Mike, the Housing Editor, got straight down to business, catching her unawares. 'Brownland targets, Victoria – you gonna be tougher than the other lot?'

'We'll do our best but new homes obviously can't all be built in cities,' she said, embarrassed at such a dismally uninspired reply. William so close beside her was distracting.

His look hadn't been a come-on, she thought, just a sudden split-second connection. But it had shot straight through her and it shouldn't have done.

'So you're sympathetic to Downsland, then?' Jim suggested slyly.

'Come off it! The public enquiry hasn't even started. We've got a very experienced Inspector . . .' She tailed off, frustrated at not having a witty comeback at her fingertips. William said nothing, distracting in itself.

He turned to her while their plates were being cleared, 'Sorry, just got to nip out. My secretary was getting something I need to see.' He sounded warm but Victoria felt ridiculously put out that he was wandering off in the middle of lunch. He certainly wasn't lobbying, she thought.

It was flat with him gone, a cast of also-rans. Jim started having a go at Ned Markham, which didn't help. 'Guy Harcourt should have got into the Cabinet, not a throw-back like Markham,' he said dismissively.

It was adding insult. Guy was the other Minister of State at the Department and the very last person she'd have chosen to work with. He was scheming, nakedly ambitious – not someone with whom you'd want to go to the last ditch. His appointment had been a real blow. His leaking to the press was legendary, too.

'Markham's only in the Cabinet because his father gave the PM an early leg-up,' Crispin, the leader-writer, said waspishly, joining in.

'What tripe!' Victoria exclaimed hotly. 'You could at least wait and see how he does in the job.'

William slipped back in his seat and touched her arm. 'Sorry about that.'

She smiled in response and then worried about Angie noticing over-friendly looks.

Things became more relaxed and over coffee William talked of having lunch with a bee-keeping earl. 'He was very full of a deadly virus that's attacked British hives. Only Neapolitan queens were immune, he told me; only in Naples could you find the perfect queen – but they quite transformed your hive. True story!'

Angie and Mike laughed but Victoria was too conscious of doing badly and could hardly smile. 'We must be off,' she said firmly, catching Angie's eye, 'and you must all be up against it too, I'm sure. Thanks so much for lunch.'

Goodbyes were said and Jim walked with them to the door. William came too. 'I have enjoyed meeting you, Victoria,' he said, 'and good luck in the new job!'

'I'm going to need it,' she answered ruefully as he hurried out of the room.

Jim saw them to the lifts. Going down, Victoria confessed to Angie, 'Not my sparkiest performance, I'm afraid.'

'Steady, though.' Angie was being diplomatic, Victoria thought. It had been anything but.

They were in the busy downstairs hall when she heard William call her name. She hesitated; Angie was a little ahead, almost at the exit. Someone coming in though, a florid bouncy man who seemed to be an old friend of hers, called out, 'Angie Newton! Long time no see!' Victoria left them and turned back.

There were messengers dangling bike-helmets, staff coming and going, a group of visitors looking vague; no one seemed particularly curious. Her heart was thudding disgracefully.

William walked her to a less-peopled spot by a bank of plants. 'I was wondering if we could have lunch? I'd very much like to ask you about euthanasia. I'm particularly interested in your father's case. Of course, you may hate talking about it,' he added evenly, mildly questioning.

She stared, her pulse quickening; it had to be just a fig leaf for Downsland. And did she really want yet more stuff written about her father? William's eyes were understanding. 'Completely off the record, of course,' he added. 'It's a personal interest.'

'In that case I'd love to,' she replied warmly. 'Will your office call mine to find a day?' She said a rather abrupt goodbye. Angie was peering back.

In the car Angie asked her what he'd wanted. 'Lunch with Osborne won't go unnoticed,' she observed coolly. 'There'll probably be a diary piece about lobbying. Always best to let the office sort these things out.'

'It's off the record,' Victoria said lamely, 'and keeps good relations with the *Post.*'

Angie made no further comment. She was in profile, her face looking wooden and immobile. Her largeness and proximity were overpowering. Victoria edged nearer the window wishing the armrest had been down.

During the afternoon there was a session on MDF board. An official taking her through all the pros and cons seemed to be letting slip his personal reservations about the necessity of a ban.

'I accept the medical evidence isn't a hundred per cent accurate,' Victoria said annoyed, touchy at his subtle attempt to exert influence, 'but you'll never get builders to wear dust masks and there are safer alternatives. And am I right there's talk of a ban in the States?'

'Yes, that's true,' he agreed dubiously. So what was his problem, then? A ban was likely to be a vote loser, though. The construction union was naturally keen, but the multitude of do-it-yourselfers wouldn't take kindly to extra costs, nor would the big outlet stores.

Victoria had a moment between meetings and went to the window. Pushing back the dreadful net curtains, she stared out. The curtain's days were numbered; some sort of transparent blinds were arriving. Marty was on the case. She was also warming up to asking him about changing the battle-scene paintings.

It wouldn't have been easy, refusing lunch with William, but it was wishful thinking to imagine that he had a genuine interest in euthanasia. The *Post*'s Editor was a tough operator who called all the shots, whose home was near Downsland: he stood to lose out financially and in quality of life if the development went ahead. He knew how to trade on his charms; he knew what he was doing, all right.

But the look he had given her when they met hadn't been calculated, she thought, connecting certainly, but also one of startled surprise. He'd probably had some sort of instinct that softening her up was the way – and he'd been more or less right. Except that now she had to sharpen up. She would keep everything neutral, talk openly about her father's case – it was mostly all on record anyway – and hope for as few unfortunate diary pieces as possible.

Barney said she took herself too seriously. He'd had a cartoon of her, *The Schoolgirl Who Always Did Her Homework,* framed and hung in the loo. He might revise his opinion, she thought now, if he knew how close she was to acting like an irresponsible fool.

Officials were filing in for the next meeting and she went back to her desk.

CHAPTER 4

The phone was a cordless one. Nattie had put it on the edge of a bookcase after her mother's irritating call about being home safely; she stared at it for a moment then returned it to its stand. Leaving it around the place drove her father mad. She was finding the stillness of the empty house, the ticking grandfather clock, oppressive; everything seemed to be chafing at her. Why had Seb suddenly invited her to a party, just like that, right out of the blue? She took a Radiohead CD out of her rucksack, put it on then leaned against the Aga, thinking he was probably wishing he hadn't and regretting it like mad.

She filled the kettle. Getting the milk out of the fridge she stood with the door open, staring vaguely at yoghurts and cheese and cling-filmed leftovers: there was nothing she felt like eating. He must be a bit interested, she thought. There'd be such shock horror at home though, about her staying in London for a party. But it would be unbearable not going, so ghastly and claustrophobic, stuck at the cottage, thinking she could have been with Seb. Just because her mother had to be in the constituency. God, it was unfair.

She made tea and went up to her room. Her old ted was tucked under the duvet and picking him up, kissing his fusty furry head, she murmured out loud, 'Think he fancies me then, Bas?' But Basil had no teddy-bear thoughts on the subject and she let him droop on her chest.

Maudie might help. Feeling in urgent need of unloading, Nattie dumped Basil and raced back down to the kitchen phone. Mauds was a real friend, you could always trust her to say what she truly thought. She was so pretty with her green eyes and pointy chin and the short dark hair that suited her face. She made Nattie feel all limbs and as tall as a giraffe. She was out at her parents' Wiltshire house for the weekend, not at the London flat. Coming back on Monday, though.

'Hi, Mauds,' she said a bit breathlessly.

'Hi! I'm so pissed off out here. Henry's on half-term, too, and he's got this friend staying who keeps trying it on. He's gross!'

Nattie had always felt slightly jealous of Maudie's brothers, especially the new little one. She said, 'This party Seb's asked me to – I mean, do I go? I fancy him, I totally do, but you know what that scene will be like; it's all a bit of a nightmare.'

'I'd watch it with Seb. I don't trust him. Suppose he's bet those shitty friends of his he can shag you? You'd still be up for it?'

'It was weird, it was like he'd just thought of it, just spur of the moment.'

'You're going to go, aren't you, whatever I say. Listen, sorry, I've got to go. Stay cool – see you Monday.'

Nattie went to the patio doors and looked out; the fig tree still had its fat splayed leaves. Her eyes misted over. Seb wasn't like his friends, whatever Maudie might think; she just didn't get him.

He probably only did drugs for show; he wasn't that into it really.

She heard the sound of the gate-latch and her father's steps on the path. He would understand about a party, Nattie knew, and be on her side. She wished her parents weren't always so close to a row. Her mother was too uptight, forever having guilt trips about her work – if it gave her such a buzz, why not just get on with it? Things had got worse between her parents recently; they were tense as hell.

Maudie's parents were so much more comfortable with each other. Staying there was always good fun, all the family games and roughing-up and stuff.

The front door slammed. 'Hi, Dad,' she shouted, and went upstairs to greet him.

Barney put down his briefcase. 'How's things, my Angel?' He gave her a big bear hug. He'd had a whisky already; she could smell it.

'I want all the news,' her father said, going to the stairs, 'but first I need a drink. Come down to the kitchen and fill me in.'

He made straight for the fridge and took out a bottle of white wine, then opened the dishwasher for a glass. 'I hate emptying that thing,' he said, getting out a corkscrew. 'Want some?' She shook her head. He went to the sofa with his bottle and glass. 'School OK? Any half-term plans? How's the lovelife?'

'Don't be so boring, Dad. There's this party on Saturday – I know we're meant to be at the cottage, but could I stay in London with a friend?' She held her breath. It had to be all right, she'd already told Seb it would be.

'You know Mum would worry, love.' He smiled. 'I could drive you up for it if you really want to go. I've got a contract to work on and the reference books are all here – and Mum's got a Saturday-evening fundraiser down there. It works quite well, actually.'

She leaned over and kissed his cheek. 'That's so, so cool of you, Dad – thanks.' She thought of him coming to collect her and how embarrassing that would be. 'You needn't come and get me or anything. I could be back whenever . . . ?'

'Don't worry,' he said, grinning, 'I've got the picture. But we'd need to leave by midnight, love, or we'd be in trouble. You just come out then and I'll be parked outside.'

He was being so irritating, trying to be understanding. The party would hardly have started but it was better than not going at all. He got up. 'We should do something about supper. I thought we might have that lemon chicken you like.'

'And I'll unload the dishwasher, Dad.' She said.

CHAPTER 5

Bob was drawing up outside the house, 'It's so good,' Victoria couldn't help saying, 'having Nattie home for half-term. She's got till Sunday week.'

'You'll have a nice lot of quality time together,' Bob replied with genuine warmth.

Victoria went in feeling buoyed. She had cleared Friday of constituency work and Barney was taking time off, too. They could all go to the cottage together the next day.

Nattie was watching television. 'Hi, Mum,' she jumped up and came for a hug.

Barney was at the Aga. He called over his shoulder, 'Hi, I must keep stirring this. Good day? You had that lunch, didn't you? Go all right? You more or less ready to eat?'

'Sure. I didn't do brilliantly at the *Post*, just about got by, I think.'

She wasn't keen to talk about it. Brushing wisps of long fair hair out of her daughter's eyes and feeling enough love to fill an ocean, she said, 'It's great having you home. Tell me what happened about your short story. Did it go in for the competition? It was very good.'

'Miss Grigson's entered it but it's rubbish; it's got no chance.'

'It certainly has! And the Banquo essay, did that get a good mark?'

'You're not getting on with your special salad, Nats,' Barney called over.

'Keep your hair on, Dad, it's only a bit of chopping.' She went to the fridge for celery, peppers and carrots, assembled walnut pieces and sliced an apple and became absorbed.

Her Banquo question forgotten and unanswered Victoria felt ignored, brushed aside. She knew it was just teenage casualness and meant nothing, but feelings of self-pity still clawed. Getting out rush mats and the cutlery, she laid the table in silence.

Barney spooned a lemony sauce over his chicken dish. It had such a delicious zesty aroma that she cheered up a bit and praised his cooking. Sitting at the table for a family meal with Nattie home, cosy together, the world seemed a better place.

'Would you like to come and see my new office tomorrow, Nats?' she asked, preparing for a look of horror at the very thought. 'We could go just before leaving for the cottage – not too early. You'd really like Marty, my Principal Private Secretary. He's pretty special.'

'Sure, why not?'

Barney said, 'I'm going into work but I'll come there afterwards and get you both.' He reached for his wine glass and eyed Victoria in a slightly suspect way. 'So. Nattie's got this party, Saturday, and I said I'd drive her up. I can work on that big contract and you have got your fundraiser, hon?'

He was using his mumbly voice and was fiddling with his fork. Victoria's pleasure at Nattie's unexpected reaction began to seep away. It was the first she'd heard of any party or big contract. She turned to her daughter. 'Who's giving this party, darling? Who's asked you?'

She shrugged. 'Just someone from school.'

'A hot new boyfriend,' Barney chipped in. Nattie looked at him, furious.

'I'm not sure about this. I hate you driving back late, Barney – you absolutely won't drink?'

'Midnight deadline, promise! It is half-term, hon, and she doesn't want to miss a party.'

He was grinning, testing her. Victoria felt manipulated and outnumbered. Nattie could have stayed with a friend and got a train in the morning. She tried not to react and give Barney that satisfaction, but she still clattered the plates more noisily into the dishwasher than was necessary.

Nattie slept in the next morning but there was still time for a bit of King's Road shopping. She was so short of clothes; Victoria longed to spoil her but she only wanted yet another black T-shirt.

They went by Tube to the office. Security men gave them interested looks, officials smiled in corridors; Victoria felt intense pride in her beautiful daughter, her wonderful foal. She had a golden look, glinting amber-brown eyes, glowing skin with all the elasticity of youth. Her whole life was ahead of her, but could it ever be free of knocks and disillusion?

Marty welcomed Nattie with his eyebrows leaping, and Sue, and even Tim – had smiles. Shown her mother's office, Nattie stared round in awe. 'You could go ballroom dancing in here, Mum. It's huge!'

They had coffee and Nattie asked Marty whimsical questions about whether some ministers worked harder than others. His response was typically diplomatic. When Barney called, saying he was outside,

Marty came with them and carried the weekend red boxes. 'Sorry about the workload, Minister,' he said, as they squashed into a full lift, perhaps mindful of Nattie's remarks, 'all this burdening you at half-term.'

'Nothing for it,' Victoria grinned, trying to hide a grimace. Somehow it would have to be done.

They set off out of London. Barney, meeting Marty for the first time, had chatted and made a few witticisms, but Victoria sensed a resentful mood.

'Marty's like a rabbit on stilts,' Nattie remarked from the back seat. 'He's sweet.'

'Seemed a bit limp and effete to me,' Barney muttered.

Victoria stared out of the car window, despairing of a squabble-free family weekend. It had felt so different with Nattie at the office. The party business was still upsetting her. Barney didn't even know when he was lying any more, it was such second nature to him. It was all too easy to feel bitter.

She turned to Nattie in the back. 'Tell me about the boy who's taking you to the party.'

'Christ, Mum! He's called Seb. He's Upper Sixth: brown hair. OK? All right?'

They finally got to the cottage.

It was one of a semi-detached pair of thatched cottages that the local landowner had been prepared to sell. Being so close to Southampton, the village of Ferndale had struggled to stay rural, but they were on its outer extremity, down a country lane and with fields on three sides.

Mrs Potter, a gamekeeper's elderly widow, lived in the adjoining cottage and her front patch of garden with its circle of bright pansies was a joy. She was so deaf it encouraged Barney in his use of loud colourful language but she always turned on the boiler for them, which was another joy. She had the most magnificent tabby she called Poor Pusskins – although Pusskins clearly wanted for nothing in life – who switched allegiance at weekends. She would be straight in the front door the moment they opened it. They almost felt shared ownership and had taken to calling her Portia for her air of haughty superiority. Mrs Potter seemed not to mind or notice the defections and any crisis of identity passed her by.

Portia was waiting on the doorstep as usual and Nattie scooped her up. 'Who's a lovely puss-cat, then,' she murmured, putting her cheek to the soft tortoiseshell fur. She was sounding a bit over-emotional and Victoria worried that it was tension about the party.

They had a late lunch and afterwards went for a walk. Calling in at the village shop they bought crumpets and then, home again, made a fire and toasted them on long forks that had been a Christmas present from Nattie to her father.

After supper Barney did some computing in the dining room while Victoria tackled her huge pile of work in the sitting room – in a two-up-two-down cottage it was easy to talk between rooms. She and Nattie were on the sofa together, a wonderfully squashy old thing with worn green covers and dramatically drooping springs. The television was blaring but she could always manage to blot out noise and concentrate.

Stuck for an appropriate word to jot in the margins of a submission, she looked up for a moment and felt worried. 'You OK Nats?' She seemed as edgy as on the eve of an exam.

Nattie gave an expressive shrug, a plea for space, and then flicked impatiently through the television channels. William's programme, *The Firing Line*, was on and she stayed tuned. The debate on drugs education in schools held her attention.

It held Victoria's, too. William was attacking a Secondary Head and being forcefully dynamic. Watching him, she suddenly longed to be touching the hollows beneath his eyes, smoothing the lines at the corners of them. He looked appealingly tired, but was passionate, animated. 'You hate me now, don't you?' he said with a sudden grin to the poor teacher whose argument – that his staff weren't policemen – William had just been annihilating. 'Why don't you get reformed addicts to talk to the children?' he demanded. 'Have round-table discussions, get their views? Get them involved!'

The fire was dying down, the television the only sound. Nattie was looking distant; mother and daughter both lost in thoughts they could never have shared.

Victoria's constituency office was in a Southampton back street. It had previously been a mini-cab depot and they still had occasional hiccups of communication. She held her surgery there on Saturdays. Just as with a doctor, anyone, whatever their political leanings, could come to her for help and advice. Constituents brought problems from mothers-in-law to Middle East war-zones, and all benefit and social security-claim cock-ups in between.

Her agent, Jason, gave up his Saturday mornings to be on hand. During the week he ran the office with the ample help of a busty secretary. He was an energetic young man with thinning fair hair, full of good intentions but an awful alarmist. Victoria mostly discounted his panics but expected to get caught out one day. He was wonderful with old ladies, any ladies, in a gentle, one-of-us sort of way.

The office comprised two ground-floor rooms of a small Edwardian house that had a bay window on to the street. Parking Barney's car, Victoria got out, only to be scowled at by an old lady buying vegetables at the greengrocer's outside display. The shop-owner, who was pouring potatoes into her tartan bag, was a supporter and much friendlier.

'How's things, Mrs James? Saw you on the news with that vicar fella the other night, the one who's trying to stop Downsland. They don't want it, do they! Can't say as I blame them.'

'Emotions are running high,' she said, feeling fed up about the Reverend Jeremy. As chairman of the Downsland Action Group he was already a thorn in her side. He was never out of the media, she had to constantly respond, and he was such a zealot, a Pied Piper in a dog collar, signing up more people daily. And given his surname everyone felt on first-name terms with him.

The office had a hideously noisy entrance buzzer. Shutting the door with relief, Victoria smiled at the people waiting on wooden chairs in the narrow passage.

'Kettle's on,' Jason said encouragingly, following her in to the front room. 'It's a packed morning. You've seen Mr Mudd waiting and that weird woman always ranting on about sewage?'

'How could I miss them! Right – I'll see Mr Mudd first.' He had a walrus moustache and a fancy for pretension; it was always a job to get him to leave.

Mr Mudd deposited a huge briefcase on the floor and then sat with his hands clasped as if in prayer. 'I am here in my capacity as

President of Ferndale Friends of the Earth, Mrs James, seeking urgent reassurance that you will absolutely reject this abhorrent Downsland project. We must protect our glorious countryside, our nation's heritage, from such disastrous wholesale destruction.'

'You're my constituent, Mr Mudd, and I'll help where I possibly can, but you know I cannot discuss my ministerial work. Friends of the Earth will have every opportunity to put their case at the public enquiry.' She smiled, willing him not to prolong things.

He did, and eventually Jason had to move him on. Mr Baxter was next. He was a primary-school teacher who wore waistcoats in the identical check to Barney's M&S shirts, and Victoria had always warmed to him. He had a gaunt face and carried all the world's problems on his thin, anxious shoulders. She'd guessed that this morning he would talk about the baby seals in Russia.

'I just wondered,' he said, sitting forward, 'if, now we have a new Prime Minister, you could ask him to appeal to the Russian President? We must do something about the inhuman clubbing of baby seals; I feel truly desperate.'

'I'll certainly write to the Prime Minister, Mr Baxter. I know he'll do all he can to get across the strength of people's feelings.'

By the end of the morning she had seen twenty-five people, including a group threatening Warfarin and acid baths for a neighbour's vast quantity of defecating cats.

Barney and Nattie had waited for lunch. There were jars of home-made jam and a grim-looking cactus on the draining board. 'You never went to Mrs Casey's!' she exclaimed.

'Dad dragged me along, too. A coffee morning, God!'

'Dragged wasn't the word' said Barney, smiling fondly.

'You're a saint.' Victoria kissed him, wondering if his conscience was troubling him. He took a steaming shepherd's pie out of the oven. 'You are wearing your halo today,' she said.

'It's what I have to do to get a kiss these days.' He deposited a Worcester dish on the small kitchen table and started to serve.

Nattie was changing for the party but taking so long that Victoria went upstairs to see if all was well. She found her daughter standing in the middle of her small, whitewashed bedroom, looking close to tears. There was a forlorn heap of clothes piling up on the floor.

She had on a red top and jeans. 'That looks just right to me,' Victoria said hopefully.

'Don't start. It's gross.' She flung off the top like a wilful toddler and hurled it at the pile. She was tall with a slender frame and well-developed breasts; she was going to a London party on a Saturday night with a boy of eighteen. Victoria thought of all the takers and willed her not to be a giver. She was too precious. 'And do you have to stare?' Nattie said aggressively. 'Am I deformed or what?' She dropped her eyes to the pile of clothes.

'Why not wear the new black top we got yesterday?'

Nattie glared but she picked it up and put it on. It looked great, clingy and sexy. She swapped the jeans for a mini-skirt and black tights. Barney was calling and she yelled down hysterically, 'I'm coming! Lay off, can't you?' Then, grabbing the man's tweed coat she'd bought for three pounds in a jumble sale, she gave her mother the most cursory of brushed-cheek kisses and was out of the door and gone.

On the Thursday of half-term Victoria was preparing for a meeting with the construction union leader. Whether MDF board should be banned was a real worry and dilemma.

Sue looked in. 'He's a bit late — I'd have some coffee and a break.'

Alone for a moment, she let in concerns about Nattie. She had been tight as an oyster about the party. Asking if she'd had fun, probing whether she was seeing Seb in the week, had been stupid. 'God, Mum, it was just a party, no big deal.'

Victoria thought it had been a very big deal, given the knife-edge state of her daughter's nerves. She was glad Nattie was now on a train to Worcester, going ahead for a long weekend with her grandparents at Brook House, comfortingly far from London and Seb. She and Barney were driving down the next day.

They always spent Christmas and Easter with her parents. Nattie had made friends locally over the years and Brook House was a second home to her. She played chess with her grandfather and took his liver-and-white cocker spaniel, Christie, for long walks. She loved Agatha too, the fat black cat who had a purr like a Porsche engine, and whose habit of slinking on to beds at three in the morning Victoria could have done without.

Brook House was part eighteenth-century, but much added-onto. It had an acre or so of garden, lavished with love by her father, John. He fed his old-fashioned roses compost that in plant terms could have matched any meal at La Tour d'Argent.

His reinstatement and a small inheritance had made Brook House possible. Victoria had no recollection of their house before his prison term, but she could remember the flat over the local garage that had been home until she was nine. Light and roomy, it had had a scrubby, allotment-style patch of land where, after his release, her father had grown vegetables.

But with the smell of petrol fumes, the constant revving of

engines, it must have been hard for her parents not to be constantly reminded of changed circumstances.

Victoria had gone to the local comprehensive by bus with several friends and her boyfriend nicknamed Ego: they had all smoked and been reported. Among those hauled before the Head and threatened with expulsion, she and the vicar's daughter had been the only girls. The boys had been a rough lot; she'd had to do their homework for them or have her knickers pulled down in the playground.

Sipping her coffee, she looked round the office. The battle-scenes had gone. She and Marty had just been on a trip to see the Government art collection. It was largely made up of donated paintings – also of gifts to Ministers deemed too valuable for them to keep – and was housed on the first floor of a warehouse south of the river.

They'd come away with a lively oil of a fallen flowerpot with a red geranium spilling out and a glorious John Doyle of Romney Marsh.

As Victoria gazed at the paintings, Marty's head came round the door. 'He's here, just coming up in the lift.'

The union leader was in the room in seconds, with Marty and Tim trying to keep up. 'Hi, I'm Mark Doherty.' He stuck out his hand. He was nattily suited with dark curly hair. 'And that's Jon, our Press Officer.' He waved airily behind him to a designer-bald sidekick following in.

Doherty wasted no time on niceties. 'You know our concerns, Mrs James. MDF is harmful, carcinogenic, our members are breathing it in – we want nothing less than a ban.'

She asked questions and tried to assess how reasonable he would be if they were to do business. Marty's eyebrows were active, his eyes darting between Doherty and her. Tim sat looking glum and mistrustful. She suspected him of inward sneers, of a preconceived conviction that she wasn't up to it, that she would be indecisive, unwilling to risk unpopularity.

The sidekick spoke up. 'We'll put out a statement that we've had a fruitful discussion and you're deciding what action to take.'

That would have boxed her in. 'No. You can say I take your concerns seriously but no more than that for now.' Doherty looked surprised. Had he taken her for a pushover?

She felt only slightly insulted, he was too likeable, but as he was going out of the door he turned and winked, which didn't help his cause.

Was she right to be thinking of banning MDF? It was a tough decision. The workers had to be protected but it was only a health hazard in very small degree. She would be accused of caving into the union and become the hate figure of every DIY shopper in the land. Simply to warn of a risk though, would be so inconclusive. You couldn't win: people either got hysterical over health scares or just carried on regardless.

Guy Harcourt was the problem – her least favourite Minister and the one with whom she had to work most closely. He would see it as a plum chance to rubbish her and put her down – he'd leak to the press that he was opposed, say she was bowing to union pressure. He would ensure the Parliamentary Party knew all about it, too, and be passionate and persuasive with the Department's three most Junior Ministers, the pussies. Getting it through was going to depend entirely on Ned, and she had no idea how he'd fall.

She looked at her watch. Nattie should be almost at her grandparents' by now.

Victoria was looking forward to the weekend and being with all the family, but before that there was a heavy-duty evening with Barney to get through: kitchen supper at Dick and June's – a penance only marginally eased by the Private View at the Royal Academy they were going to first. The invitation had come from Angus Weatherill, the banker at the Simmonds' dinner. His bank was the sponsor.

It was a new exhibition, *Erotic Paintings from the Sandling Collection*, and causing quite a stir. The reviews had been ecstatic and excoriating in equal measure and Victoria felt pleased to be going.

Her lunch with William was still almost a week away. She was impatient for it, finding it impossible to suppress her anticipation. That flash of contact, meeting him, was never out of her mind. But even supposing his interest wasn't Downsland-motivated – what then?

It didn't do to be feeling so unnervingly attracted. Life had to go on.

CHAPTER 6

That was that, Nattie thought miserably, on the train to Worcester. Half-term over, Seb was sure not to get in touch now. Just his one call on Monday and that so meanly cut off; it had been a horrible week with all the waiting and hoping.

She checked her mobile one last time then stared round the carriage feeling incredibly on edge. A man in a suit with three ear-studs was also checking his mobile, there was a woman with a bulgy little boy in a tracksuit and a Chinese girl eating from a boxed take-away with chopsticks. She was avidly reading *Cosmopolitan* and not dropping a single bean-sprout.

The journey stretched ahead. Nattie took out her copy of *Macbeth*. She read a page or two then gazed out of the window, thinking about the party again and feeling sick with embarrassment. It had been at Matt's house in Hampstead; it had a big basement den and his parents were away for the weekend. Chas and Matt were Seb's good friends. They were six-footers but he was smaller and slighter – taller than she was though.

Nothing had gone right. Even just getting the doorbell answered

– having to ring it for ages, feeling crowded with her father watching and then it hadn't been Seb who came, only some staring-eyed girl in ripped jeans who'd opened the door and gone.

Nattie had followed the sounds downstairs and peered round in the fug trying to see him. The relief of finding him had been short-lived; he'd barely even registered her, let alone shown any interest: so humiliating.

And being in that stupid skirt when they were all in jeans.

They'd been drinking beer and cheap vodka. When Seb had finally noticed her existence he had been nice and found some wine and given her puffs of spliffs, but weed never seemed to have much effect. Nothing could have helped her relax; she had just wanted to curl up and die.

And just when Seb was being more attentive, his friends had started getting at her to have some coke. It was just what she'd been dreading.

No one had even bothered to talk to her except for when they were pushing her to have a line. 'Go on, Natalia, it's not going to kill you. You might even like it.' They were high, they couldn't have cared less; she had felt as defenceless and picked on as a fly having its wings pulled off.

The excuse of the car journey had been a disaster. They'd fallen about. 'You can't smell it, darling, not coke! So your dad gets a whiff of weed! Do you really think he's never had a drag in his life?'

'Not her parents,' someone sneered. 'Certainly not her mother!'

'Lay off her, you losers,' Seb had grinned. 'I'll see she gets her kicks. Don't you worry,' he'd had his arm tight round her by then and kissed her. 'We'll leave 'em to get on with it,' he said, pulling her away upstairs. 'I want you all to myself.'

He had taken her to a sitting room, in darkness but for an outside streetlight: the curtains hadn't been drawn. She felt her cheeks burning, thinking of being alone with him. Sounds of the party had made it so hard to relax though, especially with the door not being shut.

The train was stopping at a station and she checked to see where they were. Not much further: she put away her unread Shakespeare. She felt pleased to be seeing her grandparents again. And with them around, she thought, there'd be less chance of her parents having rows.

She had resigned herself to Seb not calling before getting back on Sunday. How would he be at school? Would he talk to her? He had seemed so keen – or had it just been the coke? Her body was going all moist thinking of his kisses and touch. Why hadn't he called again?

Looking round the carriage, she saw that the Chinese girl had fallen asleep. The man with the ear-studs was talking loudly into his mobile – all about being knifed in the back by his office.

Seb had gone to get drinks and must have had some more coke; he'd come back hyper and wide-eyed, his pupils dilated, and so all over her again, kissing her everywhere. But remembering how high he'd been took away from the thrill, it didn't feel that special.

He'd been cruel about her going. 'I really do have to split, Seb. My dad's waiting; he'll be mad at me and I owe him. I'd have been stuck out in Hampshire.'

'You're too much, Natalia doll. Fab tits, though.'

'No, Seb, no more; I really have to go.'

'"Yes, Seb, yes, more, more – don't stop!"' His teasing had been mean. 'Who's a little pumpkin, then?' he'd called after her when she had finally struggled free.

She got her bag down from the rack, worrying about missing the station. The Chinese girl seemed to have gone. Nattie hadn't noticed her get out.

Seb would be different away from his friends, she thought; they were so into doing drugs. But she was sure to have blown it, being so uncool at that party. He hadn't even sent a text.

She relived his one call on Monday morning, the thrill and then the puncturing hurt. He'd been talking about the party and saying he wanted to see her again, to take her to dinner. Maybe not till the holidays, he'd said, he had things on.

If only the doorbell hadn't rung. She had just gone away for a second to let in the meter man but Seb had clicked off. It had felt as bad as being dumped that he hadn't hung on and said goodbye; it had reduced her to tears.

Her grandparents had both come to meet her. 'No Christie?' Nattie said, hugging them, longing to see her favourite dog.

'He's in the car. Lunch is all ready at home. Perhaps give Mum a quick call?'

Her grandparents were chatty in the car, Christie all over her, but Nattie was feeling vulnerable and scared; she had a sudden need of her mother. There were times when the way her mother just hugged her, literally or in spirit, without any questions or probing, made her feel really loved. Nattie was in need of that, her mother's loving arms.

She hated the way two boys at school had started bitching about her mother's new job. It was such a drag they lived near Downsland. The boys said that a Minister was always in the pockets of big business and that her mother wanted to concrete over the whole green belt – the whole crappy country, they sneered, from John O'Groats to Land's End.

It was such random meanness. Nattie didn't know how to retaliate. It would be even worse, she thought, if her parents suddenly decided to split. It would be all over the papers and the press might find things out. They'd have nothing on her mother; no one was more serious and proper. That was small consolation, Nattie thought, as they arrived at Brook House. But all the growing tension at home wasn't easy to live with.

CHAPTER 7

Victoria picked up the phone.

'Hi, Mum, I'm here at Brook House. We're about to have fish lasagna – the healthy option!'

'Sounds delicious. Dad and I should be there by supper tomorrow. Thanks for the call.' She was glad of it, and that she'd been free to take it, the moment of contact meant so much.

Nattie was always more natural, staying with her grandparents. Victoria let out a sigh – quite forgetting for a second, that Marty was in the room. They had been having sandwiches, trying to sort out a few problems.

He cleared the lunch debris and stood up. 'Almost time for the green-belt meeting. Angie's sitting in on it, if you remember? She wants to give a media view with the Downsland enquiry starting so soon.' His eyebrows suggested that was mild cause for anxiety, but he picked up the plates smiling and made for the door with his big loping strides.

Angie was late for the meeting, but soon dominating it and making her considerable presence felt. 'I hear William Osborne's wife has joined the Downsland Action Group,' she announced, giving Victoria a rather arch glance. 'I know Ursula, his wife, and she's a very private person, no campaigner. It'll be Osbourne's doing, a way he can guide and influence the DAG – though that militant vicar chairman's not making such a bad fist of things himself.'

'That's a little extreme,' an official said. 'The Action Group will have its say at the enquiry. People will calm down.' His intelligent eyes were levelled; he looked quite cross.

'You won't keep the Reverend Jeremy down,' Angie retorted. 'He's like a cork in water, popping up everywhere. He's a menace. And now he'll have the benefit of all Osborne's ruthless professionalism.'

Victoria could feel knots of tension forming. 'Sounds like I'll have my work cut out,' she said. 'With a long enquiry there'll be plenty of ructions, but at least it's happening at the beginning of a Parliament – getting the unpopular stuff over with early!' Then she wondered if she should have said that in front of civil servants.

As the meeting wore on she felt dreadfully brought down by Angie's news, and by Downsland, they were so intertwined. There had been more scuffles and clashes with the police. Sam Swayne's camp was upsetting the farmers, but he had the locals on his side. Victoria felt crossly that Ursula Osborne and her well-heeled fellow DAG members could just shut up and spare a thought and a field or two for the struggling first-time buyers. The problem was where to draw the line.

Why didn't she feel more mistrustful? She thought of William's steady eyes: was he really that good and calculating an actor?

Couldn't his wife just possibly have joined the DAG of her own accord?

Before leaving for the exhibition at the Royal Academy, where she was meeting Barney, she called in Marty. 'I'm going to recommend a ban on MDF board,' she said, more calmly than she felt. 'We can't take risks; it has to be withdrawn. Can you do a paper for the Secretary of State?'

'Yes, Minister, of course.' His vintage mandarin response gave no clue. Not knowing whether or not Marty approved was unsettling; she was feeling low enough already.

She had brought in a little black dress and changed for the evening ahead. The dress had a cut-away neckline and knowing it suited her made her feel a bit more cheered – in spite of having to have supper later with Dick and scrub-hair June. She would be drooling at Barney over her glass of Beaujolais, Victoria thought, hardly a soothing antidote to a stressful day.

Barney was waiting on the Academy steps. He gave her a squeeze. 'You look great. That's such a sexy dress, I've always thought.'

They went up the central stairs. Angus Weatherill was in the main gallery doorway. His head was still thrust forward in the bull-like fashion she remembered from the Simmondses' dinner; it made her wonder if he head-butted in the bedroom.

'Glad you could make it,' he said, grinning. 'It's quite a crush. Not sure about the paintings but all tastes are certainly catered for!'

'Mine are catholic,' Barney said, with a hint of coolness probably only apparent to Victoria. She thought he hadn't forgiven Angus for some chance remark at the Simmondses'. He could harbour resentment for years. As they moved away Angus's parting grin seemed too knowing.

The paintings weren't for delicate constitutions but she saw plenty of people she knew and enjoyed the buzz. It was more her world than Barney's. He took off purposefully though, and with him gone she looked round for William. She had hoped he might be there.

Angie could be wrong about Ursula. Did she really know her that well? She had talked about working on the same paper as William, and said his wife had never been around. Perhaps he wasn't that close to his English-rose Ursula? It was a bad sign, out of all proportion, Victoria thought, having jealous feelings about the wife of a man she'd met once at lunch.

'So what do you reckon?' She started and spun round. Nick Bates was grinning at her. He was one of the pussies in the Department, and her best hope for support on MDF. She saw he was looking at a huge painting of a tumescent penis.

'Not my style,' she said. 'Too up-front.'

Barney came back and joined them. He was being irritating, fidgeting. 'June's asked us for eight,' he said impatiently. 'We should really be off.' It was too bad of him, being so uncivil; it was only half-past seven – bad enough having to go at all.

'I guess I should be off, too,' Nick said politely. 'See you, Victoria.'

He left in cheery good grace but his smile, like Angus's, had been collusive. Was everyone sensing the prevailing lack of harmony? She rounded angrily on Barney. 'That was so rude! We've got plenty of time and June's not going to go off the boil. Nick is important to me at work, you know.'

Barney's retaliation was forestalled: a girl with a fierce black fringe came up and prodded at him menacingly. 'I thought it was you,' she said in triumph. 'I hope you're contrite, after the tennis club last week! "For every few who won't . . ." God!' She was looking insufferably pleased with herself and seemed not remotely to care or consider that the woman beside him, who hadn't merited a glance, was almost certainly his irate wife.

At least Barney had the grace to look highly embarrassed. 'Oh, come on, Joan,' he said pleadingly. 'You knew that was just a joke.'

'It's Jean. And it wasn't one that made *me* laugh, I must say.'

'Sounds like that was your loss then,' Victoria said tartly, her patience snapping. She walked off and went to the last room of the exhibition where she stood, unseeingly, in front of a canvas of two naked women sharing a very long snake. Her fury was turning to despair; it all seemed so pointless. How much longer could she go on?

'Hello Victoria.'

She swung round. 'Oh, hi – sorry, I was miles away.'

It was a complete shock, William suddenly beside her. Her heart started thumping, kicking like a baby.

He was smiling and he brushed at her hair, lifting it back gently from her eyes. It surprised them both.

'I couldn't see you,' he said, his smile trying to excuse and further explain. 'How are you? I was wondering if you might be here. Are you enjoying the pictures?'

She wrinkled her nose. 'Not much: they're not really my thing.'

'Nor mine. The Goya's opening on Tuesday though, and that should be wonderful. Are you going? I could have a ticket sent.'

He couldn't do that: he couldn't tempt her with visions of a quiet post-Goya dinner *à deux*. 'Sorry, I can't,' she said. 'Fred Buckley's giving a lecture, and I've promised faithfully to go.'

Next Tuesday was just before they were due to have lunch, in which case they'd have been seen together twice in as many days. Rumours would start. She looked round. The crowd had thinned but a man with a slight squint was close enough to have heard their exchange. Fortunately, he looked more of an art buff than a reporter.

'What's Fred talking about?' William asked.

'Euro-American relations: the Atlantic partnership.'

'Interesting. Bit out of area for an ex-Home Secretary, isn't it?'

'It's something he's really passionate about: he doesn't want Europe flexing its muscles and America turning to the Pacific Rim. He thinks he can help people see the dangers.' Fred was an old friend and she knew his views.

William stared at her then gestured to a nearby painting, a muddy abstract. 'What do you reckon on that? I'd say it's an orifice but I'm not entirely sure which.'

The man with the squint who had begun openly listening had the bright eyes of someone keen to enlighten. Victoria stared past him though, making it hard for him. She could see Barney advancing with a great black scowl on his face that she thought was entirely defensive — as it most certainly should be.

She would have to do the introductions, and the prospect made her feel rebellious, but to her great relief William distanced himself. He moved away and began making conversational asides to an elderly woman who had come up to peer at a painting.

It was enough of a disconnection. Barney assumed she was alone and coming straight up, he hissed at her rudely, 'Come on now, for God's sake. It's after eight.'

'You don't have to nag,' she hissed back. He was glaring like a scolded bully but at least he wasn't looking around; he would have recognized William from *The Firing Line* and possibly remembered the editorial lunch. She felt glad to have been spared an extremely awkward meeting.

Barney stormed off again, clearly expecting her to follow. She turned to say goodbye to William whose chat with the elderly woman seemed to have run its course.

He and the man with the squint must have heard the bickering. Embarrassed, she said 'My marching orders, I think,' then, turning more directly to William, added, 'I'd really better be off. It's next week we're meeting?'

'Wednesday,' he said, holding her eyes. 'I'm looking forward to it.'

She looked down, repositioning her handbag in readiness for leaving. 'Must go,' she said.

*

William watched her weave through the thinning crowd in her eye-catching black dress. He saw her link up with her blond prick of a husband at the door. They'd had a very recent row, he thought; she had come into the room looking distracted and upset.

'It's how you read it,' the man with the squint pronounced, making him jump, 'for individual interpretation.' William got his drift and gazed dutifully at the orifice painting, finding it hard to keep a straight face.

'It does repay study,' he replied gravely. 'Well, guess I'd better be off.'

Dave, his driver, was waiting in Piccadilly. They got on fine. Dave was a fly East Ender with nicotine fingers and slicked-down black hair. A bit of a stereotype wide boy; nothing passed him by.

'The office, Dave,' William said.

He kept his head turned to the window. He was back in the

Academy, catching sight of her, feeling her hair, soft as goose-down. Lifting it away had been an instinctive reflex. She'd looked taken aback but had known it was an unconscious innocent gesture. He smiled to himself; the word innocent didn't entirely fit.

They got to the office, still half an hour before the first edition. Striding down corridors, William thought of the Skeat pictures reaching a million or so households by morning. He felt tense, lacking in his usual certainties. Bugger that. It would sell papers. Doing his rounds, he was quick to find fault and yelled at people, but most knew when to keep out of his way.

Seeing the first edition, the reality, he felt little better. A newspaper proprietor's wife and a well-known female columnist locked in a bare-tit clinch, fleshy cavortings in a St Tropez back-street dive – it wasn't in the *Post*'s normal run of things. People would think it offensive and kick up. And Skeat's expletives when he saw those pictures wouldn't be too pretty. William wondered if he had allowed his intense loathing of the man to cloud his critical judgment. He couldn't help thinking of Victoria's reaction. She was bound to see the pictures as crude, intrusive and nothing else. She was too much on his mind.

The copy read well. The columnist running a rampant campaign against pop stars and personalities who set bad examples had given them a rich seam to mine. Stupid bitch. But journalists didn't have to practise what they sounded off about, unlike politicians. William checked the rest of the paper and then went for a routine session with the Night Editor.

He was a crusty old cove, set in his ways; he would have divorced his wife before changing sides of the bed. He loathed having to alter the first edition. However, William persuaded him to move up a heartrending story about a teenage suicide pact. It made the pictures of Skeat's wife and the columnist seem even more sordid and he went back to his office with a sense of unsettled frustration.

George fell in step. 'Quick half?' he suggested annoyingly adding, 'Oscar's not going to be a happy bunny, is he? What do you reckon he'll do?'

'Yell at me down the phone, I guess.' William turned with ill-hidden irritation and grinned. What the hell did George expect him to say – that Oscar would sack him and crown the fucking Deputy? 'I won't have a drink,' he said, 'bit knackered. I'm off soon.'

He went into his office and shut the door; he had no intention of going. Working at his desk he was absorbing little, and he finally sat back and lifted the phone. Calling GD was a bit extreme in anyone's book but fuck that, he wanted to.

Waiting for an answer, he pictured GD, lank hair and moles, scurrying to take the call in some dark cabbagy-smelling passage. Private dicks, snouts, were a sad breed; called Gold Dust by journalists they were mostly broke and living in places like Dalston or Ponder's End. GD had once come up with a hot story about an errant Dean and they'd kept in touch. They had an understanding. William knew a useful thing or two about GD's past.

'Want a job?' he muttered, when GD came on the line. 'Whatever you can get me on Barney James – as in husband. Five hundred.'

'Urgent?'

'Quite.'

It wasn't all that over the top, William decided. In fact, he reckoned it could justifiably be charged on expenses – it was good stuff to have on file. The focus was going to be on Victoria. She would be steadily more high-profile: useful to know about it if she had a rocky marriage. He thought that was likely. How could she possibly have fallen for that boorish blond berk?

He stared at the blue-leather double photograph frame on his desk: Ursula and the girls on one side, Tom on the other. Tom was in school-grey trousers leaning against a tree, grinning and looking so young. He was nineteen now, at art college, living in halls and away from home. All poised for the rush to the future. William hoped he wouldn't get there too fast.

It wasn't a great picture of Ursula. She was smiling into the sun with her brow furrowed. Her flaxen hair was held back with combs and he preferred it loose. She had a contained, refined quality that had been part of the attraction. Was it now all part of the trouble?

The girls were looking sweet. Emma, fair as her mother, and little Jessie with her violety-chocolate eyes. She and Tom were dark, Tom the image of his father – so people always said.

He felt intense paternal love almost like a physical pain and got up and went to the window. The river was looking silver-plated in the moonlight. Gazing out on to the winking, glittering city William thought of all the saddos and druggies, the loneliness and greed. And somewhere out there, Victoria was at home with her ghastly Barney.

In his mood of introspection he began thinking about marital nothingness. His life with Ursula was a plateau, a tundra; there were no breathtaking hills, no heart-stirring views.

Was he to blame? Was it his lifestyle, his job, the hours? Or was the widening crack in their understanding just a marital fault-line, a natural flaw that had slowly become more pronounced? Ursula gave him clean shirts and inscrutable looks when he left for London, but where was the love and the hugs? He thought of Lampedusa's cynical description of marriage in *The Leopard*. 'Flames for a year, ashes for thirty.' But it needn't be that way; people could grow closer as well as apart.

It was midnight, time to get off. Commuting hadn't had a hope, he thought; he'd tried, he'd done his best. And Ursula might hate coming to London for a few short night hours but it wouldn't hurt her to make the effort once in a while. She hadn't been to the flat since Oscar's last dinner and that silly row, which had actually been quite funny.

'Are you an opera fan?' she had cheerily asked the lugubrious Ian Fuller and it had sung out in a conversational lull like a cut-glass accent on the Tube. The man had just been sacked as Covent Garden's director, kicked out in a blaze of publicity. He shouldn't have shown his irritation, William thought, but there had been pictures of Fuller in every bloody paper. It had made Ursula look foolish when she wasn't.

He and Ursula were fine; they had wonderful children and a perfectly pleasant life – just a bit semi-detached. The fault was in him, not her. He should try seeing it from her point of view and not crash out at weekends and duck the neighbours' parties.

He didn't want to. He didn't want the weekend to come. He just wanted to stand at his window all night, thinking about Victoria. About her wide eyes, the feel of her soft dark hair: about a moment of meeting that had arrested his brain. And while his mind had been stationary she had climbed right in and stayed. He was feeling some inner force at work. It was powerful and baffling, exhilarating and frustrating in the extreme.

Having lunch with her would get noticed. Skeat was nothing if not vengeful, and the *Courier* would be on to it even before the table was booked. Jim would mix it. The diaries would spin lobbying stories. Being up-front was always best, he thought. He would choose a media haunt – possibly somewhere like Christopher's? Certainly not a quiet bistro.

So they would have a nice little chat about euthanasia in full view of the world and then what? Nothing. She was having lunch to keep in with the *Post* or because it had been hard to refuse. Even because of an attraction, but not – as the Downsland Minister – out of a burning need to jump into bed with him. Whereas he, William thought, was being driven mad with it.

Dave was waiting downstairs. He took out her cuttings folder from his middle desk drawer and thumbed back. *Victoria James takes Southampton East . . . with her husband, Barney, forty-three.*' That affected Election-night kiss for the cameras, God, what a poser. He flicked open his briefcase and put in the folder, locked it and went out to the lifts.

He was in at seven next morning, keen to see the later editions and know how the Skeat stuff was playing. The heavies pontificated. The tabloids, apart from the *Courier*, had just lifted the pictures while crediting the *Post* with gross invasion of privacy.

There were sounds of Margie arriving. Minutes later she was buzzing with Oscar on the line. 'Got the earplugs in?' she said.

'Shit,' William replied.

'What the fuck do you think you're playing at?' Oscar blasted. 'Do I give you *editorial freedom*,' he ponced up the phrase, 'to zap my good friend Ivor Skeat low down in the balls? No reference to me, you just go right ahead. Fuck you, Bill – do you think I need this?'

Oscar had a Buddha-like body and spindly legs. William dared to imagine he was quite valued by Oscar — whose rage, he sensed, would work through. 'It'll shift papers,' he said, 'and we're hardly bashing the good guys. Skeat's had it coming for years. I don't see why he needs the kid-glove treatment.'

'Yes, you damn well *do* see why! He's going to want his pound of flesh. I'd sack you this minute, Bill, if I had any goddamn sense, and if it wasn't for the fat severance packet.'

'It's me he'll go for. I can handle it — I'll watch my back.' William thought it wise to keep Oscar talking and asked, 'Harold Reid's no mate of yours, is he?' Reid was a fat-cat friend of Royalty and could easily be one of Oscar's too. 'He's over-stepped it,' William carried on when that was cleared, 'and it could be quite big. He makes his millions out of loo-rolls — appropriate commodity when you think of it — and still has to cheat and fiddle. We'll get him; it'll take time but we'll splat him from a great height and get the credit, too.'

Oscar liked that but said threateningly, 'Skeat's not a man to cross, Bill. You just keep your head down and stay outta trouble, or there'll sure as hell be some.'

William swivelled in his seat and gazed out of the window. October sun was streaming in. He wanted trouble; he wanted Victoria.

His telephone never stopped. The morning conference ran on; he had a queue of people to see. Margie brought him letters for signing. As she turned to go, William said, 'Fred Buckley, the ex-Home Secretary, is giving a lecture next Wednesday. Can you get me the details?'

'Will do. You're late for your lunch and Harry's still waiting.'

'Better send him in,' he said with a sigh.

He left the office soon after eight and Dave raced him across London to *The Firing Line* studio. The programme was live and went out at nine on Friday evenings. Ursula complained about the loss of Friday nights, but she had no complaints about the new tennis court, he thought.

The debate that night was on food labelling: hard to sex up but William did his best. He stayed on drinking with the production team afterwards when he should have been going home.

He eventually went out to find Dave among the mêlée of waiting cars. He got in the back, yawning. 'Think I need a kip,' he said, wanting no chat. 'Sorry it's got so late.'

'All overtime,' Dave tossed back, doing a nippy three-point turn.

They were the wrong side of London; it would be nearly one before he got home. He did have three bloody weekend nights there, William thought irritably, feeling the effects of whisky on too little food. He sometimes went in to London on Sunday afternoons for the Monday paper but never broke his rule of getting back home for the evening. Tom came most weekends but left after Sunday lunch. It was William's special time with the girls; he checked their homework, gave them vocab tests.

He remembered they were on half-term. Victoria had a daughter who was probably on half-term, too, he thought. Sixteen: was she giving her problems? He imagined everything patched up between her parents, after that row in the Academy, an intimate family weekend.

Clear of the City, the Jaguar purred. Jazz filtered back – Dave knew his tastes. William felt cocooned and coaxed into indulgence; he felt the loosening of the anchor of his marriage and he let the current take him.

He was picturing more than lunch, seeing her face, taking it in his hands. She was married. The press called her 'Miss Priggy'. He remembered a cartoon about a schoolgirl who always did her homework. And there was a real world out there, media butchers who would carve them up and feed them to the printing presses. Was she going to risk that? Was he?

Dave slowed down; they were going through Brearfield, William's local market town on the Surrey-Sussex borders, familiar, friendly, but stultifying. They turned up a lane and went in through his white five-barred gate, always kept open, that had *Old Vicarage* painted on it in black. The house was 1860s, built by a rector for his seven children and fifteen horses, so the records said. The stables had long been converted and sold off.

William pushed on the central brass knob of his glossy black front door, thinking Ursula would be asleep or pretending to be; he stood guilty of making himself late with that in mind. He hoped she would blame the office if he were in an inattentive fog all weekend. It would be hard not to be. He felt gripped; he had a goal, a need, and he lived by conviction and drive – a belief that determination and wanting it badly enough was the way to win through.

CHAPTER 8

It had been a terrible weekend, desperately anticlimactic. Victoria had had such high hopes. Seeing her parents, having quality time with her daughter. But William had been so much on her mind and Barney's every word and gesture had grated. He'd monopolized Nattie, with all the cooking – and sucked up as usual to his mother-in-law, Victoria had felt maddened and had ended up snapping at everyone like a bad-tempered bitch with her puppies.

They had just dropped Nattie back at school in Newbury and were driving on to London. The thought of a Sunday night alone with Barney filled Victoria with dread. Her backlog of work did too; it had been piling up over half-term. And she hated to think of Nattie seeing them at each other's throats all weekend, all the barbs and veiled looks. It made her ashamed.

She touched Barney's arm. 'Can we wipe the slate?'

His eyes flickered. 'That's a way of saying I should share the blame, is it? That's rich!'

It was an understandable reaction. She transferred her guilt to her mother, Bridget, who had tried nobly to be ballast all weekend and keep the peace. Her mother's perennial sweetness to Barney was exasperating, Victoria had never felt able to confide things about him. Her gentle dimpled mother had quietly taken an opposite line to her father and encouraged marrying him for the baby's sake. Telling tales of violent temper flashes or tennis-club flirting would have been cruel.

Barney had his eyes on the road. 'Can't you bloody buck up a bit?' He sounded close to blowing a fuse. 'I did just say something. It's like talking to someone's sodding voicemail.'

'Sorry, love, I'm just so behind with work. Nattie seemed very on edge, getting back to school, didn't you think? I do hope it's not all to do with the new boyfriend.'

'Give her a break, she's entitled to her moods.'

And I am to mine, Victoria thought, fast losing the urge to be sweet and try harder.

Even her father, John, had got her on the raw. He'd been critical about MDF and it had been hard to take. His judgment was always so sound. They were very close; he understood the things that motivated her, her private passions. Memories of the time of his imprisonment were hazy but Victoria knew the circumstances. She felt fiercely proud and protective.

Her mother, an able physicist, had selflessly given up her career to look after the family. Never a complaint: it was in part her nature but also a feature of her generation. Now, though, she was busily involved locally; she had a life of her own. It was John, the keen follower of politics, who asked all the sharp, pertinent questions.

They had been for a walk, she and her father, after church that morning, a little tradition of theirs that Victoria loved. Out in a field she had told him in confidence about MDF board.

'There is a real health risk, Dad. I'm sure it's the right thing to do.'

'You're seriously thinking of banning it?' He had sounded incredulous.

'Yes, on medical evidence – workers' respiratory problems. Of course, I may not get it past my colleagues. Guy Harcourt has it in for me, he thinks my job's positive discrimination!'

'Can't you just give it a health warning, like cigarettes? Respiratory ills can be caused by many things and I should think the risk is infinitesimal.'

'They're thinking of banning it in America.'

'So? We do things differently here and I don't see people keeling over like ninepins.'

She had felt put out and provoked. No squeezes of the arm or assurances that she had the facts, not he, had helped. The damage had been done.

Barney was going over Hammersmith Bridge; they were nearly home. Her need of her father was suddenly acute. She was thinking about the finite time left with him, of his thin bony body, the white hair sticking out under his cap. His faded tweed jackets smelled of wood fires and Christie. She was in need of his hugs and love – of a release from Barney.

It wouldn't do, she told herself, unpacking the car; the onus was on her to make more of an effort. She smiled at Barney. 'Thanks for doing the driving, it's nice to be home.'

'Don't look so hang-dog about it then,' he said unfairly. 'What's eating you, exactly?'

'I think it was Dad, getting me down. He doesn't agree with me over an issue of health safety in the construction industry.' She hoped that sounded routine enough not to get him interested. Barney liked being involved, but he wasn't entirely to be trusted.

There was a distinct autumn-evening chill and the Aga's warmth was welcome. They weren't over it yet; the atmosphere was still strained as Barney made some supper, soup and cheese on toast. Victoria cleaned the cheesy grill afterwards, in the spirit of doing her bit.

As she pulled off her rubber gloves he came close and kissed her. It was a hard, passionate kiss and she had so much work to do. 'Later, later – backlog first,' she said, trying to make light, hoping no hint of impatience was showing.

'Oh, sorry if I'm keeping you.' He pushed her away brusquely.

'I must get some work done, love,' she said, touching his lips, 'get some under my belt and I'll finish the rest, first thing.'

She went up to the ground-floor sitting room. It was a seldom-used room but soothing and pleasing to be in, with an amber-marble mantelpiece, a Chesterfield covered in textured cream. There was an old Turkish rug bought on an early holiday. Her desk was under the back window and looked out over the fig tree, settling down to work she felt full of relief.

Reading housing projections, Marty's occasional little notes in the margins, her thoughts flitted from Nattie to Barney to Guy Harcourt and MDF. But William straddled them all like a Colossus. She imagined what lunch could lead to. But it couldn't be allowed to go anywhere; that was the reality, the harsh truth of it.

'I think you've done enough now,' Barney said rather menacingly, appearing after only half an hour. He came behind her as he often did, and parting her hair, gave her neck a little bite. 'My turn now,' he murmured, 'and you'd better be good!'

She had been so stroppy and withdrawn all the weekend. She locked away her work with the smallest suppressed sigh, and stood up with a smile.

He took hold of her wrists, staring. 'You've been very distant.' She shook her head as if to dismiss that, but he kept his eyes fixed on hers. Then, taking her arms behind her, he spun her round so that he could keep her wrists clasped. 'But you're going to make up for it now,' he whispered into her hair, walking her in front of him to the stairs.

He was rough and dominating, as though trying to force her to take notice; he couldn't bear being made to feel unwanted. She meekly played her subjugated role but afterwards lay in bed, sore and deeply depressed. He would have known her responses were faked; he knew all about women's sexuality.

In the past, Barney's sex-drive had been a powerful pull, transmitting waves. He was given to excess and sexual adventures – like a gambler he couldn't stop – but he always wanted them with her, too. He cared in his own way and he was generous to a fault: dinners out, beautifully wrapped presents, armfuls of scented flowers. But for all his bantering charm and cocky outgoingness, she thought, he badly needed bolstering and had no sense of self-worth.

She lay awake for hours; her life seemed capsized, a mess. Parliament was back, and her workload even greater. The State Opening was on Tuesday, and all MPs had to have signed the book and been sworn in beforehand. Somehow that had to be fitted in next day. And then Wednesday was the start of the Downsland public enquiry – and the opening of the Goya exhibition. It had been right to resist going to that, she thought. No, it hadn't. She was lying in bed thinking of nothing else.

The first day of the Downsland enquiry was going to be murder. The DAG's chairman, the Reverend Jeremy, would give endless interviews; she'd be dashing to studios, constantly expected to respond, the pressure intense. Sam Swayne would never be off camera – in one of his billowing white shirts and looking more the swashbuckling hero or romanticized slave than a troublesome young protestor. There was little chance of getting to Fred Buckley's lecture, let alone meeting William at the Goya.

Sleep refused to come. The photographs of Ivor Skeat's wife splashed in the *Post* bothered her – although Nick Bates, her friend among the Department's Ministers, had argued the case on the day.

'You're such a stickler, Victoria,' he'd teased. 'Think of all the poor suckers with golden careers full of promise that Skeat does in every Sunday. He's had it coming.'

'But targeting his wife – that's such disgusting intrusive journalism.'

'So they got caught? It was in a public place. Osborne sure won't be Skeat's flavour of the month, though!'

She made it to the Commons next afternoon, in time to sign the book in the Chamber before the State Opening. She was there co-incidentally with Rufus Coram, who had been confirmed that day as her Shadow. Thin-faced, with bright, mean, challenging eyes, he made her think of a bird of prey; he'd certainly be swooping and rooting out any juicy facts to use against her, Victoria thought. She felt his match on the floor of the House but he was clever – he knew his way round the Westminster village, the media, and he had the ear of his leader. He would be chipping away at her reputation and giving slanted stories to the press in his typically scheming way. She hoped it wouldn't all be believed.

The splendour and pomp of the State Opening wasn't new to her but it was for Barney. Tickets for backbenchers' families were limited and drawn in a ballot, and in the past he'd told her not to bother. Ministers' spouses had special seats, though, and he'd decided to come.

She didn't see him afterwards, as both of them had to dash off, and by the time they were having supper together her mind was on Rufus Coram again. Confiding her fears about him to Barney, it was clear he wasn't interested. He'd wanted to talk about the State Opening. 'So how was it in the spouses' seats this morning?' she asked belatedly. 'Were you the only man?'

Barney affected a bored look but he was obviously very full of it. He glared. 'There was the most appalling cock-up, if you must know – a ridiculous business with the seating.'

That was hard to believe of an occasion that ran like Royal clockwork. 'Surely not!' she exclaimed. 'Whatever happened?'

'Well, I find this tiny gallery above the Lord's Chamber after a load of wrong directions and then get this! The card on my seat says, *Mr Victoria James*. I mean, I ask you – what kind of morons are supposed to be running this country?' It was rhetorical. 'But I had a delightful Mrs Simon Elliot next to me.' Barney stuck out his chin. 'A pretty blonde thing.'

And wife of the Deputy Chief Whip, Victoria thought, who was far from delightful himself. 'If you can have Mrs Simon Elliot,' she ventured, 'why not Mr Victoria James?'

'You know very well why not and if you don't, you're not the woman I married,' Barney said impatiently, 'and you're interrupting my flow! It was a minute gallery, no knee-space at all. I liked looking down on the elevated birds in their *décolletée* and tiaras, better than bald male pates, but where were you when the MPs poured in and the Queen got going?'

'There's a sort of pecking order – the PM and Chancellor, Foreign and Home Secs. Junior Ministers get trampled on by pushy back-benchers.'

'You leave them all standing,' Barney said with genuine pride, surprising her as he often did with his mercurial changes of mood.

She made it to Fred Buckley's lecture the next evening. It was in Church House, a smallish bright hall near Westminster with comfortable seats in semi-circles. Sitting a row from the back, wistful about the Goya, she was glad for Fred that the hall was nearly full: an audience of MPs, researchers, journalists and Americans.

It had been as hellish a day as expected. The Downsland enquiry had opened to angry, shoving crowds, and the police were out in their numbers. The Inspector had somehow managed to get the proceedings off the ground, but on television the scene had looked grimmer than a first day at the sales.

Her interviews had been tough going. 'How can the Government possibly justify such a costly enquiry, Mrs James,' a sharp young political commentator had asked, 'with such an overwhelming weight of opinion against this purely commercial development?'

'We are acting fairly and responsibly. The law requires that these proposals are given proper consideration; an enquiry is absolutely necessary – people must be allowed to put their case.'

'Isn't Government simply in the pockets of a powerful consortia of developers?'

'That's absurd. The question is whether this is the right place for a development of this size and nature. When we have the enquiry's findings, everything will be taken into account.'

She thought of Nattie watching the news with schoolfriends. After the impassioned outpourings of sexy Sam Swayne, the Government line would sound dull, dry and defensive. Would William, seeing it, think her just another politician, drearily uninspired?

'We must protect the European-American partnership . . .' Fred got started, speaking strongly and clearly, and it made her think of William's voice. It too was authoritative, one of the things that so attracted her. She tried to concentrate on Fred's talk, and wondered casually why he hadn't been brought back into Government – probably due to some private grudge of the PM's.

Someone coming in late was moving along the row behind, the back row. She half-turned and saw it was William. He hadn't come to hear a lecture, she thought with a hammering heart as he sat directly behind her. What was he playing at – just flirting and having fun? There were journalists in the audience. It was no good being a moth to the candle-flame, secretly hoping, as she had all day, that he might somehow turn up – softening her studio make-up, worrying about her safe trouser-suit. Plain colours and clean lines were best for television, MPs were advised.

Fred was on his peroration. When the clapping started, William touched her shoulder. 'Don't rush away,' he said. 'I just need a quick word.'

'I thought you would be at the Goya?'

'I did go, briefly, but I needed to see you – I had something I wanted to say.'

Fred had started taking questions and she turned to the front again, her cheeks burning. When he took the last one, finally, William called out, 'What about the irresistible pull of self-interest?' People turned and she was glad not to be in the same row.

'That's the crux of the problem,' Fred replied fervently. 'We need to warn of the consequences, the risk to world stability. Now if the *Post* were to take it up . . . There's wine at the back,' he called as a general exodus began.

In the scrum she saw Fred moving in on William. He wasn't missing such an opening, she thought with frustration, unsure whether to stay or go.

'Congratulations on the job!' She turned; it was someone from the Foreign Office, a Downing Street policy adviser. 'Some of us had rather hoped you might come to the FO,' he said in a friendly way.

'It might have been less fraught than Downsland,' she laughed.

William came to join them. 'Could we have a quick word, Victoria?' He gave the policy adviser a witheringly dismissive smile and the poor man took his cue. Alone with her, William said, 'I just wanted you to know our lunch has nothing to do with Downsland. It's a personal interest, your father's case. I'd hate you to think other than that.'

'But Downsland will leap to people's minds.'

'True. But the Skeat press is gunning for me now, not you. I'll take the flak!'

'I did hate those pictures.'

'I couldn't stand the hypocrisy of that column – nor can I stand Skeat! It was just too good a chance to miss. Try not to think too badly of me.'

How could she, when he looked at her like that? 'I should go,' she said with a grin.

William said he should too, and left first. She went to tell Fred what a good speech he'd made and then hurried out to find Bob. The Westminster street was eerily quiet, a desert of shutdown offices. Bob drove her home and he seemed to know when to leave her to her thoughts.

Hadn't she promised to do supper? Had Barney said he'd be late? Everything had gone out of her mind. It was a question of trust, but William must have his motives. Was it too much to hope they could possibly be as simple and straightforward as hers?

CHAPTER 9

Victoria liked getting in by about eight in the morning with time to see the cuttings covering her area. They were always waiting on her desk in a stapled pile. A full spread of newspapers was provided too, all neatly laid out on a side-table.

She turned to the papers first, anxious to see the *Courier*. It had a regular diary columnist, Blake Hardy, whose bite-back pieces about politicians and personalities were a must-read for MPs. As she'd expected, there was a late insert, a couple of lines about William at the lecture – his strange appearance at a non-event talk by Fred Buckley (who he?) on the Atlantic partnership. Had the *Post* Editor got the wrong hall, Blake Hardy queried, or had Osborne naturally assumed that a few pompous jottings in his little organ could cement Euro-American relations at a stroke?

No mention of her being there. It was a bit slack of them not to have made the Downsland connection, but it would be a different story having lunch.

William must have been prepared for a diary piece; he'd asked a question and been quite up-front. She thought of him calling it out and Fred wanting to take him up.

Hearing a sound, she saw Marty had come in. Private Secretaries never knocked, they just discreetly appeared. 'Angie's on her way for the media update,' he said.

He discussed a meeting at the Treasury later that morning. Victoria was trying to win VAT relief for home refurbishments. It wouldn't be an easy meeting and she didn't want it running into lunch.

Angie was in her usual black. Drawing up a chair and never one for preamble, she got stuck straight in. 'You're wanted on *Question Time*: December sixteenth. The programme's skewed to Downsland by the sound of it. Your Shadow, Rufus Coram, is on with you and Bertie, that roly-poly chef with the starred restaurant near the site. William Osborne is on, too, I hear. You've got lunch with him soon, haven't you – about euthanasia?'

'It's today, actually,' Victoria answered, annoyed at Angie's pointed emphasis.

'Well, you should get his measure at least. Useful for *Question Time*,' the woman said grudgingly.

Angie ripped through other media bids, and then, returning her chair to the conference table, she said as a parting throw, 'The *Courier*'s out to get Osborne now after his attack on their columnist and Ivor Skeat's wife. They'll try and pin lobbying on him. Jim Wimple might talk it up too – he doesn't hit it off brilliantly with his boss.'

'I'm sure his boss can well handle that situation,' Victoria shot back sharply.

She smiled at Marty a bit ruefully when Angie had gone. 'Well,

I'd better get off to Prayers now,' she said. 'I'm quite nervous – I don't expect unanimity over MDF.'

Prayers was a misnomer for the Ministers' meeting, she thought. With no Private Secretaries or officials there, Ministers never held back, and things could get quite heated.

'I'm sure the Secretary of State will agree with your decision,' Marty said deferentially.

She hoped he was right. It was Ned, after all, who had the final say, who was boss.

She made it to his splendid office and took her seat at the table. All five Ministers were soon assembled and Guy Harcourt talked about a Local Government issue. It was his area of responsibility.

There was to be a small separate meeting immediately after Prayers for her to set out her case for a ban. She was tense, about to be tested and her lunch with William was too much on her mind.

Ned explained the extra meeting. 'Victoria wants to do something politically sensitive. I'd like the views of all of you.' He smiled at her. 'Over to you, then.'

Everyone turned except Guy, who kept staring out of the window annoyingly. She glanced down quickly at her paper that only Ned had seen and then, feeling mightily unprepared, did her best to present a compelling case for a ban.

Guy brought his eyes back. He had a politician's face, with skin the greyish sheen of uncooked pastry and slicked-down brown hair, but he was quite good-looking. He wore ambition like a sharp suit; you couldn't miss it. Victoria thought bitchily that his divorce must have been quite an inconvenient little glitch. After his reputed liaison with a television presenter – one with a well-trodden path to her bedroom door – his wife Sarah, an Earl's daughter, had upped sticks with the children and retreated to the family estates in Northumberland.

He looked at Victoria with disdain. 'You're seriously suggesting yet another regulation, a ban on MDF? Spare us more red tape, Nurse James!' He forced a laugh.

She brushed at a bit of fluff on her skirt and then lifted her eyes to face his sardonic stare. 'You'd compromise people's health so construction companies can squeeze a mite more profit?'

He gave a dismissive wave. 'And why shouldn't they? Spell out the risks; let people run their own goddamn lives.'

The Department's three pussies divided two to one. Justin, who was godly but very anti-regulation, and brogues-and-hockey-sticks Olivia were for Guy. Olivia had an impressive brain but had always been sweet on him. Nick Bates, though, was supportive, as Victoria had hoped.

'If we don't ban it, Europe will,' he said. 'We should get in first.' She felt grateful and forgave him a too-personal smile.

Ned rocked back on his chair-legs with the tips of his fingers touching; he let the arguments run then landed his chair with a muffled thump on the carpet.

He wound up the meeting giving no clue as to his opinion, neither vetoing nor supporting the ban.

Victoria immediately had to dash off to the Treasury. Ministers always went there, the Treasury team never played away. Their home ground had miles of disorientating corridors, cunningly designed, she thought, to put any poor supplicant at a disadvantage.

She went with Marty but an official came with them in the car and she couldn't really talk about what had happened over the MDF issue. It was frustrating. Guy wasn't going to walk all over her, she thought bitterly, still shaken by his rudeness. She blamed him for her deflated confidence. She had needed to be brimming over with it to have any hope of success at the Treasury. And at lunch too, it would have been a life-jacket, a way of keeping a hold on her feelings. She wanted to see William far too much.

At the Treasury they eventually found the high-ceilinged office of the Financial Secretary, Martha McCann. She was a fluffy blonde who wore a lot of make-up but she had a steely hold on the purse-strings and wouldn't likely cave in.

She waved them to a vast table and she and her own lieutenants sat opposite: they were like two little warring platoons.

VAT wasn't paid on new-built houses and it seemed only fair to exempt home refurbishments, but Victoria's reasoned arguments simply made Martha more resolute. It was a lost battle from the start. Martha used Treasury speak, saying she would give it 'consideration' and that 'with the greatest respect' it would be very costly and open-ended. 'I'd call it jam on the icing,' she said complacently.

'It would be logical and sound,' Victoria complained, as she and her team prepared to leave. She felt despairing, thinking that perhaps the rottenness of her morning equated with the sins of her longings for lunch.

There was an hour to go. November had arrived unremarked but the weather had turned. A violent downpour had just started and she was thankful Bob had said he'd be waiting in the basement car park; she didn't want to be a wet rat at lunch. She had taken almost as long as Nattie deciding what to wear and had finally chosen a well-fitting honey-coloured suit.

It was hard not to feel some symbolism in the stormy weather: heavy sulphurous clouds, dramatic thunder and the torrents. William had chosen Christopher's in Covent Garden, a media haunt and about the last place you'd take someone you wanted to get off with. Was that the idea though – a bit of a bluff? Or was she reading it all wrong anyway?

She turned and looked ruefully at Bob. 'It's been a bad enough morning without this.'

'Not helping the traffic,' he replied stoically.

He leaped out and held a big black umbrella over her when they arrived. The restaurant was on the first floor up a curving stone staircase, and with the rain forming rivers of water in the street it could have been a Venetian Palazzo. She stood at the foot of the stairs collecting herself, then, bending her head forward, she tossed back her hair and went on up.

The restaurant had pastel walls and a cheery mid-Atlantic bustle. William's table was pointed out to her and making her way to it, she smiled at journalists she knew. Toby, a friendly ebullient MP was there, having lunch with a woman in an in-your-face hat. He called out loudly, 'It's the White Queen! Hi, Victoria, not with your Black Knight today?'

'Hi, Toby,' she called back, cross. He was drawing attention to her, something she could do without.

William stood up and greeted her with sophisticated ease. He was wearing a navy suit and a red tie. He pulled out the table that was against the wall and she squeezed in to sit facing him. 'Sorry, bit of a squash,' he said, sitting down. 'Who's your Black Knight?'

'Oh, that's just Joe Reynolds, my Pair. It's a Westminster bad joke. We're good friends and that tag's sort of stuck. I mind being called the White Queen though. I don't feel at all regal.'

'No, you're not that,' he said, regarding her thoughtfully, leaving her wondering. He grinned. 'Fred's pushing me to use a piece on the Atlantic partnership. It would justify coming to his lecture but it's heavy going. I've got Carl Hancock trying to sex it up.'

She'd had her run-ins with Carl, who wrote for the *Post*. 'Carl needs sexing *down*,' she said. 'He writes like an angel but he's such a lech. Why can't men see it has the opposite effect? It's a bit like those paintings at the Academy – they were so *un*erotic!'

'Remember the man with the squint?'

'Yes. Did he explain that picture's finer points when I'd gone? He did seem to be longing to.'

'He said it was for individual interpretation. Each to his own orifice, I suppose, though with his eyes that could be difficult! Sorry, that's a bit squintist – and I should be getting the wine.'

While he looked round for a waiter she glanced at him quickly. She liked his dark hair that was greying a bit at the sides. It needed a cut but he would hate making time for those things. She wanted to touch it, to smooth his attractive thick dark eyebrows. He had good features: a straight strong nose, an appealing mouth. She remembered a line in Trollope's novel *Can You Forgive Her?* Something about a man's firm handsome mouth that befitted a good husband. Was he that – a good family man with an interest in euthanasia?

'I'm glad we could have lunch,' he said, bringing his eyes back.

A waiter came and he ordered a bottle of Pouilly Fuissé and mineral water. They looked at the menus. She chose vegetable terrine and halibut. 'I'll have the same,' William said, and the busy waiter hurried away.

She was facing into the restaurant and suddenly saw Guy Harcourt. He was having lunch with the *Courier*'s political sketch-writer – who chose that moment to look her way. She imagined him saying that the *Post* Editor seemed very taken with Guy's fragrant colleague and Guy sticking in the Downsland knife. It couldn't be worse.

'Harcourt needs watching,' William said.

God, he missed nothing. He'd seen Guy, known where she was looking. She stared, wide-eyed, thinking she had to be a lot more careful. 'He's very able,' she said primly. 'We work closely together.' William was grinning as though that was protesting too much and she gave in and smiled. She shouldn't have; it was revealing and lowering her guard.

The waiter brought their terrines and leaned over the table, depositing her plate. As William moved helpfully aside, his knees brushed hers. It was accidental, incidental, but it was contact and she knew they were both aware of it.

'You wanted to talk about my father's case?' she asked, longing for the touch of his knees again.

'Sure you don't mind? That sentence for euthanasia seemed harsh and it must have been an incredibly difficult time for you all. How did he come to be tried? Did you have complete faith?'

The last question was a surprise and quite hurtful. It seemed ridiculous, so much not the issue. William would never have asked that if he'd met her father.

'Of course we had faith,' she said passionately. 'It simply wasn't like that. We couldn't have been more proud and supportive of him.' She didn't want such probing personal questions, but she said levelly, 'I was very young. My brother, who's four years older, had it harder, putting up with the teasing at school.' William was watching her over his wine. 'I'm very close to my father,' she added simply.

'But he did end a life. Haven't you ever worried about that, or discussed it in the family?'

'We've never needed to, that's the point. We love him.'

She told William about her father's patient, an intelligent ninety year old with all her faculties whose eyesight had gone and whose liver had been shot to pieces from a tropical illness. She had been so close to the end, in desperate pain, and had coerced him, sanely and intellectually, into letting her go. He'd given her the most marginally increased dose, but her companion had chosen to make trouble.

'It could have been bitterness over the will,' Victoria said, 'the few hundred pounds the old lady had left my father, although he'd immediately given that to charity. He served thirteen months of a two-year sentence but no one's been to prison for euthanasia since. It would never happen today.' William was staring and she looked down, fiddling with her piece of bread, worrying that she was being too open. Glancing up and trying to backtrack she said, 'What's your particular interest? Do you feel strongly about legalization?'

'I'll tell you on *Question Time*,' William answered, smiling. 'Euthanasia's sure to come up with you on – you know we're on same programme? You'll be a very distracting influence.'

She dropped her eyes again. William had his back to the room but she didn't have cover from the journalists and other MPs in the restaurant. She picked nervously at her bread. There would be a dig about lobbying in the *Courier*. Guy would talk – certainly to his friend in the Whip's office, the mean-minded Simon Elliot whose wife Barney had called 'a pretty blonde thing'. Toby, sitting quite close by with the woman in the hat, was a gossip.

The waiter brought the main course and refilled their glasses; Victoria refused more wine. 'But your father's practice took him back,' William went on. 'Wasn't that a huge tribute?'

'Yes,' she said proudly, thinking he must have read every cutting, 'and it meant a lot, but there were still people out to make trouble.' The memories came flooding back. Her father with his head in his hands; she had gone to comfort him, a small child, and been hugged very tight. Her mother had cried at an anonymous letter.

To her absolute horror, she felt her own tears pricking. She kept her head bent trying to stem them, fiddling with her bread again, distractedly rolling it into little grey balls

'I think you need another piece,' William said, smiling and giving her the one from his plate. His knuckles rested against hers. 'I shouldn't have made you talk about it.'

She had to look at him then, he'd sounded so gentle. He was staring at her again and it was hard to cope. She fished in her bag for a tissue.

She had felt each knuckle, felt it in the pit of her stomach, in her veins. And he knew; he would have seen it in her eyes. 'Sorry,' she said, blowing her nose. 'I don't know what came over me.'

'It was my fault for bringing back memories. Tell me about your brother. What does he do?'

'He's a neurosurgeon. His wife's an illustrator of children's books and they've got four of their own under ten.'

'And you've a daughter, Natalia?'

'Yes, we call her Nattie. She's in her first year of A-levels – as the oldest cousin she has to sort out all the squabbles.' Victoria thought of the mess of toys and bikes in Robert's big house in Barnes and felt wistful.

'She's at Newbury School, isn't she? You happy with it?'

'Quite. I worry about her boarding; it's hard to know what's best.' She was talking far too personally. The press must never get near Nattie. Sitting up straighter and feeling a need to regain some control, she enquired stiffly, 'Your wife must find newspaper hours quite a trial?'

'Before I forget,' William said, grinning, 'you might like to know that on the day you were appointed, Jim was going round saying you were the one to watch.'

'There are so few women,' she said dismissively, aware that William's blatant change of subject was giving her a dangerous lift. He wasn't wearing her down that easily and she said determinedly, 'My husband isn't best pleased with the workload. Luckily, he likes cooking.'

'But you're enjoying the job?'

'Loving it.' She felt a need to qualify that. 'Well, it is a bit daunting and hard on home life.'

'Is that to do with how little you see your daughter? It's my big problem,' William said, smiling easily. 'My two girls are ten and eleven and in day school, but I hardly used to see any more of them when I was commuting. I've got a son of nineteen, too. He's at art school in Camden, living in halls – he wants his independence.'

The coffee came. She wondered if William mentioning that he no longer commuted had been deliberate. Her heart was thudding loudly, the colour rising to her face.

'I must go,' she said. She didn't want to, the sense of finality was awful.

'I'll get the bill.' He wasn't pressing more coffee on her or giving any hint of possible future meetings. It was a terrible letdown. It was the right and proper thing.

With his eyes down signing the bill, William said, 'I'm at the Commons on Monday night, speaking to the all-Party Media Group.'

He looked up. 'Could we have a drink after that, perhaps? It should finish around eight.'

'Monday's late-night voting,' she said, playing for time. 'It might be a bit hard getting away. Perhaps we could have a drink at the Commons – the Pugin Room or somewhere?'

He tucked back his pen and held her eyes. 'Central Lobby at eight?'

She nodded, feeling like a racing-car driver who was failing to right a spinning skid. She thought of leaving the table together, of the journalists watching. 'Better rush,' she said, getting up. 'Thanks so much for lunch.'

'I'll just hang on for the waiter. Wait for me downstairs. I've got an umbrella, I can take you to your car.' He said it with authority, something she wasn't used to. 'It's pouring, you'll need a bit of help.' William stood up to pull out the table.

CHAPTER 10

Victoria stared ahead out of the windscreen. This couldn't go anywhere. It had to be just a drink. It was going to be so hard though, getting through the next few days – especially the weekend. She couldn't let anything happen: absolutely nothing more than a drink.

Lunch with William, a titillating piece in the *Courier*, a drink in a Commons bar; the rumours would be whirling like leaves. Worse still, the *Courier* would spin lobbying and that was professionally harmful. People would murmur about lack of judgment, flightiness; they might think it out of character but it wouldn't enhance her chances of promotion.

Of course William could be cleverly manipulating her. But it didn't feel like that, it really didn't. Talking to Di might help. No need to mention names and Di was completely loyal anyway.

She got through to her just before leaving the office. 'I need some help, Di. Can we meet?'

'Barney problems?'

'No. Someone I've met. We've only had lunch – we talked about euthanasia.'

'Everyone has to start somewhere. Monday? One o'clock at Uno's?'

'Thanks!' It meant scrapping a working lunch with Marty, but he wouldn't mind.

Di would tell Gerald, she thought, but in a way that preserved the confidence. She and Gerald were an unlikely couple; he was much older and had just had a huge heart bypass but Di entertained him with gossipy witty stories and was nurse, lover and good friend to him. She had a heart bigger than Wembley Stadium.

The couple had no children and lived in a funny little in-fill house near the Chelsea Embankment, not far from Hartley Street. Di had carved a niche for herself in the art world with her paintings of beautiful façades. She was never short of clients. Victoria wondered if she did occasionally extend her remit; she had once confessed that painting people's houses had certain logistical advantages.

Marty came in, to see her to the car with the boxes. He had his startled-rabbit look, and she suspected some niggly problem. 'The Opposition are adding to your workload, Minister,' he said, smiling ruefully. 'They've made their half-day slot on Tuesday a debate on housing.'

She stared at him in frustration. 'That's such a bugger!' she exclaimed, aware it was a slightly extreme reaction but it meant so much extra work on Monday night. She didn't want to have to cancel the drink. Whatever the downside or William's motives, some invisible thread was tugging, some bat-like undetectable irresistible call.

Bob took the weekend boxes from Marty and put them in the boot. It was only Thursday but Fridays were spent in the constituency. The weekend ahead with Barney loomed. Her father maintained that

shades of her feelings showed on her face like the colours of the
rainbow. 'Don't grow up and be a spy,' he used to warn. 'You wouldn't
last two minutes.'

Leaving next morning, she stopped before reaching the motorway
to buy the *Courier*. There was something in Blake Hardy, as expected,
and it was grim. It said sarcastically that the *Post* Editor was to be
seen with Cabinet Ministers at the Savoy on occasion, but he had
been spotted attentively lunching an inexperienced middle-ranker,
the comely Housing Minister Victoria James. Could the closeness
of his home to the controversial Downsland site just possibly have
been the spur for this cosy liaison? James was the Minister in charge.

She thought it bordered on the libellous and it got her blood up.
If she wanted a drink with William, no low-down Skeat columnist
was going to stop her. Driving on, her fulminating rage began
draining as steadily as sand in an egg-timer. It wasn't that simple.
She was part of a team now, and also happened to be married.
There was Nattie, too.

The Southampton streets were clogged and Jason was in one of
his usual flaps. 'It's put back the whole day! You'll be late for the
Small Business meeting and there's the pharmaceutical visit.' Her
lateness might have been altering the course of history. 'And you've
got Mrs Biggs's wine and cheese tonight.'

'It'll all work out, Jason, don't look so glum.'

She felt wretchedly glum herself; Di had to talk some sense into
her. It was raining and raw and she set off for her first meeting
filled with the thrill of William but feeling morbidly in harmony
with the weather.

*   *   *

Barney was driving to the cottage, battling with the Friday traffic. The rain wasn't helping, nor was his headache. It was the brandy; he should have gone straight to bed the night before instead of getting going on that. Victoria had been trying so hard to look asleep though, and it had got to him. She mightn't believe him about being out with a client but it wasn't pique at his night off, he thought; her mood was different this time. It had to be something deeper and more fundamental.

He put off thinking about it and revisited his evening with Mary. She was such a shy, studious little mouse with her fierce specs and frown. That was a turn-on in its way but she had other, well-hidden talents too. He felt amused at her guardedness when he'd started quizzing her about her own firm of solicitors.

They were a cut above his, he thought bitterly. Simmonds & Key were safe, plodding and going nowhere fast. Lincoln's Inn had seventeenth-century grey-stone çalm, ancient passages to the Law Courts, but as anyone with a clue knew only too well, it was the last bastion of middling solicitors. He hit the steering wheel with the heel of his fist.

Was Mary getting over-keen? For all her uptight professional primness she was showing the signs. Better cool it a bit. He liked her though; she had a good body and she was a giver – so much the opposite of Dick's wife, June. He had an image of Mary in seamed black fishnets and a corset and thought about buying them for her. And getting her to wear the tights to the office: he enjoyed the idea of her clacking down the corridors in fishnets. It would give those fucking smart-arse achievers at that firm something to chew on.

God, he felt lousy. The wipers were making an excruciating sound, even in heavy rain. The lights changed to red again and the traffic still hadn't moved. A boy was working the line of cars, selling roses. He looked so sodden. Barney lowered the window. 'How much the lot?'

'Gimme a twenty?'

He fumbled in his wallet. The man behind started up his horn and Barney cursed viciously. He exchanged a note for the roses and then, shutting the window, furiously held up two fingers to his driving mirror. The bugger behind probably couldn't even see; he felt tempted to storm out and give him the sign hard up to his window.

The roses were limp with the rain and a bit of a sickly salmon colour, but they'd cheer up with a good drink in a bucket of water. Would Victoria be pleased or just try and look it?

What the hell was wrong with her? That piece in the *Courier* had been a dismal double whammy – certainly a way of concentrating his mind. Dreadful rag, he would never have seen that diary piece if the receptionist hadn't had it open at the page.

He'd been reading it over her shoulder. 'Is it me perfume?' she said, turning with a grin.

'It's driving me wild with distraction.'

'No, it's not, you've been reading the bit about Mrs James!' Stupid cow, that receptionist.

Victoria couldn't let herself get taken for a ride by William Osborne. But wouldn't lobbying just make her more likely to decide the other way? She was so fucking stubborn. She had to deliver on Downsland. God, it would be awful if she didn't, after all the nods and winks to Roland Chalfern, assuring him that the scheme would go through. William Osborne was a real operator, though; sharp as tacks on *The Firing Line*. He'd use any dirty underhand tricks to stop a development that threatened his home.

Barney needed Victoria to be on side. Chalfern had something going with Downsland and it had to be big. He played things so close though. It was a bit rich when even his solicitor wasn't in the loop. Ideally, Hugh should be told about the problem, Barney thought, but perhaps not quite yet. He'd insist Victoria be told and she'd immediately have to declare an interest. She would be moved, sidelined, given some dead-end slot. Then Chalfern might schlepp off and take all his lucrative business with him, which was half the bloody firm.

Why would she have had lunch with Osborne in the first place? She wasn't born yesterday; she knew about lobbying and that the media would have a go.

Could she be seeing him? It would explain a lot. Hard to imagine it being Osborne, normally, she'd run a mile from the press. And there was Downsland: surely he was the very last person? What's more, the man could look scruffy and beardy and was quite a bit older. Would she really go for that?

If there *was* someone, Barney thought, it was far more likely to be an MP. How else could she manage any meetings?

His headache was getting worse and he put a hand to his temple. She couldn't do this to him. It was her dependability he loved. She'd been off him before; it was probably just pressure of work. The bloody job always came first – even before her husband and daughter.

He arrived at the cottage and parked on the hard standing. Getting out, he felt stiff and aching. Victoria opened the front door, wearing her coat. 'Hi! It's Mrs Biggs's do tonight – remember?

I was nearly having to rush and leave you a note – have you had an evil journey?'

'Don't ask!' He leaned back in for his bunches of roses. 'I bought you these,' he said, piling them into her hands. She made the face she reserved for one of his more gross extravagances, which a few mangy roses certainly wasn't, and kissed his cheek by way of thanks. 'I'll come to that fundraiser if you give me a minute,' he said, 'tired as I am.'

He had a sense she was trying to put distance between them. He didn't want that; it was making him feel even more rock bottom. She wasn't going anywhere on her own.

Later that evening Barney had to let out some of his suspicions. 'I saw the piece in the *Courier* today. Wasn't it all too obvious Osborne would want to lobby? He lives near Downsland. Whyever did you have lunch with him?'

'He's got a particular interest in euthanasia,' she replied. 'He'd told me when I was at the *Post* – we'd fixed to have lunch then. I'd expected there'd be some silly diary piece but you can't let things like that rule your life.'

Barney felt exhausted and unsure what to think. He had a feeling in his bones of mounting suspicion and a hurt sense of rejection but what she had just said had a ring of truth. Victoria was straight dealing; it was another of her qualities he loved. He didn't press it. He didn't want to think too hard or keenly, he just wanted to be close to her, to feel her warmth.

'You're a bit on edge,' he said, switching off the bedside light. He was showing his feelings, but he wanted her to be aware of them and feel some guilt.

She touched his cheek. 'It's all the hassle of Downsland, darling.'

'Fuck Downsland,' he said succinctly, and drew her to him in bed.

CHAPTER 11

Uno was a small Italian restaurant in Pimlico, friendly and very noisy. Di was there, in a tight charcoal sweater-dress, turning heads with her handsome looks and tremendous boobs, gesticulating and attracting attention, just what Victoria didn't want.

She pushed through to join her. Uno was a much-loved old haunt but the tables suddenly seemed far too close for a private talk. They caught up with general news till Di said, grinning, 'Tell me all now, you old prude. I can't wait – you're glowing!'

Victoria gave a sketchy account, guardedly, very *sotto voce*. 'I can't get involved, Di. I only have to cross my legs and some pressman's taking a picture.'

'I do see they'd get more excited if you uncrossed them. Is he an MP?'

Victoria looked round anxiously. On one side of them, a beautiful young man was gazing into his friend's eyes and on the other, two businessmen were struggling to entertain some silent Japanese. It seemed more or less safe. 'He's a newspaper editor: he does other things too.' Di would work out who he was without any trouble.

'Doesn't it help if he's press himself?' she asked, looking intrigued.

'Hardly. His rivals would think it was Christmas! And he's just made a serious enemy of one.'

The waiter arrived with their tagliatelle, bright with asparagus-tips and pungent with fruity olive oil. He brought Di's glass of white wine, poured Victoria some water and left.

'But surely an MP's private life is less of a big deal than it used to be?'

'Not really. Gays can do their own thing, except on a common, but try being married! He is, too, of course. I'm acting like a lovesick teenager, Di. We haven't even held hands. But we're having a drink at the Commons tonight and that must be that. I've just got to accept it.'

Di studied her. 'You don't want that, nothing's clearer. And you may be a whiz at politics but your private life's a mess. You should have left Barney years ago. Why can't you go with your instincts and just see what happens? Take it step by step. And for God's sake, don't start worrying about his wife. For all you know, she's got a nice little scene with a tasty librarian in Tonbridge.'

'Dorking,' Getting a blank look Victoria explained patiently, 'It's nearer Dorking than Tonbridge.' She got cross then when Di started cracking up. 'You don't understand! I'm not a free agent. A press demolition job on me could have repercussions for the whole Government.'

She thought of all the hounding and dissecting, the constant exposure. It was impossible to get across how intense the pressure could be. Di couldn't really know and she was so irrepressible anyway. She also had it in for Barney.

They ordered cappuccinos. Victoria was finding it hard to think responsibly, seeing William in hours. 'Want a lift?' she offered, 'Might as well make the most of Bob while I still can, before I'm sacked . . .'

'That's more like it! I do understand – more than you think.'

In the car, Di said in a coded whisper for Bob's benefit, 'And no losing sleep over Tonbridge. It's more her problem, remember – you've got quite enough of your own.'

'That's morally challenged and heartless,' Victoria whispered sententiously but they were soon giggling behind their hands in the back seat like girls at an office party.

At eight o'clock Victoria went to wait in Central Lobby, her nerves taut as violin strings. Under Di's bad influence she had cut corners with work for the debate but now all her uncertainties were creeping back. She had got everything out of proportion. William was just flirting, amusing himself. He'd been coming to the Commons anyway. Ursula had joined the Downsland Action Group.

Barney's interest in Downsland, too, was troubling. Surely he couldn't have lied about Chalfern? He might be barefaced about his women, but professionally – surely not? He was a responsible solicitor and intelligent. It would be the end of her, Victoria thought.

She looked round the splendid hall. It was a pivotal meeting-place, lofty and circular with green benches against the walls but also a throughway that led out in four directions. Monday was late voting and there were a lot of comings and goings, with visitors and MPs, watching policemen and attendants. The sight always made her feel a humbling sense of awe, all the more so as a Minister. Parliament's making of laws, the seamless binding of history and tradition with the needs of now; it was precious, to be guarded and never toyed with.

MPs were criss-crossing, hurrying. Simon Elliot, the Deputy Chief Whip, wandered in and sat down on an opposite bench. Her heart sank. He must be meeting someone. Barney might have liked his nice wife at the State Opening, but Simon was a malicious shit with an almost congenital need to do people down. He was looking across, studying her; she hated the feeling of his eyes on her legs. And in a clingy red wool dress and heels he would see she had taken trouble with her appearance. William only had to walk into Central Lobby for the *Courier* piece to leap into Simon's mind.

She was desperately trying to decide what to do when a voluminous elderly woman sailed into Central Lobby like a stately liner and made straight for Simon. 'I saw those googly eyes, dear,' she boomed, 'but you're stuck with me tonight. Dinner with your old maiden aunt!'

She was in fringed purple, splendidly eccentric. People looked amused but he was struggling to suppress embarrassed rage. 'Wonderful seeing you, darling Aunt Delia,' he drawled with puke-making unctuousness. He jumped up and practically propelled her out of the hall.

William was just coming in as they left – from another direction, but Simon had eyes everywhere. She thought it possible he had seen him. William was with some of the Media Group he'd just been speaking to. Tall spare, he looked so much more interesting than any of the ill-assorted bunch of MPs. She desperately wanted to be alone with him.

'Quick one?' Brian Evans, the Group's chairman was pressing. 'We can't have you getting away with that sneaky line on press intrusion.'

Victoria studied her hands, heart thudding, dreading William's reply.

'Thanks, but I've got a meeting with Victoria James and I can see she's waiting.' She looked up and he smiled over at her.

'You come for a drink, too, Victoria?' Brian Evans called out.

She got up to join them. 'Sorry, too short of time, Brian.' He was such an interfering twit.

'I do need a word later,' he persisted. 'Small housing problem and an idea of mine.'

Couldn't they leave her alone? Questions in the House, debates sprung on her and then buffoons like Brian Evans whinging and pushing potty schemes. She tried to sound firm and workman-like but friendly. 'Perhaps during the vote – I am very pushed tonight.'

'We'd better get a move on then,' William said, taking her arm.

Walking out of Central Lobby she could feel the eyes of the entire Media Group on their backs. As they turned the corner out of sight, William said scathingly, 'How can you put up with the likes of Brian Evans? He's got the intellect of a Teletubbie.'

'That's a bit harsh, there are lesser talents around this place!'

They passed Strangers dining room where Members could take guests. Looking in, Victoria saw Simon and his aunt, reading menus. It was one less worry. And going into the Pugin Room, Guy Harcourt and Toby, both of whom had seen her at lunch, were nowhere around.

It was a smallish bar with a wood-panelled bay window over-looking the Thames, another place where Members could entertain.

They found a free table and she ordered two glasses of white wine. 'You often have drinks and supper with Joe Reynolds, your Black Knight?' William asked, looking round as though the bar was reminding him of Toby's joke about her Pair.

'Sometimes, but only in the canteen – there's strict segregation in Members' dining room! Do I gather from Brian Evans' remarks you were passing the buck on press intrusion?' she queried, smiling.

'I just suggested that for some people publicity was sweet oxygen.'

'Suffocating for others,' she came back sharply. 'You must agree it's gone too far.' She didn't want to be sparring, sitting in tub-backed leather chairs, like distant islands. She wanted contact, to be anywhere but where they were.

'Of course it has,' William said, 'and those Media Group thickos couldn't even see I was on the defensive! I had to talk about something though, and it's very topical and on my mind.'

She wondered if that was to do with Skeat. Someone at the next table wisecracked and William lobbed one back. They were getting nowhere, but wasn't it better that way?

'Sorry I was so embarrassing, talking about my father at lunch,' she said.

He looked at her; he seemed quite on edge. 'You weren't. I wish we could have talked more about it. There's never enough time though – just like tonight.'

That seemed pretty final. She felt punched, so sure that something, somehow, had been going to develop. 'It's an impossible life,' she said limply. Had she really thought he would spirit her off to a candle-lit dinner and hold her hand?

William leaned forward, his elbows on his knees. It brought him closer and he said under his breath, 'I need to talk to you. Can we have a walk on the Embankment or something?'

It was like a scattergun to her thoughts; they went flying in all directions and she struggled with how to react. 'I'll just sign for the drinks,' she said with a quick smile. 'It is a bit complicated. I can't be out for very long.'

Her coat was in her room and she suggested he wait in the passage near the riverside terrace. It led to the canteen and also to the underpass that went directly into the Tube station. It would be the most unobtrusive way of leaving, she thought.

Getting her coat, she decided it was too great a risk and she should apologise, say there simply wasn't time. As she squirted on some scent, she changed her mind. Leaving with him, just being seen walking in the street – was that really such a sin?

She turned into the corridor, where William was looking at prints of the old Parliament in ruins before Pugin redesigned it. As she went to join him, Joe Reynolds, her Pair, called out from behind her, 'Quick canteen supper, Victoria? I'm just on my way.'

It seemed such a coincidence after William's comment in the bar. As Joe caught up she said, 'Thanks, but I've got a mass of work, I'll take a rain check.'

'Hold you to that.' He chatted with William. As a Minister in the last Government, their paths would have crossed. Then turning, he said with a grin, 'See you later then, Queenie,' and went on ahead.

'Joining your Black Knight later?' William asked a bit dryly.

'Oh no, he just meant the vote – and we go through our separate lobbies at that.'

She took William down a wide stone passageway, past a photo booth and cash machines, and out by the post deliveries door. They went along a covered walk that bordered Speaker's Court. One or two hurrying people eyed them but an Editor and a Minister wasn't such an uncommon sight and not everyone read the *Courier*.

From the Tube station they took the exit to the Embankment.

A biting wind greeted them, coming up the steps. Victoria shivered and tied the belt of her camel coat more tightly. It was a moonless night, dark and cold. Crossing the busy road she felt very exposed to passing cars, glad when she and William were by the low stone barrier wall and could look out at the river. They stood side by side, staring out on to the blackly swirling Thames.

'Thanks for coming,' William said.

'It was hard to talk in there.'

She kept looking ahead. The wind was lifting her hair and she gave another shiver. William touched her arm and the Pugin Room seemed a million miles away.

His hand stayed resting on her arm and she turned to meet his eyes. He stared without smiling. 'I'm sorry, this was a bad idea – it's too cold out here. We could go to my flat though, and have a drink and talk there? It's small but near here – walking distance, actually.'

'It's this side of Charing Cross,' he continued. 'Perhaps if we start walking you could decide if you think there's time?'

It was sensitive of him, she thought, helping her not to have to reply.

He took her arm crossing over the road, but they kept well apart down a silent Whitehall street whose looming buildings looked faceless, grey and immutable. She felt confident he didn't have some sort of cynical entrapment in mind – more worried about how often he took girls to his flat. It made her think of Ursula, but she tried hard not to. Her need was too overwhelming, it was overriding sane thoughts and sensibilities and her feet kept walking.

'I had to see you,' William said. 'I was desperate you mightn't come.'

She didn't answer but felt an elated swell. He was striding out very purposefully and she was in heels, hardly able to keep up. 'You're going a bit fast for me,' she said.

He turned and grinned. 'That could be taken two ways! Sorry, I'm so keen to get there – to get you in the warm.'

They crossed Northumberland Avenue. Turning into a narrow street, a drunk pushed past but she thought he was beyond recognizing anyone. William took a cut-through alley that came out to a terrace of Regency houses that were offices, she thought; they had nameplates and looked shut up for the night. The street was on an incline and at right angles to the river.

'Mine's that block on the corner,' William said. 'They're mostly company flats, I think, or overseas owned. I never see anyone.'

It was a modern building. As he keyed in a code she felt watching eyes all around, hidden cameras, relief when the heavy door swung closed. 'It's the fifth floor, the top,' William said.

The lift was small and they had to stand close. Looking down, she saw he had a bunch of keys in his hand with one selected and firmly held. His other hand was beside hers and the back of it was touching. So lightly, it might not even have been intended. The sensation was electrifying and it was hard not to give a shiver.

Her face was tingling with the warmth of indoors. Unlocking his door, William said, 'It's very tiny and impersonal, very unlived-in. I never bring anyone here.'

She went into a small hall and looked around. There was a door to a sitting room; she could see a brick-coloured sofa, and another door that she assumed led to a bedroom. Down a small passage there looked to be a little kitchen.

A watercolour drew her eye; it had a translucent quality and seemed almost to float. '*Berwick Bridge*,' William said, clicking the latch and following her eye as he turned back. 'Painted by a friend of mine. He died not long ago from lung cancer.'

There was genuine loss in his voice that surprised her slightly. 'I'm sorry,' she said inadequately. 'It's very soft and delicate.'

William nodded, then smiled. 'It's warmer in here. Shall I take your coat?'

Her coat had a tie belt and he picked up the ends. It felt so intimate a thing and she was trying to hold back. Everything seemed so uncharted. He sensed her resistance and let go the ties but then he traced over her lips with his fingers instead.

'You're going too fast again,' she said, smiling weakly. 'This isn't talking.'

'Yes, it is. We've done the other sort, all through that tormenting lunch when I wanted to kiss you so badly I could hardly look at you. I was despairing, desperate to get it across without making you even more wary and guarded.'

She looked down. He put his arms round her and pressed her head to his chest. It was a comfort, a breathing space, easier than talking. She could hear the thud of his heart – or was it hers? He smoothed her hair gently then tugged at it and made her look up into his eyes.

He kissed her. The feeling flooded her. It was engulfing. She felt him undoing her coat, his arms slipping inside round her waist and she arched and pressed against him. She needed his body hard and tight to hers, his kissing, touching teeth, his tongue in her mouth – the full force of his passion. There was no more holding back, no last hair's-breadth of inhibition. She felt swamped, ecstatic; she was aching with desire.

'If you hadn't come,' he murmured, 'if you'd changed your mind . . .'

'But I shouldn't be here. We can't do this.'

He got her out of her coat and flung it on a chair. He flung off his jacket, too; he'd been without a coat in the cold wind. 'I had to make you understand what it wasn't,' he said, clutching her and pressing his cheek to hers. 'It was you, nothing but you.'

He looked at her. His hands spread down her body, over her breasts and back up again. They held her face. There was a question in his eyes; one she didn't know how to answer. 'We haven't sat on a sofa and talked,' she said, 'which would be one way forward.'

'You know I'm serious, this isn't playing games?'

'And the rights and wrongs?' Sixteen years of being faithful to Barney, she thought.

'There aren't any. It's happened. You're here – and there's nothing more right than that. It's high stakes but your beautiful eyes are very wide open – you know the risks. We'll talk all about that later. Later we can talk for hours.'

They went in the bedroom and nothing felt more right than that. She didn't think about Ursula as she stepped out of her red dress and it stayed in a crumpled pool on the floor.

William held her jaw and kissed her. His fingers slipped to her neck, along her collarbone; he told her he would never let her go. He kissed the crescents of breast above her bra and she felt impatiently for the clasp. He held the flat of his palms to her nipples, tantalizing her before the exquisite sensations. She wanted to believe the things he was saying, that they weren't simply the language of passion. The lovemaking was so right, the sense she had, of how they fitted.

She felt so complete. Taking him in, wrapping him in her limbs, she had a feeling of coming home. It was uniquely exhilarating. It was there in a second of stillness, in the height and heat of the moment. And lying locked together in ecstatic exhaustion it was overwhelming. She wanted to go on holding him for ever. Putting off the unravelling and separation. If he rolled away it would be final, time to get up and go.

He lay in her arms for a long time. Eventually he sat up keeping hold of her hand. 'I'm a terrible host,' he said. 'We've got some champagne. Come in the kitchen while I get it, I need you with me.'

She unhooked a dressing-gown from the back of the bedroom door, feeling overtaken by sudden shyness. Sounds of Ursula's key turning in the lock had begun to prey on her mind. Swamped in white towelling, she felt irrationally much more prepared.

The kitchen was tiny, more of a galley. William got a bottle of champagne out of a fridge that had nothing much in it, just milk and a couple of beers. He certainly didn't cook, she thought. 'I hardly know you,' she said, putting her arms round him from behind.

He turned. 'You know me intimately, that's a good start. And you'll soon know everything there is to know about me. I like you in my dressing-gown!'

'Do you always keep champagne chilling for these eventualities or was I such an open book?'

'You had to come, I'd have found a way.' He kissed her and took a couple of glasses out of a cupboard. He reached for a biscuit tin, too, and prised off the lid. 'There's no food, I'm afraid, only this cake.'

It was a crumbly fruitcake, very obviously home-made. It was stuck with almonds and sat there, squat, square and accusing. She stared at it. Ursula sent him up to London for his weekdays with a cake in a tin. She couldn't do this thing. 'William, sorry. I've got to go.'

He was naked and holding a bread-knife. He stuck it in the cake and turned to face her. 'Only back to bed,' he said, kissing her forehead, 'to drink champagne,' he kissed her eyes, 'and eat cake. And you've got to get to know me.' There seemed no argument about it.

The bed-head was padded in a fabric to match the curtains: plain navy with a border of tiny acorns and leaves. There was no escaping Ursula.

William rested the plate of cake on her bare lap and she steadied it with her knees. 'I've got to go and vote,' she said, clutching her glass, feeling alive to him beside her.

'No, you've got to ask lots of questions and catch me up. I know everything about you.'

'You don't,' she said. 'You know very little. It's not all in the cuttings . . .'

'I have got one question. How could you possibly have married that man? He's not for you.' The intensity of his tone came as a shock. 'Sorry, these things aren't for tonight,' he said, touching her cheek – aware, she thought, of surprising her. 'Tonight's just for us.'

She smiled, though still feeling a bit unnerved. 'Well, I'd better get on with my homework, then. Have you any brothers and sisters? Where did you grow up – where's home?'

'Near Stroud. My father had a small printing business – birthday cards, that sort of thing. My brother went into it but I left and made a lot of tea on the *Barnsley Echo*.'

'How did you get from there to the heights? Did you have to service an Editor?'

'Certainly not! But it was vaguely in that sort of area. I was at a Town Hall meeting during the miners' strike and I picked up a particular look between a union boss and the local baronet's wife. I did some digging. It was quite a big story and got me noticed.'

'I see.'

'Don't be so hard! The union boss was done for misuse of funds and the baronet's wife ran off with a heavyweight boxer.'

'And that makes it all right? I think I'd better ask about your birthday.'

'My birthday,' he said, grinning, 'is the twenty-seventh of June.'

'You can't possibly be the same day as me!'

'I can. I got quite a buzz out of seeing we shared a birthday. I'm forty-eight.'

She looked round the room. There were piles of books on bedside tables: a mahogany chest. A tortoise-shell tray on it had a jumble of cards, keys and change. No sign of scent or make-up or a woman's dressing-gown. 'Your wife's not at the flat much?'

'No, she's only here occasionally. She's called Ursula.' He left it at that.

'Doesn't she worry you might be doing just this?'

'I've never given her any particular cause.' Victoria thought about being one of his non-particular causes. 'Till now,' he smiled, and taking away her glass he moved to kiss her.

She held him at bay. 'You haven't got any family photographs around.'

'I put them in a drawer in case you came.' It was an honest answer at least. 'It's not the time for this,' he said, 'not tonight.'

He made love to her. It was gentle, more familiar this time. She was on her side, facing him and he kissed the tip of her shoulder. 'Even without all the rest I'd love you for this little bone.'

'That's your way of saying I'm too thin?'

'You're perfect. Slender as a mermaid and quite as graceful, especially in bed.'

'You've made a study of mermaid physiology?'

'You'll always be my mermaid now,' he said, and then frowned as his mobile started up. 'Fuck it! I thought I'd turned it off. It'll stop soon.'

She stared past him at the bedside clock. 'My God, it can't be ten! I've missed the vote. The Whips will kill me.' She had gone to the hall for her bag and her own mobile but still hadn't heard it. 'Mine must have been on silent,' she said, 'I usually have it on me.'

'Not easy tonight,' he grinned. He got up and fished in their clothes. 'I'm turning them both off – no more interruptions! You can tell the Whips you felt feverish and went to bed.'

It was no joke. And the drink in the Pugin Room was sure to get back to the Whip's office, what was she going to say? Was it better to call immediately or leave it till morning?

'I bet you knew exactly what the time was and you just didn't tell me,' she accused with half-genuine crossness. 'It's all your fault! Don't you want to know about your call?'

'It'll be the office, they can handle it.' He squeezed her hand. 'And you can, too. I'm very glad you weren't clock-watching! Our drink might get back to the Whips, but no one's going to imagine

I carried on any lobbying in bed.' It was exactly what they would be imagining, she thought.

He pulled her on top of him and trailed his fingers over her. 'My beautiful, graceful mermaid.'

She was back, held in his arms, and the real world outside had ceased to be.

CHAPTER 12

It was very late but William felt comfortably settled. 'You can't go,' he said, tightening his grip. 'Stay the night, stay for breakfast – you can't go!'

She kissed his cheek and wriggled out of his hold. 'I've got to, this very second. I've missed the vote, and I haven't mugged up for my big housing debate tomorrow. Plus there's Barney.'

'Will that give you problems?' he asked stiffly, feeling resentful.

'I'll say I worked late. He trusts me. I don't think he'll be imagining anything.'

She didn't sound at all sure and she was tensing up, getting dressed in a hurry. William got half-dressed too, but he couldn't take her home and risk being spotted by a sharp-eyed cabbie.

Victoria sat on the bed to pull on her tights and he kneeled down to help. 'You'll come tomorrow, even for ten minutes?' He put his cheek to her calf. When she didn't respond he rose and sat on the bed, needing to say it more urgently. 'You must, I've got to see you.'

'I can't come here again; you know that. Don't make it even harder.'

'What do you mean, you can't come here?' He felt the frustration building. 'You don't want to? You don't care? Didn't it mean a fucking thing? Well, it did to me!'

The cabbie was ringing the bell. 'You're the one making it even harder,' he said.

'Don't rant! And we can't talk about this now. I'm desperately late and I can't keep the cab waiting. But tomorrow's out, anyway, with this debate and a dinner I've got to speak at right after.'

'Wednesday, then? You've got to, we must have this out seriously.'

He scribbled his contact numbers and she gave him hers for her mobile and private line. She went to the door. 'You'll be OK?' He kissed her. 'For Christ's sake, call if you get problems.'

'I'll be fine.' She got out of his arms and into the lift.

'I can't possibly last till Wednesday,' he said as the door was closing.

When the main door slammed, William shut his own and leaned against it, feeling angry and determined. She wasn't walking out of his life, not now.

Her scent was still faintly lingering in the bedroom. He took the glasses and bottle to the kitchen, and seeing the cake-tin, remembered he hadn't called Ursula. There were times when he didn't; it wasn't a problem. Barney was, William thought, as he got back into bed.

He was feeling physically tired but sleep was eluding him. A plume of hatred had risen up within him like a poisonous cloud. It was the thought of her with Barney.

He was still feeling unsettled by it and contemptuous in the morning. But on his way to work, images of Victoria took over and he played through them in his mind as though on a digital camera. Her most intimate smile, her sweetly cross face, arguing. He had to see her again. He wondered about doing a piece on mermaids in the paper. Dave left him to his thoughts but then in the mornings Dave had his head round the three-thirty at Kempton Park.

Early in the office, he read the other papers. They all had pictures of Harold Reid with a brace of Royals; only the *Post* hadn't featured it. He was thankful Oscar had no links with Reid and hadn't vetoed going for him, the Financial Desk was convinced of Reid's insider dealing. He was a toiletries tycoon, he'd made his money, bags of the stuff, and yet he still had to cheat and fiddle. William felt disgusted by a dishonest, arse-licking social climber, nothing would give him more satisfaction than to expose him.

The more Reid was seen with the great and the good, the further he had to fall. Why hadn't the *Post* used that photograph? It was an irritant, a jarring note: a cold shower waking him up to the hard light of day. Jack had been on duty; he was useless, not up to the job.

They might fail to nab Reid but either way it was vital to keep it under wraps. William thought of lying in bed with Victoria, talking for hours. Had it been rash, telling her? Reid was in with the Prime Minister, a supporter, very pro-Government. He still felt he could trust her.

She had been shocked and disbelieving at first. Pleading Harold's case, calling him a witty philanthropist who sponsored a hospital in India. It had really got to William; he wasn't having her think that. 'So if an infinitesimal fraction of his fortune goes to charity,' he'd argued angrily, 'then it's fine to break the rules?'

'Of course not! But you said yourself it's impossibly hard to prove insider dealing.'

She was too trusting – except where he was concerned. He wasn't even sure he'd really got it across that it was far from a bit of shagging. And she was still mistrustful over Downsland. If anything, he thought, taking her to bed made it more likely she'd allow it than not: a sort of reverse bias. She certainly wouldn't be influenced – Victoria James had a very stubborn brand of integrity.

It was too early to call. He got some coffee from a machine and took it back to his desk. He sipped it, feeling the caffeine kick and thinking about GD. Private dicks left a bitter taste, but GD had emailed some findings over the weekend and it was useful to know about Barney's women. GD had said he was into sex shops. Was that for home use or away? God, the thought of him with Victoria . . . She must know he played around. Was she jealous? Was this all about getting back at Barney?

But it hadn't been like that, William thought. It hadn't, when they'd met with her wide-eyed look and dropping of her guard. It hadn't, in all her attempts to hold back. Nothing had been calculated at any stage. And she'd taken a real risk. She would know very well that the slightest hint or sniff of a rumour and Skeat would start throwing the book.

Barney himself was the problem; there was a hard-to-read flicker in her eyes, talking about him. She didn't love him, but it wasn't a flat relationship like his own with Ursula. There was some sort of need or hold or commitment, William thought, and he didn't like it.

Half-past eight. If he left it any longer, Victoria would probably have gone into a meeting. He picked up the receiver on his desk and stared out at a grey drizzly day. His pulse was racing as he punched in her number and got through.

'Hi, I'm missing you. Was it OK at home?' He felt a smile breaking out on his face.

'Sort of. I'm in an early meeting – call you back?'

'Soon as you can.'

He clicked off, intensely frustrated, and squared the papers on his desk.

A couple of minutes later, he heard Margie getting in. She was soon in his office being brisk with schedules and letters for signing. Her red hair swishing; she was trim and neat in a tight jumper and short skirt.

The morning conference got underway. If Victoria called now, William thought, with his executives so close at hand round the table, they might pick up signs. George, his Deputy, would love to alight on a weak spot, and they all had professionally keen eyes and ears. He remembered the fun when Harry on the News Desk had started smelling of after-shave. They'd all been merciless. Yet he still couldn't bring himself to switch off his mobile.

The talk in conference was about the Health Secretary, Chris Hartstone, who was in a furious funding battle with the Treasury. He wanted money, lots of it – for more rehabilitation units for addicts, extra training for doctors, hospice care within hospitals and so on – but the Chancellor was swatting him away with an amused flick of his elegant hand. He might appear easygoing, a laid-back sophisticate, William thought, but the Chancellor was made of iron-ore. He did not bend. All the same, the Health Secretary, with his high, domed head was a proud, prickly bugger: what would he do?

'My hunch is Hartstone will jump,' Jim Wimple said, chiming

with his thoughts, 'or at least threaten to. We could do a quizzy piece, "Health Sectretary to resign?". Funny chap, Chris – a loner. He's not popular. Victoria James sticks up for him but she's about the only one.' She'd worked closely with him in Opposition, William remembered. How close?

'Hartstone won't go,' he responded tetchily. 'No one ever resigns and the fucker's only been in the job a few weeks.' He canned it. Others agreed; they all thought Jim off-beam.

William felt on edge for the rest of the conference, and as his office began clearing, his earlier irritation resurfaced. He asked Jack to stay back. George did, too.

William glared. 'Why didn't we use the Harold Reid photograph, Jack?'

'We decided to go with the other Royals' pic,' he said anxiously, with his gormless stare. 'We think they're about to split. We're working on it.'

'We were expecting you back,' George chipped in. 'I called. I even left you a message and accused you of shagging – we couldn't think what was up!' He chortled at his own pathetic joke. William didn't react but when they'd left his office he thought he'd better see what George had said.

He fished out his mobile and stared down at it. It wasn't his. It must be Victoria's and they'd got mixed up. Shit, she would see some dreadful crude shagging line from George. Shit, it was about the worst thing he could have said. Shit, shit.

George returned on some pretext or other and got into defending Jack. He hadn't chosen his moment well.

'That's just so much crap,' William snapped. 'That was an old news story Jack ran and the Reid pic was topical, useful. It just won't do. I don't pay him ninety grand to have his hand held. We're not having any passengers here. Jack either shapes up or he's out.'

George looked pained.

William felt a bit bad and added more civilly, half-honestly, 'Actually, I didn't get your message, George. I seem to have mislaid my mobile.'

George appeared slightly mollified as he left the room once more.

Alone, William turned on Victoria's mobile, impatient to find any messages that might help him get more under her skin. He began imagining living with her and all the professional conflicts that could arise. He would need to pass on any new messages, he thought, which was a valid excuse to call – though she might, of course, never speak to him again after George's.

There were just two. A Whips' instruction to all her Party's MPs. *Do not respond to the* Post's *Health Survey.* Twitchy about the mavericks going 'off message', he thought, amused. It wouldn't stop them.

The second message brought him up sharp. *Need to meet urgently. On the brink, C.*

He stared. *C* had to be Chris Hartstone and Jim had been right all along! It was the tip-off they needed. If they ran that story, 'Health Secretary Threatens To Resign', they'd be ahead of the game. But Victoria would know he'd seen Hartstone's message and she'd never believe him if he said Jim had got there on his own. It was no way to gain her trust. He felt skewered; he couldn't win.

Need he tell her about it at all? Chris Hartstone probably would himself though. He'd ask if she'd got his message and why she hadn't been in touch.

She still hadn't called – because of George's message about shagging? Calling again and interrupting a meeting would be counter-productive, he thought. Texting? But by now she must have discovered the mix-up and might not look at any more of his messages. Had she even found George's, he wondered. The best course was probably to both text and call. She'd most likely have the mobile off in meetings but she might just look again later, out of curiosity, and two chances were always better than one.

Scrolling down, he found messages from the previous night. There was one, *Division imminent*, advising about the vote she'd missed, but there was also one from Barney.

Where the fuck are you? It transmitted a lot. Lack of concern, impatience, anger but feelings of need, too. William felt a deepening of his loathing.

The leader writers were waiting in the outer office. As he buzzed Margie to send them in, he was thinking of a form of words to text Victoria that might somehow make amends. It made him feel better, more in touch, and his mood softened slightly. He wanted the session over with quickly, to be alone again and able to text and make his call.

*

Victoria's officials were advising on out-of-town shopping. She was settling in with them, a working pattern established, and they seemed quite well-disposed. But that was dependent on her maintaining their impression of her sharpness and ability, and she was in a world of her own today, finding it hard to come down to land.

'There is new evidence on traffic movement, Minister,' Mr Binks, her least favourite official, said sniffily, looking suspicious. She struggled to pay more attention and sat up straighter.

'Can you give me all the fine print on that?' she said brightly, and he embarked on meticulously detailed analysis of traffic patterns that was clearly going to take some time.

She wondered if Nattie had seen the piece in the *Courier*. But a diary column mention of lunch and lobbying would be as a Sunday-school outing to the coverage if the media picked up on a liaison. A single innuendo story could do so much harm. And last night with Barney had been an amazing stroke of luck, one that certainly wouldn't happen again.

He had been asleep, half-propped against the bed-head with a near-empty whisky bottle and glass on the table beside him and the light still on. She had switched it off, holding her breath, and crept to bed incredibly grateful.

In the morning he'd been up first and had left the room. She hadn't had to face him until going down to the kitchen. But he'd been leaning against a worktop watching as she came in and his features had been set in an unyielding stare.

The questions had come fast and furious, hurled at her like balls out of a tennis machine. 'Where were you? What were you doing? There was only the ten o'clock vote, I checked. Not so much as a call. So unlike you – how could you be so inconsiderate? Your mobile was off, too. Perhaps,' he said coldly, 'you would like to explain what in fact you were doing, out till after one? You weren't back by then, I know.'

'I was back soon after. I'd no idea it had got so late, I had so much work for the debate.'

He crossed over to where she was standing and glared. 'And why was your box here, ahead of you?'

'We brought it here at about seven. I thought Bob could do with an evening off since I'd be working late – he dropped me back at the Commons.' Coming home had given her a chance to shower and change. 'Sorry, darling, but I had told you about the debate, remember? And you know I never have my phone on at the Commons.'

'You have it on silent,' he muttered. 'You're usually keen enough to check. Can't you loosen up?' he complained. 'The country won't grind to a halt, you know.' She thought pride had stopped him from asking the more penetrating questions she'd been dreading.

Barney had looked drained, upset. He knew she never worked late at a deserted House of Commons, she brought the work home; he was no fool. Seeing William had no future; it was fraught, madness, and could only cause heartache and harm.

Mr Binks had exhausted the minutiae of traffic patterns and was looking expectant.

'Very helpful,' she said, hoping that would apply, whatever. 'But in any event the South is saturated with supermarkets. I shall be taking a tougher line.'

There was just time to phone the Whips' office between meetings. MPs had their own particular Whips and Jock was more easygoing than some. But she still felt anxious, missing a key vote was no joke, and she was unsure of his reaction, even with a first offence. A formal written reprimand would come her way, but perhaps, since Jock was usually sympathetic, he might put in a good word.

She thought it wise to check her mobile first, in case the Whips' office had been sending furious messages. She slowly absorbed it wasn't hers. Working out what must have happened brought a smile but she was soon thinking with alarm of all the ramifications.

It could be serious, William seeing the Whips' 'on message' instructions and colleagues' private comments. He had a journalist's instincts and the *Post*'s interests at heart, after all.

She played back his messages feeling slightly like a voyeur, but they would need to be passed on.

Hearing the voice message he'd ignored from last night. She felt weighed down. *For your ears only . . . No show, Bill? You must be shagging!*

Had that been it, just an available shag? And a blindly naïve one, she thought. It couldn't possibly have gone on but that in no way lessened the hurt. Everything about last night had seemed as remote from a one-off shag as a whole book of love sonnets. No tears, she thought, feeling devastated, remembering she had yet to call her Whip.

It took an effort of will to pick up the phone. 'Sorry, Jock, I'm really sorry. I seem to have lost my mobile. I'm afraid not having it on me and missing the reminder was the probem.' It was a pathetically thin excuse. 'When I'm busy I do tend to rely on it,' she added.

'In future don't.'

'It won't happen again,' she mumbled, shaken by his unexpected curtness. It was humiliating, a cold telephone slap in the face, worse than expected. It would be noted in her file and cause speculation in the Whips' office – especially when that drink in the Pugin Room got back to them. Simon Elliot might have seen William in Central Lobby. There was the *Courier* piece. And Whips only got to be Whips by being sharp and watchful.

It had all ceased to matter, she thought, fighting to keep control. There could be no more contact. Her intense happiness, her briefly wonderful love affair was over. Like so many political careers it was abruptly ending in tears.

'They're here for the meeting,' Marty said, appearing in the room. 'Shall I get them in?'

She nodded. His eyebrows were jumping, he was looking anxious but it was easy to work out why. Calls were always monitored and she had stupidly called Jock on the office line. Marty must have heard her crawling feeble excuse, and he was so astute; he'd be thinking hard. He'd known she had cut corners for the debate and stood him up for lunch. He would know, too, that she wouldn't lightly miss a vote . . . It was a bad situation.

She tried to be throwaway about it. 'I'm in disgrace with the Whips! I've somehow managed to lose my mobile.' William's was out on her desk; she slid it into her suit-jacket pocket thankful that Marty was distracted by colleagues and officials coming in. She didn't want him thinking her capable of blatant lies.

The meeting was for a final run-through on the housing debate that afternoon. Before then she had lunch with the Chairman of the Campaign for the Protection of Rural England, which she thought would be hard going. Unlike William he would be single-mindedly and openly lobbying on Downsland.

Things had just got underway when William's mobile suddenly rang – quite as loudly as it had done in his bedroom the night before. She tried to act as though it was perfectly normal for her mobile, supposedly lost and anyway always on 'silent', to be at full volume and causing a disruption. Nick Bates stopped speaking. Feeling appalled at forgetting to turn off the ringtone, and studiously avoiding Marty's eye, she dived into her pocket. People looked mildly irritated but Nick said indulgently, 'Take your time.'

In her embarrassment she flicked up a text and then stared, taken aback. It was for her. *Crude deputy ... Not for real. You are. Desperate for call.*

She said collectedly, 'Sorry about that, Nick – interesting point you were making.'

The debate would be fine, she thought, suddenly less worried. The facts stood up. Her spirits came splashing up like a bucket of water from a well. She failed to panic about Marty. Her reaction had been extreme. William *did* care. She had to see him one more time.

The morning ran on, making her badly late for lunch with the CPRE Chairman. Marty went away to get word to him, and alone for a moment, she saw a chance to call William. The telephone rang though, just as she was reaching for it.

It was Barney. 'I'm sure you've forgotten,' he said a bit smugly, 'since you were so busy at the weekend, it's tomorrow we've fixed to see Nattie's school play.'

She *had* forgotten. 'But things have piled in, darling. There's a seven o'clock vote now, it was always a danger, and Ned's asked me to speak in his place at a House Builders' Federation reception. The vote's on a Three Line Whip, too, not a Two Liner when I could have paired.' A small majority made pairing easier in general but not with key votes. 'And the Whips won't let me off, you can be sure!' Not after Monday's fiasco, she thought.

'Why not? You're always so conscientious. Couldn't you at least ask? Does your daughter count for so very little these days?'

That really stung and she fought back. 'That's ridiculous when Nattie isn't even in the play. I'm sure she'll understand I've got to vote. And we're seeing her on Sunday, after all.'

'I did say you mightn't be able to make it,' Barney said pleasantly, suddenly changing his tune. 'It starts early – hard, coming from London on a weekday.'

'What time?' She needed to know how long he would be there since she couldn't get to William's flat much before nine. 'Just in case I can make it.'

'Six-thirty,' Barney said. 'See if you can.'

He could be home as early as ten and it wouldn't do, being late again. Marty was back, looking agitated, and she sprang up. 'Barney just caught me! I'm off to lunch right away.'

It was impossible to ring William from the car but she tried Nattie's mobile and got through. Pouring out excuses and apologies, she said, 'I feel awful, Nattie. Say if you want me there, if it's important. That comes before any vote.'

'Christ, Mum, give us a break! It's a rubbish play, who cares? I bet Dad's only coming because of Miss Jones, my history teacher – there's some mutual fancying going on there!'

No wonder Barney had decided to sound so amenable, Victoria thought crossly.

'Did you mind that bit in the *Courier*,' Nattie asked, 'about your lunch with William Osborne? Maudie was quite jealous. She's got this thing for him. What's he like? Did he come on strong about Downsland?'

'Of course not. It was a working lunch – on a quite different matter.'

'A couple of boys are being a pain about Downsland, Mum. They live near there in Sussex. I don't really know what to say.'

'Tell them there's a public enquiry and their parents can write to me. Don't let it get to you, Nattie.'

'They say you'll be on a "kickback" but I'm not sure what that is. It's money, isn't it?'

'Yes, it's a sort of bribe and I'm certainly not! Nothing like that goes on, you can be sure.'

'Can't you get that across? I hate people thinking you're on the make. Their mothers are friends with Mrs Osborne and they think she'll get the *Post* to do a big campaign.'

'I doubt that.' Victoria was embarrassed at the turn things were taking and worried about Bob overhearing. 'No one gets special treatment, neither developers nor protestors. That's why there's a public enquiry.' They were almost at the Savoy. 'See you Sunday, love. So good talking to you and I hope it goes well tonight.'

She walked into the Savoy Grill where, according to the *Courier*, William sometimes came for lunch. It was a huge letdown that he was nowhere to be seen.

The CPRE Chairman was a balding retired businessman, a backer and friend of the theatre. He was new in the job and an energetic lobbyist, pleased with himself, too. There was no need, he said, to desecrate virgin land when so much land that had been used for other purposes was available. He pressed the virtues of these brown-field sites as the perfect panacea. People could live close to their work, he said, and help fight global warming by not using cars. The countryside, he insisted passionately, was our proud heritage, as much a part of us as the English language.

Victoria resisted giving counter-arguments, like the vast cost of brownfield sites, most usually in cities, children losing touch with rural ways. He seemed so convinced she wanted to give Downsland the go-ahead it would only have confirmed him in his view.

'Of course,' he said, eyeing her balefully, 'you've had luck with the *Post*'s Editor.'

'What do you mean?' She stared back at him, her heart starting up.

'Well,' he said, 'it's common knowledge he lives near Downsland but no rival paper's going to speak out against that monstrous proposal and be useful to him, are they? They're all such cutthroat operators. And Osborne won't campaign himself; he's too scared of being attacked for nimbyism.'

'The Downsland Action Group is a strong voice,' she muttered, feeling fed up. She was still letting her eyes rove, looking in vain for William.

'I guess Osborne will have his ways.' The Chairman was talking across her. 'It matters and it affects him, and he's a powerful man. I'm sure he'll be working overtime to win *you* round!'

She minded intensely the Chairman's condescending tone and suddenly felt desperate to get away. He had a foppish manner and he was touching her on the raw.

Lying shamelessly, she explained that the timing of her housing debate had been advanced and she was really sorry but she was going to have to hurry off before coffee. She told him he was a wonderful ambassador for the CPRE.

On the short trip back to the Commons – along the Embankment past the place where she had stood with William the night before – she tried to get her thoughts on to a saner footing. It was a risk seeing William again, even just once. But she needed to, in order to end it properly and to be sure he understood the reasons why – although he should know them better than anyone, she thought.

Bob was drawing up at the Commons. She got out at Members'

entrance and went to her room. There was the debate to get through, another difficult night of hiding her feelings from Barney, the whole of the next day. It mightn't work out; anything could go wrong, it might have to be postponed. Nothing was going to stop her. She had to see William one last time.

CHAPTER 13

It hadn't been a good day for having lunch with Carl Hancock. William was on his way back to the office and wishing he'd cancelled. Carl was a useful contributor who wrote brilliant, outrageous pieces; he was good for some well-informed hot gossip but he spread it around like silage, too. No one was more indiscreet.

'You're looking a bit shagged out, Bill,' he'd said. Hardly well-timed after George's message and a bit rich coming from an old roué like Carl. He was wild-haired, opinionated, never out of his grubby Garrick tie. He probably screwed in it, William thought – he did enough of that.

It was taking too long to get back. Victoria still hadn't called and being stuck in the car with Dave was as frustrating as being in a getaway car with a flat. William thought he would call again himself a bit later; he had the excuse of passing on her messages and making his peace about George.

The traffic was slow, stodgy. They took the back doubles but still inched along. William stared into dirty back-street shopfronts feeling thwarted and caged. A black fishtail vase in a junk shop caught his eye and he asked Dave to pull up.

The shop was full of auction job lots: part china services, bundles of silver-plate fish forks, brass coal scuttles, cracked mottled tureens. There was some good stuff as well, small items of furniture and paintings. A Laura Knight charcoal aroused his suspicions, and handing over three pounds for the mermaid-tail vase, William asked casually, 'How much is the sketch over there?'

The heavy-lidded man minding the shop looked at him languidly. 'Couple of thou and it's yours.'

'And the Jessie Keppie watercolour?'

'Five hundred. And before you send your reporters sniffing around, Mr Osborne,' the man sneered, 'it's genuine house clearance. The old biddies snuff it and the relatives just want to get rid of the stuff. They haven't got a clue. It's the property they're after.'

'I'll stick with the vase,' William said, despairing at being so easily recognized. He couldn't even keep his head down in a South London junk shop.

Getting back to the car, he rooted about in the glove pocket for the bundle of compliment slips that lived there, scribbled on one and handed it to Dave. 'I'll walk, but can you go to the florist's for me? I want flowers sent with this slip to the Housing Minister, Victoria James. Margie has the address. And see if they'll use this vase. It's just a little joke; we talked about marine life the other day.' Better some sort of lunatic explanation than none, he thought.

'What kind of flowers?'

'Nothing garish. Yellow and white, perhaps,' he said. Flowers to thank someone for help over lunch wasn't so unusual. Her office would most likely put it down to lobbying but that wouldn't matter too much.

He set off on foot and cut down to the river by the Tate Modern. It was a filthy day, and apart from a few tourists and students in woolly hats, there was hardly anyone around. He sat down on a chill seat looking out to the Millennium Bridge, whose design made him think of flying fish, and took out Victoria's mobile.

As she answered he forgot the icy wind off the river, the wintry monotone day. 'I was about to call myself,' she said. 'I've just got to my room at the Commons – sorry I couldn't get back to you before.'

'You minded the message from my Deputy? Was it really bad?'

'Quite illuminating actually.' She wasn't upset; he heard her smile.

'That bad! But you found the text from me? I've got to see you. You will make it tomorrow? And tell me it was OK with Barney? I've been worrying about that, too.'

'I got by. Not with the Whips, though. That was real black-mark stuff, awful.'

She was evading talking about Barney and he wanted to know why – what went on in her life, how things really were. 'Say you'll come tomorrow,' he pressed, feeling excluded.

'I'll try, but it has to be the last time. I wish it didn't. Last night meant so much.'

He refused to take that seriously, feeling sure he could persuade her. His need to see her was acute. 'Promise you'll make it – for however little time? I'm at the Savoy tomorrow. If you text when you're leaving I can be at my flat in minutes.' He was almost forgetting Hartstone. 'Oh, and I've got pager messages for you,' he added.

'Embarrassing ones?'

'There's one from the Whips you might rather I hadn't seen and a personal message which says *Can we meet urgently? On the brink, C.*'

Victoria was silent – probably worrying he could easily work out C's indentity.

'Thanks,' she said eventually. 'Look, I must go or I'll be late for the debate.'

He admired her self-control. 'Don't go, not yet, I want to tell you something. You see, in conference this morning – before I'd discovered the mixed-up mobiles and found your message – we'd actually discussed the chances of C resigning. Jim thought he wouldn't stick around since he's so deeply pissed-off with the Chancellor but I thought that was fanciful and said so. I won't go back on that, I won't abuse seeing that text.' He was impatient for her response. 'Say something, can't you! Don't I get a word of praise for all this virtue?'

'I really am very grateful. I'll have a quick drink with C after the debate. I think I can stop him – we do get on. See you tomorrow, all being well.'

William resented her obvious closeness to Hartstone. Had there been anything between them? He wanted to know. It irritated him to think the drink she was intending to have with Hartstone meant she'd be rushing off to her dinner afterwards and unlikely to go back to her office and find his flowers.

The chill was beginning to penetrate and he saw with some alarm that an elderly couple had joined him on the bench; how could he have been so unaware of them coming?

'Hi, how you doing,' the man said amicably, standing up. He had an American accent.

'Cold, isn't it,' William said, relieved that his call probably hadn't meant anything to them. He watched the couple's solid departing backs, their identical spread-flat bottoms in baggy beige trousers, thinking that people grew to look like each other as well as their dogs. Too much sitting around on park benches, he decided, springing up and striding away.

At the office he got busy but during his reading hour, between six and seven, Victoria was back in his thoughts. Distracting images of her astride him, lying facing him: the inviting look in her wide flecky eyes.

He gave up on work. Margie was still in the office and he asked her to see if Beverly Leander was around. Bev had just won Fashion Editor of the Year award but she often looked a mess herself, to his untutored eye. She was auburn-haired and tiny, devoted to high platform shoes.

'Hi, Bev,' he said as she came in. She was wearing a grey loose-knit sweater like a string-bag; sure to be Armani or Donna Karan. He got two beers out of the fridge and they went to sit down. 'Just a little idea I had, Bev, a fashion spread with a mermaid theme.' He stretched out his legs, wondering if he'd just taken major leave of his senses.

She looked amazed. 'In December, Bill? Be on the kitsch side even in summer, but fill me in,' she said with an eager grin, as though not forgetting who was boss.

He put down his glass and clasped his hands behind his head, struggling to come up with a line. '"Mermaid Fashion for a Sea of Christmas Parties", something like that?'

'Could work,' she said, brightening. 'There's loads of sequinned stuff out there, plenty of gold and silver. How about "Shimmer

Like a Mermaid in a Silvery Second Skin" or "Make Waves This Christmas, Dress Like a Mermaid"?' She got quite into it but must be thinking he was off his trolley – or had a girl in his life.

More restraint was certainly needed, William told himself. It was hard though. He had the feeling of flying, of being lifted high.

William was in the office early next morning and impulsively called Victoria again. He wanted, without actually asking, to find out what had happened with Hartstone. 'I hear you saw off Rufus Coram in the debate,' he said. Jim had reported back. 'And the dinner went OK?'

'Your flowers picked me up, or I'd have gone to sleep on my feet. It was black-tie and I'd rushed back to the office to change after seeing Chris – I mean C – and found them. You'd no business sending them, of course. They're on the conference table in that fishy black vase! I think C's going to be OK,' she continued. 'I got him to calm down. Trouble is, he gets things so out of proportion. He just needs his hand held, so to speak.'

William felt impatient. Hadn't Hartstone got a bloody wife for that? He said, 'You promise to come tonight?'

'I'm busy till half eight or nine and I can't be late home again. Barney's at Nattie's school play. She isn't in it, which helps as I couldn't have gone, what with the voting.'

William read a lot of guilt into that – and that Barney was encouraging it. But at least she was opening up a bit, he thought, before remembering the big Downsland Action Group meeting that night. It was sure to get publicity and revive Victoria's suspicions.

*   *   *

Margie got in and soon after, Oscar called. They talked sales, offers, a lawsuit being brought by a prima donna. Oscar demanded more attacks on the Government.

'We've hardly needed to, with the Chancellor slagging off Hartstone so publicly,' William said, a bit defensively, 'and new governments do deserve a breather.'

'They've had a whole bloody summer vacation,' Oscar snorted. 'I'm over in the New Year, Bill, and I wanna do some dinners. Who's going places? Who do we ask?'

'Victoria James is a new face,' William said unthinkingly, wanting any chance to see her, even at dinner with his proprietor. He kicked himself. She'd be asked with Barney. And he would be a shadowy insubstantial figure in the background, he thought acerbically. Oscar's dutiful Editor. Playing fifth fiddle to fucking Barney.

'The Minister who's a looker?' Oscar yelled down the phone. 'Good plan. Fancy her, then? Think of some others, too.'

Preparing for the morning conference, William had a few wistful twinges. No other paper had the Hartstone resignation story. They could have been setting the agenda, getting people talking, interested, questioning the Health Secretary's future. Virtue seemed a very bland pudding.

'We could still run with the Hartstone story,' Jim said. 'It would be quite damaging for them and stir things up a bit.'

Just what Oscar wanted. 'Too late now, we've missed the boat,' William said firmly, 'but you were probably right and I was being over-cautious.' It was quite a concession and the executives round the table looked surprised.

As things were winding up and his room clearing, he asked Jim to stay back. With Oscar demanding scalps it seemed a good idea to get a political overview.

'How do you see the landscape, Jim? Tell me the weak spots, who's vulnerable and who's on the up. I think it's time we did a bit of gingering.'

'The Chancellor's riding high. He'll keep harrying Hartstone, and we can give him a helping hand there. Ned Markham's probably the weakest link, I'd say. He's not a total slouch but he's such a toff old-guard throwback, we can have some fun with that. Guy Harcourt should have got that job: he's sharp and I'd like to start saying so.'

None of it would please Victoria. 'Harcourt's a scheming obnoxious shit,' William snorted. 'He deserved to miss out. And the public's right off political nasties – they're in the mood for a softer, *mea culpa* image.'

'Don't you believe it. They may say that, but they love all the dirt and in-fighting. Sure Harcourt's a shit and he'll go to any lengths, but he's got talent, too.'

Jim was being annoying and inconvenient, and he had a maddening habit of masticating his words, speaking interminably slowly. William felt tempted to start arguing and citing the few decent politicians. Chris Hartstone was one, he thought grudgingly, surprising himself. Tight-lipped, unbending, the Health Secretary had no discernible charm but at least he'd got there playing it honest and straight.

Jim was picking at a tooth, in a little reverie. He had a very PC partner in the Civil Service, two small children and dry right-wing views; William couldn't piece it all together. 'Who's the coming talent?' he asked, beginning to get bored and looking at his watch.

'Nick Bates isn't the lightweight he's taken for and there's Victoria, who, as I've said, could go far. Downsland's tricky, though. The DAG could give her trouble. That Rev Jeremy's a formidable operator. You must be very pleased!'

William was beginning to lose his cool – was Jim deliberately trying to irritate him? His mobile bleeped then and he felt sure it must be Victoria. Something new about Hartstone? He hoped she wasn't crying off. He'd have to call back, no other way. Jim was as alert as a guard dog and would pick up on the most imperceptible nuance or softening of tone.

It was Ursula. William's sense of anti-climax was extreme. 'Any problems?' he demanded briskly. 'You OK? I am quite busy—

'You're making that clear enough,' she said crossly. Jim went to the door gesticulating that he was leaving. 'It's just,' Ursula went on more hesitantly, 'well, it's the big Downsland meeting tonight, remember? Jeremy was wondering if you'd send down a reporter and crew – just to cover it, not to take sides or anything. Just to cover it.'

'For Christ's sake,' William snapped, as the door had closed behind Jim. 'haven't I said often enough I'm staying right out of it? Try the Editor of the bloody *Parish Gazette*.'

'You'd only be reporting it, and tell me what's wrong in that?'

'Plenty. Look – I've got to go.' She had a point; he was taking his Downsland stand to unreasonable extremes. He said more contritely, 'Sorry, darling – I'll ring back.'

The call had been unsettling and he felt short-changed, a powerful sense of letdown that hung around like low-lying mist and refused to disperse.

He had a lunch to get to. Signing a few quick letters he found himself wondering which way Victoria was leaning on Downsland.

She'd probably be for it on balance: wanting starter homes for young families, split families, single parents. She would be a lot less keen if it were her own constituents' backyards at risk, he thought sharply.

Downsland was the wrong place for that development; the infrastructure simply wasn't there. He could never argue it with her; she'd always suspect his motives. But, cynically selfish as it might be, his house wasn't that near and should hold its value. His focus was London now. His heart was no longer in his home. How was he going to win her trust?

Leaving for Soho, he asked Margie to get him another mobile. He was going to win through, he thought, and a separate one might be useful. Anything to avoid getting so psyched-up at every call.

Dave was driving along the Embankment and as they neared the Temple Gardens William said he wanted to get out and walk. He felt too confined in the car.

Coming out by the flower-stall at Embankment Tube, the stallholder had a cheerful dig about the *Post*'s racing tips. William bought flowers to make amends. Early narcissus: jonquils. It was only November, he thought, they must be imported. He was close to his flat and nipped in to leave them in water. He put them in a vase on the coffee-table, thinking how Victoria's career was taking off and that she might not come.

He hurried up Villiers Street. Two girls coming out of a Starbucks asked for his autograph. He pictured them reading a shock exposé, lurid headlines about his steamy affair with a Government Minister. There was Ursula, his job. Shouldn't he accept that for all his burning need and gnawing hunger, it had to end? That Victoria was right: he had to be responsible and accept there was no way it could go on?

*   *   *

The *Post* was sponsoring Women in Health's charity dinner and fashion show that night. William shaved, put on his dinner jacket and left for the Savoy at eight. He was a little late and the lady chairman who was waiting at the River Room entrance was glancing this way and that. He was her principal guest. She looked like a Christmas card robin, he thought, with her barrel frontage and shiny red frock.

'We're so delighted,' she exclaimed, relieved to see him. 'So sad your wife couldn't be with us, too.'

'I'm afraid she had a commitment in Sussex tonight,' he said with a polite smile.

A first course of seared fresh tuna and salad leaves was served. Sultry, bored-looking models in wisps of gauze that left nothing to the imagination sped up and down the catwalk. His shiny red chaperone was annoyingly asking if her teenage daughter could do work experience at the *Post* and he was just summoning the energy to reply when his mobile vibrated in his pocket with a text coming through.

He read it and looked up ruefully. 'Sorry, but I've got to dash. A bit of excitement's cropped up that needs my attention. I'll do my very best to get back.'

CHAPTER 14

Victoria was studying the vending machine, trying hard not to be noticed. There'd been no cabs in sight coming out of the underpass and the Tube had seemed best; quicker and less curiosity-causing than walking, hurrying down dark streets alone.

Her hands made tight fists: no weakening. All the gossip and rumours would soon start. William should never have sent flowers and that telling note. *Thanks for the help at lunch; it was so fruitful.*

Marty would have read it. It had come right after a missed vote and he was so intuitive. The fishtail vase had got Sue intrigued, too. 'Isn't it unusual, Minister! Most florists do them in water bubbles, these days.'

There were few people on the platform at Westminster; even so she felt vulnerable and exposed like a tiny Russian doll, bereft of all her protective outer-selves. It had to end. They couldn't escape the press for two minutes. And William's wonderful passion would soon plateau out and trickle away to nothingness like great roller-coaster waves on the sand.

A train came. A man sitting down opposite her had the look of a researcher, she thought, or a Commons clerk or journalist. Was he covertly watching with Westminster eyes, wondering why, with a Government car outside Members' entrance, she was travelling with her head bent so low on the Tube?

Getting out at Embankment she was thinking of the need to resist even a kiss. To fall into William's arms would be to kick away, as a thug with an old man's crutches, her only means of support – her pride and dignity. She was there to say goodbye, not to cling to him as though dangling from a top-floor window-ledge.

The street was lit by a crescent of moon. She rang the bell. William had texted the code but it seemed inappropriate to use it; too familiar.

He was there waiting as the lift opened. Neither of them spoke and he kept the lift door held back with his foot. He was in black-tie, though without the jacket on, and she thought how well the crisp white of his dress-shirt suited him.

'Can I get out of the lift or it'll be time to go down again.' She gave a small grin and he did too, looking slightly abashed. 'But I'm here to say goodbye,' she said as he put his arm round her and they went into the flat. 'I hadn't expected the dinner jacket,' she went on slightly awkwardly. 'Have you just ducked out of some big do?'

'Only a charity fashion show we're sponsoring. I told them I had a little crisis but it's actually a very big one.' He pressed her closer in his thin, fine shirt. 'None bigger!'

Inside the hall she thought of walking in only two nights ago. She was wearing the same belted camel coat and couldn't help her eyes going to the picture of Berwick Bridge. William's eyes were on her but he made no move.

She took a breath and said, 'It has to end.'

'I don't agree.' He was looking at her intently. Her heart was hammering. Why wasn't he even taking her coat? She needed contact, touch and feel, the reassurance of heavy pressure and then the guts and will to resist it. 'We'll go in the sitting room,' he said. He went to the small brick-red sofa she had seen through the door and held out his hand. She hung back a moment before going to join him and sitting down. Staying stiff and upright and still in her coat, she concentrated on doing what had to be done.

A rectangular Perspex coffee-table in front of the sofa had a vase of scented narcissi on it, a bottle of white burgundy and two glasses. There were tall china lamps on side-tables, books, music equipment and a flat screen in the wall. She was looking round, playing for time. Jazz was on in the background but turned right down; it sounded like Dave Brubeck. She hoped the flowers were nothing to do with Ursula.

William poured some wine but left the glasses where they stood. 'I know you haven't got long, though I hardly think Barney will be rushing back.' He was remembering about Nattie's play, she thought, and he was probably right, but his scornful tone was surprising.

Her hands were twisting in her lap. William unravelled one and began sucking thoughtfully on her fingers; she felt guilty at their compliance but didn't pull away.

'I don't want it to,' she burst out, 'but it has to end – you must surely understand why.'

He brought down her hand but didn't let go. She could feel the sexual tension between them, the intense pull, and he began speaking, completely ignoring what she had just said.

'I worried about pressing you so hard to come tonight. I didn't want you having problems or George's crude message giving you completely the wrong picture. I dreaded that. I'm obsessed with winning your trust, you see, but I know it's got to be earned.'

He offered her a glass of wine, but she shook her head. 'I had a walk at lunchtime,' he went on. 'I made myself think about all that's at stake, all the worst possible consequences.' So he was ending it. She felt completely irrationally hysterical. 'But even knowing what it would do to Ursula, I can't let go. I can't lose you, not now – it's unthinkable. We'll find ways and get by. You'll see.' His smile had enormous tenderness.

'There aren't any ways.' She dropped her eyes and could hear her heartbeat loud under her breastbone. 'I can't see you again and that's an absolute final decision.'

She wanted to undo her words. He would never begin to understand what strength it had taken to make that dull flat statement that had sounded as though she didn't care.

'Thanks, nice, mustn't get too entangled – that's all it meant to you, is it?' His eyes glittered. 'Well, you may be able to flick off your feelings like a fucking light switch but I can't. If the job's that important,' he challenged, 'if that's your true motivation then I want to hear you say so, up-front and to my face. You owe me that, at least.'

He was reaching into her, probing into deep corners in a way Barney never could, touching her, testing her will. But even feeling the full force of him, she still hung on.

'You know my feelings,' she said angrily, 'and that was cheap, flinging the job at me. Just think about it, will you? You've got a family, another life, a responsible job. You're well-known, high-profile. We're married, people we love would get hurt.' But taking this sane sensible course, she knew, meant she would be the one to suffer instead.

'I want to be part of your life,' William said. 'You don't love Barney, I know you don't, but I don't know what he does mean to you. Tell me that, tell me what goes on.'

It was an unfair demand, they were unanswerable questions but his eyes were burning into her, making her feel alight.

'I'm not going to start quantifying my feelings, I've taken a decision and that's that.' She felt sure her eyes would be giving her away.

'I want to know. Tell me things, talk to me.'

'I haven't asked those sort of questions about Ursula.'

'Try me. Ask anything.'

'You're determined to make this even harder, aren't you? I'm going now. I have to.'

'Just hear me out,' he said more reasonably, taking hold of her arm as she began getting up. 'Stay just a few minutes more.'

'It's getting late,' she muttered, sitting down again, tying and untying the belt of her coat.

His eyes were on her face, not her fidgeting fingers. 'Suppose I don't see you for a while? I won't try and get in touch. We both stand back a bit. Then if we meet again, and you're still this determined, perhaps I'd be more able to accept it.' He reached for her hand. 'I know what I'm doing, I'm full of certainties but I need you to be feeling them, too.'

'How long would you give this trial break-up?' she said

guardedly, feeling her defences crumbling. His hand was smoothing hers, lulling her, luring her. It wouldn't do.

'*Question Time*'s in two weeks,' William said. 'It's pre-recorded, over by nine; there'll be a way of meeting afterwards.' He pressed her hand to his cheek. 'I'll work something out.'

'Two weeks is hardly a test,' she said, trying not to give in. 'There'll be all the same obstacles, nothing will have changed.'

He brought her hand to his lips, brushing on her skin with a butterfly touch. 'We're going to get there.'

She got up. He did too and they stood facing each other. Their bodies were so close. It was late, almost ten, and Bob was waiting at the Commons. 'You had better go,' he said gently, touching her face.

She went to the door but couldn't leave. 'Will you kiss me?' she said, turning.

He came close and held her shoulders. 'I can't. I couldn't cope, the way I'm feeling. If only I could get you to understand.'

The look he was giving her was far too tender, far too forceful and she knew it was locking her in. She should never have agreed to another meeting. It was going to be an unbearable two weeks, an incredible strain.

William let go of her shoulders, kissed her head and went out to summon the lift.

Barney wasn't back and Victoria was grateful for the breathing space. There was some spinach soup in the fridge. She heated it up and spread out her work, trying to look well dug in. She didn't feel like eating. Forcing down a few spoonfuls, she thought about Nattie seeing splash headlines and of William's three children. And Di might have joked about Ursula's passions but they were far more likely to be roused by Downsland than any tasty 'Tonbridge' librarian. The image Victoria had of her was of a homemaker, a beautiful, dutiful, adoring wife. William said she did research for a headhunter's firm and was very self-contained.

It seemed a good time to call Di. Her brand of bullish honesty might be cleansing and cathartic.

Di listened in silence. 'You really don't want to believe he's serious, do you?'

'Di, we've had one wonderful night – he just wants an affair, badly enough to take risks but he's probably sure of his saintly possessive little wife staying loyal.' Jealousy she shouldn't be feeling was spilling out.

'He sounds pretty hooked to me, and he's tough – you might just have met your match. I can see the job's a complication; you've got all to play for. You'd make a good Foreign Secretary – our answer to Condoleeza Rice – but others seem to have managed it fine in the past.'

'For God's sake, Di, can we get real?'

'Look, you've agreed to meet him again. At least go with an open mind. You owe nothing to Barney in my view, less than zilch, just remember that.'

'Why can't you find any room in that great big heart of yours for him, Di? He's not all bad, just very complex and insecure.'

'Yeah, well.'

'He does need me,' Victoria told her. 'He thinks people sneer and are all against him. It's hard to turn my back, knowing his lack of confidence and how he depends on me. I'm his comfort blanket. I'd be causing pain, risking so much, and my feelings for William could be all in the heat of the moment.'

'Isn't that the point of this cooling-off time?'

Victoria had no answer to that as Barney was at the door.

He came in peering round a bit as if he half-expected to see someone there. She asked after Nattie and the play. Barney poured himself a whisky and his initial guardedness soon fell away. He got going on the awfulness of some parent or other, and the mutual tension gradually eased.

She lay awake long into the night. She felt trapped, a captive in her darkened bedroom. The tanks of reason were rolling, advancing and there seemed no way out of their path.

Going into work the next day she thought of William calling on the two previous mornings. If he were feeling half as desperate as she was, mightn't he just pick up the phone?

The cuttings were on her desk as usual, the newspapers on the side-table. Top of the pile was the *Post*, and her insides gave a lurch. She picked up a broadsheet and tried to concentrate on an article about economic forecasts in the medium term.

Her private line started ringing and telling herself it was Barney, she let it ring. It didn't stop and she gave in. 'You can't call,' she said crisply elated at hearing William. 'It won't work.'

'Don't sound so cross! I only want a little help with Harold Reid.' She was the opposite of cross but didn't want to talk about Reid. 'It's so notoriously difficult proving insider dealing,' William carried on, 'the best hope is through friends and contacts.'

'I don't see how that affects me,' she said suspiciously, minding being put in that category.

'It's a very long shot but can I try you? You know Reid's great Think Pink bash the other night . . . our night? We didn't cover the party but we'd sent a cameraman. I've been going through the pictures. They're mostly of fake flamingos, girls in pink G-strings – the whole tasteless caboodle, but with five hundred of Reid's closest chums there I was hoping for a pink-cheeked predator businessmen or two. A photograph of Reid with anyone involved in a subsequent take-over or iffy share dealings would prove nothing, but it's back-up if we get a breakthrough.'

'I still don't see where I fit in.' She was eying the door, hoping Marty wouldn't come in.

'Well, for instance, in one picture Reid's talking to the chairman of Toothpaste for Pets. That company was in a bad way, but right after Reid's party there was a sudden hike in the shares and then, surprise, surprise, it's just been taken over!'

'Why did that company ever fail?'

'Not enough cats and dogs with bad breath? Can I email you a couple of photographs? You might just know something about someone that gives me a lead.'

'All right,' she said cautiously, 'but it'll be a waste of your time. Can it wait till tomorrow when I'm in the constituency? I'll have a look when I get to the cottage if Barney's not back. But then you must agree to no more calls before *Question Time.*'

'I hate the thought of you at a cottage with Barney all weekend. I can't stand it.'

His sudden ratcheting-up of the emotional tone caused fresh turmoil. 'I am married to him,' she said, desperately.

'How can you be? How can you have stuck it out? He's not for you.'

* * *

Driving to the constituency the next day, Victoria tried not to look at her mobile in its holder – on the principle of a watched pot never boils. Marty rang twice, Angie, too, with press bids, but William didn't call.

Jason had his usual string of vicissitudes. He had lined up visits to a school, the local hospital and plenty more, but she could only think of getting to the cottage and finding an email from William.

Opening a new village hall in the early evening, she told the councillors and local residents how very sad and frustrating it was to have to rush away and miss the wonderful spread of cheese and pineapple on sticks, sausage rolls, mini scotch-eggs, cakes, orange juice and tea.

The cottage was warm; Mrs Potter had turned on the heating. Victoria opened her laptop on the kitchen table but Portia kept jumping up, putting her paws on the keyboard and insisting on being fed.

She found the photographs, and a careful, circumspect note from William asking her to ring, not email her reply. There was one man with Reid who looked vaguely familiar, in spite of his party pink 'Dame Edna' specs. Then she remembered sitting next to him at a fundraising breakfast. He was an in-house lawyer for Ice Kings, a frozen-foods giant, and his enthusiasm for acquisition had made him a little less forgettable. 'It's like chasing a bird you fancy,' he'd said, and the trite remark had seemed to afford him much private amusement.

Was it worth passing on? At the back of her mind was a feeling of unease at the thought of the *Post* doing over a possibly innocent Harold Reid. He was a contributor, a staunch supporter of the Prime Minister. Also, a good friend of Guy Harcourt's – which counted against him. Still, she needed contact with William: any excuse to hear his voice.

She told him about the man in the pink specs. 'It seemed odd to me, an in-house lawyer for Ice King laughing so hard at his own joke. Perhaps they're after a chicken nuggets business, or something to do with birds.'

'I'm sure there's a reason,' William said grittily. 'Thanks. We're going to get Reid.'

'But prosecutions are incredibly rare – must you be so ruthlessly Reid bashing?'

'He's a dirty cheating hypocrite. Can't you even trust me on that?'

'No, you're too obsessed with getting him,' she said, feeling hurt.

'I had to talk to you,' William said quietly. 'I had to stop you putting down the phone.'

That reduced her to a liquid pool. And the call was ending badly. 'I'm dreading the weekend,' she mumbled, 'feeling too much in limbo. It was a terrible plan of yours, having another meeting.'

She deleted his email and began making risotto. Barney would have had a long drive and a hot meal would be welcoming. Things had to be given a chance.

Softening the onion in butter and olive oil, stirring in Arborio rice till it was glistening and translucent, she was thinking of past impasses and roadblocks in their marriage when she had so nearly left him but found a way round. Mostly problems over girls, obscene photographs of him with one once, found hidden in his tennis kit. And the times he'd hit her, too.

She remembered an extravagant holiday in the Caribbean; they had squeezed it in between Christmas and the start of term. Nattie had been eleven, she and Barney playing paddle-tennis with young locals on a Tobago beach in the late afternoon. The sea had looked like folds of silk, the waves barely breaking.

A skinny little boy had yelled out to Barney, 'You're useless, man, a real loser!' He'd had a huge happy white-teeth grin but got no reciprocal smile.

Something as minor as that could swing Barney's mood. He'd been so sour, Nattie had got upset, and the next night he had drunk himself into the ground and erupted in a violent temper.

But no solicitor's appointment had been made, she thought, adding frozen chicken stock to the rice. Barney made it in ice-trays to have in handy cubes. He had been so sweet and humble back home; she just hadn't been able to do it.

He sometimes drank vodka and tonic steadily from breakfast on with a bottle of mineral water at his arm as a sort of pointless cover. He would never admit to having a drink problem and, Victoria thought guiltily, she was always so busy with work, she had never found the time for a really concerted, if stressful, attempt at helping him overcome it. Nattie would have had to know too, and she was so devoted to her father.

She heard him parking on the hard standing and turned off the television. *The Firing Line* had been about to start. His timing always did for her, she thought resentfully.

He came in looking grey with exhaustion. 'There was a great pile-up, it's taken almost five fucking hours.' He put down food carriers and kissed her. 'Something smells good. God, what a filthy drive. I'd wanted to be early and surprise you.' The thought of that was cause for alarm. He knew what to look out for, how to creep up on her, she thought. He knew all about deceit.

He deposited the bags on the kitchen table. 'God, that drive. I was so impatient to get here.' He came over to her, untied her apron and pressed her back against the stove. He turned off the heat under the risotto. 'Impatient for my wife.'

'First things first,' she said, laughing, feeling him hard, backing off. 'Supper's ready – you can make do on a drink for now.'

The meal was awkward after that, but Barney drank most of two bottles of wine and mellowed.

She was first upstairs. The bedroom radiator was tepid, it needed bleeding. They had kept the original Victorian fireplace with its pretty grate and pine surround, but had never got round to having a fire. Barney came up and stood watching her undress. It was just a body, she thought angrily, and it was hers, hers to decide when and how it was used. She felt cold, miserable, wanting to be left alone but, scrambling into her nightie and bed, she said cheerfully, 'I can't imagine life without an electric blanket.'

'I'll warm you up,' Barney said tritely. He sounded low, as though he were the one needing warmth. The small brass bedstead creaked as he got in. Switching off her light and settling down, she was dreading his approaches. She felt him push up her nightie and rest his hand on her stomach. 'I love you,' he said, rubbing gently.

It was new currency, not something he normally said and she couldn't say it in return. Putting her hand over his, she murmured, 'Lower, lower!' It was a phrase from an old film that had always made them laugh – what Mia Farrow had told a friend she'd said to her lover in similar circumstances. The lover had lowered his voice instead of his hand.

'You can't say it, can you?' Barney muttered bitterly. 'The feelings aren't there. Oh, forget it, I'm going to sleep.'

He was sounding as prickly and unreachable as a conker in its spiky shell but when she touched his arm, he didn't shrug her away. 'Don't be cross,' she said. 'It was just a little joke and I'm sorry, but don't let's go to sleep without a cuddle.'

On Sunday at breakfast reading the papers, Victoria put hers down. 'I'll go for Nattie. Aren't Chelsea playing and you'd like to watch?' She didn't want to sound over-keen.

Barney looked up from a news section. 'Sure you can spare the time?'

He was choosing to make her job the culprit, she thought, using it, hiding behind its skirts – not wanting a showdown. He seemed more interested in her red boxes than usual, this weekend. Snooping and surreptitiously trying to peer in them, affecting a sort of sniffy canine disdain, as though considering lifting his leg. She was careful to keep them locked. With her files out the night before, Portia had curled up in the empty box and gone to sleep.

On the way to Newbury she thought of every excuse to call William but there was no question of it. He was home on Sundays. She imagined a close-knit family scene and it hurt.

Nattie was outside school, waiting.

'Why hasn't Dad come?' she asked, getting into the car.

'Chelsea are playing,' Victoria said, feeling cast in gloom by the question. She set off and then turned with a smile. 'How's things?'

'Fine.' Nattie's head was bent; she was using one nail to clean under another.

Victoria glanced at her daughter's delicate profile through her fall of hair. Her skin was flawless but the occasional spot always sent her into a decline. Nattie needed time to unwind, she thought, aching for closeness.

She drove on and said after a while, 'I thought we'd make the Christmas cake today.' Barney wasn't into cake baking; he put it in the same bracket as weeding and making beds – women's work. 'What do you think, Nats?'

She looked up from her nails. 'Got all we need?'

'I think so,' Victoria said uncertainly. Barney was the keeper of the store cupboard. 'But Alldays is open.' She felt on a sudden high, a rather inexplicable one since thoughts of Ursula's cake that first night at William's flat had probably sparked the whole idea.

They made the cake after lunch and had quite a companionable time. Barney pottered down to Alldays for them and got the mixed fruit and peel. After tea he and Nattie set off; he was dropping her back to school and carrying on into London.

Alone at the cottage, Victoria went to pieces. She sat at the kitchen table thinking William might be at the office; he sometimes went in on Sundays in the afternoon, he'd said. She wanted to call but didn't. It made her wonder if realism and sanity would really prove her allies. Why was she resisting when she felt life would never be the same, always pointless and empty. Sanity had to prevail.

It was time to lock up and go – to get back for another evening with Barney. She laid her head on her arms and started sobbing. She stayed there a long time.

CHAPTER 15

The night before *Question Time* Victoria's heart was swooping and diving like a bat. Going home from a Commons' dinner she told Bob it was her first time on the programme and she was feeling nervous. She felt wry at the understatement.

'Mr Osborne's on with you, isn't he?' Bob said. 'He'll be a friendly face.'

She thought of William's unwavering locking-in look as she'd left his flat. 'Hardly friendly when you think of *The Firing Line*,' she laughed. 'And my shadow, Rufus Coram is on too, Bob – and he'll want to draw blood!'

'It'll be all right on the night,' he assured her, turning into Hartley Street.

Barney had the television on but he was working at the kitchen table. He looked up as she came in and grunted, 'What kept you? I'd expected you back sooner.'

'I was at a Fred Buckley dinner for his constituents and the questions dragged on. Want some coffee? I do if I'm going to get down to any work. Can I switch that to *Newsnight*?'

'Do whatever you like. I will have some coffee.'

Victoria put on the kettle and watched the news headlines. Petrol prices were going up and the French were threatening to ban British lamb. Either might come up on *Question Time*.

The morning papers were briefly discussed, front pages flashed up on screen.

The *Post*'s front page had led with petrol prices; the lamb scare was pushed further down, but there was a jaunty strapline banner across the top of the page which caused her to stare in amazement. 'Beverly Leander's Mermaid Look for That Sea of Christmas Parties: Shimmer and Shine, Dress Like a Mermaid'.

William had to be behind it. The blood rushed to her face and she went scarlet. It was certainly a novel way of communicating. She got on with making the coffee. 'You're not getting ill, are you?' Barney accused, looking across. 'You look flushed.'

'I am feeling a bit hot.'

'Give you some problems, wouldn't it, having to take time off?'

His sarcasm and lack of solicitousness was infuriating. She dumped the coffee by his elbow and said sharply, 'I'll be up at my desk.'

It was impossible to get on. William's wonderful gall was giving an extraordinary feeling of intimacy, of being there in his thoughts, and she couldn't resist sending a text. *Mermaid Fashion was editor's idea?*

One came straight back. *He had mermaids on his mind.* She glowed: small fists were hammering at her chest as she tried to work and a small private smile was playing. When she leaned to plug her mobile into its charger though, the smile faded. Barney was in the doorway and it was hard to know how long he'd been there.

He said coolly from the door, 'What was that smile about?'

'Just a text – some silly joke about mermaids that's going the rounds.'

'Who's texting you at this time of night?'

'Just a late-working journalist. For heaven's sake, darling – so I looked at a text!'

'I thought you said you had work to do? I've turned out the lights downstairs, I'm going to bed.'

'I'll be up soon.'

She had been trying to be warm and compliant but he wasn't making it easy. They had reached a point where all the bickering and tension was almost a relief. It was cover, a way of keeping her distance.

She wanted space, room to love. Her thoughts never left William. He had called twice more in the agreed no-contact period. Once with the excuse of updating her on Harold Reid. Her lawyer friend's wet little joke about chasing birds, he said, had been to do with his frozen-food company, Ice King, being after a niche business called Brinkley's Duckling. Shares in Brinkley's had shot up after Reid's party – and now Ice King had just acquired it.

That proved little, Victoria thought, but sloshing dirt around about a respected figure like Harold Reid would be in William's interests: very good for sales.

His other call had been more disturbing. No excuse, he said, just need. Marty coming in had cut it short.

Sighing, she locked up her box and went up to bed.

*

Barney felt her foot touch his bare calf. 'You asleep?' she whispered.

'Trying to be,' he answered impatiently. He had been waiting long enough for her to come to bed. Wanting her, knowing she didn't give a shit.

'Don't be like this,' she said, but putting distance between them, beginning to fiddle with her night cream in the dark.

'You can put on the light – I've said I'm not asleep.'

He was feeling irritatingly aroused but he wasn't going to crawl or ask favours of a frigid icebox. She could have it her way.

It had to be an affair, he thought, and it was serious. Did he just lie back and take it, do nothing? She probably wanted a showdown; an excuse to walk out. Would she really do that though, with her new job and such vaunting ambition? Things had been bad before. He just had to keep acting as though nothing was wrong. It was probably an MP who'd move on soon enough. She wouldn't risk the press getting a sniff. The affair would run its course.

There was the Downsland worry, too, the fear of Victoria discovering that Chalfern, the firm's biggest, most valuable client, was involved in that development. He appeared to have a lot more at stake than the shares in the biggest consortium that Barney knew about. Chalfern had been far too delighted at Victoria doing Housing and Planning and he seemed to assume she would be on side, convinced of it. But if there was any trouble, if he thought she wasn't sound . . . He was too big an egg; they'd be lost without all his lucrative business.

She'd been late home again. Fred Buckley's dinner running over, she said. Could it even be Buckley? Surely not: he was too old and had run to fat. You never knew though. It might be worth a call to his office in the morning just to check.

Barney thought about her dreamy smile, staring down at her mobile. He suddenly wondered if the text might still be there and had an urge to creep down and look. She probably wasn't asleep; it would be better to do so very early in the morning before she was up. That mermaid line had been pathetic; she was a useless liar.

He woke well before the alarm and slipped out of bed and into his dressing-gown. Padding down, he was listening out, tense. He found the text: *He had mermaids on his mind.* It came as a surprise, almost a letdown. No protestations of love, but it had to be the one; it fitted. She hadn't even lied. Her look had been so wistful, so . . . intimate? He felt curiously chilled; the hairs at the back of his neck were quivering, as though some harm awaited him round the corner, some terrifying apparition or flashing knife. It was a powerful presentiment, a fear that she was inevitably going to leave. He felt infinitely low but quite determined that she never would – whatever it took.

He was halfway through shaving when the thought came to him that he should have looked at 'sent items'. That text could have been in response to one from her.

Just then, Victoria came in the bathroom rubbing sleep from her eyes. 'You were up before the alarm. Bad night?'

'Bad as any other.' He cut himself then and needed the styptic pencil. He asked after *Question Time*, beginning to feel less angry, and wished her luck. 'It's pre-recorded, isn't it? You'll be able to get home and watch it with me, won't you?'

'Think so, although it's possible I may have to stay on a bit.'

He went into work thinking of checking up on Fred Buckley, and tracked down the number of his constituency office. A geriatric-sounding woman answered. 'I'm writing about after-dinner speakers for *GQ* magazine,' Barney said cheerily. 'You had Victoria James last night, I believe. How was she? Did you feel you got your money's worth?'

'Oh, she wasn't paid! Just kindly helping out a colleague. It was a lovely evening. All the anecdotes she told and she took such trouble with the constituents' questions.'

Not Fred Buckley. Who, then? Barney swivelled in his office chair and looked out of the draughty sash window, feeling hatred that seared like boiling oil. He wanted his wife back. Didn't she even care about Nattie?

God, if he ever got near the bastard . . . whoever he was. No one was going to walk into *his* life and trample all over his territory, *no one*. He wanted his hands on the scumbag's neck, to be feeling for his oesophagus and squeezing hard. There wouldn't be much left of him, given half a chance.

Then he thought of Victoria doing her first *Question Time* that night. He had been putting her edginess and their miserable problems down to his near certainty that she was deep in a serious affair, but could she simply be more nervous about such things than she let on? Had he been too quick to judge?

He wished he hadn't been so sour and suspicious over the text. It had been about mermaids, whatever that meant. Never getting it quite right, he thought morbidly, was the story of his life. She was the success. He needed her, she had always cared and understood him; she couldn't leave, not now, he couldn't bear it. She was everything he had.

CHAPTER 16

It was almost time to go. The red dress Victoria was wearing for *Question Time* was hanging on the back of the door. It was plain, good for television, but chosen as a reminder of her first night with William, and now as one for their last.

Bob drove her to the studio on the South Bank.

A young gofer met her and took her to Make-up. The bulky make-up man was in his fifties, with a lot of rings and ear studs. He set to work with colours daubed on the heel of his hand and kept up a stream of calming girly chat.

The gofer came back and took her to a room where the panel and chairman were having drinks and sandwiches. It had a hideous neon strip and staying near the door, taking stock, she felt glad of the make-up man's artistry.

William and Rufus Coram were talking together, Bertie the chef was nattering with the chairman, and the other two panellists, an American writer and a left-wing cleric, were studying plates of sandwiches with dubious expressions. She was the only woman on the panel; there were more often two.

'Hello, Victoria, ready for the fray?' William had caught her eye and was calling her over; he wore a navy suit with a blue shirt and tie. Her heart stopped but she tried not to show it in her expression.

'I was hoping you'd go easy on me, an old hand like you,' she smiled, coming up.

'All's fair in love and war,' he said, his look too direct and revealing.

'He's buttering you up for the kill,' Rufus sneered before casually wandering away.

They were getting through the programme. The warm-up question had been about a tug-of-love child, then Downsland had been batted around for ages. Rufus had been bitchy, William had sat on the fence. Victoria tried to keep facing the studio audience so as to avoid eye-contact. She thought of meeting him afterwards and felt as if on Death Row; the audience had ringside seats.

The legalizing of euthanasia came up; her father's case had made that likely. William talked of exceptional circumstances, dreadful incurable suffering, old, desperately sick patients pleading to be let go. He said then, with convincing passion, 'Doctors must be allowed their own judgment. A compulsory second opinion would be extra protection.'

He was putting her father's case; Victoria felt unsure whether to be immensely touched or suspicious of his reasons. Both, possibly. She thought it wasn't William's instinctive view; he had strong convictions but he was probably bending with the wind. It would be a wonderful comfort to her father, watching at home.

The chairman was looking at her. 'I'm sure you agree with that, Victoria?'

'No, I don't, I'm opposed to any form of legalization. Relatives can exert such heavy moral pressure and the medical profession isn't immune from greed. We must always do all we can to protect the sick and old from exploitation.'

She got little applause, speakers from the floor argued: William had carried the audience, she hadn't. Also, she had never spelled out her views so explicitly at home. She hoped she wasn't undoing William's good work and hurting her father.

The last question, put by a bald man making his point in a sequinned jacket, was in the Christmas spirit. 'Why should girls wear all the party glitter and not men?'

Men needed toning down, she said, floundering, not given more chances to show off. Others on the panel gave similarly tame answers but William, who was last, had a very confident glint in his eye.

'George IV once took his seat in the Lords wearing a black velvet coat covered in pink spangles and shoes with high red heels,' he said, 'but I'd rather have seen them on Victoria any day!' She thought a camera swung to her. 'We actually had a feature on glitzy clothes in the *Post* today: *Mermaid Fashion*. Now I can't quite see Rufus, or even Bertie here, in one of our sequinned boob-tubes,' the audience was loving it, Bertie the chef being loud and roly-poly, 'but Victoria – well, now you're talking! The mermaid look was just made for her.'

Her cheeks burned red as traffic-lights. She had no quick comeback – it was too personal, too familiar – and she'd told Barney the text had been about mermaids. It couldn't be worse.

The chairman talked about being off the air till January. Then he said with a grin and his customary caustic edge, 'And I think

William deserves our congratulations. That must be the first time in history anyone's ever got a Minister to blush!'

It was close to Christmas and an end-of-term atmosphere prevailed as the panel said their goodbyes, but Victoria was thinking peevishly of being the butt of jokes about blushing Ministers. William was on a lengthy mobile call; one or two people in the audience sought her out but she couldn't keep hanging around. His plan, if he'd ever had one, wasn't working and she had to go. The thought of not seeing him, of going back to watch the programme with Barney, of anticipating the mermaid embarrassment, brought her close to tears. She waved an airy goodbye to William and went out in misery to find Bob.

He was nowhere to be seen. Waiting on a windy pavement with her coat tightly tied, feeling cold and desolate, she was thinking numbly of the wonderful night, the hours of loving and talking, the incredibly powerful sense of something real. She remembered William describing his children. 'Emma's very fair like Ursula; the other two are dark. Little Jess is the one I worry about – she bottles it all up.'

Her mobile indicated a text. It was from Barney, but this time it came as a great relief.

Still no Bob, or William. A flattened beer-can went clattering down the street and there were putrid scraps of paper being gusted around. A fat man in black leathers with his hair in a ponytail let his whippet crap on the pavement; a woman pushing a baby-buggy at nine at night had to dodge round it. She should be re-housed and living in Downsland, Victoria thought.

Bob drew up and got out apologizing. Then William, who seemed to have carefully timed his appearance, turned up beside her. His nearness was affecting; she felt desperate for a brush of his arm, physical contact of any form.

Bob immediately started talking about *The Firing Line* and Mrs Bob being a fan. William smilingly cut him short and then said, 'Glad I caught you, Victoria – there's that small party, remember? You were thinking of coming? It might be quite fun.'

'I could come, I suppose, just for a bit. Where's it happening?'

'It's off the Strand. Shall I come in your car and show the way?' Getting in, he directed, 'Anywhere near the Savoy, Bob,' and then called his own driver to release him. 'Sorry about Mermaid Fashion,' he said, turning to her with a grin. 'Will you ever forgive me?'

'Not lightly. I didn't know where to look!' She sat forward. 'Can you go on to the Commons for me, Bob and leave my box in my room? I've got to call in on my way to the constituency tomorrow, I can pick it up. There's no need for you to come back, it's a private party – taxis will be easy in the Strand.'

Was it all very obvious and implicating? Would Bob be drawing his own conclusions, watching in his driving mirror as they walked away?

*

William unlocked the door of his flat, intensely relieved to be there. He wished he felt more confident. Two weeks on and he still had no certainty of winning her round. 'Some coffee?' he said formally, touching her cheek. 'Wine?'

'Coffee, thanks, that would be nice.'

'Let me take your coat.' He helped her out of it and hung it on one of the brass hooks alongside the door. There was a tiny D-table in the hall; she was noticing an envelope addressed to Mr and Mrs William Osborne on a pile of unopened post.

She looked up from it. 'Why are we here? What are we doing?'

'Finding a way round.' She stared a moment, then went to an upright chair just inside the sitting room and sat down, crossing her legs in a way he found intensely sexy. She was lost in her own thoughts, looking forlorn, and his heart did a flip.

'Don't go away, I'll just make the coffee,' he said, smiling. 'Be right back.'

In the kitchen filling the kettle, he tried to imagine leaving Ursula. Would her life actually be so very different? But there were the weekends and holidays, he thought. Her friends would feel they had to rally round and she would loathe that with a passion, she was so fiercely independent.

'Shouldn't you turn off the tap?' He started and turned; Victoria was in the doorway. 'Water's pouring all down the sides and out of the spout,' she pointed out. 'What were you thinking about so hard?'

'My marriage – avoiding thoughts of yours.'

'You're still not turning it off,' she complained, coming and doing it for him, tilting the kettle to tip out some water.

She was too close. He dumped down the kettle, held her jaw in his dripping hand and turned her face and kissed her.

She broke away and stood with her back to him, clutching on to the worktop. The only sound was an insistent tick of the clock on the wall. Her head was bent, her hair falling forward and he fastened on a small bone at the nape of her neck, wanting to touch it. 'I shouldn't have done that,' he said. 'I'm sorry.'

She swung round with her big eyes gleaming like a tiger's. 'Think of your family,' she shot out. 'Think of the headlines,' and left the kitchen.

He caught up with her in the hall and grabbed her arm. 'What headlines?'

'You know perfectly well. "Housing Minister Is Home-Breaker". "Victoria and Her Slick Willie",' she glared. '"Editor and Minister in Secret Love Tryst".'

'That one's no good.'

'Why not?'

'Too soft. But I'll give you a job if you're sacked.' He was walking her into the sitting room.

'You could try being a bit less flippant,' she muttered.

'Sorry, you think I'm not serious. I've never felt more so.' He pulled her down with him on the sofa. 'It's too late, can't you see? You're trapped, done for. I'd stalk you, I'd sleep in a bloody box in Whitehall, I'd write incriminating things. I'd . . . I'd boil your bloody rabbit.'

'The rabbit died a long time ago – natural causes.'

'I'm sorry to hear that.'

She started to cry then, her mascara running, the studio make-up in streaks. Her shoulders were heaving and he hugged her tightly to him. 'It's too late,' he repeated, kissing her buried head. 'We're in this now, there's no going back.'

She got more in control, sniffing and blowing into his offered hankie. Her lips were trembling and he needed to kiss them. 'It's hard to talk about love,' he said, 'when you're married to someone else and your youngest child still calls you Daddy and holds your hand – but what I'm feeling is very real,' he kissed her lowered eyes, 'and very strong and wonderful.' She looked up and stared. 'And built to last.'

'But it's fantasy land, hopeless. Barney's already convinced I'm having a roaring affair. He caught me reading your text last night and he'd looked at my mobile by morning, I could tell. I stupidly hadn't deleted your message. And then on *Question Time* you have to go and talk about mermaids! He knows it all, now.'

'He doesn't for sure,' William said guiltily, thinking she could have deleted it.

'It's lucky,' she said. 'He sent a text tonight asking me to tape the programme as he was going out – his friend Dick had some crisis. I can forget to do that and get by this time, but for how long? And have you thought about Emma and Jessie and their schoolfriends seeing the *Courier*? Or how Ursula would feel? Loss of trust is devastating. The bottom would drop out of her life.'

'Why did you stay with Barney?' he demanded. 'You'd lost *your* trust.'

She looked at him with wet panda eyes. He felt for his handkerchief again and gently wiped at them. 'Ursula will see the mascara,' she muttered.

That was too close. 'I often have my female staff in tears,' he said sharply. 'You've known a long time, haven't you – about Barney?'

'That's irrelevant.'

'No, it's most certainly not.'

She looked down at her fidgeting hands. 'It's just a part of his nature.'

'The part that made the bottom drop out of *your* life?'

'God!' she said, her eyes flashing up again. 'Are you so perfectly virtuous and faithful? What right have you to sneer and stand in judgment?'

'Every right. Tell me when you found out and just how long ago it was.'

'Before Nattie was born, if you must know.'

Whatever had possessed her to stay all those years – the sex? The thought consumed him, he felt corroded by jealousy. He said lightly, 'How did you discover?'

'Seeing him – which at least left no area of doubt! We were away for the weekend; the head of my old Chambers had asked us, he'd just inherited a big estate. I'd felt pleased, having a baby on the way and still a pupil. I'd been worrying they might turf me out.

'Barney spent a lot of time with a sloe-eyed girl who was also staying. She was pregnant too, but less advanced; the husband or partner wasn't around but I'd thought nothing of it. It was May, fantastically hot as I remember. On the Sunday morning I was mooching around in the grounds and saw some lovely red poppy heads in a wildflower garden. I wandered closer and then I saw Barney's head, too. He was fucking that girl having someone else's baby and she was fucking my husband, crushing all the pretty flowers in the grass.'

It was an unexpectedly bitter outburst, the scene obviously still vivid, still with the power to hurt. William felt seething rage at Barney's inexplicable hold. 'What did he say about it?' he asked.

'Just that it was all in the heat of the moment, which was probably true but I was young and pregnant, very naïve. I got in his car and drove straight back to London.'

'You'd married him because of the baby?' The dates were in the cuttings.

'Yes. Against my father's advice but I was sure it would work.'

William got up and shoved his hands in his pockets. 'I never made the coffee,' he muttered and started for the door.

'I don't love him though.'

He stopped and turned and she met his eyes.

'Do you love me?'

'Yes – but it doesn't solve anything.'

He dropped down beside her. 'Yes, it does. It solves everything. We're going to take risks for a while, but I won't let you down.'

'You're not seeing sense – you're determined to live in this fantasy world.' Her eyes were misting up again.

He kissed them and tasted the salt; he kissed her mouth and couldn't stop. 'It doesn't feel much like fantasy to me.' He was hauling her to her feet with his mouth still on hers. He didn't let go and they made slow progress through the door.

Victoria was tucked into his side, just where he wanted her, where she fitted; he rested his head on her sweet-smelling hair. His feelings weren't easy to describe. Nothing was certain, but he felt released from all the draining stress and tension of the past weeks. The past years too, he thought.

She had stayed with Barney sixteen years; she had been determined to make it work, perhaps even to prove something to her father, but that wouldn't have been enough glue. There had to be more to it than that.

She shifted and looked up at him. 'I need to say something. Please listen. I'm going to be out of London for two weeks over Christmas and you'll have more time at home. Will you think about things –

about Ursula? We *are* going to get found out.' The look in her eyes
was so earnest he had to smile.

'We won't get found out quickly,' he said. 'I do know how it works.
I'm not going to take stupid risks, I'll get you through Downsland
and then after that . . .' He kissed her; they were difficult words but
he thought she understood. They had to get there first. 'After
Downsland' was a long way ahead.

She was getting dressed, washing her face; she came back in from
the bathroom, scrubbed of her make-up and looking lovely, saying
she had to go.

'You can't, not till I know when I'm seeing you again.'

'It won't be easy with Christmas. But it's late now. You've worn
me down and I haven't stuck to my resolve. You'll be writing me
off in the *Post*, saying I'm lacking in vertebrae.'

'We'd rate you as no toughie but suggest there's a human side.'

'Don't you go thinking I'm a pushover or expecting any inside
information.'

He carried on teasing her but his thoughts were already back on
Barney and they would continue to be when she had gone.

She was at the door with her smiling wide eyes. 'Bye, then.'

He gripped her shoulders. 'I want all your heart, not just a share.'

She looked startled, but she put her cheek to his and then she
was gone.

CHAPTER 17

William's street was deserted though there was pub noise coming from the alley. People would be drinking outside when it was warmer, Victoria thought, and seeing her movements. She hurried to the Embankment, knowing that taxis would be impossible now in the Strand with people coming out of the theatres, and she desperately wanted to be home ahead of Barney.

Safe in a cab finally, she couldn't hold back. She let in a great swamping gush of happiness. It was an opening of the floodgates; letting in dreams which receded when she thought of Jessie holding her father's hand.

Barney was calling, just getting out of his car when she reached home; she hadn't been in time. 'Why are you only just back?' he demanded. 'And why the taxi? I suppose that means you haven't taped it? I saw up to the euthanasia question at Dick's; you were doing fine but I wanted to get home and watch the rest with you.'

'*Question Time*'s off air for a while now and there was a small party so I had to stay.'

They were in the hall under a halogen spotlight. 'I thought they made you up,' Barney said suspiciously. 'You haven't got much on. And you look as if you've been crying – I thought you'd just been at a party?'

'Of course I had make-up on but the studio stuff is so awful, I scrubbed it off.'

Barney looked deeply disbelieving but also quite pleased, as though he thought tears a hopeful sign, the end of a love affair not the beginning.

He took his coat to the under-stairs cupboard in his tidy way and she followed his example – hers mostly lived on the newel post. He hung it up for her. 'No red box tonight?' he said grinning, but it was a come-on. He was nudging his thigh between her legs.

She eased away. 'I'm dying for a hot bath.'

'Don't be ages,' Barney called meaningfully as she went towards the stairs.

The thought of sex with Barney that night was an anathema, tarnishing, like being a prostitute; the guilt though, was in the sense she had of letting William down. It had been a unique and extraordinary evening, and she was in love.

The constituency office was cold; Victoria's feet were blocks of ice. People were talking about a white Christmas but Jason was zealous about heating bills. He brought them coffee in Southampton Football Club mugs. It was instant, not entirely dissolved, too milky and not hot enough.

'Mrs Casey missed the Wednesday lunch-club,' he said gloomily. 'She's in one of her bates, even refusing to do her sponges for the Christmas Fayre.'

'Mrs Biggs rubbing her up again?'

'Something rotten. She's got tight-pressed lips the whole time, like a child who won't eat.' Jason ran mournful fingers through his thinning ginger hair.

Victoria's thoughts strayed. William had called on her mobile early, just as she got in the car. He'd gone to the office when she left, he said, and seen the end of *Question Time*. 'But I had George, my useless Deputy, breathing down my neck. He thinks I'll get called "the man who made a Minister blush"!' She hoped George was wrong. 'When I got back to the flat later,' William went on, 'your scent was still there, but not you, it wasn't you. I hated thinking of you with Barney.'

He said jokingly that Ursula had queried his sudden keen interest in euthanasia; it was a throwaway line but it had cast a cloud and seemed to blight the call.

Jason coughed. 'Victoria? I do need you to tell me what to do.'

'Oh yes, Mrs Casey – I'll see if I can get Barney on the case. He'll sweet-talk her round if anyone can, she thinks he's God's gift.'

It was the Chamber of Commerce Christmas lunch. Very jolly with crackers and hugely substantial courses, the turkey came with three thick rashers of bacon and a long sausage curled up like a mosquito-coil. Victoria kept her speech brief, but was still late visiting one of the many nursing homes in her constituency.

Wizened hands hung on to hers, sunken eyes glazed over as Matron moved her on; food stains on lacy wool, facial hair, a flickering television. The old people were seated in a communal circle but individually wrapped in layers of loneliness.

It was Nattie's school carol concert that evening. Driving on to Newbury, Victoria was feeling helpless and sad after the nursing home. She had called the office to check timings and saw no way

of meeting William in the three days left before Nattie's term ended.
They were going straight on to the constituency and then to Brook
House for ten days of Christmas with her parents.

It was pitch-dark already, at five o'clock, raining and cold. She
stopped in a lay-by needing to call William; pulling up behind two
huge articulated lorries, she locked her doors and picked up her phone.

She explained how hopeless it was to think of meeting and
reminded him that he'd said Ursula was in London for a couple of
days.

'But not Monday,' he shot back quickly. 'What's wrong with
Monday?'

'There's a Lancaster House dinner for visiting European environment Ministers.'

'Can't you come on the way – even for five minutes?'

'It's too tight, impossible. But I'm back on the third of January
and it'll be very quiet. Can we meet then? Can you take time off
in the day?'

'I'm not waiting till then! I'll drive to Newbury tonight, straight
from *The Firing Line* and meet you somewhere after your carols.'

'Barney's on his way there from London.'

'Fuck him,' William said. 'Fuck Barney.'

She agreed to try for Monday but knew it was a bad idea. She
ached and craved and strained for him but her sense of duty had
hold of her, like a well-trained dog. And Christmas was a time to
test their feelings, she thought piously; a time for Nattie and being
a family, for sticking more twigs in the nest.

Newbury School's main building had a huge flagstone entrance-
hall; now thronging with parents all noisily hunting down their

beloved offspring. Finding Nattie was easy; she stood out looking golden, as though pinpointed in a beam of light in the jostling maelstrom.

'So nearly Christmas!' Victoria exclaimed, hugging her and feeling overcome.

'You're not often first, Mum. Dad *is* going to make it?' She looked anxious.

'I'm sure he will. It'll just be the traffic.'

They were being eyed by a group of two boys and their parents; were they the ones living near Downsland, Ursula's neighbours? Victoria willed them not to come over and start talking; Nattie would want the ground to open up. People were being summoned to the assembly hall though, an exodus beginning.

Barney made it just in time. He pushed his way to his seat. Parents gave him curious looks, this blond head-turner married to a Minister. They belonged to golf clubs and never missed school plays. Victoria thought how much more prurient their looks would be if her love affair suddenly became headline news.

She thought of Nattie's boyfriend and whispered, 'Which one's Seb?'

'Shush, Mum! He's over by the pillar, beside the boy with the ears.'

They stood to sing 'Silent Night' and Victoria stared across. Seb had a sallow face and long brown hair, but when he turned she saw the attraction must be his arresting light eyes. He looked bored and cynical, too knowing. She felt on a metronome arc, a constant rhythmic swing between passionate hopes for the future and prescient fear.

*   *   *

Monday was completely overrun by Christmas, quite out of hand. It was Environment's day for questions in the House; the sketch-writers would be watching her performance, it mattered how she did; she had written answers to get out, last-minute cards and presents. She wanted to rush out and buy one for William but there wasn't a chance. The more the day wore on, the more a dash across London for minutes in his arms seemed like lunacy.

She sent texts: *What if only five minutes?*

Come for two.

Formal dinner, will be all done up.

Leave off the lipstick.

She had chosen to wear an oyster-silk suit with a stand-up collar and a cleavage-boosting neckline. It looked good, though possibly not ideal for Lancaster House.

'I need to make a detour,' she said to Bob in the car. 'I know we're short on time but I do want to meet a friend at Charing Cross.'

'Be very tight,' Bob said dubiously. 'Traffic's absolute murder round there.'

He had understated the traffic. She fixed on her watch feeling mounting hysteria, but finally had to accept defeat. At least Bob wouldn't see her in a state of flushed disrepair. 'It's no good, we'd better turn round,' she said flatly, starting to text.

'What a shame for you,' he said.

Press cameras flashed as she got out at Lancaster House, and inside, a plummy-voiced girl requested she go straight to the State Room. The others were all assembled, dinner about to be served. Crossing the Grand Hall in all its gilded splendour, Victoria stopped. 'Sorry, but I really must make a quick urgent call.' She had to; she couldn't stand it.

Plummy Voice looked a bit sniffy but opened the door on an empty office and said she would go and explain to the organizers.

With the door closed, Victoria leaned against the wall and reached William. 'I'm desperate,' she whispered. 'There was nothing I could do. But there's the BBC party tomorrow. Can we meet there – or are you doing other things?'

'That's it, is it? A coded chat at a Christmas party and then you just go away?'

'Don't be like this when I'm missing you so badly already.'

The door creaked open and Guy Harcourt peered in. She hurriedly straightened up and instinctively covered the phone. 'I thought you should know,' he said, giving her a cold hard stare, 'that they have all been waiting quite some time.'

'I'll be half a minute – I'll catch you up.'

He left the door ajar and she angrily, noisily, kicked it shut. God, he was a rude snooping shit, so eaten up with curiosity. She gave William the gist, but then had to race. Being one of the hosts and so conclusively late was quite a black mark. Ned seemed relaxed enough though; he told her he liked her stunning dress.

Over a polite dinner with their European opposite numbers, she and Guy, the spying creep, were full of bonhomie. He was a deter-mined enemy though, and having seen her at lunch at Christophers, he wouldn't need many more clues. William's promise to get her safely through Downsland suddenly seemed sheer whimsy.

Guy was going to need fighting, she thought; he was devious and scheming and out to get her, but she had to win. Everything depended on it. Everything.

CHAPTER 18

There was a picture of Victoria in the *Standard*. She was arriving at Lancaster House in a glamorous revealing evening suit. William, on his way to the BBC party felt another eruptive flash of the kind that hadn't helped his behaviour the night before. George had been in despair, giving him pleading looks like a timid wife with a husband picking fights in a pub.

Being about to see her was helping, and the latest circulation figures were out. They were up. Just a little, but it was against the current trend and quite satisfying. He would tell Victoria it was entirely due to Mermaid Fashion – if he could tell her anything in a roomful of circling media sharks.

The party was at Broadcasting House and being given by the BBC Chairman. Dave drew up in Portland Place and William got out, clutching his present for Victoria. It was a commissioned piece, boxed and wrapped in brown paper. It had cost quite a lot and he was about to take considerable risks with delivery.

He smiled at the girl checking names for the party. 'This is for

Victoria James. I'll try and see her to remind her, but can you stop her going off without it?'

'I'll try to, sir.' She was very young with a lopsided smile, not the sharp-minded type to jump to conclusions, he hoped.

No sign of Victoria but the room was packed and it was hard to move. Keeping his eyes skinned he chatted with little enthusiasm to Carol Knightly, an insipid blonde television reporter whom he had always found too pushy.

'Do you always look over people's shoulders at parties?' she enquired coolly.

Pinioned in her ice-blue gaze, he gave what he hoped was a winning smile. 'I just have a bit of business to do, someone to see – can you ever forgive me!'

'You might have to buy me lunch,' she said with a look of minor triumph.

He had no out. 'It's a deal. We'll do it in the New Year.'

It was less fraught, talking to a sports commentator, easier to exit from – although he spotted Victoria with the BBC's Chief Political Editor, seeming well dug in. He saw how animated she was, making her mark, and he was impressed.

When the moment was right he intervened and got her alone. In the crush conditions he could press a foot to hers. 'I've just had this month's figures,' he said smiling, wanting more than a shoe, 'and at this rate we'll be overtaking the *Sun*. It's all down to Mermaid Fashion, of course.'

'I like this touching faith in Mermaids—,' she began, but broke off with a warning look on her face. He stepped back and glanced round casually. Carol Knightly had been about to tap him on the shoulder – couldn't she give him a break?

'You must meet Vince, our man in Moscow, William,' she said officiously. 'He's a fund of fascinating stories.'

Vince was also drunk to the gills and promptly spilled champagne all over Victoria's black jacket. William pulled out a hankie and dabbed ineffectually where he could. Carol smiled sweetly. 'Such a tough time you're having with Downsland, aren't you, Mrs James? You must be really longing to get away for Christmas.'

Margie was going through the schedule. William was still feeling irritated at being bounced into lunch with Carol Knightly but perhaps it was no bad thing, Margie never talked but it would get round, he thought. Better mild gossip about Carol than Victoria creating a storm.

He'd had a shock calling Victoria earlier that day, her last in the office. He had reacted badly to her firm insistence that there was no chance to meet. She'd been shifting the blame, reminding him of the Harry Potter film he was seeing with Ursula and the girls that night. It was an early showing, they were getting a train; he could easily have bailed out.

It was Victoria's dinner with Barney and his father that was the problem in his eyes, and he'd said stubbornly, 'I won't last two weeks. I'll turn up. I'll drive to Ferndale.'

'You can't do that, or take any more risks like you did with that present! I haven't had a chance to open it yet. You must give some hard thought to the realities.'

That had got him mad as hell. 'I'll give hard thought to how much I love you, I'll—' He had stopped dead then, staring in fascinated horror. His door had opened and he'd been shouting, he couldn't fail to have been overheard.

George had been coming in. 'Sorry, bad time,' he muttered and went out again.

He'd looked amazed, nonplussed but he must have been paddling fast, William thought. He wasn't a total slouch; he would hardly have believed it an early-morning passionate outpouring for Ursula. And Victoria's blush had registered – George had commented on it and his cogs did click into place once in a while. But, so early on a working day, wouldn't the busy Housing Minister have seemed a rather unlikely recipient of such a heated declaration of love? William could only hope so.

He called George back in and asked confidently, 'So what's new – what did you want?' Lounging back, legs stretched out under the desk, he thought George was looking, as well as understandably pop-eyed with curiosity, quite juiced-up. The Washington story, perhaps? That might have got him barging in so early. There was talk linking Britain's Ambassador, Sir Rodney Hammond, with an American senator's wife called Roxanne.

'Just found an email,' George said, pulling up a chair and blinking like an excited owl behind his pebble specs, 'about Hammond! A brassed-off staffer's been spouting. Washington's got a lead and they want the OK to go all out for it now.'

'Hold on, George, I'm not sure about this – It could backfire, infringement of privacy and all that. Hammond does his bit out there – so he's doing this Roxanne as well, but that's no big deal. It needs some careful sober thought.'

George's chubby chops wobbled in disbelief. 'Come on, Bill, it's a big story, for Chrissake! It's Hammond's fucking fault if he can't keep it zipped. He knows the game.'

Hounding an able Ambassador, disrupting diplomacy – and for

what? Cheating on his wife? Victoria would hate the double stand-
ards. She'd probably know Hammond's reputation, but that was a
fine distinction and one she was unlikely to make.

It would certainly be a hot story. And he was giving himself away
with his caution, giving George clues. 'OK, we'll see what they
come up with,' he said with more authority. 'It does make Hammond
more vulnerable. We can square it – the public has a right to know
and all that – though it'll need to stand up.'

Tough on Lady Hammond, he thought, but Roxanne's senator
husband was a dry humourless bugger if ever there was one. Hardly
surprising she should have succumbed to a smooth clever woman-
izer like Hammond.

George got to his feet with a little chuckle. 'Sir Rodney's come-
uppance – one up too many!' William groaned. How *did* George's
nice bright wife possibly stand him?

He spent a tense morning worrying about the phone call, about
Washington – about how little progress he was making with Harold
Reid. He might bend the ear of his accountant on Reid, he thought.
They were having lunch that day.

At his usual quiet table at the Savoy Grill, he skated round Reid.
He liked his ruddy-faced accountant who was semi-retired and more
into golf than clients; the man was loyal and to be trusted. William
stared at him thoughtfully. 'Here's a hypothetical situation. I suspect
a big name of insider dealing but can't prove it. I think there's more,
that his company's cheating on its shareholders in some way –
maybe fiddling a million pound bonus, something like that. How
easy would any of it be to prove?'

His accountant was rubbing his nose as he formulated an answer.

'You'd need a whistle-blower, somebody constantly on the lookout. The company could be inflating its profits – a Finance Director in on it, perhaps. Suppose, say, there were six divisions, the losses of one or two could be quietly missed off the Annual Accounts – that mightn't be too difficult to track down. Any good to you?' He smiled.

'Who'd be a whistle-blower though, what sort of person?'

'I've got a godson working in just such a company, he's a bright lad. I saw him this weekend and he actually said there was some-thing that didn't seem quite right.'

'What did you say? What did you tell him to do?' William felt a shot of journalistic adrenaline of the kind he hadn't felt for an age, a sense of coincidence, luck and timing just somehow clicking into place.

'I told him to keep his eyes open and have very sharp wits. If there's really some creative accounting going on, it could get quite unpleasant. This purely hypothetical company, William . . . is it by any chance a manufacturing one?'

'They make loo rolls and stuff,' he said, feeling elated as it became clearer that they had a fit. 'I don't suppose,' he said, lowering his voice a whisker, 'your godson would be able to encourage anything helpful into the bins instead of the shredder? We know about handling refuse and it would be hard for anyone to point the finger then.'

He changed the subject and soon signalled for the bill. Out in the Strand the two men cheerfully parted company and went their separate ways.

Back at the office, William set a few wheels in motion but then felt flat. Reality began creeping in. Deeply satisfying as it would be to nail a cheating bastard like Reid, it was way down the line, a very long shot.

The Hammond story was far more of the now, imminently likely to explode. Downing Street wouldn't be pleased, although the Foreign Secretary had it in for Hammond and would enjoy seeing him squirm; they had a longstanding feud.

Victoria wouldn't like to see the Government under pressure and the daily evidence of his own hypocrisy, William thought. He felt unsure of her reaction.

He wanted more dirt on Barney, all the help he could get. Smut was going to be needed, probably the only way in the end. When the time was right.

After a discreet call to GD and some expensive tailing set in train, he felt better. GD would keep it under wraps, he knew.

He prowled round the building. He wanted Victoria to have opened his present before her family dinner that night. She was putting Barney and her father-in-law first, he thought. Surely she could have dreamed up some excuse for not going. She couldn't start developing a conscience; there was no one lower than Barney.

She was too locked into the marriage. He wanted contact, not a Christmas apart with that shit making free. And his own life at home wouldn't be easy, keeping up a façade with Ursula. He had needed to see Victoria to get through.

CHAPTER 19

Barney's father, Quentin, lived alone in a low-stone hillside Cornish cottage, by choice, in the grimmest of conditions. Victoria was fond of him, although on their rare visits she never got as far as taking off her coat. Gin and his passion for orchids kept him alive. He would be lyrical describing the silky sensuality of his cymbidiums, his creamy phalaenopis. He grew many varieties in a grey-painted greenhouse, a small tropical haven lodged against his outside kitchen wall.

The cottage was a midden, empty gin bottles, half-eaten tins of corned beef with a fork still stuck in; it was dangerous sitting down without first making a careful inspection of the chair.

In London Quentin stayed at his club in Pall Mall, which was where they were having dinner. Victoria hurried through tall studded blue doors and clattered up a wide wooden staircase to the first-floor bar. It was comparatively noisy, but Quentin and Barney were morosely silent, sunk in green-leather armchairs with their respective gins and whiskies. She felt infuriated that Barney failed even to get up and greet her.

Leaning to kiss Quentin's rheumy old cheek, she said, 'Wonderful to see you. Sorry to be so late — my last day in the office and it was murder!'

'Better go in now, Dad,' Barney said, downing his whisky and patiently helping up his father. He was refusing even to look at her; she thought it was her lateness.

In the dining room, people were talking in murmurs and the clink of cutlery dominated. Predecessors on the walls peered down dyspeptically out of cumbersome frames; there were white table-cloths, a domed sweet trolley but no Brown Windsor soup on the menu. They ordered potted shrimps and fillets of lemon sole with spinach.

Quentin reminisced about old consulate days in Madras but he was meandering, drunk. Victoria pressed him to come to her parents' for Christmas. He slowly shook his head. 'Hate turkey, dear thing,' he said, leaning to squeeze her hand and trailing his tie in the spinach. He was rolling his head from side to side.

'You should come, Dad,' Barney pressed, but Quentin just went on slowly shaking his head as if he had quite forgotten to stop.

Sherry with the soup, quantities of wine, all the gins and whiskies, Barney was drunk, too. Quentin had to be helped to his room and it was very slow progress. Barney was gentle and patient though, even in his own condition. He was always so sweet with his father, Victoria thought with sudden affection.

Getting in the car though, and with Bob seeing his condition, she felt differently. Barney certainly wasn't being sweet to her. What right had he to be so sullen and maudlin when he was far from blameless? There was June and all the others.

They were outside number 16. She loved the house and its fig tree in quiet leafy Hartley Street. It was almost Nattie's holidays; she had to try, had to give.

Barney went off unsteadily up the path but she stayed behind to give Bob a festive bottle. 'I won't see you now till the third of January, but have a very Happy Christmas and New Year,' she said warmly.

'And yourself,' he replied. 'You take good care, now.'

She lay listening to Barney's breathing. He had taken Alka Selzer and crashed out on the bed without a word. He must be asleep, she thought; he seemed insensible. There hadn't been a chance to open William's present at the office. She knew it would be better waiting till morning, when she was alone in the car, but she was too impatient. Either way, the problem was where to hide it.

The grandfather clock sounded like a ticking time bomb as she crept downstairs. The present was in a carrier of other presents from the office. Barney hadn't seen it, she thought. He'd gone straight in and to bed. He had no reason to come snooping.

She tried not to crackle the brown-paper wrapping. Inside was a cardboard box and inside that, in plenty of tissue paper, a small silver statue of a mermaid sitting on a rock. William had had it inscribed on the base. *Caution in love is fatal.*

She found a note in the box. *It's part of a Bertrand Russell quote. 'Of all forms of caution, caution in love is perhaps most fatal to true happiness'* – do heed his words!

She held the statue and let the tears run down her cheeks. It was solid silver, a lovely delicate thing. The lump in her throat refused to go away; she couldn't swallow. She wanted to believe in a future with William, but it seemed a far-fetched dream. He was in the full flight of a passion that couldn't possibly last.

Barney was still uncommunicative in the morning. He saw her off, all packed up for two weeks over Christmas, in a churlish mood. He was staying another night in London. She tossed the carrier of presents on to the back seat of the car. Nowhere in the house had seemed safe, especially with Barney there on his own.

The office seemed the only solution. She called Marty and said she'd stupidly forgotten something in her desk and was dropping in on her way.

She tucked the box behind a pile of envelopes in the bottom drawer of her desk. Squatting to hide it, she realized that the inscription was incriminating whoever might see it. Getting up again, she saw that Marty had come in. He wouldn't pry into her things. She thought, it would be all right.

'We'll send down as little work as possible,' he said, with his gentle smile.

'Thanks – and I hope that means you're easing up a bit, too. And thanks for having the office party in January, Marty, it was so thoughtful and kind.'

'We knew you wanted time with Nattie.'

She said her farewells for a second time and hurried to leave London.

Cars were queuing up at Nattie's school, girls shrieking, horns honking, presents being swapped. It took time, but they finally heaved in Nattie's kit and got away.

She was excited, talking about making mince pies, picking holly and doing a tree at the cottage – just a little one, she said, as they were going to her grandparents.

At the cottage Portia was waiting to be let in and Nattie scooped her up. Victoria felt released as she unpacked the car, glad of a night on her own without Barney, and the chance of late-night calls to William. Putting away clothes, she laid carefully in the drawer a new turtleneck cashmere sweater that had been bought for 3rd January. It was the soft lavender colour of distant hills, a colour that suited her.

Nattie went to bed early, tired from the end of term.

In bed later, Victoria lay wakeful, listening to the sounds of night. The wind had died down, the forecast warning of a hard frost. She heard a long drawn-out strangulated shriek and wondered if it were a barn owl: possibly a rabbit caught by a fox?

The Firing Line was off air for the holidays so William would have Friday nights at home. The thought was depressing; she didn't want Ursula drawing him back in. It made her all the more impatient as she lay waiting for it to be late enough to call.

In her heart she didn't believe he would ever really leave his family but he gave her confidence, a feeling that he wouldn't let her down. Would Christmas have changed things? Would he be less certain of his feelings when they met in two weeks' time?

CHAPTER 20

Barney had another headache; they always seemed to coincide with the Friday drive. It had been forgivable starting on the brandy, he thought, alone in the house and after such a depressing evening with Mary. Her timing, talking about her firm's new business, couldn't have been worse coming right on top of Hugh's news. And he could have hit her when she sensed his mood and tried so hard to be sympathetic.

He had just been leaving the office when Hugh called him in. Hugh with a scotch in hand had been a bad sign; he usually sped straight off home to his frizzy-haired Mandy. And he'd had less of his naturally superior way. He could be so bloody patronizing, Barney thought, remembering the time when, introducing him to a new client, Hugh had said that Barney gave the firm their colour. God. Well, there was no one greyer than Hugh, the pinstriped bastard. He was a pompous tedious prick.

He had offered a drink, then walked about while Barney perched on a corner of the desk, and finally, after looking hard at his manicured nails, come to the point. 'Sorry about this, old boy, no easy way. We've lost Squires and Taylor.'

He had been expecting bad news but it still came as a shock. 'But that's half our bloody business! And they've been doing great – sports gear is booming.'

'That's just it. They think they're in the big league now, and they've gone for one of the top six. I'm sure I need hardly say this, but Chalfern's pretty key till we land some new business.' That had clearly been the reason for singling him out for this meeting. 'I'll, of course, be telling everyone in the partners' meeting tomorrow,' Hugh said, as though reading his thoughts.

'No worries,' Barney said confidently, downing his mean little whisky. 'I can handle it. Roland even fancies Victoria!' Hugh didn't know the half of it, he thought. Chalfern's big shareholding in the leading Downsland consortium was only the tip of the iceberg; he felt convinced there was more. Chalfern was too uptight in meetings, too keen to let it be known that Victoria had to deliver that development or else.

It might have been wiser, mentioning the shares to Hugh, but he was so correct. He'd want Victoria told, come what may, and then she would run to Ned Markham, get herself moved and Chalfern would shift all his business out of spite. It was fucking lose, lose all the way.

Without Downsland she'd be out of the limelight, Barney realized, accelerating forcefully as the car in front got going, and just when her high profile was starting to pay dividends. The dinner they'd been invited to in the New Year with the *Post*'s proprietor was a case in point. It was bound to have an influential guest list; it could even lead to new business – and what a satisfying smack in the eye for Hugh *that* would be.

He thought it would be all right. Victoria would want Downsland to go ahead: more housing was needed and she'd be keen to do the right if unpopular thing. A General Election was a long way off.

He couldn't be sure, though. There were effective lobbyers around, like William Osborne. She'd had lunch with him, and Osborne had been at it again on *Question Time*. A piece in a diary column, next day, had talked about him getting her to blush.

And the politics of it couldn't be discounted. The local MP was lobbying strongly, always on television. Could it be him? Or possibly even Osborne?

The road ahead was clear and he put his foot down. How could she be so disloyal? Even coming late to dinner with his father – probably hot from a fond Christmas farewell and an exchange of presents, with whoever it was.

Barney was battling with his headache and his mouth felt like the furred inside of a kettle. The urge to challenge her was growing; he was spoiling for it but he knew that could tip her into leaving. He didn't want that, he felt cold at the thought; nor did he want the whole bloody world sneering. However bitter the pill, he just had to sit tight. Her conscience would get to her in the end, he thought; it would run its course. God, he felt ill and depressed, so raging mad at her. It was a good thing Nattie was home to keep the peace.

His daughter came out of the house as he parked. 'Hi Dad, you're late. Supper's ready and you're not to be rude about it after all my hard work.'

He was distracted, seeing Victoria in the light of the doorway. He still wanted her, fucking disloyal bitch, with her wide serious eyes. 'What's this gourmet feast then, Nats?' he said, grinning and planting a kiss. 'I'll be critical, mind; the unvarnished truth is always best.'

'It's lamb with red and yellow peppers. I've peeled the peppers and used lots of fresh rosemary – and that was so typically mean of you, Dad.'

*

Victoria helped unpack the car and tried to make light. 'I like this new idea of the unvarnished truth,' she joked, and Barney scowled. He was in an inflammatory mood, she could smell and feel it in the air like humidity.

Nattie regaled him with all her doings over supper, the presents bought, the cards hung. She said Mrs Potter next door had given her two very old bottles of stout off her larder shelves. 'She's got tins ten years out of date in there, Dad. She wouldn't let me chuck any. I took her in some of my mince pies and do you know, she sniffed them!' Nattie was being wonderful, but she would soon sense the mood and she hated rows.

There was another hard frost overnight. Victoria went in the kitchen and pulled up the blind on a crisp bright wintry scene; the garden and field beyond were glittering and crystallized, like crushed diamonds. She wanted to feed the birds but thought Nattie would love doing it when she surfaced.

Barney was up later than usual, too. He was in a black depression. He had slept as far apart as the bed's dimensions allowed: a relief but still worrying. Victoria wondered if there was some other problem on top of the home-grown ones.

He came silently into the kitchen. He cut slices of bread and stuck them in the toaster, viciously ramming it down. 'Does the frost mean your golf with Dick is cancelled?' Victoria asked, knowing he'd have had to leave a lot earlier. He shrugged. She worried about him hanging round all day; she had her surgery, people to see.

'You know Giles and Margaret are coming tonight,' she reminded Barney. 'I don't suppose you'd do the shopping and perhaps cook your special honey roast duck?' He looked slightly mollified.

It was Victoria's last surgery before Christmas and few people turned up. A beekeeper was one. Jason had warned her he was coming to complain and she'd done a bit of homework. He certainly came in with an unhappy set to his brow. His hives had succumbed to a virulent virus, he'd been virtually wiped out, he said, and what, he asked, was the Government going to do for him by way of compensation?

Nothing, Victoria thought, but she said reassuringly, 'We do understand the importance of bees for crop pollination and wild plants as well as honey. The National Bee Unit spends well over a million pounds per year on disease controls.' She paused, thinking of William's bee story at the *Post* lunch and needing a diverting moment, 'I believe, um, am I right that Neapolitan Queens are immune to that virus?'

'Good heavens! How on earth do you know about that?' He left smiling, suggesting a visit to his bees and with no more talk of compensation.

She went home after a light surgery, thinking about the evening ahead. Giles was a wonderful constituency chairman and he and Margaret would be a neutralizing, reassuring influence, but they were bound to pick up that relations were strained.

* * *

'You do get the duck-skin so crackly-crisp and tender, Barney,' Margaret Royston enthused. She was a great doer of meals-on-wheels but top Chinese-restaurant-style crispy duck wasn't a regular in her repertoire. Barney grunted but looked pleased; he pulled the cork on another bottle of claret.

Nattie had made a trifle with proper eggs-and-cream custard; the raspberry jam was from the Roystons' own fruit. Everyone praised it.

Giles talked about the Christmas Fayre. 'A man spent nine quid at the tombola trying to win a doll in an orange crocheted crinoline, just fancied it, he said – we had to fiddle it in the end – and Mrs Casey's sponges went, well, like hot cakes! Jason tells me you chatted her up at the Joneses', Barney? We've got you to thank for that! You both do so much,' he went on. 'We are all so very proud of Victoria, she's working her socks off, but she always has time for us lot down here.'

Barney was collecting up the pudding plates and he stood holding the pile. 'It's me she never has time for. I'm way down the pecking order these days.' He went out to the kitchen.

No one knew quite what to say; it had punctured the mood. The candles flickered in the small, beamed dining room that just took the pretty mahogany table and six Regency chairs; Barney had bought them in a fit of extravagance early in their marriage. They made awkward small talk until he returned.

'Are you interested in politics at all, Natalia?' Giles asked, which Victoria didn't think was the most diplomatic route. She waited anxiously on Nattie's reply.

'Only in a back-row sort of way. Mum's workload's a joke.'

That seemed to be siding with Barney and it hurt. Victoria began smoothing in guilt like body lotion, worrying that she should have been at home more. Nattie was hiding behind her fall of hair, but she was clearly distressed and embarrassed.

The Roystons left understandably early. On the doorstep Giles squeezed Victoria's hand. 'A nice long Christmas break will do you both a power of good.'

'You're right,' she smiled, thinking how desperately she longed for an extremely short one.

Nattie took off to bed with a muttered good night, but Barney did help to clear up.

'Bear with me, love,' Victoria said pleadingly. 'It's such early days in the job.'

'I've got no option, have I? You do your worky whirl and I just satellite round your sun.' Turning round from the sink, his face was coldly sardonic.

'Don't be sarky! I know I've been a bit wound up, but this is my big chance and I really want to prove myself and get through Downsland as creditably as I can.'

'And after that? Life's suddenly going to change, is it?'

She had no answer.

On Sunday night in a last-minute flurry, she and Nattie were on the floor in a sea of wrapping paper. The presents for her brother's children were too big for single sheets and Nattie helped tape joins. 'Normal people buy four-metre rolls,' she complained. She looked up. 'Are hand-warmers really OK for Grandpops, Dad?'

'Fine.' He was still being impossible, monosyllabic even with Nattie. He chucked down his paper in ill temper and got up to refill his glass. 'I can't believe all the crap written about the nightingales at Downsland. It's so irresponsible of the Sundays, giving space to crackpot environmentalists.' He finished one whisky bottle and opened another, pouring himself half a tumbler. He glared at Victoria. 'You should be countering, being pro-active. If you don't start soon . . .'

Her hackles rose. 'If, what? Can't you even finish a sentence?'

Nattie went to the door. 'I'm going up. I can't bear this. You'll come and say what to pack, Mum?' Victoria nodded. They were leaving early next morning for her parents', while Barney was going back to London for two more days. He drank his whisky in silence when Nattie was gone.

Victoria found her daughter on the bed, hugging her knees with a T-shirt stretched over them. 'Why's Dad being so awful?' she asked plaintively.

'He's probably just fed up about the golf.'

'For God's sake, Mum, don't treat me like a child.' She was looking so young though. 'I do hate it when you row. I've packed my Zara black dress for New Year. Anything else happening?'

'Nothing much. Uncle Robert and the gang are coming on Christmas Eve, Mabel and Freda on Christmas Day.' Victoria drew the curtains and kissed the top of Nattie's head, then picking up Portia she went to the door. 'Love you, Nats,' she said. Portia's purring was a soothing, comforting rumble.

She decided not to go downstairs again and got undressed, but Portia rubbed insistently against her legs and made it clear she wanted food.

Barney came in. He leaned against the fireplace and carried on ranting about Downsland. 'It should be half-built by now. The French just get on with it. You should be massaging public opinion, deflecting all these nature loons. Why aren't you fighting back?' he demanded aggressively. It was the drink, Victoria thought, determined not to rise.

'Nightingales are in decline,' she said equably, 'and people care, they have a right to their views being heard. I'm going down to feed Portia now and put her out.'

Barney came closer; he was reeking of whisky. 'No, you're not, you just listen to me for a change. They're cranks, freaks, scrounging yobbos – don't give me that apologist's crap.'

'Leave it, Barney, will you? I want to go and see to the cat.'

He stood between her and the door. 'You'll bloody well stay till I've finished.'

'For God's sake, keep your voice down.' She couldn't bear Nattie to hear.

'You'll have a lot to answer for, if you screw up.' He was talking far too loudly, sounding far too interested in Downsland. 'I sometimes wonder if you're up to that job of yours,' he added with a goading sneer.

She ignored the jibe and squatted down to gather up Portia. 'Come on, puss, I'll find you some scraps. Can you please get out of the way now, Barney?'

'You're staying here.'

'No, I'm not.' She tried squeezing past, but he roughly pushed her backwards. There was a kelim rug; she slipped on it and fell against the brass bedstead, catching her hip on the iron rim of the springs. It really hurt and she couldn't help crying out. Portia leaped out of her arms.

'Be quiet, can't you,' Barney muttered. He helped her up, then clumsily tried to kiss her. His breath was bad and she angrily pulled free. Turning away, she caught a look of such rejected fury that she knew he was losing control.

He swung up and hit her. His hand made sharp contact with her cheek, but he caught her upper lip too and she tasted blood where a tooth cut in. With the sound of the loud crack they both stood stock-still. Nattie's bedroom was right across from theirs.

'I'll go and feed the cat,' Barney mumbled and left the room.

Her lip was stinging; she sat down on the bed and, supporting her arm at the elbow, pressed a hand to her throbbing cheek. Barney would have gone in earlier to say good night, she thought, and he never closed doors. Nattie could so easily have heard. He had been drinking much more openly that night too, which upset her.

He came back upstairs. 'I've brought you some tea,' he said, coming to the bed. He sat down and nestled the mug into Victoria's hands. 'I gave Portia those scraps and put her out, but you know she gets in through the top little loo window? I've closed it for now.'

Weirdly she felt quite relaxed with him. He was being humble and she had more of the moral upper hand. The air was somehow cleared, the extreme tension over. Was this to be the pattern – a lurch from crisis to crisis until she was headline news or Downsland reached its completion? And if by some quirk of chance they made it, could she then just look Barney in the eye and walk away?

They didn't speak getting into bed, but with the protection of darkness he started talking in a conversational way. 'I'll go very early to beat the traffic and try not to wake you. Only one more actual working day! Hugh's party is the most tedious bore, but I should be able to leave lunchtime Christmas Eve.'

'You'll make my excuses to Hugh and Mandy?' She turned on her side, making it clear that that was her good night. Her lip was smarting badly and the pain was reminding her of what had just happened and where they were at.

Sleep wouldn't come and Barney was lying on his back, wakeful too, sensitively keeping well away and leaving her as much space as possible.

He reached out across the bed. 'Hand,' he whispered cautiously as though uncertain whether she would choose to hear or respond. She gave him her hand; he held it a moment and then they both settled on their sides and were better able to find some exhausted sleep.

CHAPTER 21

In the morning the kitchen door banged shut and Nattie went out of the back gate and into the field beyond. Victoria watched from the bathroom window, thinking a walk when it was only just light was a bad sign. She packed for the visit to her parents, trying to keep occupied. Life felt in chaos. Her lip was noticeably swollen, her cheek tender. Even getting on jeans had been painful; the bruising on her hip had spread like a spill of ink.

Waiting for Nattie to return was causing such tension, the need to have her back, the dread of facing her with a swollen lip. Victoria made tea and told herself to stay calm.

She jumped when Nattie suddenly came in the back door and hung up her anorak on one of the hooks beside it. When she turned, her eyes were puffy from crying. She must certainly have heard the row.

'It's much milder, isn't it,' Victoria said blandly, 'and it looks like rain. Was it a nice walk, though? Did you have breakfast yet?'

'I'm not hungry. Why is your lip so swollen?'

A straight question was unexpected, and terribly disconcerting.

'I fell against the brass bed. I was holding Portia and slipped on the rug.'

'You've got scratches on your hand, too.'

'Oh, that was Portia, leaping out of my arms. Dad went and pacified her with some food!'

'Why was he drinking so much?'

'I don't know, probably some problem at work. Have a cup of tea, darling, then we had better get going. Gran'll have lunch waiting for us.'

They locked up and left. It was a grey changeable day; the wind had got up, making driving a strain, and the milder, murkier weather was still more lowering. Victoria longed to get to her parents, to have them lifting spirits, asking no questions. She wanted Christmas to be taking over, the cooking and all the presents: the cousins' arrival.

Nattie was stubbornly, miserably silent. Victoria rehearsed saying, 'Whatever you heard, Nats, it was just a flash of temper. It meant nothing, put it out of your mind,' but the disillusionment had happened and no amount of equivocation could make it go away.

They had left the motorway and after a last weary half-hour were seeing the sprouting housing estate on the outskirts of Troomley. The village green came next, then the post office run by warty old Mrs Perks, and the pub, the Crooked Man. Finally they turned in at Brook House. The garage door was open: her father must be out. Victoria parked so he could get in.

Her mother came running out, beaming. 'I was just starting to worry!' Victoria tried to catch Nattie's eye at the predictable line, but Christie was leaping up and distracting her. 'Nattie, love!' Bridget exclaimed. 'You look so pale. Don't go and be ill for Christmas.'

'I'm fine, Gran.'

'And you're white as a sheet too, darling.' Bridget looked at Victoria concerned. 'Have you had a little fall? Your lip's a bit up – quite becomingly,' she added, overdoing being sensitive. 'Is it an allergy, perhaps? Dad might have something to help it.'

'It's nothing, Mum, just a fall. It'll go down. We're both fine. Dad doing his trolley stint at the hospital?'

'He's due back any minute but said to start lunch. It's fish pie, Nattie, the one with smoked haddock, and I put in some mussels, too.'

Victoria's father didn't comment on her swollen lip, for which she was grateful. Nattie was subdued, but sitting at the kitchen refectory table, life seemed more bearable. It was a rambling kitchen, in need of modernizing and smelling of dog-basket, but it was home. They would manage Christmas, Victoria thought.

The office had sent a red box to Brook House by government car that morning. Her father gave her his desk to work at; it was in an annex off the sitting room and she cocooned herself there after lunch.

Before starting work, she took out her mobile. It was her last chance for a quick call to William. She had asked him not to text since her mobile wasn't safe from Barney; he had honoured that and they hadn't had any contact since Friday.

There was a string of texts from him, all demanding she call. They swelled her heart. But they suggested he knew Barney was back in London, and she deliberately hadn't told him, not after all the talk of his driving somewhere close-by to see her. That had seemed wrong with Nattie at home, a risk too far.

They talked in murmurs. The electricity flowed; she thought of him holding her jaw in his little kitchen the talk of love that had so overwhelmed her. 'How did you know Barney wasn't around?' she asked, 'to be sending all these texts this morning?'

William seemed to hesitate. 'I rang his office and checked it out.'

'But what made you even think to?'

'I am a newspaperman, remember.'

'Yes, and I must never forget it,' she said, wondering about the tiny pause, 'but in spite of that I still . . .' Her father looked in, saw she was on a call and went out. It was time to end it. William said he'd been about to leave, and would be home till Boxing Day afternoon. Three days of undiluted family life, Victoria thought.

Her father came back. 'I wanted to get you to come for a little walk,' he said. 'Nattie and Mum are going to Tesco's.'

'Love to, Dad – and Christie's heard the magic word!'

There was a thin unappealing mist of rain; it wasn't walking weather. John asked after the office, how things were going with MDF and then mentioned *Question Time*.

She said ruefully, 'You weren't too hurt about my euthanasia answer?'

'No, it was pretty sound – and I did have that very warm endorsement from William Osborne.'

'Is that by way of saying his answer was better than mine?'

Her father smiled and squeezed her arm. They went into the church car park and over the stile. There were sheep but Christie was well trained and they let him off the lead.

They walked on a bit and then her father turned to her. 'Did Barney hit you?'

It sounded too stark and harsh a question in the middle of a wet field.

'He didn't mean anything by it, Dad, he just lost it for a moment. He's very low and upset – and it's me he's upset about, you see?'

'There's someone else?'

'Yes. And Barney knew immediately, almost before it had happened. It's quite serious, Dad, but so complicated, I know it can't have a future.'

'Because of your job – because he has a family?'

She nodded. 'Three children, and two of them are younger than Nattie.'

'But you love each other?'

She smiled. 'It's all so new, he's probably just very swept up.'

'But you're going to leave Barney now, aren't you – whatever happens? It's time, darling, it always has been.'

'Don't go on, Dad. It would be impossibly difficult right now. I'm so much in the public eye with Downsland – you must see that?'

'That's always been your problem, summoning up excuses. Don't leave it too long. I only want your happiness, darling, and you are nearly forty . . .'

'Thanks!' She wanted hope, reassurance, to be told that of course her love affair had a future, that William would free himself and everything would be wonderful. 'I will make the break,' she said, 'but in my own time, when it feels right.'

'There's never a right time. And don't be worried about putting pressure on this man; he'll do what's right for him. It's for you, darling, you must do it.'

'In the summer, perhaps, Dad. Barney will make it really hard

– he'll talk to the press and do anything to try and stop me. He really cares.'

'Funny way of showing it,' John muttered. He whistled for Christie and they turned for home.

They were nearly back at the stile when he stopped and stared at her with a thoughtful frown.

'What is it, Dad?'

'That wasn't the first time he's hit you. Tell me honestly.'

'It's been very rare, I don't expect you to understand. He's so kind in many ways, and a good father to Nattie. Don't think the worst.'

'I do – and you can't go on putting it off. You must end it now.'

There was no one else tramping the wet field but she still glanced round instinctively. 'It's my life, my mess,' she said, angry. 'I even love Barney in a way.'

'And what's it doing to Nattie, do you think? She's a young adult and obsessed with her own life, but yours is impinging on hers. She seems very knocked and upset. It would be better for her, too, if you make the break; have you even considered that?'

She could tell he thought he'd hit home. He went on ahead but when she caught up he had a gentler look and then he slung his lean old frame a little stiffly over the stile.

Victoria's brother Robert and his family were coming for Christmas Eve lunch. Nattie was putting the pastry tops on a batch of mince pies; her head was low and Victoria felt the weight of it. They were alone in the kitchen. 'Nattie, darling,' she said tentatively, 'they'll be here in a minute. Can we have a quick hug? It is Christmas.'

'I know very well it's Christmas,' the girl muttered, but she turned and accepted her mother's arms.

As Victoria drank in the warmth of contact, she felt the brush of wet lashes; it was a chink, a loosened brick in the wall. It had had to be asked for though, it hadn't been spontaneous. And once released from it, Nattie made for the door. 'I do know it's Christmas, but I wish to God it wasn't,' she blurted. Looking back, she ran out of the room and upstairs and slammed her bedroom door.

Robert's car drew up shortly afterwards and disgorged its boisterous load; then Barney got back. The family were gathered together, the young cousins whooping and shrieking – even more loudly when Nattie eventually turned up, looking pale. The whole hectic Christmas show had somehow got itself on the road.

CHAPTER 22

'I want a hug for them!' Barney was holding out his arms. Victoria thought he was genuinely pleased; he loved old glass and she'd found him some Georgian rummers in a Southampton antique shop. 'And of course they're a great excuse for some really decent wine,' he said, grinning.

'You never need any excuses.' She got up from the floor and went to sit beside him on the sofa. 'And you got Mabel and Freda completely tiddly on the sloe gin and cherry brandy at lunch. They had bright pink spots on their powdery old cheeks!'

'We had to hold their elbows all the way down the road, taking them home,' Nattie said. Her grandmother, with her tired feet up on a fireside stool, smiled indulgently. Christie was flat out on the hearthrug, his paws twitching in a dream, and Agatha was there too, looking vast; no cat was more spoiled.

John took no part in the conversation; he was staring at the fire with his head half-screened by the wing of his favourite faded blue armchair. Victoria directed a meaningful look his way. She was cross with him; he was being incredibly cold and standoffish, sometimes not even answering Barney and he was keeping it up, even on Christmas Day.

Nattie, in charge of the presents under the tree, got going again. 'Here's Dad's to you, Mum,' she called, 'and now can I open one of mine?'

Victoria unwrapped a toggle-style winter coat, a rich deep brown with embroidered fastenings; she put it on over her Christmassy red sweater and skirt and did a little twirl. Nattie said she looked like a Cossack or a lion tamer. Bridget thought it was very swish, much smarter than the old one, very generous of Barney.

'I've never been that keen on her old camel thing with the belt,' he said.

Nattie had been given money but she couldn't have been more thrilled with Barney's surprise present of a digital camera. 'It's a serious one, Dad, it's fantastic!'

Victoria, too, was finding it easier to be sweeter to Barney and more tactile, partly to compensate, she thought, for her father. But she hadn't, since the row, yet been required to cope at night.

At breakfast on Boxing Day though, everything Barney said and did seemed to jar; even his chair seemed too close to hers and he was giving infuriating exaggerated groans. 'Feeling hungover?' she enquired stiffly, reaching for the coffee.

'God! My mouth feels like an Ethiopian taxi-driver's armpit.'

Nattie looked up from a book. 'That's such a racist remark, Dad.'

'Give us a break! Shall we try out the camera when I'm not feeling so fragile? The light should be fine after lunch; we could take arty pictures down by the brook.'

'Nice idea,' Victoria said. She had been thinking obsessively about how to call William, who was back in the office that afternoon. 'I'd better go to the shop before it closes,' she said, getting up. 'Mum wants some more onions.'

'I'll come, I need some air,' Barney said quickly, transparently, as if she wasn't to be let out on her own.

They walked down to the green. Mrs Perks's post office and shop stocked the basics, a few tired vegetables, newspapers and cards. Barney bought the *Post* instead of his usual paper and Mrs Perks's overweight daughter grudgingly looked up from a magazine to serve him.

Back home he made a fresh pot of coffee and sat at the kitchen table reading the paper. It was a skinny Boxing Day edition and Victoria wondered if he had a half-formed or even a strong suspicion about William. He was normally such a faithful reader of *The Times*.

John came into the kitchen. 'Your Press Office rang,' he said to her, ignoring Barney. 'The *Post* want a call. It's to do with New Year resolutions.'

'Thanks, Dad,' she said flushing, even though she knew, as he gave her the name of a female journalist, that it had nothing to do with William. 'You could do with making a resolution or two,' she said defensively to Barney, 'like giving up drink, at least until Lent, for starters.'

'And you could resolve not to nag! There's a Bible saying, "It is better for a man to sit on a corner of his roof than to suffer a nagging wife". I could spend a lot of time up there.'

Her father went out and left them, noisily closing the door.

Victoria watched from the sitting-room window as Barney and Nattie went down the front path to try out the new camera; his arm was on her shoulders and her hair, almost as fair as his, was touching it.

It was her moment to call William and she thought the garden would be the most private place. John was watching the racing on television and Bridget was sewing by the fire. Victoria wondered how much her mother knew or had been told. She usually took Barney's side so hearing of violence would be a great shock to her, but the thought of a break-up would be too.

Victoria turned from the window and wandered out. She went to a damp bench in the garden and brought up William's number. A little shiver attacked her spine. He might sound subtly changed. Ursula and he might have reunited while he'd been home; his children might have touched his heart and conscience.

There was office background noise when he answered and she had to wait while he got to his room. She had chosen a bad time and tried to say so but William talked over her, questioning her so keenly and aggressively about her Christmas that she got flustered and answered in platitudes like a young shop-girl with an arrogant boss.

But how could she tell honestly of all the cold undercurrents, of Nattie's distress and what had led to it? It was William's own fault, she thought peevishly. He made talking about Barney impossible.

'Tell me about your Christmas now,' she demanded, trying to turn it round.

'Not much to say. I was surrounded by Ursula's family and felt tired the whole time. My mother-in-law's quite a trial – she doesn't approve of me, apart from the television show. I like Ursula's diplomat brother though, who was back on leave from La Paz. He's got a feisty wife – she'll probably slow up his advancement – and he'd brought Tom some cocaine tea he swears is harmless, that the diplomats drink for the air in the high altitude. Tom got mad when I said Sussex didn't have that problem!' Victoria didn't laugh; it sounded too normal a family scene.

'You're being distant,' William said. 'What's happened, why are you off me?'

'I'm not, but you make it so hard to explain things. Christmas hasn't been great, you see. I had a row with Barney before we got to my parents'.'

'What about?'

'Nightingales – but it could have been anything,' she said quickly, thinking of the Downsland implications. 'It was really more to do with you.'

'If Barney's tied up in Downsland in some way,' William said, as quick as a flash, 'you could be in trouble. People are always digging, and if there's anything to find out they will.'

He sounded hurtfully matter-of-fact. She retorted, 'Is the *Post* digging too?'

'Don't know,' he said, which seemed honest. 'Possibly. Jim Wimple could have got a tip-off. We do get them, the *Courier* too: any paper does.'

'But there's nothing to dig,' she said, nervously defensive. 'Barney has a property client – the one I told you about once – but there can't be any links. I am married to a responsible solicitor – he'd have told me.'

'You really believe that?'

'Yes, I do,' she said angrily. 'Must we fight like this? You're making me think that getting in first on some cheap mudslinging story is all that really matters to you.'

'You're all that matters.'

He had a quiet way of saying those things that made her feel such boundless longing, such intense need she wanted to jump straight in the car and drive to London. The excuses flowed into her head; she'd forgotten a charity soup-kitchen visit, there had been a request to do some media. Her bruises gave her pause though, and the conflicting pulls made her say ungraciously, 'You're not being at all easy, you could be more gentle.'

'I don't feel it. I'm missing you, I can't stand you being there.'

She suddenly felt confused and raw-nerved. She thought William hated Barney almost more than he loved her, though Di said it was all about sexual jealousy.

Her need for contact was acute. She said, 'Remember, the day I'm back will be very quiet. If you can spare the time and you want to, we can have the whole afternoon.'

A local farmer and his family had a regular New Year's Eve party with party games and charades. They all enjoyed it, Victoria less so if there was Scottish dancing.

Everyone called Nattie the belle of the ball. A year on she had a little more confidence and entered more freely into the games — much less coy in the orange-under-the-chin game, getting on very well with the boy next to her in the team. He was on the phone next day, politely and shyly asking to speak to her; he lived on another planet from her boyfriend Seb.

The day after that, their last, Barney left before lunch. He had been getting wound-up and withdrawn. She thought, perhaps, it was her father's drip-drip effect or he was anticipating her lover being back on the scene. Or it could be a date with June.

She was seeing William in hours, and struggling to contain the high-voltage shocks of elation to her system. As Barney drove away, it felt as if a tight brace on her chest had stopped clamping and she could breathe.

It was another damp mild day; there were crocuses and the first daffodil shoots. Her father was in the garden and she went out to him.

He was standing back in his thick sweater and sleeveless puffa, white-haired, surveying his old shrub roses with pride. 'I should take my little saw to them. People disagree but I think January's a good time for pruning.'

'You were tough on Barney, Dad. He must have been very hurt.'

'Good thing too.' She glared but her father went on with a warm smile, 'Are you quite longing to get back?'

She melted. 'Yes, but it's so hard to see him, Dad, with all the press. Thanks for not asking names!'

'I didn't need to, it was obvious. I knew, watching that programme. I knew when we talked – it showed in your glow – but don't worry, I won't even tell Mum!'

Her father was everything to her. When, after an early supper, she was leaving for London with Nattie and giving him a last heartfelt hug, she couldn't help the tears.

In the car Nattie tuned the radio to a hip-hop station; it made talking difficult but during a phone-in, a tedious discussion on wheat-free diets, she turned with an unexpected smile. 'Thanks for your New Year resolution, Mum, but I know work makes it hard.'

Victoria had taken a risk and given the *Post* a corny resolution about keeping contact with loved ones; she had liked the idea of William seeing it and hoped it wouldn't make the Whips think she wanted to spend more time with her family. Nattie's reaction seemed more than she deserved.

'The job does have its problems,' she said with a quick smile. 'Dad gets very fed up. It causes a bit of friction.' She was longing for Nattie to take the opening, but in vain; changing tack she asked with some trepidation, 'Will you see Seb this week?'

'Might.'

'Are you quite keen?'

'It's no big deal, Mum.'

'You'd say though, if it gets to be a relationship, if anything's ever a problem?'

'Like I said, it's no big deal.' Nattie drummed her fingers on her knee. A glimmer of progress, a tiny step forward and then, as always, they seemed to take one back.

There was another phone-in. A woman with a voice as affected as Hyacinth Bucket's droned on about weight-loss, but she suddenly said rather arrestingly to the guest dietician, 'My partner and I favour oral sex. Can you confirm if there's a calorie count involved?'

It was after nine in the evening, Victoria thought, struggling to keep a straight face.

The dietician was reassuring. 'About the equivalent of a small broccoli salad, I'd say, nothing to worry about. I'd carry on if you enjoy it.'

Sneaking a look at Nattie did for them both; they started to splutter and soon got completely hysterical. A small broccoli salad seemed such a quaint culinary idea.

The house was in darkness when they got home. Victoria thought Barney must be out; if he'd gone to bed he would have left the hall light on for them. She saw Nattie upstairs, kissed her good night and then took her red box to her desk.

Switching on the sitting-room light, she got a shock seeing Barney in an armchair. 'What on earth are you doing here in the dark?' He didn't answer. 'If this is about Dad, I'm sorry but I didn't tell him, I never would; he drew his own conclusions. Christmas is over now, can't we just draw a veil?'

'Sure, over anything you like.' He got up and pushed past her out of the room.

He brought her tea in the morning, the day she was meeting William. 'Well, it's back to work for another whole bloody year,' he said with forced breeziness, putting the mug down on the bedside table. 'Hope it's a better one. We lost Squires and Taylor, you know, just before Christmas.' He was painstakingly avoiding her eye.

She couldn't believe he hadn't told her but he could never bear to admit to anything approaching a failure. It helped to explain his moods though, and she swung out of bed and put her arms round him. 'Why on earth didn't you say, you old silly. It's not your fault, for God's sake. Something'll turn up. Things do – like Hugh getting Chalfern at a Harrow sports day.' Stupid, that, reminding Barney of one of Hugh's successes. 'You'll find the next big one,' she said, trying to make amends but wanting him just to go.

She longed for a scented bath, to dress in her best underwear, her new cashmere sweater. It seemed harsh, his uncanny choosing of that day to be unburdening himself and in need of her supportive care.

He had made toast and coffee, but she couldn't eat and feared her monumental impatience must be pointing bright as a laser to something going on.

She smiled. 'Two whole weeks since Bob's been waiting outside. Better be off now, darling. Can you say hi to Nattie from me if she's up before you go?'

Barney walked with her to the stairs. 'It'll be very quiet, won't it? I don't suppose you could take some time off and come round the sales?'

How could life be so mean? 'Sorry, darling, I've got a lot to catch up on. I do need this day. Look, why don't we skip going to Ferndale? I'd only have to cancel one New Year wine and cheese.' She was overdoing it, trying too hard to be enthusiastic but she pressed on. 'Nattie would certainly like staying in London.'

'I thought you wanted to cut down on her time here? Oh, forget it. The last thing I want is to slog round in the weekend crowds. It doesn't matter.' Barney's brittle hurt was turning the knife. 'I should go to the office, anyway – what's left of the place.'

'Plenty's left, darling. And Chalfern must be the firm's biggest fish now, and you look after him. Hugh owes you a lot.' She felt Chalfern might have been better left out of it. 'I had better go.' She kissed his cheek, ran up the stairs and out of the door.

He could always turn things sour; even with all her singing anticipation he was casting a shadow over her. She couldn't share with William how wretched she felt. Barney was still the one gaping crater in the path of their understanding.

CHAPTER 23

'I think there's only you and Nick Bates in today.' Marty was telling her she was being rather over-keen, coming into the office. Ministers created work and the heat would be on again in days.

'I'm only here for the morning,' Victoria reminded him, aware of her thudding heart.

There were a few things to be dealt with, minor but intractable enough to keep her focused, and they went over the long-term diary too, the fat stapled sheaf of pages with everything detailed to the minute. Marty had two copies for her; one was probably meant for Barney. She wondered about giving it to William, to help with timing calls.

Nick Bates called up during the morning. He wanted to have lunch and she suggested the following Tuesday; he had a bit of an eye for her but he'd been a good friend on MDF. She imagined it was to do with work or even, possibly, some depressing gossip; Nick knew what was going on. He was sometimes dismissed as a lightweight but she thought him able and politically quick. Still in his thirties and unmarried, he had a moon-shaped face and an engaging puppy-dog manner; you almost wanted to pat him.

At twelve-thirty she packed up, telling Marty she was going to the Commons first, before doing some personal things, and would walk there; she didn't need Bob. 'I'll be back around five for the box,' she said. 'Perhaps Bob could be here then? Call me any time, of course, if I'm needed.'

'Have a good afternoon,' Marty said pleasantly. 'We'll expect you back later.'

As William's door clicked closed and she was in the headlights of his intense gaze, she had no thoughts other than her raw desire. She wanted to be backed against the wall, feel his tongue in her mouth, his body hard on hers.

'It feels like a year at least,' she said, desperate for him to pull her close.

He traced round her lips and she sucked on his fingers. When he took them away and stood staring, she stared back in a panic. He had seen reason, he was feeling torn; he was thinking how to explain a responsible change of heart. 'What is it?' she asked. 'What's wrong?'

'You were so wrapped up in Barney. Why didn't you get in your car and come to London? I needed you to – I even thought you might. Does *he* always come first?'

She thought about being so ruthless with Barney earlier that day; it would be pointless to try and tell about it.

'You've got no answers?' William demanded.

'There aren't any, you know that. My car keys were in my hand on Boxing Day but it was hard. There was Nattie . . .' He knew her feelings perfectly well, she thought, and he must sense her overwhelming desire, standing there, trembling-lipped, straining for him to kiss her.

'If I take you to bed,' he said, leaning closer, 'you don't get any lunch till four.'

'Why then? That's when you have to go?'

'No, that's when we might have a break. I got in a Fortnum's hamper.'

Time ceased to be or matter. He loved her in a way that over-powered her; she felt out of control, terror at the thought of losing him. Even smothered and in his arms, she could hear the rumble of London five floors below and it sounded ominous. There were those in their lives whose feelings mattered, who would suffer, and there were people out there in the city bearing grudges, coldly bent on doing them down.

William asked how her hip had got so bruised though there was only the faintest roseate shadow remaining. She gave him an edited account of her fall.

The stout wicker hamper on the coffee-table contained quail's eggs, lobster quiche, tomatoes on the vine, figs and champagne.

Victoria leaned against the arm of the sofa with her legs over William's and sucked on a fig. It wasn't allowed, this joy; she would be incarcerated, held in chains, the Chief Whip her guard. She reached for her bag on the floor. 'I've brought you my work diary in case it helps with timing calls – but can I really trust you with it?'

'I'd pay good money for this,' he said, grinning and flicking the pages. She moved closer to read it with him and had hardly a qualm about the insights it might contain.

He found times for meeting, events they would both be at. An

MP's birthday drinks the following week was one and he wanted her to come to the flat afterwards.

'I can't, we're taking Nattie to a play,' she said. 'But I'm meeting them at the theatre. Barney's not coming to the party. My best friend, Di Faulkner is, I think, though. She knows.'

'Dinah Faulkner, the artist?'

'We're old friends from Oxford days. When I was so wound-up about seeing you we had lunch. She told me to trust to my instincts. She's a bad influence!'

'So I owe it all to Di. Take care though, even with close friends. Suppose for instance you'd given her a lift? Bob hears a chance remark, he hangs out with other drivers and it gets repeated, someone thinks there's a few bucks in it . . .'

'We weren't swapping secrets like girls in the dorm,' Victoria snapped, knowing it was just what they had been doing. 'God, that really makes me rise.'

'Just what you're doing to me.'

'No, I'm not. Don't brag, you're exhausted. And anyway, I've got things I want to talk about – Oscar Bluemont's dinner for one. You'll be at that, won't you?'

He put down the diary. 'Yes, but I can't promise to behave if Barney's around.' He took her face in his hands and kissed it. 'Leave him now, while the press have nothing on us. Don't wait.' She stared at him, feeling mesmerized. 'I couldn't see you for quite a while and I'm not sure I could stand it, but the press would be desperate to find out who else was involved; they'd be watching like hawks. But don't you see, it's so much the best for you? You can't go on with him, I can't stand it, and doing it before we can be linked, there'd be less hurt all round.'

She couldn't, just like that; it felt too soon and it would be impossibly hard leaving Barney. For all the hurt and wasted years, her sense of time running out, she still felt tied; his deep-down dependence on her was almost as binding as love.

His potent sexuality, too, had been a hold but no longer. Her need of William was stronger than anything she had known and not to see him as he was suggesting made her feel in anguish. There was Downsland too; Barney would stop at nothing in what he would say to the press.

Her eyes hadn't left William. 'I couldn't bear not seeing you. And you know the problems in doing it now – you have them too, remember? You must understand.'

'But you'd be the one most hurt by the publicity. And Ursula doesn't know but Barney more or less does. He's never going to understand or accept it whereas she might, given time.'

His wife would never be that obliging, Victoria thought, feeling bitterly dismissive of that. William was deluding himself.

She wanted to ask if he still slept with Ursula but found it an impossible question.

'It is true Barney probably has an idea,' she said evenly. 'He's asked questions, he's bought the *Post* when he never normally does, but he'd talk, he'd give interviews to the press. Believe me, he could make it bad. And people like Guy Harcourt certainly could, too. I will leave, but in the summer. I can't now.'

'And risk getting found out in the meantime, which would be even worse?'

That was below the belt. 'Have you forgotten about your promise to see me through Downsland?' she goaded, not letting him off.

'You've got a bloody answer for everything!' He stood up. 'And you're unbelievably stubborn. I'm not letting up though. Come on, let's have some coffee.'

'Nick Bates wants to have lunch,' she said, following him into the kitchen. 'I hope he hasn't been picking up rumours. I'll find out soon enough on Tuesday.'

'He's probably just on the make. Where's he taking you?'

'I think the Cinnamon Club, it's near the office. Why?'

'I've got to have lunch with Carol Knightly. I might come there too, if she's free.'

'Why have you "got" to?' It was unexpected and made her feel quite put out.

'Because I looked for you over her shoulder at the BBC party and she was cross.'

'And you expect me to believe that?'

He pressed into her side. 'Your phone's vibrating,' he said, grinning.

It was. The office wanted a call. 'I hate to trouble you,' Marty apologized, 'but can you do a radio clip on the Downsland skirmish, that farmer's tussle with Sam Swayne?'

'It'll have to be on a mobile,' she said, anxious about doing it from William's flat.

When she gave the interview he was being teasing, molesting her, being quite impossible; she impatiently turned her back and tried to concentrate. 'The police have their job to do,' she said crisply into the phone.

'But the local community is solidly behind Sam Swayne. Passions are running deep.'

'I know all about the passions of local residents,' she snapped, 'very well indeed.'

*   *   *

She got back to the office and found Marty looking concerned. 'You missed a call – your uncle from Australia? He's just hit town,' he said.'

'But I haven't got any uncles, certainly not any Aussie ones.'

'I did think he sounded more Fleet Street than Down Under. I told him you were tied up in a meeting, just in case it was someone snooping on your movements.'

'That's a relief!' she exclaimed, immediately worrying in case she'd sounded too fervent. Given Marty's perspicacity he might start wondering what she had actually been doing.

Talking to William later made her feel no better; he was being too calming, telling her that reporters tried it on the whole time. 'They don't,' she said irritably. 'I don't get regular calls from uncles in Australia.'

She worried the whole weekend about the reporter's call. For some reason, it brought back all of Barney's suspect phone-calls over the years, the picking up signs, the staring at unexplained bills. Nattie was being a worry too, very withdrawn and in a world of her own. Term started soon, so it could just be nerves.

The MP having the birthday drinks was a rebel, one of the awkward squad who had plenty of friends in the press. Di had painted a picture of his house once and knew him well. Victoria felt on a high at the thought of William and Di meeting. Going into the Reform Club though, and looking back, she happened to see Bob sauntering over to a group of other drivers. He might casually mention to William's driver about taking them to the Strand after *Question Time*; Dave would know exactly where his boss lived . . .

The party was packed, full of loud MPs and even louder members of the press. In such a male-dominated room finding Di wasn't difficult; she was in a low-cut burgundy suit and the magnificent pair were at full thrust like rockets about to be launched.

Di grinned. 'You're not getting all wound-up over Tonbridge, are you, I hope?'

'She's got a name,' Victoria whispered, glaring, 'and I am – very much so.'

'We'll get him away,' Di said, 'even if it has to be a joint effort!'

'God, Di, I'm not sure I want you to meet him at all.'

They found William having an argument about jury trials with his bumptious right-wing contributor Carl Hancock. Carl's pen flowed but he jumped on any female in sight and his views were extreme. 'Two visions of loveliness,' he said, easily distracted. 'Which one's yours, Bill?' God, he was crude, Victoria thought.

'Hello, William,' she said neutrally. 'Good Christmas? This is Di Faulkner.'

He pulled out all the stops, and ended up asking Di out for dinner that night. Victoria watched Carl taking it all in. It was for his benefit, she knew, but William did seem to be piling it on.

She forced a smile. 'I must be off. I'm seeing *Private Lives* tonight with my daughter.'

'I'll buzz,' Di promised. 'Say hi to Nattie from me.'

The Coward revival was in a small theatre with red plush seats, opera glasses and an old-fashioned crush-bar; it made all the jeans and trainers seem out of place.

It was in the Strand, a bad location; the play passed her by. Barney had to repeat a question in the interval and coming out later she couldn't help peering round. She thought Nattie noticed; she was giving her mother curious looks. It was a flat, sad evening.

By morning, Victoria had worked herself into a state of childish pique about William and Di. She was chilly during his early-morning call, didn't ask after his evening and when he brought it up himself she didn't pursue it.

Di rang immediately afterwards and launched, unasked, into a blow-by-blow account. 'He took me to dinner at the Ivy – said it might get in *Private Eye*. Any publicity's fine by me. But before you get too po-faced and uptight, you old prude, it's all a ruse, just about wanting me as a front – he says I'm a magnificent one!'

Still smarting about Carol Knightly, whom William had called a decoy, Victoria kept silent; she thought he had quite enough fronts already.

'He's really got it in for Barney,' Di went on. 'If he finds out the full picture, there could be trouble.' Di knew Barney occasionally lost control. She had asked outright once, just as Victoria's father had done at Christmas. 'You should tell William, really,' Di advised. 'Oh, he's taking me to the theatre, by the way. I said I was a novice at platonic relationships and he'd have to hold my hand.'

'And what did he say to that?' Officials were coming in and sitting at the table.

'I don't think I'd better tell you!'

'I think you better had,' Victoria snapped, only half-aware of the officials' embarrassed shuffling of papers.

'He said in the circumstances it was the very least he could do.'

She put down the phone. Di had no business goading her like

that. It rang yet again and she was surprised when it was William calling back.

'Just so as you know. I'll be at that restaurant at lunch – say yes if you love me?'

'Meeting starting.'

'You can't be this heartless!' She most certainly could.

In the Cinnamon Club later with Nick Bates, there was a columnist lunching an ex-Prime Minister and two backbenchers plotting like prison inmates. The restaurant was a converted library and the best tables were against pleasing wood panelling. Nick's was stuck in the middle: he wasn't well-enough known.

'You seem a little quiet, Victoria,' he said earnestly. Hardly surprising since William had just come in with Carol, who was looking, Victoria thought, fatiguingly anodyne in a powder-blue suit with annoying fur cuffs.

'It's been rather a testing morning.'

He chatted on but finally, looking slightly sheepishly, got to the point. 'There's something I felt I should tell you, that I suppose might not come as a complete surprise.' He stopped. Her mobile had started buzzing and he waited while she felt in a pocket.

It could be Marty or the Press Office, even the Chief Whip. 'Sorry,' she said ruefully aware that she'd disrupted him at a delicate point.

It didn't read quite as expected. *Cocksure little squirt, he's coming on too strong. Put him down.* At least, she thought, William wasn't completely wrapped up in Carol.

She looked up again, 'Just a press bid – Downsland means I get so many requests for interviews. Do carry on, Nick.'

'Well, this is a bit delicate but you see, my sister's best friend who's a solicitor is, well . . . seeing Barney. I couldn't decide about telling you,' he ploughed on hurriedly, 'but in the end, the press being what they are, I thought it might get out.' He looked at her anxiously. 'It did seem best. Of course, if you'd ever like a chat, perhaps over a drink or anything . . . ?' He dried up, sensing her stony-faced reaction.

He was using it as an in; she felt furious at the cheap shot but kept control. 'You shouldn't get involved, Nick. Personal relationships, people's marriages, are complex, never as they seem. And if *you* know, how many other people has your sister or her friend told?'

He pleaded forgiveness with his puppy-dog eyes. 'I'll tell my sister. I'll sort it, I promise.' He looked so forlorn that she softened; he had such an engaging way.

Her mobile went again. 'It'll be just another press bid,' she said smiling, ignoring it.

When she and Nick walked back to the office she hadn't once caught William's eye.

During an afternoon session though, while Mr Binks, the most punctilious of all her officials, was into the small print of energy efficiency in the home, it was hard to look raptly attentive. She loved William's productive energy, the way he seized life by its neck and shook it – the way he made her feel so much a part of him. His second message had said he loved her.

Mr Binks was eyeing her. He asked, in a tone dripping with condescension, if he had explained things satisfactorily. She nodded slowly and gave him a Delphic smile.

Talking to William later, she said she liked his second message more than the first.

'That squirt Bates was on the make though, wasn't he? I was right?'

'He wanted to tell me Barney's seeing his sister's friend. And Carol of the fur cuffs – what did you talk about to her?'

'I said she should have her own show; it bought me time for keeping an eye on you. Dirty chat-up line that, of Bates's, but I suppose he could have his uses. I'm feeling more magnanimous now I can swap Carol for the magnificent Di.'

'Di's leading you astray – "a novice at platonic relationships"!'

'Does she tell you absolutely *everything*?'

CHAPTER 24

William was shaving at the office before Oscar Bluemont's dinner; he seldom shaved in the evening, but with Barney there he didn't want any adverse comparisons.

He shushed his razor and glared into the mirror. He hadn't seen Victoria in a week and felt in a determinedly foul mood. No chance of any eye-contact or touch of her arm. He could handle it better, William thought, if she wasn't still sharing that bastard's bed.

Out of the office bathroom window, London looked lit-up and alluring, even though it was February, cold and bleak. He thought wistfully of being in some far-distant place with her – the luxury hotel outside Washington where Hammond and the Senator's wife had been spotted came to mind. It was one he knew, the Inn at Perry Cabin. But wherever it was, they would only be spied on through a long lens and be done for – just like Hammond and Roxanne, he thought morosely.

That story wasn't helping his mood, either. The Senator husband's PA had told all. She had dumped Roxanne deep in the shit and most likely brought down an able, if disliked Ambassador, too. It was a hot story but nailing Hammond wasn't bringing the usual adrenaline kick. William couldn't care less about pressure from the Government or a backlash on intrusion; it was his own newfound niggling sensitivity that was the problem, his edginess about the hypocrisy.

He splashed cold water on his face and patted it dry. What with there being no breakthough with Harold Reid, a lawsuit from a transdresser upset about the *Post*'s phraseology, the need to be civil to Barney . . . he had every right, William thought, to be wallowing in sour resentfulness.

He went over the guest-list. The television interviewer, Jack Hale, and his well-connected wife were coming. So were the Chairman of a television company and the head of a big insurance broker, with their wives. William had paired himself off with the *Post*'s star female feature-writer, toothy Jane French. Ursula was mercifully still refusing to come to any of Oscar's dinners, still prolonging the row after the last one and accusing him of lack of support. It was just an excuse; she hated coming to London.

Victoria said the guest-list had made a big impression on Barney; that he was after new business for his firm. Who did the cunt think he was? No company chairman or head of an insurance firm was going to toss *him* a crumb. It might keep him occupied at dinner though, trying to win over their wives.

Oscar had taken a private room at Gordon Ramsay's at Claridges. William mingled with the early guests and when Oscar and Bella, the svelte blonde fourth Mrs Bluemont, had arrived, he thought it was all right to slip out. It was just possible Victoria and Barney might come separately.

They arrived together. She had on a fussy formal coat. He hated it; he wanted the one that had special connections for them. He was feeling irrationally livid about it as she rather nervously introduced him to Barney.

'Shall I take that very smart coat for you?' he enquired with heavy sarcasm.

'It was a Christmas present from Barney – he thought this was just the occasion.'

'Oh, yes?' he said, warmed by her smile but refusing to melt.

'She's hard to get into new things,' Barney chipped in. 'She lives in her old ones.'

'Oh, yes?' he repeated, then got more of a grip. 'Come on through and have a drink. The Bluemonts are here – we all mostly are now, I think.'

Under her coat she had on the little black dress she'd worn at the Academy and he remembered his first glimpse of her through the crowd. She was looking just as stunning; the junky silver earrings were eye-catching and fun, and not, he thought, something real from Barney. Going through the restaurant to the private room she got plenty of stares.

Oscar was loud, greeting them, prancing about on his spindly legs yelling, 'Where's the champagne?' The waiter was already proffering tall glasses of Dom Perignon.

'You're getting great coverage, Victoria,' Oscar declared, 'but no human interest stuff. Hey, Bill, why no big spread on her? Why no nice sympathetic piece by Jane?'

Jane French turned at the mention of her name. Her interviews went right to the bone; she could worm out steamy revelations people must wish they had never made.

'Victoria's Press Office isn't having any of it,' William explained.

There was an exquisite first course of wild mushroom tortellini. Victoria was on Oscar's right, Jack Hale on her other side. William was sitting opposite and could look at her, which was bad for his frustrated need. He exchanged a few desultory words with Bella Bluemont, who was studying her nails – keen to display her clunking great diamonds, he thought. Barney was next to the insurance broker's wife; he was chatting her up, as expected, and also putting back quantities of an excellent Château Talbot.

The wine flowed. Mrs Insurance Broker was hanging on Barney's every word. She had marble eyes, a palpitating mouth like a landed fish and a freckled cleavage that heaved. William thought it a lost cause, he couldn't see her husband swapping solicitors.

Jane French was a Charlton fan and talking football. A top footballer had just badly beaten up his girlfriend – a case currently attracting huge publicity.

'He has that vast talent,' the television company Chairman was saying. 'His footwork's pure poetry yet the man's such a disgusting base brute.'

'I'm about to interview the girlfriend,' Jane said. 'Is there something peculiar to footballers that makes them so violence-prone?'

'God, those pictures of her black eyes!' Bella said, suddenly coming to life.

Jack Hale and his wife pitched in; it became a table-wide discussion.

'Poor buggers. They're put on pedestals, expected to be paragons, role models,' Barney observed.

William's stomach turned. 'So you have to be a paragon not to beat up your girl?'

'But they're under such pressure, footballers of that calibre. They get so stressed out.' He was drunk, but could he seriously be saying that? William writhed with contempt. Sometimes, with supreme effort, he could consciously decide to stay in control, but not at that moment.

'So that's all right then, is it? A bit of stress on the pitch, a bad day at the office and you get home and lash out. Is that it – is that your yardstick?'

Barney shrugged dismissively and picked up his wine glass. William wanted to knock it out of his hand, splash red wine all down that immaculate cream shirt, stain the tailored charcoal suit. He stared at him. 'I haven't had an answer, have you got no answer?'

'Cool it, Bill,' Oscar said. 'What's happened to that damn wine waiter? We need more wine, more action around this place, for God's sake!'

'We're having plenty of that,' Jack Hale said, grinning.

William couldn't be in the same room as Barney. Finding it hard to restrain himself he got up and pushed in his chair, 'I've got to go, paper to edit.' He felt the whole table staring, Victoria's wide eyes on him, but nothing could have stopped him from turning his back and walking out.

He went out of the hotel's side entrance into Davies Street. There were no staff desks there, no one to chat or accost him, just a little-used Ladies' loo beside the door. Out in the street and refreshed by the icy air, he could think more clearly. Oscar would be OK. People blew their top – it wasn't a hanging offence. But, he thought, if Barney hadn't previously had much of an idea, he would certainly have one now.

Possibly it wasn't quite as clear-cut. Someone having an affair would never have picked a fight in so uncompromising a way; they would more likely go out of their way to be easy and accommodating.

Barney had been condoning thuggery. It was appalling – and if he didn't see that much wrong with it, did it mean he was even capable of it himself?

The idea took hold and William felt an urgent need to put the question to Victoria and gauge her reaction. The cold was beginning to penetrate. He had left his coat in the hotel half-deliberately – in the fanciful hope she might come out looking for him.

He went inside the door and saw her right there in the passage, standing near the Ladies' loo, glancing round. He felt overcome.

There was no one about. They stared at each other a moment and then he went very close, and with the back of his hand touching hers, he looked her straight in the eye and said, 'Has he ever hit you?'

'Not now, we can't talk now,' she muttered, looking quickly about.

The bastard had, William thought, otherwise she would have denied it instantly. 'I have to know,' he pressed, and then he couldn't stop himself from kissing her with all his coursing passion. He broke away just as quickly, leaving them both shaking. He'd done enough damage for one night. 'You'd better get back in,' he said with effort. 'Sorry I lost it in there.'

Two women were approaching the Ladies, the wives of expense-account businessmen or clients, he thought; they looked not really in the know. Victoria made an easy-to-overhear polite remark about an excellent dinner and then went away and left him. It hadn't been possible but he would have liked some heartening sign, some re-assuring gesture of forgiveness.

*   *   *

They spoke the next day; when she was on her way to Southampton.

Through the night he had added more layers to his hatred of Barney, sealing it, making it hard and glossy like papier-mâché; he knew he should keep it more in check. A memory had nagged at him in the night, something that had registered but been lost with time.

In answer to his first question, Victoria impatiently told him she was fine. She began cheerfully telling what had happened. 'Jane French said it was work-overload and that you constantly let off steam and ranted at everyone in sight! She was good and loyal to you. And when we got home, Barney just airbrushed you out – he erased the row, no more mention. He was full of the glitz, the wines, the Montrachet and the wonderful Château Talbot, Bella's rocks the size of gull's eggs!'

'He *has* hit you, hasn't he? I want to know. I want you to tell me straight.'

'I can never talk to you sensibly about him. You simply refuse to hear or even try to understand. You just sound off and do this!'

'Do what?' She wouldn't fucking-well admit it, but it was obvious he had.

'William, can't you just cool it? And you must see it's even harder for me to leave now. Think of Jane French, Jack Hale – he's in television, he talks – people would know you're the one involved. You're in it now, don't you see? You've put yourself there.'

He did see. 'But you're not safe, that's all the more reason,' he muttered.

'Don't be silly. That's the least of your worries – have you ever seen me with two black eyes?'

'I never get to see you at all.'

He could hear Margie arriving; he had to go. There was the weekend and also no chance of Monday, he was doing television, but he pressed hard for Tuesday.

'I can't, there's a special Grand Night at the Inner Temple,' Victoria said. 'It's a big dinner, I must go. If I said I was ill, Barney might want to stay home; he's bad at going to things on his own.'

One day he was going to have to get better at it, William thought.

During his morning conference, the niggling memory struck home. While George was asking how Barnes, the Foreign Secretary, would react to the Hammond story, he suddenly remembered sitting next to Victoria at the *Post* lunch and noticing a bruise on her face. He had been studying her profile and wondered how she had got it.

After the conference he asked Margie to put him through to Oscar; an apology was needed and it couldn't be postponed.

'Sure rubbed you up, that blond bugger,' Oscar chortled, giving the impression he'd been quite entertained. 'You got some private feud going – some dirt on him or something?'

'He fucks around, and I've thought for a while that, given who he's married to, there might be a story. We've been keeping an eye.' William was mindful of the *Post* picking up GD's first pay tab. 'Never met him before,' he added casually. 'Not sure I need to again.'

Oscar chuckled and then offered his opinion that Victoria had a lot more spark and chutzpah than some, and could go far.

'I'm considering a campaign on domestic violence,' William observed. 'Any thoughts?'

The idea seemed to go down well, but he would wait till he had seen Victoria, he thought, before deciding for sure. He might have been going over the top.

Doing the rounds during the morning he passed Jane French in the passage. 'You certainly weren't taking any prisoners last night,' she said, grinning.

'I did rather overreact. God what a loser – you'd have thought Victoria James could have done better.' He tried not to overdo it or sound too on-guard. Jane was sharp.

'Must be those model looks of his,' she said infuriatingly, making William fear some telltale black shadow might have flitted across his face. Jane was best mates with Bev Leander, and if she hinted at a thing going with Victoria, Bev might click with mermaids and *Question Time*.

Did it matter if his staff had a good idea? Better they didn't – George, especially.

Over the weekend, Ursula said he seemed very listless; perhaps he was due a thorough check-up? He told her he hadn't the time. Tom was home – though he spent all weekend painting a picture of eyes, the same pair everywhere, all over the canvas. He was clearly in love; William hoped his own feelings in that department were a little less on show.

Dave always drove him to London on Mondays. He couldn't talk to Victoria from the car and he'd missed her when he got to the office. He felt in need of contact but had no chance to call before lunch with the Foreign Secretary. He sent a text but then cleared his mind to be ready to fence with Barnes.

At his usual table at the Savoy Grill it amused him to watch Barnes's surreptitious half-glances at the nearby mirrored column.

Vain or not though, the Foreign Secretary was quick on his feet, darting about the political spectrum with alacrity. William thought they were both performing well, with neat fencing steps.

Barnes waited till the coffee but then looked craftily over his cup at his host, 'Doesn't come from me, old boy, of course, but Downing Street's a touch twitchy about the Washington scenario. Hammond can be a bit of a liability, thinks he'll never get his feet wet . . .' It was a clean thrust. The Foreign Secretary bore grudges and clearly wanted to see an old adversary take a tumble.

'Highly thought of though, and a good buddy of the President's,' William said mischievously, causing a darkening of Barnes's expression. Then: 'But I'm afraid this story's getting up momentum, and if it breaks it's likely to have long legs.'

A thinly veiled look of satisfaction shone light into Barnes's glowering aquiline face. William felt a morsel of sympathy for the smooth Ambassador. Sir Rodney Hammond being brought down by his sex life was just too close to home.

When he finally managed to talk to Victoria, he had to get the breaking story off his chest.

'You're saying you've got the proof and are about to do a big exposure – that Hammond's wife is going to get a rough ride? Ever thought of glass houses?'

'I can't defend it, it's my job. Don't stop loving me.'

'I can love you with my eyes open as well as shut! Good luck, tonight, with the Press Barons programme.'

'I wish to God I wasn't doing it. You can't seriously be going to that tedious Inner Temple dinner tomorrow, with all those puffed-up, opinionated lawyers?'

'There are a few of those in your own profession.'

'Pomposity isn't endemic,' he muttered. She was defending Barney again. William didn't want to be in a television studio; he was starved of her, hungering, and wanted to ask her, face to face, the question she'd been refusing to answer on the phone.

CHAPTER 25

Victoria stood at her office window. Dusk was falling and a flurry of snow was turning to sleet. William wanted answers, she thought, but even a more rational man wouldn't understand. It was a choice between disloyalty to Barney or lying.

Monday nights were late voting and Marty came down with her as she left for the Commons. 'I've put a note in the box on MDF board,' he said. 'You'll be pleased – the Secretary of State agrees with you.'

'How long before we can announce it?' she asked, delighted.

'Depends. The Secretary of State has to get approval from the relevant departments and it might have to go to a Cabinet committee. All being well though, a couple of weeks, I should say.'

He had an encouraging smile and she was grateful. But driving off with Bob, her confidence began draining. Guy was leaking like a wonky tap to the press and stirring up the backbenchers, getting them to air their misgivings. Then there were the arch deregulators in the Cabinet who would be determined to block a ban. And though her decision was taken and she thought it right, she wished her father did too.

She signed letters in her room until the Division Bell and then went to vote.

Crossing Central Lobby with her Pair, Joe Reynolds, he suggested a bite of supper.

'Mind if it's fairly quick?' she said. 'I do want to catch that Press Barons documentary at nine.'

'William Osborne is doing it, isn't he – your chum? You were with him the last time I wanted to have supper.'

She thought Joe wasn't placing any special emphasis, just seeing a slight coincidence. He was a good friend, too. She said, laughing, 'You'll start a rumour, saying things like that. You know what this place is like.'

'Now there's one rumour I wouldn't mind starting . . .' He gave her a playful hug.

She sensed they were being watched and saw a lobby correspondent moving away. Victoria knew her; she was an irritating Sloane type, always mixing it. Shit. She was sure to get some annoying unhelpful little item into her paper's diary column. It was one they had delivered at home and Barney would see it.

No point worrying, she thought, setting off for the Members' canteen with Joe. They had a quick meal and went their separate ways.

In the morning, Victoria snatched a glance at the paper while Barney was making the coffee. There was an inevitable diary piece, a pointless bitchy bit of innuendo.

It was hung on the canteen supper: *East meets West across the Bosphorus but at Westminster, opposites meet across a cosy table in the canteen. Housing Minister Victoria James and MP Joe Reynolds – dubbed by colleagues the Black Knight and the White Queen – were intimate over*

their egg and chips and in a world of their own. What the Whips have to
say about this chummy fraternization goes unrecorded, but sources say they
are just good friends. Quite so.

'Something about you?' Barney queried, bringing her coffee.
'You're looking cross.' He took the paper and his own face became
black as thunder. 'That's all I need! Every single lawyer will have
seen that – they'll all be sniggering into their soup at tonight's
dinner. You could have thought of that when you were cosying up
to Joe.'

'God, Barney, you can't be taking it seriously? You know journalists write that sort of drivel every day. I had supper with Joe, I
get on with him – you've met him, you quite like him.'

'I'm less keen on some of your other friends.'

It was the first mention, the first indication. William's rude humiliating attack, Barney's own terribly misjudged remarks; nothing said,
nothing else on their minds. They had stepped carefully round the
row at Oscar's dinner, evading it all weekend, treating it with a kind
of silent wary reverence as though it were a coffin in the room.

Barney was scowling, drumming his fingers on the kitchen table;
he hadn't finished. 'What are you going to do about that piece?
Can't you sue?'

'That would be the most ludicrous over-reaction! It's nothing, a
bit of fluff – no one could take it seriously. I must get to work.
See you at dinner tonight – and do put it out of your mind.'

At the office, William called and when he too started on about
Joe, she really lost her rag. 'It was a canteen snack, not a seduction
scene. We had fish pie, not egg and chips – how can you even waste
breath on it? My constituents have more savvy; they know a thin
news day. I was in good time to see the Press Barons' programme,

and if you want my opinion you were excellent, not in the least deferential – but then no one would ever call you a proprietor's poodle.'

'Sorry,' William said humbly.

'Your pet tycoon, Harold Reid, is giving me problems,' she said. 'Guy Harcourt wants to appoint him Chairman of the Audit Commission.'

'Remind me what that does?'

'It's the Local Government watchdog. Guy decided he's the most eminently respectable businessman around. I know telling me about insider dealing was in confidence, and I'll honour that, but professionally I should be acting on my inside knowledge and trying to stop Guy making a risky appointment. I feel put on the spot.'

'I didn't do what was in my professional interests with the Hartstone resignation story, remember. It'll do Guy good to get egg on his face. You need to toughen up.'

'But say you expose Reid and then Guy finds out about us,' she said thoughtfully. 'He'd suspect I'd have known it was in the pipeline. His thoughts won't be sweet.'

'Since when have Harcourt's thoughts ever smelled of roses?' William snorted.

Sue was coming in with briefing and Victoria ended the call.

'The papers aren't very encouraging this morning on MDF,' Sue said, rather obviously and irritatingly. She and Tim were good Private Secretaries but only Marty knew what *not* to say.

'We had to expect leaks and murmurs about a potential ban.'

'I wonder how it got out though?' Sue observed. Was she being disingenuous?

*   *   *

Changing for the dinner that night, Victoria thought of Guy's enthusiasm for Harold Reid. She had felt artfully in the know in the Ministers' meeting and said, when asked her opinion, that Reid seemed almost too good to be true. William was so fired up and convinced of being able to nail him, she hoped it wouldn't turn out like a greyhound race, a case of always chasing but never quite catching the hare.

Her burgundy chenille dress had a low cowl at the back and was full-length; she lifted it clear going upstairs to the first floor of the Inner Temple Hall. She soon spotted Barney's blond head in the mêlée of legal worthies having their pre-dinner drinks. Making her way to him, her dress was getting looks; she wished they were from William.

Barney glanced at her but didn't smile or say hello. He was talking to a vast bald barrister, who transmitted a look of pained apology, a plea not to be tarred with the same ill-mannered brush. Victoria saved him his embarrassment and went off crossly to look at the seating-plan. Finding herself between Barney and a judge not renowned for his warmth and compassion did nothing for her mood – the food had better be good.

Barney barely exchanged two words with her at dinner. He was forced occasionally to converse with the matron in sapphire-blue spectacles on his right, but he was downing the various wines as fast as his glass was filled. Victoria heard the rumble of voices and outbreaks of laughter, clinks and clatter; she looked down the table at the heraldic shields and historic paintings and felt sad. Barney should have been in his element, not drinking himself stupid over a nonsense bit of innuendo and allowing himself to be knocked off-course.

The Simmondses were seated diagonally across the table; Mandy's flesh-coloured fussy silk was so unbecoming it was a small comfort, but the woman spitefully brought up the Joe piece and evened the score. Barney heard her. 'Joe Reynolds, I'll have you know,' he declared in a wine-soaked, carrying voice, 'is an effing raving queen.'

The immediate table was stunned into silence, but talk soon got going again and Victoria went to the loo. Closeted in a cubicle she decided she couldn't risk a call, but she sent William a heartfelt text. *Having a stinking vile lousy loathsome time.*

Barney had left his car at Lincoln's Inn and came home in hers. He sat slumped beside her, a pale shade of green, and she wondered if he'd had a day on vodka. His stumbling exit from the car was something she had rather Bob hadn't seen.

She felt relieved to get indoors, but Barney went to lean on his hands on the narrow hall table. His head was hung low, almost hitting the wall, his hair dangling.

'Please let me help you to bed,' she tried.

'I don't need any of your fucking help – you couldn't care anyway.'

She stood back as he started up the stairs. He had got halfway up and turned round again; the sweat was pouring down his face, which was the colour of wet putty. He jabbed at her while trying to steady himself. 'You think you're above the likes of Dick and me, you with your celebrity friends.'

'That's so crazy and ridiculous! We need to get to bed and get some sleep.'

He had reached the landing. She caught up and tried to put a steadying arm round him but he flung it off, as though it was poisonous or diseased.

The back of her hand hit one of the spindles and she gave a cry of pain, but a sound came out of Barney too, a small embarrassed groan; he bent double over the banisters then and was violently sick.

The smell was pungent; she wanted to retch herself. He stood up swaying and she went to steady him, braced in case he flung her off again and pushed her away.

'You get to bed, I'll clear up – don't worry about that,' she said, trying to sound soothing, but she should have known not to draw attention. Barney so hated mess.

'And have you privately sneering like everyone else tonight?' He took hold of her arms, his fingers digging in. 'I'll clean up my own mess – just leave me alone.'

He pushed her back against the wall and a picture, an old print of Chelsea, came unhinged and slipped to the skirting. The glass splintered but it stayed in its frame. She felt wobbly.

'You couldn't care less what those people tonight were thinking.' Barney wiped some sick from his chin with the back of his hand. 'They're not part of *your* world, so who cares?' He took hold again, gripping, shaking her hard. 'Well, *I* care, do you hear? They're part of mine.'

'Barney, stop! You're hurting and we're too close to the stairs!'

That seemed to register. He stared drunkenly but dropped his hands and moved slightly away. He looked suddenly so wretched, it made her long to get him to bed. She came forwards from the wall but then something seemed to snap, it was as though he felt threatened in some way; he put out his hands and with his face contorted, all the bitterness mapped, he gave her a brusque shove, forcing her to step back.

She trod on her dress and lost her balance, her foot slipping half off the top stair.

She grabbed wildly at the handrail but her hand slithered and lost its hold. With a scream and an icy gut-wrenching feeling of pure fear she fell backwards down the stairs.

Her first sickening thought was that her back might be broken; she didn't dare move. The edges of stairs were pressing into her; her left shoulder and arm were pinned against the banisters halfway down the flight, the pain was sharp as whiplash. There was vomit by her face with bits of undigested food in it. Feeling overcome with nausea, she turned her head the other way.

No broken back, she thought with flooding relief, or she couldn't have moved her neck freely. It encouraged her to try and get to a sitting position, but somehow she had first to get herself pointing the right way. Using an elbow she started edging her bottom down a stair at a time, till she managed not to be lying downhill.

Kneeling upright and hanging onto a spindle, she looked up. Barney was sitting on the top stair with his elbows on his knees, his head buried low in his hands. 'I need help,' she said, starting to sob loudly. 'Barney, don't just sit there, for Christ's sake! Come and help – I could have broken my back.'

He looked up; he was as white as a sheet. 'You fell – I had nothing to do with it. I couldn't have stopped you. It was your dress, it was an accident.' He was terrified of what she might say or do, she thought. He knew how bad it could have been.

'Forget how it happened, who cares? I just don't want my legs giving way if I try and stand. Can't you bloody come and help? I want to go to bed, Barney, I'm hurting.' She broke into more hysterical sobs.

He got her upstairs, gently, mindful of her pain; he helped her undress, helped her ease into bed. 'I'll bring you some tea now,' he said, smoothing her forehead, 'and you should have a shot of brandy. I'll clear up as best I can downstairs; it's my mess. I think it was some shellfish at lunch, but I'm better now.'

She felt as though a lid had been lifted, steam let out, all the pressure released. The pain was bad, she was shivering and couldn't stop crying; she thought it was just the shock. An awful thought began taking hold: she would be covered in bruises and William would see them. She tried not to think at all. Sleep would help but there seemed little chance of that.

Barney brought her the tea and brandy and suggested a sleeping pill. She didn't know he had any and felt slightly alarmed; she'd been brought up to mistrust them. 'Perhaps I should take one,' she said dubiously, longing for some peace.

As she heard him busy downstairs her eyelids began to close; there was a powerful smell of disinfectant. Good thing it was a season for well-covering clothes, she thought drowsily. Her face should be unmarked, but William's reaction didn't bear thinking about.

The sleeping pill's chemical balm was working; very soon oblivion came.

Waking up in the morning, she was aching all over and feeling darting pain at the slightest movement and she couldn't shake off the effects of the pill. Barney came in with more tea and said he would call the office; she told him to leave that to her. He looked terrible. He had a kind of hollow, emptied look – gaunt-cheeked. He was shaved, dressed but he could hardly have slept at all.

'Feeling rotten?' she asked, her eyes closing again. 'Will you be OK at work?'

'I'm fine, but I'm not going in. You must stay in bed today and you'll need help. What are you going to tell the office?'

She heard the quaver in his voice and opened her eyes. It was no bad thing if he was worried. 'That I fell, I suppose,' she said vaguely. 'But I don't want help, I just want to be alone. It was a bad scene, Barney. I'll get over it – but in my own time. You go, now. Perhaps tell Bob, can you, as you leave, to go back to the Department,' she was drifting again, 'and wait for a call?'

The telephone woke her. It was Marty. Seeing with a shock that it was well past nine, she told him what had happened and blamed a loose stair-tread. He urged her not to come in but she said she probably would at some stage.

She lay back on the pillow, aching in every limb and worrying about the missed meeting on brownfield targets. Marty said Di had rung on the private line, but that he had just missed other calls. His polite way of saying the phone had been put down, she thought.

William must have been wondering what was wrong; she wanted to call him but her mobile was in her bag down in the hall, and if she used the home phone, the number would show on the bill.

It had been terrible, ghastly, but the bruises were somehow protection, always the way of regaining the moral ground. Barney was clearly terrified that she might tell it as it was. She had never done that before – so was he worrying about someone else seeing her body?

Di called and insisted on coming round. Victoria wanted to be up and dressed and slowly got her legs out of bed; they felt heavy as logs but they supported her. The mug of cold tea was still beside the digital clock. It looked unappealing but she took a few sips and could feel the energy kick; Barney had sweetened it. With intakes of breath and grimaces of pain, she got to the bathroom and had a deep hot bath with health salts.

She made an inventory of her bruises. The worst caused the least discomfort. Her shoulder was so bruised it looked like film make-up, but although it was tender, it didn't hurt much; nor did the hand that had caught the spindle, though it looked bad. Her back was agony though; getting around was going to be a slow, embarrassing business.

By the time the doorbell rang she was in a baggy grey sweater and loose trousers. The sight of Di in a mulberry angora sweater-dress was no help to a flagging morale. The tears weren't far away.

'My God, whatever's happened? You look ghostly, chalk-white.' Di jumped forward to give a hand.

'Thanks. I fell down a few stairs last night, that's all.'

Di was wonderful. Busying around, getting her propped up and comfortable on the old kitchen sofa, making tea – just being there. She didn't ask unnecessary questions or interrupt, but listened carefully as Victoria, who had started off feeling quite tight-lipped and resentful, was soon letting it all out.

Finally though, she said caustically, 'So it was what you might call an accidental push?'

'Don't assume the worst, Di. Barney was really sick as well as drunk. He wasn't seeing straight; nothing he did was deliberate. I haven't yet contacted William. I'm supposed to be seeing him tonight, but I don't think I can.'

'No,' Di said, considering. 'It wouldn't be good. You must rest

– you'll be better able to cope tomorrow. One thing, though: I'm sure by now William knows how hard you find it to lie. For that reason, if for none other, my advice to you is to put in a bit more work on perfecting your story. It's not one he's going to believe.'

CHAPTER 26

William felt surprised when Di called him at the office, but he quickly connected it with Victoria's fall. She had used the direct line and, with Margie beside him going through the mail, he had hammed things up a bit, answering, 'Hi, Di. Wild party last week – I liked your sculptress chum with the green thigh-boots.' Margie had made herself scarce.

Di wanted him to go for a drink that night. She suggested ten. It was a good time, after the first edition but still three hours away, and he was impatient to know what it was all about. Victoria had insisted she was fine, that she had just slipped on the stairs, but she would never take a morning off lightly. She had gone in later though, so why wasn't she coming to the flat?

He started wondering about the circumstances of the fall. Her text from the dinner had seemed joking but it could have been implying a row. Hard to imagine that Barney had pushed her down the stairs though, that was going a bit far.

It was his reading hour and the time he usually called Ursula. He glanced at her picture on his desk and it sparked off a stray thought about her poetry. She had a real gift. Her early poems had been powerful, bleak and black, all about her father dying. That had happened not long before they'd met. He had been on the Barnsley *Echo* and she still a student at Leeds.

All that chasing up the motorways to the university, William thought, in an old Ford hung together with string. He had soon moved on – got his break and gone off to London. They had only met again quite by chance, buying a morning paper – one of life's strange twists and turns. Would Ursula make a new life if he left? He thought guiltily that if he mucked up her present one, she might at least be inspired to write more poetry. He picked up the phone and made his duty call.

Di lived close to the Chelsea Embankment in a tiny Regency terrace off a cul-de-sac; quite a test for the taxi-driver. He had decided not to go with Dave.

She poured him a whisky, single malt, and waved at a sofa with an ethnic throw. He was just sitting down when a bald glistening head appeared round the door. 'Hi, I'm Gerald. You're being looked after? Good. I'm off to bed.' Di must want a private talk, William thought; her husband seemed well-primed.

'I'm not really sure about getting you here,' she said, bringing over the whiskies, 'and Victoria doesn't know, incidentally, so don't let on.'

'She's OK though?' He took the glass Di handed him, staring keenly at her.

'Sort of,' she said, coming to sit beside him. 'Well, no – it was a backwards fall downstairs, awful, ghastly. An accident, she says, but she's panicked you'll think Barney pushed her.'

'You're not implying he did, I hope?' William felt shocked in spite of himself.

'Who knows? No, forget that, I'm sure he didn't. I'm just showing my prejudices.'

'Ones I share,' he said. Her words and their significance were hitting home. Victoria had obviously been underplaying it; she could have been paralysed. He felt the chill of sudden panic.

'Look, this is difficult,' Di said. 'I'm trying to ride two horses, staying loyal to my good friend and taking risks with you – but I don't know how sensible you'll be.'

'Not very. Am I right to think Barney has knocked her about?'

'Still does. She's got a blind spot where he's concerned; she makes allowances, invents excuses. People do.'

William wasn't having that. 'People?' he said sardonically. 'Professionals like Victoria? Where's this going, Di?'

'I just wanted to get across that you should go gently. Victoria's in shock and she's a mess of bruises. She'll tell you the truth, almost. My advice is to leave it there.'

'But? There was a but, before. You've dropped off the but, the other horse.'

'Sharp arse! It's just this. If you choose to do anything about Barney – as I think you want to – she mustn't suspect you've had a hand. She loves you to death, but she'll resent it and want to protect him. She thinks he's vulnerable, insecure. I'd call it unstable, myself.'

He looked her straight in the eye. 'And what do you think I want to do, Di?'

'Get Barney out of her life, however things map out with yours. Won't be easy.'

'Thanks for the whisky,' he said. 'Sharp arse!'

* * *

That night, William slept poorly and had a bad dream. His hands had been on Barney's throat, but as hard as he squeezed and pressed, Barney just kept on grinning and leering and affectedly chucking back his hair. He had tried kicking the grinning face into submission but his foot would never quite reach; he had woken up finding himself kicking out at the duvet.

A difficult day lay ahead. He wanted to sack Jack, his Assistant Editor. During the morning, he sent for the Managing Editor to look at the contract. Two-year rolling, Jack on a hundred thou; it was going to cost. The Managing Director or Chairman could give problems, William thought, trying to remember if Jack was in with either of them. It might be worth some advance groundwork, buying them a few drinks and letting slip reminders of stories Jack had goofed on – nice guy that he was.

It was a brutal business, sacking: a cleared desk and you were out that very day, escorted to your car by the security guard. But he had a paper to run, William thought defensively; there were more jobs than Jack's at stake if the *Post* started going downhill.

At seven he left the building and took a taxi home. At the flat he changed into jeans and an old navy sweater. He chose music to suit his mood – Bob Marley followed by Brahms – then sat drinking whisky while he waited, thinking over his talk with Di.

She had said Victoria would tell him almost the truth; did that mean saying tripped instead of shoved? He passionately needed to see her, but was he being selfish, asking her over? He knew there couldn't be much chance of sex. Shouldn't she have seen a doctor? Perhaps she had. He felt on the fringe, left out of her life.

She rang. 'I'm just leaving. I got held up – a call from the Party

Chairman. Interesting one. It's to do with the Italian elections, a rally in Milan.'

He was in no mood for political rambles. 'For God's sake, I just want you to get here.'

I was actually hoping,' she sounded rueful, 'you might manage a trip *there*, to Italy?'

How had he been so slow? 'Oh,' he said. 'Well, I just might. That's all the more reason for you being here now. But are you really all right to come?'

'Just a bit stiff. Marty's been such an old mother hen, as you wouldn't believe.'

He hadn't been prepared for her pallor. She was so washed-out and pale, her skin looked translucent and, sinking down thankfully on the sofa, she looked whiter still. He poured a splash of whisky in a glass, held it out and as she took it he saw that one of her hands was shockingly bruised. It had a thick livid mark on it, as though hit by a poker. 'Did you fall on that hand?' he asked, rigid with hatred.

'No, it hit the banisters. It really doesn't hurt though.'

They were silent a moment but she was giving the almost-empty whisky bottle looks and he felt he was being lumped with Barney. 'For God's sake!' he said. 'I'm not drunk, and even if I were paralytic, I wouldn't hit you and knock you around. Is that what you want though – some rough stuff?' She lowered her eyes.

He felt bad and apologized, but didn't stop. 'That's what Barney does when he's had a few, is it? Please look at me. I want you to explain how you can go on living with him – *how*? There's no

more contemptible behaviour, in my view – no one could begin
to understand. You've no idea how angry and hurt I feel. It's
pretty fundamental this; if you love someone, wouldn't you want
to share something like that? You lied about the row at Christmas.
I can remember a bruise then. And I'm sure you've told Di – you
trust her more than me?'

Victoria's wonderful eyes were filling and all his anger drained.

'You make it so hard,' she said. 'Di *does* know, but only because
she asked outright once. My father did too, at Christmas, and then
put on such a cold front all the time we were there. Barney wasn't
hitting me when I fell, he didn't encourage it. I tripped.'

'Backwards downstairs?' William shot out; she still wasn't being
straight with him.

'I stepped back. Don't fight, can't you let it be? I am leaving him
in the summer.'

He thought of Di's advice. Victoria was looking so defensive; he
tried to be less combative but he had to ask. 'Tell me what happened,
I do need to know.'

'He'd just been sick, he felt awful about it, the mess and everything, and he shrugged me off when I tried to help. But I did trip
backwards, that's the truth. It was an accident.'

'A sort of accident – almost the truth?'

She hung her head and he felt he'd won a great battle. He wanted
to hold her so badly. He touched her face, her neck; he had a hand
inside her jacket, kissing her. 'If I'm very gentle can I take this off?'
he whispered. 'I want to see your bruises and make a fuss of you,
cook you supper – hear all about Milan.'

'You can't cook, I thought?'

'True,' he said, easing down the sleeves of her tweedy jacket, 'but you could sit in a chair and direct.' He loved the silk shirt she had on underneath. 'I've been missing you so desperately,' he said, undoing the buttons. 'It's been the purest hell.' He broke off as he saw the bruises; they were appalling. 'You must see a doctor,' he said, horrified. Her shoulder looked bad enough to have been kicked and beaten, but it was the small bruises on her arms that held his eye. 'Those aren't from a fall,' he challenged. 'Barney was shaking you, wasn't he?'

'A bit,' she said mildly. 'He was upset about the Joe piece. He thinks the whole world looks down on him, me included, and of course he feels dreadfully threatened by you.'

His loathing was spurting like blood and as hard to stem. 'I can't let you go back,' he pressed, using all his persuasive powers. 'You're not safe. I'll book a hotel room, find you a flat. I'll fix protection. You just say you're separating, it'll be fine.'

He was taken aback when her eyes flashed furiously. 'I'm doing no such thing,' she said in a steely voice. 'I'm fine, quite safe. Barney feels desperate about what happened. It was an accident but in iffy circumstances, and now I have the upper hand. I couldn't leave now, in this condition. It would cause gossip, press speculation, questions about timing. You'd be brought into it, too; it wouldn't be good for Ursula.'

William felt tense as fuse wire; he got up and went to switch off the music. She came to his side and leaned her head into him. It was hard not to respond and he turned and kissed her sweet-smelling hair. 'Will you take me to bed,' she said without looking up, 'and let me take care of things? But I'm not sure you want it, in this mood.'

He wanted it. They went to bed and she did the looking-after;

he had to let her. He was holding her head, his fingers in her hair: loving her, needing the physical release but knowing his frustrations would remain. There was an endgame and he wasn't there.

When she was lying beside him he stroked her arm, feeling overwhelmingly protective. He thought of a life of fighting his own battles, never wanting or needing to offload. Now he needed Victoria, her approval; she felt part of him as no one had before.

Freshly determined, he took hold of her hand and kissed it. 'I want to do something that'll make you hysterical with rage,' he said, 'but don't explode till you've heard me out. I want a picture of your shoulder. I've only got an old Polaroid camera here, so there's no negative – just a single picture that's never going to leave this flat. It'll be in my safe and no one, not even Ursula, has the code. I need to feel there's some rainy-day insurance, something in the locker if anything else happened and you needed proof. I need you to trust me and to understand. It'll help me handle my fury.'

She had sat up looking as though he'd just been giving a reasoned rationale for castrating Barney. 'Try and see the sense,' he said, sitting up beside her. 'Call it humouring me, if you like.' She was speechless; he fetched his camera without waiting for her words to come, praying his old Polaroid had some film.

He came back to find her stubbornly turned away. She half-looked round, saying, 'I don't want this,' but he took the shot. She was in profile. Her appallingly bruised shoulder was clearly visible and one breast was in delicious outline, too.

'If that ever sees the light of day,' she said, sounding close to tears, 'I could never speak to you again. You would have destroyed my faith in everything I hold dear.'

'It's three-quarters back view,' he assured her not quite truthfully, rubbing the Polaroid's reverse side. 'Just head and shoulders.' He peeled off the picture, glanced at it and squatted by the safe in his bedroom cupboard. He slipped it inside and slammed the door. 'Safely locked away,' he grinned. 'And now it's time for food and Milan!'

He carried a chair into the kitchen and made her sit there. 'That'll feed at least five,' she observed as he tipped a packet of pasta twirls into a pan of boiling water.

She was still sounding cool and he said, kneeling beside her, 'Tell me about Milan; tell me you love me.'

She smiled and he felt lifted. 'With the Italian elections coming up, the Chairman wants me to speak at Giulio Tourellini's convention. They think he's in with a real chance – they're off Europhile lefties, tycoons all the flavour again. It's from Thursday to Sunday, last of the month. I'd go as the Government's representative. I dutifully asked if it wasn't one for the Foreign Office, Magnus Fern or someone, and the Chairman gave me such a blatant positive-discrimination answer!'

'What?' William squatted at her feet.

'He said Magnus hadn't got the legs for it and that I'd charm the pants off Tourellini. But I'd rather be doing that for you . . .'

'On the last Thursday in March,' William said, getting up and hunting out a jar of sauce, 'Liverpool are playing AC Milan in the quarter finals of the Champions League – in Milan! I'll chat up the Sports Editor, get him to suggest I come along. He knows I'm a fan.'

'I can see where your priorities lie.'

'I'd have to come back overnight on Friday to do *The Firing Line*, but I could come out again for Saturday night. What about Barney though?'

'I think I can deflect him, at least for the Thursday, if not the weekend. What would you tell Ursula if you do get out again?'

'I'd say I was chasing a very hot story, which would be true.'

William tried to persuade her to stay the night with Di, but didn't push it. As soon as she'd left and he'd heard the main door close he called GD and arranged to meet him at a snooker club in an hour. It was ten, time enough to go back to the office first. He took the Polaroid from the safe, put it in a small envelope into an inside pocket of his jacket and hurried out of the flat.

Just before eleven, he called down to Dave. 'I need to go to a club off Old Street — shouldn't take long.'

The club was on the ground floor of a warehouse; it had about fifteen or twenty snooker tables and fruit machines lining the walls. GD was up at the bar nursing a beer and chaser.

William bought GD another, a whisky for himself, and as GD unwrapped himself from his barstool, he picked up their drinks and followed him to a Formica table. GD was a small man with receding, lank fair hair and a few moles. Nondescript to his finger-nails, which were very clean.

William handed over his precious envelope. 'I want two copies and the neg, and I absolutely must have the original back. Got that? Your life depends on it.'

GD tucked it away inside his stone-coloured anorak with a minimal nod. They downed their drinks and parted company outside. GD scurried off into the night. Waiting at a traffic-light, William briefly saw him from the car window going towards the Tube and melding into his murky backdrop. It was taking a hell of a risk.

*   *   *

The weekend was a terrible strain. On Sunday William drove himself to London to put in an afternoon at the office; he was in cords and a casual jacket, his usual Sunday gear.

The lawyers had finally passed the Hammond story and it was planned for Tuesday, but there was Monday's paper to deal with and he had arranged to meet GD at the flat at six. GD was on time. The handover of the Polaroid and copies was effected smoothly.

Back home, he tested Emma and Jessie on their spelling but his attention was wandering and the girls got quite cross. He thought Ursula couldn't fail to notice too, though she seemed quite distracted herself. She had never commented on the gradual drying-up of their sex life, no hints dropped or seductive ploys, but she wouldn't anyway, she was so self-contained.

Dave picked him up bright and early the next morning, and on the way in, William planned how to spin his domestic-violence campaign. He would discuss it in conference, he thought, and get along his best women writers, Jane and Bev.

He rehearsed what to say. 'Fifty-two per cent of our readers are women, and domestic violence affects people across the board. Scratching the surface won't do. I want you all to dig deep – this has to shock. Find professional women prepared to talk, get onto MPs, JPs – the police, doctors. Call up the charities. First copy in four days. Pictures are key and the news desk should hit it, too.' Perhaps not 'hit', William thought; hardly the ideal word.

Jane, who must have gossiped about it, would bring up the footballer's-violence case to point up a link with Oscar's dinner. It was worth preempting her, saying that the campaign followed on nicely from her interview with the footballer's battered girlfriend.

He would tell Victoria the same, he thought, and that he had set it in motion right after Oscar's dinner. She would think he was rubbing Barney's nose in it, but she might be encouraged to imagine it was William's final settling of scores.

Hammond and domestic violence was all good for sales, but not for Victoria. Jim was even planning an ambush on MDF. Should he warn her in advance, William wondered. There was not a lot to be gained.

He longed to be in her arms. There were over two weeks till Milan. He felt it would never come; there would always be more hilltops over the brow and never the magical view. The waiting was hell.

CHAPTER 27

Victoria had changed her mind hourly about the photograph. William had a naked, identifiable picture of her in his safe and she didn't like it. But after days of vacillating, the decision suddenly seemed clear. There were no circumstances in which she could let the picture be used; she could never do that to Barney. It had to be torn up and at the first possible moment. She could only go to the flat the very next night; the evenings after that were terribly busy, right up to Milan – always assuming that worked out. Her bruises were still very bad too, but that was a different problem. The Polaroid had to go.

There was also the planned domestic-violence campaign that would spell things out so uncompromisingly; especially now that Barney would be sure William had seen her bruises. He had brought it on himself but it seemed unnecessarily harsh.

It was early morning in the office and when William phoned she told him her concern about the Polaroid. He wanted to talk about fitting an alarm through to a police station. 'I've arranged it all. You can just tell Barney it's standard – necessary security for Ministers.'

'But I'm not a security risk,' she laughed, flattered at the lengths he was going to.

'I might make you become one,' he said.

She talked about MDF. 'It's had to go to a Cabinet committee. Ned's going to have a fight on his hands to get it through – but you don't know that!'

'I do know. Jim hears everything from Guy Harcourt – even the breakdown of pros and antis in the committee. There's a waverer, so if Ned can swing her, you may be OK.'

News of a waverer was encouraging and she had news of her own. 'Harold Reid becomes the new Chairman of the Audit Commission today,' she said. 'Guy thinks he's a pillar of rectitude.'

'According to my mole, Reid's company has obsolete stock on the books, inflating the price on the market, *and* they're falsifying invoices to boost sales,' William said with satisfaction.

'Why does Reid do it? Why take the risk?'

'It's obscene when he's so filthy rich, but I guess it just becomes a nasty habit – one he's had for years.'

She felt full of zest after his call. It did look bad about Reid; Guy might seriously regret his choice of Chairman. But she felt less zippy, thinking it was clear Guy was winning over Jim on MDF. The *Post*, she suspected, was going to be against the ban.

Just then, Tim, who had responsibility for Downsland, came in. Always overdoing it a bit with him, Victoria asked brightly, 'Isn't the Inspector's report about due?' The public enquiry had been wrapped up in early January and it was already late March.

'You can reckon an Inspector takes as many days to write the report as the enquiry took,' Tim said, telling her what she knew perfectly well. He wrote her off as ornamental, she thought, and never credited her with any ability. 'We expect it end of the month or early April,' he added.

'How long will the officials need, checking it over?'

'Oh, about three to four months, I'd say.' He gave a complacent smile.

That really got to her and she completely lost her cool. 'That simply won't do. If the Inspector can write the whole report in under three, then the officials can check it in two. I want it with me in two months' maximum, a decision announced by July.'

Tim looked quite cowed. He mumbled something about seeing what could be done and scuttled away.

They try it on, she thought, still shaking, finding it hard to calm down.

She was feeling bereft, frustrated at the lack of chances to see William before Milan. There was a spring media party at Downing Street but that would involve more caution than contact. She thought of the inscription on William's silver mermaid, that caution in love was fatal, and had an urge to take the statue out of the drawer.

Neither the box nor the mermaid was there. She looked in every drawer. She bit on her lip; she wanted to cry.

When Marty came in, she had to summon up some composure. 'I had a box in that drawer that seems to have vanished. Any ideas where it could have gone, Marty?'

'I, um, think Barney took it, the evening of the Christmas party. I popped back here and he was looking for something. He said you'd asked him to collect a few things.'

'Oh yes – how very stupid of me. So sorry! Are we starting the meeting now?'

'Not quite yet,' he said gently, and then with his long strides he
was out of the door.

The mermaid was probably at the bottom of the Thames. How
could she ever tell William? Perhaps Barney hadn't been able to
bring himself to hurl it away; he loved pretty things. There might
be some hope. No, there was none. It was hopeless.

Still another ten days till Milan, Victoria thought, going into the
Department on Monday morning. She was anticipating the papers.
After all the revelling in the scandal, all the lurid dissecting, the
Hammond affair was finally on the wane.

The Sundays had tracked down past loves of the Ambassador and
a leggy lovely with a triple-barrelled name had told all. But against
the odds and to the Foreign Secretary's certain chagrin, Hammond
was showing no sign of resigning. He was damaged goods though,
Victoria thought, his future tarnished and dulled.

The newspapers and cuttings were on her desk, neatly arranged
as usual. The *Post* was trailing the domestic-violence campaign that
began the next day, but what was filling the papers were all the
depressing reports of a backbench rebellion over MDF board.

Ned had persuaded the Cabinet committee and she had made a
written statement to the House announcing the ban. But things had
been falling apart ever since; the rumblings of disapproval from
backbenchers were becoming a full-throated roar and the political
journalists were prowling like ravenous jackals.

It couldn't be allowed to go on. After the Ministers' meeting,
Victoria approached Ned and asked for a quick word. The moment
his Private Secretary had left the room, she said urgently, 'I can't

let all this discontent fester, Ned. I want to talk to the Parliamentary Party and try to win them round. What do you think?'

'High-risk strategy,' he said, eying her dubiously. 'Might be quite bad for you.'

No caution, she thought. Back in her office, she called the Parliamentary Party Chairman. He said she could speak at their Wednesday-evening meeting. The Number Ten media party was the same night. If she'd been given a really hostile reception and it turned out a disaster, she might not want to go.

William said he admired her guts. It was small consolation; in his leader column that morning he had called a ban on MDF board 'as loopy as a crocheted doily'.

Wednesday came. Walking along the Committee-Room corridor and into a large wood-panelled room packed with pugnacious colleagues, Victoria thought it wasn't only a liaison that could set back her career. Doing badly now could have serious consequences.

The MPs were mainly seated; a few were standing at the back. Some gave friendly glances, many more didn't. She sat facing them with no papers to rest on the low pew-like wooden surface in front of her. The Chairman confirmed she would take questions, but the key measure of success with the Parliamentary Party, the crucial mark of a triumph, was to be asked no questions at all.

She rose to her feet and skipped the pleasantries. 'I know many of you have deep concerns about this ban, that you feel it's a regulation too far, but I do believe there are some cases where we have an absolute duty to protect the public – whether from terrorists, criminals, untested drugs or contaminated food – and the risk in fibre board. The bonding agent is hazardous and cutting the board creates very fine dust, dangerously easy to inhale, and few DIY enthusiasts wear masks and goggles. The dust can cause dermatitis, asthma; it causes nasal cancer in rats and the carcinogenic risks are known. There are acceptable alternatives, we cannot take risks with people's health.'

She carried on, offering more facts and some historical parallels, and ended saying, 'It's our most fundamental duty to protect people from avoidable harm. Why else are we all here?'

The agonizing suspense was shortlived. The banging on desks said it all. There were no questions and the Chairman declared the meeting closed.

Downing Street parties were held in an L-shaped pair of adjoining rooms on the first floor; people were encouraged to start in the smaller one and go through to the larger. It was a poorly-adhered-to circular flow; party-goers weren't a very orderly gang.

Victoria was in good time and stayed downstairs chatting to the sweet white-haired woman on duty in the entrance hall; she more usually watched over the Cabinet Room and looked after the Prime Minister's visitors. A long passage with a beige-patterned carpet edged in red led ahead to the Cabinet Room; off to the right was the Cabinet waiting room. Victoria vividly remembered being shown there that October afternoon when she became a Minister.

People were arriving and making their way upstairs. It was time to go and circulate.

Victoria smiled at the elderly woman. 'Could I ask a favour? I was hoping to have a quiet word with Mr Osborne, who's coming tonight. There's a matter I need to discuss. Would it be possible, do you think, to use the Cabinet waiting room?'

'I see no problem. It isn't needed, you shouldn't be disturbed.'

'Perhaps I could leave my briefcase there?' Victoria said, thinking it wise to remind herself exactly where it was. She left the brief-case. The room had a couple of low tables and chairs, not very romantic; the difficulty would be going in and out.

Upstairs, she basked in compliments from colleagues. She was teased and quizzed by the media, her unexpected triumph causing a stir. A bid had come in for her to do *Newsnight* and journalists wanted quotes. Her eye was on the door though. When William was framed in it her insides did a complete turn. He was never self-aware; his dark hair was cursorily combed, his navy suit the worse for a long day, the light-blue shirt tired-looking, but at that moment her need of him was more than she could contain.

'Well done, Victoria!' She turned round resentfully. The *Question Time* Chairman was grinning. She knew he loved mixing it and braced herself, but then Chris Hartstone came up too. 'You've sorted out your colleagues on MDF,' *Question Time*'s Chairman eyed her wickedly, 'but now how about Downsland? Which way are you leaning there?'

'She's certainly not going to tell you that, or even me,' William said, coming to join them.

'Hi, William, I needed some help with all this harassment,' she said, relieved.

Chris Hartstone had stiffened; he resented William and was obvi-ously feeling left out. He turned and went away.

Question Time's Chairman stuck around. 'Did you buy any of those mermaid frocks, Victoria, after William had been so keen on seeing you in one?'

She retaliated but saw William's eyes travel to his Fashion Editor, Beverly Leander, who was within hearing distance and grinning as widely as if she'd just found a diamond in her canapé. Mermaid

Fashion had been her Editor's idea, Victoria thought, and Bev was no fool.

After more geeing-up, the Chairman moved on but then the Prime Minister joined them. 'Powerful domestic-violence campaign, William. We've strengthened the law but the problem is getting women to report it. Your campaign could really help.'

He didn't linger and finally they had the chance of a word alone. William praised her triumph and then said, a lot less audibly, that she was irresistible and he was being driven to distraction. She whispered instructions for him to go downstairs and ask the lady by the door to show him to the Cabinet waiting room. He told her she was showing an impressive lack of caution.

She went to the loo to rearrange her underwear. Some instinct had made her put on a dress that morning, chestnut brown, mid-calf length. Trousers would have been more of a problem.

When she had quietly closed the waiting-room door and William had lifted her arms round his neck, she whispered, 'Downing Street this week, Milan the next – am I doing OK?'

He moved her behind the door, loving her passionately, feverishly. She clung to him feeling exultant. Hitching her up against the wall and discovering she was knickerless, he managed, 'This how you dress for the office?'

'Not every day – and no Sharon Stone moment at tonight's meeting either.'

Afterwards, he told her he couldn't live without her, that something had to give. She was trying to get him to keep quiet, to tidy herself, now in a slight panic about the dangers of leaving the room. They could talk in Milan, she thought.

Approaching the sweet helpful woman, Victoria thanked her and then turning to William, remarked, 'Glad we made some progress, you were very incisive, as always.'

Beverly Leander was by the coats, which was slightly alarming. Victoria hung back chatting to the elderly lady, glad of her brief-case, and William went ahead. Hurrying past, she saw he had stopped to help Bev into a silvery bomber jacket and she heard him being asked if he'd had a good time. She hoped that two people arriving at the coats from an unusual direction couldn't quite be held as proof positive of a flaming affair.

Leaving Downing Street, she thought of all the secrets the building must have absorbed through the centuries, the emotions felt, the passions and dramas that had unfolded within those historic walls. She thought, too, of the *Post*'s pious outrage, had two people in the public eye been caught *in flagrante* in Number Ten. She and William had risked careers and reputations, but lived up to the inscription on William's silver mermaid.

Victoria had a lump in her throat, thinking of the little statue that was lost for evermore.

CHAPTER 28

Barney sat watching his wife on *Newsnight*, bitterly resenting her triumph with the backbenchers over MDF. She was countering tough bantering questions with glowing ease. He himself saw little prospect of new business and felt outshone, like a poor relation, a slight embarrassment – better kept out of sight and out of the way.

Images from the *Post*'s latest domestic-violence pictures swam before his eyes. A second day of that ludicrous campaign; the feeling of betrayal was with him constantly. Victoria wouldn't have talked up the fall but a newspaperman seeing those bruises could make real trouble. She would never let him, she couldn't possibly; it wasn't her way. He just wished he felt more certain.

It had been glaringly obvious it was Osborne, if only he could have seen it. Even the dyke Press Officer at the Department, that Angie woman, had been dropping clues at the Christmas party. 'Keep up your guard with the press, Mr James. There are editors after her, your wife's in such demand!'

Barney pinged off the television and went straight to bed. He heard Victoria coming back and didn't call hello. She'd stay down working, he thought resentfully.

Going to the office the next morning, he was dreading a third day of the violence in the home campaign; he avoided the corner shop and bought the *Post* in Sloane Square. He got to Lincoln's Inn, parked and looked at it in the car. Then he slowly mangled it, a few pages at a time, squeezing viciously until he had a mess of scrunched-up paper balls. He stuffed them in his briefcase and went out to look for a bin. One missed and the wind took it to a gutter. Barney went to where it lay and ground it in violently with his polished heel until the last of it, bar a few torn slivers, was through the grill to the sewers below. Where Osborne belonged, he thought.

He gave a quick self-conscious look round then went back in through the gate and hurried to his office. His hands were black.

'Morning Karen, light of my life,' he called to the receptionist. She was reading the *Post* and barely lifted her peroxide head.

'You're very cheerful this morning.'

'Try me on a good day,' he threw back and went off to wash his hands, raging.

Coming out of the washroom, he couldn't avoid a morning exchange with Hugh.

'Remember that nice client with the decorative boxes business, Barney?' his boss said. 'You'd never believe he was a wife-beater. It's all over this morning's *Post*. Mandy pointed it out. His wife finally cracked and left him, apparently, and she's given an interview.'

'And how much do you think she's being paid?' Barney demanded impatiently. He muttered about needing to get on and made for the sanctuary of his office.

On his Friday-night drive to the cottage, he was knotted up with rancour at the thought of Victoria watching *The Firing Line*; domestic violence was the subject for discussion – what else? He put his foot down, determined to deny her that pleasure.

He couldn't make it before the start and as he walked in the door, she was coming out of the sitting room. 'Supper's ready,' she said. 'Bad drive? How was your day?'

'A laugh a minute, actually.' He glared and pushed past into the sitting room, not bringing himself to give her a kiss. He went up to the television and felt it. Still warm.

Victoria came to the door with a bottle. 'This all right – shall I open it?'

His hand was still on the set. 'Why don't you watch your programme?'

'I've seen quite enough television. I thought we'd eat, if you're ready?'

Over the meal he was more in control. Her chicken and tarragon dish wasn't bad and he said so.

Victoria was looking at him. 'You haven't forgotten,' she said, 'that I'm going to Milan on Thursday? I'm quite nervy; they want me to say my piece in Italian! They think Tourellini has a good chance of winning. Italy is back on tycoons again after its little flirt with socialism.'

Barney thought Osborne could well go chasing out after her, to Milan; images came to him of them soppy-eyed in candlelit trattorias, having hand-holding strolls.

'I was thinking of coming out for the weekend,' he said with a yawn. 'Be a nice break.' He eyed Victoria keenly for any reaction.

She smiled easily. 'Do you good. We wouldn't have much time together though. The convention's in a stadium on the outskirts of Milan. I'll be stuck out there all day, but it's such a brilliant city. You can get out on the roof of the Duomo and there's the most stunning view. The Poldi-Pezzoli has Botticellis and Tiepolos, and there's a really exquisite Bernini bronze, if I remember rightly.'

The thought of sightseeing alone didn't fill him with joy. Osborne might not go. He had his filthy paper to edit and *The Firing Line* was live, he'd be stuck over that. They'd be pushed to get much of a weekend.

Barney began thinking of the German girl he'd met at a Chalfern drinks party; she was expecting a call.

He stared at Victoria. 'I suppose if you're going to be out at a sports stadium all day, I should maybe go down and see Dad.'

She got up and opened the dishwasher. 'We'd have the evenings,' she said, turning back from it. 'There's only one duty dinner on the Saturday, and of course you could always come out to the stadium? The speeches will be mostly in Italian, but there'll be headphones with translations, I'm sure.'

'No, it's time I went to Cornwall. I'll come and meet your plane on Sunday. I could be passing Heathrow anyway if I decide to drive.'

Victoria seemed neither to be hiding feelings of relief nor looking in the slightest disappointed. She obviously couldn't care less, he thought, feeling eaten-up with bitterness.

She cared about her work though, and was instinctively cautious. If Osborne was pushing to come to Milan, mightn't she try to dissuade him? Barney felt torn. It would be forced and strained if he went, so humiliating. He had his pride. And if ever he was justified in being off the lead a bit . . . Osborne would tire in time, he just had to stick it out, and grin through gritted teeth and bear it.

CHAPTER 29

Victoria squared her papers, her impatience impossible to contain. Ned had wanted help with a big housing speech but he knew she had a plane to catch. It was too bad of him.

Bob had more sense of urgency. He revved up like a Ferrari driver, but they still only just made it.

She began to relax in the check-in queue but then went cold inside. Her briefcase – it had been behind the seat, she hadn't got it with her. Bob was already halfway back to London. He could take it to the office, she thought, calming down, and Marty could fax her speech to the hotel. That arranged, she felt better. Then her heart started racing again; she usually took her contraceptive pill at the office and had stuffed the packet in her briefcase in the rush. She hadn't even taken it yet that day.

'No window seats left now,' the BA ticket girl said in a slightly accusing tone.

'What? Oh, any seat, anything's fine.' Need she tell William? The odds on getting pregnant were so remote – especially wanting it so desperately.

*   *   *

In Milan, a girl with glossy black hair and wearing a Tourellini badge stepped forward. 'Come, please,' she said with an attractive smile. Victoria followed and they went out to a minibus where three other visiting Ministers, similarly just arrived, were waiting. She was the last and they set straight off for the hotel.

The Polish Minister told her all about his trips to England, his portfolio, his problems with his opponents. The Swede didn't speak. The Dutch Minister's right eye had a distracting tic. The attractive girl's mobile never stopped. Talking into it, tucked under her chin, she handed out passes and an invitation to lunch next day with Tourellini. Victoria thought a more Mad Hatter-ish bus ride would be hard to imagine.

The Hotel Gallea had tall potted palms in the foyer and an elderly pianist playing 'As Time Goes By'. It was solid and dignified. She loved it. Italians cherished their old buildings, she thought. No Chalfern character had been allowed to replace it with a slick modern monster.

The Tourellini office had invited a few British MEPs from her Party. Ben Norris was one, and checking in she heard him calling to her. 'Cyril and I are just off for a bite at Luigi's,' he reported enthusiastically. 'Jolly trat, great food, you should come along.' He had a girth to match his expense account and was puffing out lethal garlic fumes like a benign podgy dragon. His colleague, Cyril Greene, was a wilting stick of celery by comparison.

'Love to,' she said. William was at his football match and wouldn't be with her before eleven. 'But I must be back by ten – I've got a speech to write.' She hoped Marty had faxed the one already written.

Shaking Ben off later wasn't easy, but her room made up for everything. It was sumptuous; it even had an oval ceiling painting of cherubs and fluffy clouds. The bathroom was a black-marbled palace with voluminous black towels. She texted William her room number and then couldn't wait to sink into a luxurious pampering scented bath.

There was a knock on the door and her pulse started racing. Getting out of the bath, she grabbed one of the huge towels and hurried to the door. 'Who is it?'

'Someone to turn down your bed.' The shivers of relief were sweet. William came in and double-locked the door. 'Made it!' He was in a pink shirt and blazer, grinning and carrying a briefcase that he dumped in the small entrance hall where they stood.

She hugged him tight. 'Weren't you seen getting in? Tell me how you managed it.'

He had such a grin. 'You haven't asked! We won: three nil – it was brilliant!' Football was far from her mind. 'I decided,' he said, kissing her, 'since no one's particularly tuned into your being here, my best bet was to walk in very purposefully as though meeting someone. The stairs aren't in the front desk's line of vision so I just came right on up.'

'Why aren't the press tuned in? Is there no interest in the Tourellini rally?'

'Foreign stuff always gets cut, it makes the Foreign Ed mad as hell. There's little interest in European politics and an Italian pre-election rally is hardly big beer.'

'But don't forget there are British MEPs here.' She told him about Ben and Cyril as she was leading him into the bedroom.

'I've brought champagne,' he said, taking off his blazer, 'but not much else. I was hoping to share your toothbrush.'

He looked up at the ceiling painting and round the room. The walls were salmon pink, the curtains beautifully hung, a silky green-gold; there was handsome walnut furniture and a television perched rather incongruously on a tall pillar-like plinth. 'Let me have your towel,' he said and, leaving her naked, he draped it carefully over the television set.

'It's not a parrot, it doesn't need covering up for the night.'

'It's a blot on paradise.' He sat down on the silk-covered bed. 'The girl in *A Dance to the Music of Time*, he said, pulling her between his legs and kissing her breasts, 'opened the door to her lover with nothing on.'

'I had something on, it doesn't work.'

'Not clothes – and don't be difficult! I want to say something. You do know, don't you, that when we're through all the hard stuff I want to marry you. Is that what you want, too? Could a mermaid handle a greying old hack?'

'A bit of grey at the sides is quite distinguished.' She put her arms round his neck. 'I'm getting cold. Can you get another towel or take me to bed?'

'Why are you playing for time?' He studied her, stroking her hair.

'Because of all the hard stuff – it's a virtual proposal, not a real one.'

'You've got no faith.'

'And you do know that mermaids have bad-hair days just like mortals and get ratty-tailed. Have you thought about that?'

'Never! Mine's a shining-haired paragon and I can't wait to get her to bed.'

She pulled the bedcover round her shoulders and watched as he found glasses and opened the champagne. 'I've got a problem,' she said.

He came beside her and bent to pull off his shoes. 'What?'

She explained about being late and the forgotten briefcase. 'My contraceptive pills are in it, you see – I take them at the office. It can't be much risk, as I'm sure the cover carries on a bit. Does it worry you?'

'Why take them at the office, why not at home?' He'd sat back up and was staring.

'It's just easier. Barney's always wanted more children and it's sort of less in his face.'

'God, you really care – his every bloody feeling matters! Do you not know the kind of a man you're married to? You've still got bruises,' he added, lifting the bedcover away from her shoulders. 'Can't you see sense.'

'Please try and understand. It's sixteen years, it's the hurting; it's Nattie. You'd feel it too, if you do get to the point of walking out on a wife of twenty years. You'd feel desperate about your children.'

'When, not if,' William smiled, but she thought he sounded more subdued.

She kissed him, thinking that at least the lack of pill-cover seemed forgotten. 'Isn't it time, now, for some of that champagne and possibly some bed?'

A thin strip of sunlight was nudging through the curtains and lay on the bed like a path; she wondered where it would lead. William's arm was flung across her and he looked very asleep, very unshaven. Swelling with love, she moved closer and he pulled her closer still.

She ordered a huge breakfast, eggs and bacon, croissants: plenty of coffee. It turned up unexpectedly quickly and William grabbed his clothes and dived into the bathroom. She hurriedly kicked his shoes under the bed. A pimply young waiter wheeled in the trolley, but when he bent down for the hot food in the warmer drawer, she felt sure the shoes must be in his line of vision. He glanced at the black towel over the television. She said the rose on the breakfast trolley was beautiful and pressed a very generous tip on him.

It was suddenly a rush but William promised to take good care leaving the room. He had a little time before his plane back to do *The Firing Line.* He was having a night at home with Ursula, but returning on the first flight out next morning – to an airport other than Milan. Less of a risk, he said.

On the minibus out to the stadium, Ben squashed up beside her. 'Do you know,' he said curiously, 'I'm sure I saw William Osborne in the hotel last night. Must be staying. Didn't I read that he lives near Downsland? Has that given you problems?'

'He knows better than to do any lobbying,' she replied.

There was a cordoned-off stand for VIP visitors, ill lit, with steep rows of seats. She stayed near the back, trying to avoid Ben, and sat worrying about William being seen leaving her room. Who else might have spotted him?

Someone behind her was leaning on her chair-back. It was irritating enough, but when a hand began playing with her hair she spun round, really furious.

She felt no less so, seeing William; he didn't know about Ben but he had no business playing with fire. And it had been a very short night, however glorious, and she didn't want him seeing her making an inadequate speech to a mass of bored Italian delegates.

Turning in her seat, she hissed crossly, 'You shouldn't be here! Ben Norris thinks he saw you in the hotel last night for one thing – and anyway, how did you get in?'

'Never travel without my press pass,' he grinned. 'My plane was delayed and I wanted to see you. There's a slight problem. An aide's asked me to the Tourellini lunch.'

'You can't possibly be at it, too,' she said, panicking. 'Not with Ben there.'

'If I skip it, sod's law he'll hear someone asking where I am. Don't look so worried, best being up-front. I'd better get off to the press box now. Good luck!'

A rep in the uniform of electric blue and red necktie came to collect her and Victoria followed in a fluster: her accent would be bad, her yellow suit's skirt was too short for the high podium and William being there made it harder still.

The Chairman kissed her on both cheeks, gave a flowery introduction and left her to it.

'*Vi porto saluti dal mio partito . . .*' She was bringing them greetings, her party was supportive; she felt it was a speech of real banality.

Maybe it was the skimpy skirt or the run of short bald male speakers but the delegates cheered as they might their football team and afterwards the press and cameramen came crowding round. She eventually got back to the stand – but only to find Ben lying in wait. 'Well done, gorgeous! Now let me escort you to our host's lunch.'

The dining room was up near the roof of the stadium with windows looking down on the delegates far below. It was long and narrow with round tables, and a small bar at one end where William was talking to the French Minister.

Tourellini was sophisticated and super-rich, highly intelligent too, she thought. Ben clung like a limpet, but Tourellini ignored him and after smoothly congratulating Victoria, invited her to join him at his table. 'They're looking after you?' he added. 'Hotel all right?'

'It's wonderful. I had such a good night.' She avoided looking at William who was still at the bar with the garrulous French Minister.

'You'll know Mr Osborne, of course,' Tourellini said, smiling. 'He's joining us, too.'

The smile said it all, but was that an educated guess? She had been so careful not to glance at the bar. 'Yes, our paths do cross at times,' she replied.

Ben followed doggedly as they went to the table and sat down beside her. She saw Tourellini looking extremely irritated as he stood seating people before coming to take his place on her other side. William noticed, too; he got up saying he'd be just a moment and she saw him go up to the glossy-haired girl from the airport. Whatever he said to her seemed to make her smile a lot; she even switched off her ringing mobile.

Ben was talking. 'You're staying the weekend, aren't you, Victoria? Cyril's off back to Scunthorpe tonight – will you have supper? I know a superb little place, *très intime*, you'll—'

'Mr Ben Norris?' He looked up. It was the girl from the airport. 'Please to come,' she said firmly. 'Your valuable assistance is needed. We have problem with our speaker from Ukraine – he asks for you.'

Her manner was charming, businesslike. Ben opened his mouth but had no words. He couldn't refuse; like Mary's little overweight lamb, where she went he was sure to follow. Tourellini directed his Chief of Staff to the vacated seat.

Victoria chatted to her host. She thought he knew very well that the *Post* would have sent a foreign correspondent if anyone at all, that he'd absorbed in a second the reason why its influential Editor had unusually come to his rally.

It was useful knowledge with his elections coming up: positive coverage in the *Post* would be very beneficial. William could handle that side of things, she felt sure, and he, too, had been clever. Ben didn't have Tourellini's sharp powers of deduction, nor had he noticed William's hand in his own removal. He had no need to be settling scores.

As lunch was drawing to a close, William stood up. 'I've got to go for my plane, sadly, but I'm delighted it was delayed.'

Tourellini got up too. 'I hope we can meet again some time, Mr Osborne.'

'I have enjoyed your hospitality,' William said, 'and good luck in the elections!'

Victoria thought it politic to have supper with Ben; she was practised at fending off advances. Over the meal Ben attacked the press, though not William personally, saying they were always nosying around, poking into MEPs' expenses. She hoped he might be less inclined to spread his bit of extremely hot gossip, but knew that was wishful thinking.

William had hidden notes for her round the room. They were wonderful but she was thinking of him at home in bed with Ursula – thinking too, that he shouldn't be getting an early flight to Florence, hiring a car and returning. Not after the rally. He was laying quite a trail and the *Courier*'s werewolves were already baying for blood.

At noon next day she left the convention and took a taxi to the town centre; where she bought presents for William – ties, a leather belt, some hand-made paper – and food for lunch. Then she went back to her hotel room and waited.

William called; he was full of apologies about turning up at the rally. He'd told Ursula that he'd been there and bumped into Victoria. 'Better she's heard it first from me if it gets picked up.'

'Will it be?'

'Don't ask! I feel really bad. I had tickets for La Scala that we'd better not use and I can't have another night at your hotel, not now.'

She felt sharp shards of disappointment. 'Where are you calling from?'

'Here in Milan, of course. I want you to take a taxi, I'll text the address; you're *my* guest tonight. When you go back to your hotel in the early morning, take in a newspaper and it'll look as though you'd just popped out.'

'Where am I coming to?'

'An old friend's flat. I've leaned on him, he's using my La Scala tickets and staying with his mother. And tomorrow,' William said, 'I'm taking you in my hire car, with your bags in the back, to a beautiful restaurant he recommends in Monza. It's a converted hunting lodge, in the middle of a vast park. I'll drop you at a taxi near the airport and then drive back to Florence, hating every minute!'

They covered a lot of ground that night, concentrating into an evening all the things people talk about over months.

The restaurant in Monza was all that William's friend had promised. It was large, on two tiers, and Victoria loved seeing the elderly couples and extended Italian families out for Sunday lunch – grandmothers and silent wine-drinking fathers, children dressed in their best. The tables had spotless white linen, their waiter was old, his skills impeccable.

He recommended the saffron risotto. It was exquisite and Victoria couldn't help thinking how Barney would have loved the place. William sensed it and taxed her with her thoughts. She retaliated by questioning whether Ursula was really so gullible about his weekend plans.

He wasn't having that. 'She'd be more suspicious if I'd had a proper excuse. No, she just got cross. You see, our son Tom's there this weekend. But I know I'm postponing the moment. I do so dread the thought of her going back over past deceptions and how they'll hurt.'

That was too honest. 'I should be getting to the airport,' Victoria said, brought down.

He asked for the bill and reached for her hand, 'We'll get through it all. We'll be sharing reading glasses, taking Saga cruises. It'll be all right.'

Outside, she leaned on the car and looked out to the park. She didn't want to go home. William turned her to him and bent to kiss her, but she suddenly saw Angus Weatherill coming towards them. She went rigid and William bent to unlock the car door instead.

'It *is* you, Victoria!' His clipped upper-crust tones arched through the air like a scythe. 'Thought I was right.' Angus came closer; he had a young blonde on his arm as though his view was they were both on dirty weekends so why hide it? Victoria hated the assumption.

'Fancy seeing you,' she said. 'I'm here for Tourellini's rally. This is William Osborne.'

William shook hands. 'And would this be Miss Weatherill?' he said with a hard grin.

'Do us a favour!' she said pertly. 'I'm Posie Macdonald.'

'Haven't I seen you in something recently, Posie?'

'I was in *Jodhpurs* but hardly your starring role,' she said modestly.

'My paper has a weekly showbiz round-up,' William said but Victoria interrupted before he could go on, aware he was angry and in danger of going too far.

'Sorry, William, I'll miss my plane. Good to see you, Angus – really must be off.'

She was silent driving away. 'His bank was the sponsor that night we met at the Academy,' she said tonelessly.

William pulled into a lay-by and kissed her with such raw hunger that her lips felt scorched and stinging. His needs were hers; he knew her thoughts before she did.

He drove off again with the speed of an Italian. 'You mustn't miss the plane,' he said harshly. 'Barney will have a nice little supper waiting, all ready and warm in the oven.'

CHAPTER 30

Victoria could think of nothing but Milan.

Barney had come to meet her at the airport and they were almost home, just turning into Hartley Street. 'You're very quiet,' he said.

'I'm not feeling that great.' She was preparing the ground, determined to avoid any advances. If a miracle actually happened she had to know it was William's baby.

'Bad luck, getting ill on a trip. You couldn't really have a weekend in bed, I suppose.'

She heard the bitter sarcasm. Getting indoors, busying about, having a poached-eggs supper, they carried on as normal but the edginess between them was serrated and sharp. It was hard to eat, hard to chat and smile. The weekend, the parting, were too fresh. Without William, only some sort of an existence went on. It would be better to leave, she thought. It was almost Easter and the school holidays; she would tell Nattie then and face what had to be done.

William had said, driving to Monza, 'What'll you do if you've got pregnant?'

'Be very glad,' she had answered with honesty, concerned and surprised that he was thinking about it when she had assumed it was far from his mind.

The decision to leave Barney sooner than the summer was calming, but she woke in the night with a sort of anticipatory fear. If some proof of Milan was picked up and there was a big exposure and fuss, then early separation would be out of the question. Her job would be on the line; they would have to lie low. William would want to protect Ursula.

Her sense of premonition was vindicated in hours. Barney woke her with tea as usual, but with a face as accusing as a prosecuting lawyer. 'You might care to look through the curtains,' he said. 'I don't advise opening them. And your mobile's been getting messages, by the sound of it. I'll be in the kitchen. Perhaps, when you come down, you'll explain what it's all about?'

She leaped out of bed and went to the curtains. The front gate was heaving with press. Polystyrene cups on the low wall, cameras being aimed at the door, angles tested: a low murmur of voices, rival reporters gassing together. Cynthia next door, the great curtain-peeper, would think it was jackpot-day.

Victoria read her messages with clawing nerves and a contracting stomach; the Press Office wanted her, media people were begging her to call – and it wasn't yet seven-thirty.

William had sent a coded text telling her to say nothing and keep calm.

Barney was pacing about in the kitchen, white-faced. 'I'd like an explanation. What do they all want out there?'

'I don't know. Some sort of gossip, I suppose.'

'So I get snide questions chucked at me, do I, leaving my own house?'

'Best if we go out together. Don't say a word. Just smile and go straight to your car. No comment, whatever they shout. Just stay silent or they'll never leave you alone.'

When she opened the door, the onslaught was frenzied. 'Seen the *Courier*, Victoria?'

'You weren't in Milan then, Mr James – you couldn't make it?'

'Was Mr Osborne at the same hotel, Victoria?'

The cameras were clicking. She and Barney finally got through and Bob had the car door open. He bundled her in. 'No stopping them,' he complained, driving off at speed.

Being pictured leaving with Barney might very slightly mollify the Whips, she thought.

The *Courier* was the worst. Her heart sank to rock bottom at the sight of a huge picture captioned *A Blossoming Friendship*, covering almost a whole page. She and William were in profile, smiling, their faces very close. She stared at it; she hadn't had the black jacket with her in Milan. There had been no cameras at Tourellini's lunch – the BBC party at Christmas, perhaps? She was sure no photographs had been taken there either. It was a mock-up, she realized – two quite different images cleverly melded together.

The copy, when she read it carefully, admitted that in the small print, and called the picture a 'representation'. The piece was still close to defamatory, talking about the *Post* Editor's newfound passion for Italian politics, his lingering stopover for a rally, the curious coincidence of the comely Housing Minister being there, too, spouting support for Guilio Tourellini. Osborne lived close to Downsland; James was the Minister in charge.

William called her in the office. 'You mustn't worry too much, they've got no proof.'

'Will they get it? Will they go out to the hotel?'

'They'll be all over it like flies! The bellboy will say you went out with two men, *uno grande, uno piccolo.* The maids will be shown my picture and hopefully just shrug and smile. Room Service will find it rewarding to check back slips but report no drinks to 507 – but you do know that the breakfast waiter's just got married and gone off on honeymoon.'

'I'm not up to jokes,' she said.

'Want some more? Tourellini's office will confirm they were privileged to entertain the beautiful signora and the British Editor. Sports Editors will say I cheered all through the match, but they can't help – sorry, mate – with where I stayed. It's my fault entirely, thinking I could slip in unnoticed.'

'Will I be tailed now? Are things as bad as that?'

'They'll watch your car – the flat in my case. It's easier watching buildings than people. But it's all proportional. If I were having an affair with Madonna, we'd be being tailed round the clock!'

William was making too light of it. Victoria got on with work, finding it impossible to concentrate. Angus Weatherill might tell City cronies who might tell the press; Ben might say what he thought he'd seen. Westminster would be buzzing, Guy Harcourt rubbing his hands. She couldn't see William, couldn't leave Barney. There was Nattie, too; she thought of sending her a text explaining it was a mocked-up picture and that helped.

The Chief Whip called. 'I'd like a word, Victoria. Can you come to my room just before the vote?' She said she would and in a panic immediately rang William for advice.

'You can tell that bugger from me exactly where to get off.'

'That's not hugely helpful.' She despaired of him still being so flippant.

'Tell him Tourellini's a sharp operator. Turn it; talk about the politics.'

'Better. You'll make a special adviser yet.'

Shortly before seven she went to the Chief's Commons office, off the Members' Lobby. He got up for her, crumpled, his saggy face unsmiling, indicated a chair and then sat back at his desk.

'You're causing talk, Victoria.'

She hadn't expected such a direct attack. 'The press will keep making Downsland connections,' she muttered. 'It's a constant problem.'

'Look,' he said in a more conciliatory tone. 'It's not worth it, believe me. You'll regret it. And you'll take all the flak – he won't. He'll get off light as two beans.'

Wholly irrationally she resented the presumption of guilt; the Chief's conviction that it was some cheap affair. She considered explaining it wasn't like that, but only for a second and instead said awkwardly, 'Tourellini could win; it was a most interesting trip.'

'So it would seem,' the Chief responded dryly. His eyebrows had knitted together and his hooded eyes were levelled at her; the secondary message, she thought, was that defiance and obduracy would get her nowhere fast.

The Division Bell rang but he didn't stir. 'Is there more to come out?' he queried.

She thought of Ben, Angus. 'Can't think what,' she said disingenuously, 'but I certainly shan't be laying myself open, if that's what you mean.'

The Chief grunted. He told her to heed his words and they went off together to vote.

She reported back to William, being slightly over-dramatic. 'I'm damaged goods now.'

'Don't be stupid. You're the Chief's star, that's why he's so cross. They're not in the business of losing you.' Feeling little reassured, she asked if he'd had trouble too, knowing that Angie in the Press Office had been overrun.

'Margie's had them all on,' he replied. 'They're desperate to find out where I stayed. She gives a very efficient, politely ruthless brush-off.'

There was another vote, and Victoria went home. All day she had been thinking about Barney seeing the *Courier*, and the other papers that had run with the story too.

She found him leaning against the Aga drinking brandy. 'Should you be drinking that?' She said. 'It does give you headaches.'

'Do you really care?' He sounded hurt and whiny, like a child with a bad graze; she wanted to make it better but couldn't. He swirled the golden-brown liquid, drained the glass and poured a refill from the cooking brandy bottle by his arm – probably only because she had questioned it. 'Dick and June have separated,' he said neutrally.

She pulled out a chair. 'I'm sorry to hear that.'

'Dick's very cut-up. He'd hardly set the world alight, even a gas pilot, but he was really good to her and she's thrown it right back in his face.'

'She's moved out?'

'Yes. I saw her new pad tonight. He asked me to try and talk to her.'

'Did you have any success?'

'No. She was too full of all your press coverage. It was a waste of fucking time.'

Victoria thought of the two weeks that lay ahead before Easter. The gossip and innuendo would be like a rushing brook, bubbling along finding new paths, even without hard proof. Could Barney live with it? William said the press always had a stash of hot stories up their sleeves but, however hair-raising, nothing could be published unless it stood up. But in their case the press could do plenty of damage with the trickle effect, and any day Angus or Ben could reveal all, or the sleuths in Milan hit gold. She sighed and Barney stared suspiciously.

He finished his brandy and they went to bed. Seeing William was out of the question while his flat was being spied on. And over Easter: ten more days of separation. When Parliament packed up on Maundy Thursday and Nattie's holidays started, she would be at greater geographical distance and in despair. Wild ideas skitted like pebbles, but there was no way they could meet.

CHAPTER 31

Barney had made no fuss about spending Easter at her parents' which, given her father's cold front at Christmas, Victoria thought was to his credit.

Scouring the pans after Easter Sunday lunch, she felt grateful that the family was on best behaviour, though she feared Nattie might be the one to tip the balance. The girl was on tenterhooks, jumpy as a cornered mouse. Perhaps it was all the embarrassing publicity over Milan, but it probably had far more to do with Seb.

Out of the window Victoria could see her father. Putting the roasting pan to drain, she turned from the sink. 'I'm going out in the garden for a bit, Mum. I want to tell Dad how great it's all looking.'

He was gazing at clumps of Pheasant Eye narcissi, resting on his fork. She went to stand beside him and put her arm through his. 'It's been hell with the press, Dad, not seeing him.' Her eyelashes were wet on her cheeks. 'I'd made my decision to leave – I was going to tell Nattie, but doing it now would be the worst of all worlds. I've got to wait. Milan's to blame but it gave me all my certainties.'

'That does my heart good to hear! I'd thought Milan very rash and impulsive, but it's worth anything that you're feeling sure.' He was beaming and his face held intense relief. 'Tell Nattie anyway,' he said. 'Tell her everything. She's not a child – she might even open up herself. My guess is she's started a physical relationship – no, more likely she's being heavily pressured, she'd be more glowing otherwise.'

'But if she's resisting, does that mean she's not sure of her feelings for Seb?' Victoria said hopefully, remembering her own instinctive reservations and dislike.

'Talk to her, try and find out. Try it, darling, but tell her where you're at first; she knows her father's failings and you've got to end it. She'll be relieved as well as sad.'

But how could she confide in Nattie? How, when they couldn't even talk boyfriends and parties, let alone a mother's great love affair? But to go on acting out Happy Families all through the holidays when Nattie knew it was so fake, would be a terrible strain. And if she had plans to see Seb, she wouldn't talk; she'd clam up even more.

'Will things come right, Dad?' Victoria asked helplessly. 'He has talked of marriage.'

'I can't know, darling, but you must end your present one.'

They left for Ferndale the next night. The Recess was a time for catching up in the constituency and Victoria wanted Nattie out of London whenever possible. Barney was going to try commuting. He never had before, but then he'd done as he'd pleased and never felt threatened. She thought he'd find it dire; he hadn't been on a train in years.

He was off bright and early on Tuesday morning and she went out to buy the papers. Nattie came into the kitchen in jeans and a torn red sweatshirt and saw her reading the *Post* over a cup of coffee. Victoria put it aside but Nattie had glanced at it rather pointedly. Pouring some Cheerios, and reaching for the milk she picked it up herself and began to read.

Victoria collected her briefcase and came back in to say goodbye. 'I'll be home by lunch, darling,' she said. 'You'll do some AS revision? Nattie, did you hear?'

'Yep.' She had her head down, far too interested in the *Post*.

At the office Victoria went through diary entries with Jason. A literary festival, a new event in the area, was being held in a splendid hotel on the outskirts of her constituency, and as the local MP, she had been asked to speak. Suggested topics were her favourite books or the political novel. She asked Jason to find out who the other speakers were.

Jason had to go out to the local newspaper and she took the opportunity to call William. He was in his office. She asked after his weekend – a light question but it carried the weight of her dreams; she needed to know that home could no longer reach him.

'I'm spilling over with bile!' he exclaimed. 'Those buggers had a watch on the house all weekend. I seriously considered bribing the lot of them with better-paid jobs. I was going to come and somehow find a way of seeing you.'

'And they'll keep watching the flat – for how long?' Victoria asked. William couldn't tell her. The ferocious entrance buzzer was going; she had seen, out of the window, her Chairman parking his car, but it was hard saying goodbye.

She was still on the phone when Giles came in the room looking very spruce and naval. Whether it was the call, her giveaway expression, but he began talking about all the recent publicity. Most constituents, he said, didn't trust the press and believed the whole thing got-up and overblown. They approved of her and were *Firing Line* fans; they thought the there'd been a few murmurs and grumbles but Jason had proved surprisingly adept at deflecting them. Giles didn't ask whether the story had any truth.

Sunday breakfast was a silent meal. They had got through the week somehow. Barney had come home each night reporting explosively that commuting and the Tube was like being fed into a sausage skin, but they had survived.

They were going back to London that night though, and the dynamics were changing. Barney and Nattie were buried in the newspapers, their tension glaring. Victoria's was open in front of her but she was missing William so much it was hard to absorb a word.

Even back in the city there would be no chance to see him. Ivor Skeat was vengefully spending unlimited money; his press hounds were baying. But leaving Barney now, in the heat of it, would put Ursula in the spotlight and herself in the doghouse. There'd be no end to the opprobrium. Nattie had exams coming up. There could be no worse time.

They were also in the run-up to Downsland with the media's attention focused. A glamorous protestor like Sam Swayne taking on the commercial fat cats was firing up whole armies of impassioned youth, all determined to save the planet and stop a new town from being built. The press loved it – and the nation's championing of the nightingales over decent starter homes. Then there were the menacing rent-a-mob troublemakers. Her leaving had to be after Downsland.

She stared across the table at Nattie and Barney's buried heads. William was at home on a Sunday but even sending a text would help. Even just getting out of the house.

'I'm thinking of going to church,' she said placidly, talking to their bent heads. 'Either of you want to come?'

Barney looked up with a flinty glare. 'Your soul needs more saving than mine.' He went back to his sports section. Nattie didn't bother to answer.

It was a sunny, late-spring day. The trees were already in leaf, the colours in the dappled sunlight, strong and sharp. Lemon, lime, yellow and black, the freshness of the day was exquisite. Victoria stopped the car and tapped out a message. *Gone to church, out about twelve.* She had to have contact and thought he would call if he could.

The small Norman church had a square tower and sheep grazing in the field beside. Going in through the arched wooden doors she was feeling calmer, glad of a contemplative hour. She sat near the back, mouthing hymns and giving muted responses. Sunlight through leaded panes made faint diamonds on the vicar's cassock. His hands were tightly clasped, giving his sermon, they looked as though they were stuck fast.

After the service, her mobile rang on the way to the car park. Luke, the churchwarden's eight-year-old son, was around, scuffing stones, but no one else. Feeling elated, she answered, walking slowly towards her car.

'I've got to see you,' William said. 'Don't try and stop me, just say when and where.'

'Exit Thirteen, the Ferndale turning out of Eastleigh. Can we meet in the village church car park at about four? It's very rural but we'll need to drive somewhere safer and well away.'

*

William told Ursula that something had cropped up: he had to go into the office right away. Keeping her back to him, she had said it was a pity in family time, and carried on turning potatoes for Sunday lunch.

He'd shot off in a great rush, throwing up gravel, but had needed to go via the office for some cover. Seeing Ursula at the kitchen window though, he wished he had remembered his briefcase, and not been in such an obvious hurry.

Five minutes showing his face at the office had turned into ten. George was there and had started talking about Skeat, still on the rampage and out for trouble. With his affair such obvious common knowledge since Milan, William had thought it typically limp of George. He was clearly desperate to probe, pathetically reluctant to ask outright.

He must be itching for a dramatic exposé, William thought, and the chance of taking over – which would be one way to see the *Post*'s sales plummet.

He was driving down the motorway hoping after going to such lengths, that he'd got out of the building unseen. He had enlisted GD's help in shaking off his tail. GD had thought of posing as a mechanic and taking away William's car, telling the car-park staff – and anyone listening – that since the Editor was in, he wanted it checked for wheel-wobble. 'Just get yourself to the pub near the Globe if you can,' GD had said, 'and then take the car and scoot off.'

William wondered if, as well as her ministerial car, Victoria's cottage might be being watched, but nothing could have deterred him. It was four weeks since he'd seen her. The risk and consequences could go hang.

He found Ferndale and the lane to the church. A tall girl with long fair hair was crossing and he slowed for her. She was in jeans, very slender, and although her back was to him, there seemed something familiar about her walk. It occurred to him that she might be Nattie and he worried slightly at her being out and about. He would have liked a glimpse of her face.

He parked in the deserted church car park under a cherry tree in blossom and settled down to wait. He was feeling quite tense enough, but when a small pudgy fist tapped on the car window his pulse really raced. Opening the window he queried, 'Yes, what is it?'

'Have you come for the MP?' The little boy was staring unwaveringly.

William's nerves weren't in mint condition. 'Why do you say that?'

'She said to get somewhere safer, I heard her. Are bad people after her?'

'Possibly. You could help,' William said conspiratorially, 'by keeping watch at the corner. But you shouldn't really talk to a stranger like me!'

'It's the time she said,' the boy declared, as though that resolved any issue about strangers. But he wasn't going and William was burning for Victoria. He also didn't want the boy seeing her get in the car. Looking round for inspiration, he saw a school exercise book of Jessie's and tore out a few blank pages. He found a felt-tip pen, too.

Handing them over he said with authority, 'You get off to the corner and take the numbers of any cars turning up; they could be useful. I'll stay here. What's your name?' he added smiling, hoping friendliness would clinch it.

'Luke,' the little boy replied solemnly.

'Mine's Barney,' William said. He was breathing more freely as Luke sped off.

Minutes ticked by. He looked at his watch. Hearing the driver's back passenger door opening he went cold for a second, but as Victoria's arms came round his neck, he felt a glorious surge. 'Where have you been? You can't do this to me! I was getting desperate.'

'Hiding, waiting – what was all that about with young Luke?'

'Nothing, tell you later. Does the lane go on anywhere useful? Luke's down at the corner and I don't want him seeing us leaving in the car together.'

'It's a road we can take to the motorway but it goes past the cottage.'

'Lie flat and I'll wave as we go by.'

Once on the motorway he stopped on the hard shoulder and she climbed over into the front. 'Better keep down,' William said. 'People overtaking might look in.'

'I don't know if you're being followed but I did cover my tracks,' she said proudly, resting her head on his lap.

'How?' He was driving with one hand, his other holding her breast.

'I drove to the supermarket, went in with my trolley and then went straight out again by a side pedestrian entrance. My car is still there and I walked over the fields to get here!'

William took an exit where he had noticed some woodland on his way to Ferndale. 'I like thinking of Skeat's bucks ticking away in a supermarket car park,' he said, turning down a road and finding a dirt-track into the wood.

He drove up it and stopped. She wasn't relaxed, he could tell; he felt panicked. 'What is it? Why are you tense? For God's sake, tell me. Is it all the subterfuge and risk?'

She stared. 'No, it's not so much that. It's the car; there's a lipstick on the floor, an exercise book on the back seat. It just makes it all that bit closer and brings out the guilt.'

He understood but he was feeling consumed with need, completely desperate. 'We don't have to be in the car,' he said, thinking there was no rug, nothing to lie on. There was the carpet in the boot, hard and prickly, covered in dog-hairs. He pulled it off its velcro strip and laid it on the damp woodland undergrowth, thinking they must be on someone's land, that there could be a shotgun-brandishing farmer. Then he took off his jacket and spread it lining-side up on top.

Victoria lay down on it. 'It's still warm from you,' she said, holding out her arms.

Her head was on his jacket, her hair spread out over the muddy ground. He knew just how much he loved her. When he lay more calmly beside her, he thought the trees seemed to have sympathetically closed in and created a perfect bower.

Back on the road again he asked, 'What did you say you were doing?'

'Just that I had to fit in an appointment. Barney was upset and it created an atmosphere.' William didn't trust himself to comment. 'Nattie took herself off on a walk,' Victoria went on. 'She wasn't back when I left – I do hope she is by now.'

'I'm sure she will be,' he said reassuringly, thinking of the girl in the lane. 'But could Luke be a problem? He's a mine of information.'

'Depends what he tells his mother. She's not my biggest fan.'

'Will Downsland be decided by our birthday?' William asked.

'Round about then.'

'I'm going to see you come what may. We'll have a very private party.'

He dropped her near the supermarket, drove fast round the motorways and was home little later than his usual time on a Sunday evening. He felt some guilt as he lied to Ursula about his doings; his guilt had facets that caught him unawares like a refracting crystal but he could also keep it at arm's length, an object held in his hand.

Seeing Victoria had made everything seem suddenly more promising; he was back in control, full of fight. Over supper, watching television, cleaning the family's shoes as he always did on Sunday nights, he was thinking about the next stage.

Rubbing away with a polishing cloth, he felt fresh piquancy though, at his inability to tell Victoria about an extraordinary letter he had received. Many personal letters had crossed his desk during the domestic-violence campaign but one had come as a shock to him and left him completely bemused. He longed to share it with her, but couldn't.

It had been from Martin Whiting, Private Secretary to Victoria James, and was written in typical Mandarin style. *I am writing to*

congratulate you on your very searching campaign. I share your concern over
this issue, a particularly disturbing problem . . .

It was no coincidence, William thought. For some reason that
he had yet to fathom, Marty was trying to get a message across;
the difficulty was deciphering it.

The letter had been written before Milan, and that meant that
Whiting must have been aware of the relationship for quite a while.
He had used the campaign as an opportunity to let William know
that – but why? And the letter clearly indicated knowledge of
Victoria's particular domestic problems, but how could that be?
Why should he have had reason to suspect anything or question
that fall? It was a mystery, impossible to see the subliminal message.

Was there one at all? Perhaps, William thought, it had been simply
to open a line of communication in case of need.

Knowing about the letter would complicate Victoria's working
relationship with her Private Secretary. Marty certainly wouldn't have
wanted her to know and must have been acutely conscious of the
risk he was taking. William felt flattered that the other man had
believed him to be sensitive enough to see and honour that; he
liked having his judgment trusted.

Whatever the reason for the letter, Victoria must never know.

CHAPTER 32

Nattie was sitting at the little painted table her mother used as a dressing-table. It was duck-egg blue with a scroll and flower design; hand-painted, it felt as if it belonged in a back bedroom in a French château. She picked up her mother's Calèche scent and squirted it on her wrists, neck and cleavage, then went back to leaning on her elbows, chin on the base of her palms and staring at herself in the oval pedestal mirror on the table.

He would ring the doorbell at any minute. She wished Maudie wouldn't keep putting him down, it was so mean of her; Nattie made a face at herself in the mirror. She got up and went to the full-length one on the inside cupboard door, and raised and lowered the front zipper of her black top and tweaked at the red skirt Seb had said he liked.

The doorbell rang. She had so many butterflies, just going down the stairs; part of her didn't even really want to be going.

Seb had a taxi waiting and was looking impatient. He gave her cheek a brush as she got in. 'Hi, you took your time. It's such a piss-off about my test. I've got the new Peugeot now — it's only a

206, Dad was so tight – and then that fucking bastard has to go and fail me! I'm taking you to supper first, we'll go to San Marco's then go home and watch a film or something?'

'That's cool,' she said, wishing they were going to the pub and meeting up with the others. It was stupid though, continuing to hold back; she had to make up her mind and just do it. She remembered a schoolfriend saying she'd been tanked-up on retsina and wished afterwards she hadn't done it, and other people saying it had just felt really right. That was what she longed for, Nattie thought, a right feeling.

They were on a bench seat in the restaurant and he took hold of her hand. 'You must help me with the wine,' he smiled, 'or I'll only drink the lot.' The friendly smile was comforting. Smiling back, she felt his leg pressing against hers; she took a sip of wine, feeling her face burning and hoped it wasn't looking blotchy and fiery red.

Seb's house in South Ken was only a few streets away but there was a chilly wind and she felt cold with no coat when they left the restaurant. He put his jacket round both their shoulders, it seemed very intimate and not in a coming-on-all-heavy sort of a way. She felt happier.

There were no lights on anywhere. 'Your parents aren't around?' she asked as they went in. Seb had a brother but she thought he was abroad.

'Mum and Dad are up North.' He had been closing the door and he turned and kissed her. It was wonderful being in his arms, but she could feel he was hard and his hand in the small of her back was pressing too insistently.

He opened a bottle of champagne, saying his dad never missed one, and they went through to the sitting room with a tray. He rested it on glossy books on a table in front of the sofa and encouraged her to sit down. It was a green-velvet sofa with deep sides and tasselled corners, voluminous; she stayed sitting near the edge.

Seb leaned back lengthwise, pulling her half on top of him, and kissed her long and deep. 'Hi, I missed you all Easter, sexy Natalia.'

'We were going to watch a film,' she mumbled, loving the kiss but not his hand under her skirt.

He got up without a word and went out. If they could just curl up together for a while on the sofa, she thought: if he could just understand not to rush her. He never seemed to.

'I thought we'd have a smoke,' he said, coming back with no DVDs and a spliff in his mouth. He held it to her lips and she drew on it, hoping it might help but it had never had any effect in the past that she'd noticed. Seb went out again for the champagne bottle.

They drank a bit, talked a bit; she was grateful, then he took away her glass, smiling, and unzipped her top.

'Relax, Natalia, it's all right, really it is.' He had her tights down and was yanking off his jeans. She realized the moment had passed for talking about not being ready; she had to let him, it had to be now. He took her hand and directed it, keeping his on hers and moving it up and down; her fingers closed round feeling the hardness and the loose skin moving with her. 'I'll use a condom, you've got nothing to worry about,' he said.

But there was a note of impatience in his voice and she needed him to be gentle. The condom out of its tinfoil casing, too, looked unsexy and surgical and somehow made her more certain the mood wasn't right. He wasn't being loving enough. After her brief moment of feeling more compliant and confident she felt herself drawing back. An uneasy sense of being too pressured, almost coerced, had taken over, instinct telling her to resist.

But he had put on the condom and his mouth was on hers and she was being pressed back on the musty velvet cushions. His arms were holding him up over her body and he was kneeing her legs apart. Part of her wanted to give in, she was feeling his urgency, but the stronger instinct was telling her to hold back; she jerked her mouth free and put out her hands, trying to lift away his body. 'Please, Seb, I don't want this. I'm truly sorry, call me a cock-tease, tell me you've had it with me, but I want you to stop.'

'You can't make me stop now. It's all right – it's really all right.'

'But I want you to stop. I don't want to do this, I'm asking—' Her words were drowned as he turned her face back and his mouth covered hers and he trapped her with his weight.

'It's OK, it's OK.' He was panting and she felt it hard, probing and pushing and then it seemed to find a rhythm and she felt the pain.

Her body was squashed and his tongue was filling her mouth, but she jerked backwards again and cried out, 'Stop, stop, it's hurting!' But there was no stopping and it was very soon over. He rolled off panting and lay beside her, his cheek by hers giving off heat and damp. She turned and bit on the corner of a cushion in her desperation not to cry.

Her first time, she thought and she had been nothing to him, a shag, a notch on his bedpost; her disillusion was as sharp as the stinging pain where he had been. He had taken her most valuable possession and availed himself, used it and returned it broken. Bitterness turned into self-revulsion, the thought of how she had so weakly let it get to that point.

He leaned over, still out of breath, and turned her face and kissed her. 'It wasn't so bad, was it? It'll be different next time. I'll make it good for you, you'll see.'

Clutching her underwear, she made for the downstairs loo. There, safely behind the locked door, she gulped back heaving tears. The stinging was bad and she had a feeling of sticky blood. There was a box of tissues; she took a handful to make a pad, wetted it and dabbed between her legs. The pad came away pink. She chucked it in the loo and then using all the tissues made a new one to put inside her pants. Her hair was a mess; there were silver-handled brushes, a whole set, on a vanity unit and she used one with distaste. Turning, she saw a few pink watery drips on the tiles and marks on an aqua-velvet stool but left them. 'I'll go now, Seb,' she said.

His smile was quite kindly. 'Thanks, Talie, we had a nice time.' He put his arm round her. 'Why don't you stay a bit?'

She desperately needed to get out. 'No, I should go now, really.'

'OK,' Seb said more carelessly. 'I'll call a cab.'

'No, I'll find one outside. I'll be fine.'

Seb came out with her. 'You were great,' he whispered. 'Sorry if it hurt a bit – it'll be better next time. I'll call, see you very soon!'

'I'm not around much,' she said, trying to keep the hysteria from entering her voice. Being out of the house and more able to breathe though, she suddenly found some backbone. She looked him straight in the eye and said quite confidently, 'I'm afraid that's it between us, you see?'

His light eyes flickered. 'Fine by me,' he snapped, and went back to the door.

She ran down the street, her breath steamy on the cold late-night air, and rounding a corner into a crescent of similarly tall houses with elegant wrought-iron railings, she stopped, panting hard, and clung to a couple of the chill iron struts; she became racked with sobs, her shoulders shaking violently. There was no one around to see. She eventually let go and half-walked, half-ran the mile or so to get home.

There she shot upstairs to her room, desperate to be alone, but her mother came chasing up and called through the door. 'Nattie, darling, whatever's wrong?'

'Go away, Mum. I just broke up with Seb, that's all.'

'I'm so sorry.'

She fell on the bed and buried her face in the pillow, but sensing her mother still there, she lifted herself up and cried hysterically, 'For Christ's sake, go now, can't you? Just let me be on my own.'

How could she face the looks at school and Seb's sneers? What could she say to her friends? She wanted to die.

CHAPTER 33

It was such a beautiful late-April morning. Victoria was with Ned in his office and he suggested walking over to the Commons together for Prime Minister's Questions.

She took the opportunity to thank him for the invitation to a big thirtieth wedding anniversary party he and his wife Claire were having at their Staffordshire home the following Saturday night. 'And it's very good of you, putting us all up,' she added warmly.

'We're delighted to – and Hugo, of course, is very glad Natalia's coming.'

The dance was as much for his sons, and Nattie had met Hugo before. 'Her term starts that Sunday evening,' Victoria said. 'She'll be tired, getting back to school!'

She wondered if Nattie would refuse to go. It had been awful, leaving home with her daughter's door still shut, not knowing how she was. She wasn't answering her mobile. It must have been a really bad scene for such desolation. Had Nattie just been cruelly dumped? Had she caught Seb out in some way? It was hard to know what else could be wrong.

'You seem lost in thought, Victoria,' Ned remarked. She made more of an effort as they walked on, right until they were sitting on the front bench in the Chamber.

During Prime Minister's Questions, she nodded and laughed at appropriate moments, or glared at the Opposition, as if by rote.

But she sat up and took notice when a normally ineffective backbencher asked what was being done about the shaming figures on teenage pregnancy. They were still showing the highest rate in Europe. The Prime Minister, who normally swatted away awkward questions with ease, hid unconvincingly behind the hoary old get-out of a review being underway. Victoria felt panicked. Had Nattie got pregnant – was it all about that?

William had thought Seb might have broken it off if she'd been holding out against sex and he wasn't getting anywhere. Had Nattie really been resisting, though? It sounded too strong-willed of her; she'd seemed so emotionally involved.

Victoria had told William about the party, and had been surprised by the amount of fuss he'd made. It was the thought of her dancing with Barney, he said. He resented it. She tried to set him straight. 'Barney never comes near me at parties! He goes motoring off like a peacock after all the talent.'

'Peacocks don't motor, they strut.'

Home that night, as early as possible, she found Nattie up in her room lying on her bed in jeans and an old T-shirt. Victoria drew up a chair beside her daughter and after getting nowhere asking questions about Seb, decided the problem of Ned's dance had to be faced.

'I know it's the last thing you'll feel like doing but I do need you to come.'

Nattie was on her back keeping an arm over her face. 'I'm not going to that party.'

'I need you there, darling. I need your support. It's hard for me too now, you see.'

It came from the heart. Nattie took away her arm and stared; she looked wretched, her eyes were raw from crying and Victoria felt an enormous wave of sympathy. 'I'd love not to be going myself,' she whispered, 'but Ned is my boss. Please come. Don't let me down.'

Nattie went on staring. 'All right – if I must. But can I be alone now? I've had some food, Mum, I don't want any supper.' She turned over then and lay facing the wall.

Victoria had her Saturday surgery to do, before driving up to Staffordshire for Ned's dance. She'd been on a Minister's away day all Friday and needed a short session with Jason in advance of the first appointment. 'I've accepted for that literary festival,' he said, beaming. 'Everyone's pleased it's come to the area, very chuffed; we are going up in the world.'

'But I wanted to know who the other speakers were before we accepted.'

Jason's face fell; he seldom slipped up. He promised to check it out on Monday but Victoria knew she was committed, that the programme would have been printed. It was being slightly over-cautious, but there were people who as a Minister it was better she didn't mix with – always one or two to be avoided.

*

The Markhams' estate had a cattle-grid entrance and a half-mile drive through peaceful parkland. Ned was out on the wide stone steps in front of the house, directing catering vans like a traffic cop. He bounded down, showed them where to park and then escorted them into a splendid pillared entrance hall. 'There's tea on the go in the library,' he said. 'You must all be shattered.'

Ned's statuesque dark-haired wife Claire introduced them to the other couple who were also staying, Toby and Jane Courtland. His eyes were a piercingly bright blue and Jane, in butter-coloured cashmere, had sleek fair hair and looked irritatingly immaculate. Barney went to sit beside her and she was soon throwing back her head at some witticism of his, showing perfectly even, very white teeth; she'd had a lot of trips to the orthodontist, Victoria thought sniffily.

Nattie was translucently pale and being very unresponsive. Hugo had detached himself from the group at the window and though showing obvious signs of adoration, was struggling with her. He was an engaging youth – shy, tall and with floppy mousy hair. 'We're all a bit travel-worn,' Victoria said, feeling for him. 'It's quite a hike from Southampton.'

'You might like to freshen up a bit,' he offered, and suggested showing them upstairs.

They left Nattie in her room looking very relieved at her release and Victoria went to hers. The room had a lovely symmetry – deepset windows with narrow box seats and there was a loosely arranged vase of tulips on a mahogany table. Her backless, satiny gunmetal-colour dress for the dance had been laid out on a canopied fourposter bed.

She was worrying about Nattie, thinking of little else, but climbing into a splendidly antiquated claw-foot bathtub, her longing for

William was overwhelming. She scrambled out shivering – the water had been tepid – deciding she had time to send a text before Barney tore himself away from the immaculate Jane and came to change.

She tapped out a quick message. *Missing you so much it hurts. Cold bath, too.*

Barney came in seconds later and while he was changing she went to see Nattie. The floorboards creaked going along the passage; they were in the back part of the house with a wonderful outlook over an expanse of magnificent lawn and extensive planting.

Nattie was in her dress, which seemed some progress. She was standing at the window with the curtains pulled back, staring out at the blackness of night. She didn't turn round. In her pink satin slip of a dress she looked like a glimpse of dawn against the dark sky. 'Must I really come down?' she muttered over her shoulder.

'Yes, darling. And you must have one dance with Hugo. He'll understand if you don't want to be up late, he's very gentle.' Nattie turned and her hurt eyes held a look of disbelief, as if she was transferring all Seb's sins, whatever they were, on to the whole male race.

The party got underway in a huge, lavish marquee that had star-like lights in its ceiling-folds and windows looking out onto the floodlit garden. Victoria heard Barney saying to a girl whose boobs seemed certain to spill out before the night was over, 'Don't I know you from somewhere?' He did love parties.

They were on different tables at dinner. Nattie was on Hugo's, Barney next to perfect-teeth Jane and Victoria found herself seated between a farmer and a political biographer.

Her table talked sheep. A terrifying woman with a gash of red lipstick and a cigarette-holder yelled across at an ample girl in powder blue, 'Do you eat your Jacobs? Bang 'em on the head?'

'Oh, I couldn't! I send them to market.'

'No stomach for it, eh?'

There was a moment's silence while everyone was contemplating the sheep-dispatching conundrum and in the lull Victoria's mobile indicated a text's arrival with an embarrassingly loud beep. Delving into her beaded bag, she bent low to read William's return message. *Miss me if the bath had been hot?*

She sent a quick response: *Miss you in all waters.* She looked up then and smiled fixedly at the political biographer whom she'd sensed had been glancing over, trying to read the message.

He was unfazed. 'You modern politicians can never be parted from those things,' he remarked with amused disdain. 'You need some of the old-guard laissez-faire.'

'It's all about keeping in touch,' she replied sweetly.

The genial farmer whisked her round the floor. Toby, the other houseguest, danced with her too. She wondered if he was anxious or angry, or simply couldn't care less that his wife was nowhere to be seen. Barney had also disappeared. Dancing, she saw Guy Harcourt's eyes narrowing in her direction. He would be scheming, plotting how best to prosper from all her Milan notoriety.

She had a turn with Ned and they stopped at Nattie's table. Hugo sensibly chose that moment to ask her to dance. Glancing dutifully at her mother she got up, looking so lovely it was jolting, and he led her onto the floor. He had cautious hold of her hand as if fearing he might lose her or she would float away.

Victoria sat at her table with the political biographer and was longing to slip off to bed when she felt a hesitant touch on her arm. It was Hugo.

'Sorry to interrupt, Mrs James,' he said, 'but I'm a touch worried about Natalia. She said she was going to the loo, but those Portaloos are in the garden and there's only one way back, yet I haven't seen her, even though I was looking out for her. It's just that she seemed a little down.' He smiled apologetically. 'I'm sure all's fine and I've simply missed her, and she's turned in, but could you possibly check? I've looked in the garden . . .'

'That's so kind,' Victoria said, feeling instant panic. 'I'll go right away.'

Every sort of morbid possibility was flying through her head as she hurried from the marquee and found her way back into the eerily silent main house. Racing up the staircase, her heart's loud thumping made her need to take gulps of breath.

Nattie's door was locked. She was there, that was something, but Victoria's thoughts were of overdoses, of all things extreme as she begged to be let in. The quavers of terror in her voice must have sounded very melodramatic, as the door suddenly opened and her daughter stared out.

She was still in her dress with the shoestring straps, shivering; her face was a tear-stained mess. Strands of fine fair hair were sticking to her wet cheeks. She must have been having a really howling sobbing cry. Victoria impulsively gathered her up and hugged her to the point of smothering. However big or small the problem, she just wanted to make it better.

Nattie felt like a small child in her arms. She was crying again and the thin young shoulders were racked. Getting closer to the bed so they could sit down, Victoria's own tears started to stream.

The comedy of two sobbing women soon got through to them; they couldn't help laughing and it was a wonderful release.

It formed enough of a bond for all the inhibitions to be suddenly swept away. 'Did Seb do something to hurt you? Is it my fault – has all the publicity been rough?' Victoria wanted to know; the questions came as naturally as breathing. 'Tell me everything, darling.' She remembered William's suggestion that Seb had been exerting heavy pressure. 'Seb didn't force you or anything, did he?'

Nattie stiffened and went ashen, and the picture became clearer.

'It was as much my fault, Mum,' she pleaded. 'I'd gone on being almost up for it and then pulling back, for ages. Something had made me hang back but he was losing patience, I could tell. I should have had the guts to know my own mind and to see he didn't care. Instead I let it get right to beyond, well, further even than anything before.'

'Did he use a condom?' Victoria interrupted.

'Yes, it was all part of trying to persuade me. But it was just my body; he hadn't the slightest interest in *me*. I suddenly saw that and also, well, that all he wanted was just to sort of put it somewhere. I tried to get him to stop.'

'And he didn't?'

'I'm sure he thought he was doing me a favour, that I'd thank him after – I had been going along with it, almost all the way. I did end it as I was leaving, Mum, but I keep thinking of the stories he'll spread at school, how I'm frigid and things. I don't want to go back. I don't know what to say to my friends. I don't want to have to see him.'

She was crying again and Victoria didn't know what to do. It was William's advice she wanted; she felt Nattie's own father wasn't the best person. 'Mum, promise you won't tell Dad?' she sobbed, as if divining that. 'I so don't want him to know.'

'I won't tell him. Can you say to your friends that Seb was so hateful you can't bear to talk about it? He's treated you abominably, but one scumball doesn't make all men bad. People will want you for *you* – genuine people, not bullying shits who deserve to be flogged.'

Nattie looked quite shocked at that but didn't comment. 'I'm still a bit sore,' she said.

'You could see our nice Ferndale doctor next weekend if it doesn't get better – anyone but the school doctor! Dad needn't know about it.' She seemed happy at that. Victoria had a progression of thought – from school to Hugo about to go to Cambridge, to his sensitive actions about Nattie's disappearance. 'How did you get in the house and up here?' she asked. 'Hugo said you went in the garden and didn't come back.'

'I couldn't bear to. I found a way in through the kitchens – the caterers let me in. But I'd been outside for ages and got so cold; I'd been sitting hating myself on a bench in a gazebo. It was a romantic night, which didn't help, the moon was making the gardens look silver and there were couples arm-in-arm. Then Dad and a woman came in the far end of the gazebo.' She hesitated. 'They didn't see me but I couldn't leave.' She looked at Victoria. 'What's happening, Mum? Will you get a divorce?'

'I think we're going to have to separate, but not before summer.' She felt something had to be said about Barney in the gazebo. 'Dad's always flirted, darling, but he can somehow keep it in a separate compartment. Now I've got so involved myself, and when I least expected to, it's very different for me.

'It's too late to repair things now, I think. I'm so sorry, Nattie. It's your Mum and Dad fucking you up, like the Larkin poem.'

'Do you really love *him*?'

Victoria smiled, she couldn't help it. 'That's what it's all about!'

'Will he get separated, too?'

'I don't know. He's got younger daughters. I think he loves me. Look – I must go and tell Hugo you're found. You won't talk about this, will you, darling – not even to Maudie? The press can make it so bad. And be nice to Dad. He loves you so much and he's feeling low; he wants me to stay. And about school: you've got exams, keep your dignity, you'll sort rubbish like Seb. He's only there one more term. He'll soon be gone and that terrible experience will be behind you for good.'

At school they unloaded Nattie's bags and took them up to her room.

They stood around outside by the car after that, as though waiting on a station platform for a train's arrival, the moment nearing for saying goodbye. When they really had to go, Nattie gave each of her parents a quick kiss on their cheeks and walked away towards the building. She went in through the open door and didn't look back.

CHAPTER 34

William was going over schedules and dates with Margie. 'Where exactly in Hampshire is the hotel for that literary festival?' he asked, wondering how close it might be to Victoria. 'And do we know the other speakers?' He had agreed to talk on literature and journalism, the conflicts and links, but was beginning to wish he hadn't; it would take time and thought.

Margie mentioned a few names – a poet, one still flying the flag for metre and rhyme, a playwright who was a good friend of William's, a couple of authors and then she paused. 'Victoria James is speaking too, I believe. I've asked for the programme to be sent.'

Chances were they wouldn't be speaking on the same day. But as well as feeling as starved of contact as a castaway, frustrated and desperate to see her, he needed to talk to Victoria about something not easily discussed on the phone.

It was a delicate problem involving Roland Chalfern. The man was always a danger zone, but now it seemed the *Courier* had discovered some links with Downsland – which was seriously bad news for

Victoria. Typical of Barney, having a suspect property-speculator client, William thought contemptuously.

He wondered if Jim might have more information. It would be a real giveaway asking, but they were all in the loop anyway. It was pointless worrying.

Jim confirmed his fears. 'The *Courier*'s pretty cocky. They say Victoria's in deep shit.'

'Know what they've got exactly?'

'No. I'm told their source is Chalfern's Company Secretary who's sore about a missed bonus; he's been sounding off apparently, saying his boss hits the jackpot big-time if Downsland gets the go-ahead.'

'See what more you can find out, will you? Can't have the *Courier* stealing a march.'

Jim left, looking full of himself, milking his role as confidant to the full.

William went to stand at his window. There was a filmy haze over London, a heatwave on its way. He wouldn't tell Victoria, he thought, and get her worried, at least not until Jim had reported back, but he wanted to share notes with her about the festival.

'We're even speaking on the same evening,' she said when he called her. 'But I'm going to have to tell the Chief Whip. I'll say I accepted in good faith, not knowing you'd been asked and it would cause a lot more press interest if I pull out than if I don't.'

'Will Barney come?'

'He's got a golf-club dinner, but I'm not sure if he'll scrub that when he hears.'

'My worry is that Ursula may want to come. The festival's her sort of thing. She's never once mentioned all the publicity, but if

I tell her you're speaking it might put her off a bit – or at least help me to know more where I stand.'

He talked about it to Ursula at breakfast the Sunday before the event. The girls had had theirs and gone to feed Jessie's guinea pig. He looked round the big sunny kitchen where his wife spent so much of her time. It had tall sash windows, one looking out on to the front circle of gravel, and she often stood there talking on the phone, seeing friends arrive.

She was silent while he took her through all the speakers. 'The poetry slot's the night before, which is unfortunate,' he said, thinking the opposite, 'but do you want to come?'

'What's a politician doing at a literary event like that? Why is *she* muscling in?' Ursula's cornflower-blue eyes were coolly levelled at him.

'She's the local MP and there's interest in the genre of the political novel – and in any case, why shouldn't she have literary interests?' His wife's expression told him exactly what she thought of all politicians, female friends of his or not.

She put back the lid on the marmalade jar which he traditionally left off and remarked, 'I've got better things to do that evening. But it is one of the very few nights you can have here with us in your own house. I'm not really sure why you still call this place your home.'

'Sorry, sweetheart, it's just a one-off.'

There was no question but that Ursula was assuming an affair. She had a husband who was absent in every way and she was for once facing that fact more squarely in the eye.

The girls came back in the kitchen and no more was said. He

left for London on Monday morning; life back in its rhythm. She gave him a fruitcake to take with him; she didn't always, not since the Monday Victoria first came to the flat. At the door she kissed him goodbye with her usual lack of emotion.

The week got underway but Jim had nothing further to report on any Chalfern–Downsland links. William wondered whether he was standing back. There had been a slight air of tension since the assistant editor's sacking, cautious murmuring like an uncertain audience at a lecture. Jack had been liked. But he was too ineffectual and lacking in colour, his popularity limited, William thought. The mood would ease; the Jack issue would soon fade. It had been right, he wasn't questioning his own judgement, but he still felt uncomfortable and bad at himself. Sacking was rough.

On Wednesday William's accountant rang with some hot news on Harold Reid. His young mole in the Chief Accountant's office at Reid's company had found what would make all things possible. It was vital evidence, rough sheets of stock valuations that had been altered and could nail a cheating crook. Any vague Chalfern concerns faded.

William didn't sleep much that night but by early morning the altered valuation sheets were on their way to being in the *Post*'s possession. He couldn't have felt more on a high.

Victoria was pleased for him but far too worried about Guy Harcourt's appointment of Reid to the Audit Commission and his loss of face if Reid were exposed. She feared he would blame it all on her and try to get even by any means. William was tempted to retort that Harcourt could get stuffed, but curbed his natural abrasiveness, she had shown such understanding about Jack.

She seemed concerned about her monthly questions session in

Parliament the day before. Her Shadow, Rufus Coram, had apparently raised Downsland and taken a swipe at their relationship. William's thoughts swung back to Chalfern's supposed links. He hadn't told Victoria, hadn't wanted to get her too alarmed but it seemed likely Rufus had been hinting at that, rather than having a dig at the two of them.

He thought of checking on Rufus's question and brought up www.hansard.com on his screen. Everything said in Parliament was there for all to see, recorded word for word.

Mr Rufus Coram: 'The Government is due to announce its five-year housing target: will the Minister take into account the likelihood of Downsland going ahead and can she tell us of any high-level or personal representations she has received?'

The Housing Minister Mrs James: 'The Honourable Gentleman well knows that with the report on the public enquiry as yet unpublished I can make no comment on Downsland.'

William felt sure something was up. But Reid was so much the hot issue at this moment, the lawyers needed to be squared before he could alert the Serious Fraud Office. And he still had to write his speech for the literary festival that weekend.

The sponsors and organizers of the festival were offering special weekend packages, hoping to make the event a big draw. He and Victoria were speaking either side of a drinks reception; she at six, he at eight, and both had been invited to a small dinner afterwards. A crack public relations firm had been employed and William cynically wondered if it was hoped their joint presence would create spin-off publicity. If so, it was working. A posse of press and flashing cameras were waiting as William walked up to the hotel's front door.

Those reporters who knew him yelled out cheerful jibes. 'You've missed half her speech, Bill, is she staying for yours?' Others were less good-natured.

He pushed through into a well-appointed reception and waited with the organizers for Victoria to finish and the audience to spill out. More people kept arriving; it was going to be quite a crush. He thought though, they could have a private word. Margie had checked and been assured that no press would be allowed in the reception.

As the clapping died and swing doors were pinned back, a young man with fair hair and rimless glasses was the first out. He introduced himself as Jason, Victoria's agent, and was giving a clear impression that he thought William very important in her life, a man to make contact with. He seemed under no illusions.

William couldn't get to her; Victoria was being fêted, busy with people asking questions. She was looking beautiful, sylph-like in a fitted black dress but very pale, he thought, almost as white as the day after her fall.

He wanted to know she was all right and to have a moment alone, but she came up to him with an elderly couple – her Chairman and his wife, Giles and Margaret Royston.

'Everyone's dying to meet you,' Margaret said breathlessly. 'We're all huge *Firing Line* fans!' She kept him talking long enough for Victoria to have got surrounded by others again.

The modern extension of the country-house hotel was overheated and very crowded. Victoria was surrounded; William talked to a whiskery octogenarian who told him jovially how much they approved of their MP, and then to an ample woman in puce who asked, trotting alongside him, if he wore make-up on television. He was desperate.

He had almost reached Victoria again when he saw with alarm that she was in difficulties. Her pallor was more pronounced, her luminous skin damp-looking and drained; she was about to faint. As she started swaying, her eyelids fluttering, he lunged forward and caught her just as her legs were giving way. He stood supporting her against him, casting round in helpless panic for help.

'We must get her lying down,' the lady in puce said efficiently, taking charge. She held open the nearby swing doors and he lifted Victoria's limp body and went through, back into the conference hall, where he laid her on an expanse of carpeted flooring.

It had all happened so quickly, and only a small circle had noticed. Margaret Royston, who had followed through the doors, said reassuringly, 'Just a little faint. She probably hasn't eaten all day and it's so hot out there. She's stirring now, she'll be fine.'

Victoria was trying to sit up. William knelt beside her and started smoothing her hand. 'Are you all right? Don't rush it; you gave us quite a shock.'

'Mr Osborne was so quick, the way he spotted you were going,' the lady in puce said admiringly. He had half-forgotten she was there. 'Do you think, dear,' she added smiling, 'you could be pregnant?'

His pulse started to race but Victoria handled it marvellously. 'I very much doubt that, Edith,' she laughed, 'at my age! I must get back now, so everyone can see I'm fine; we don't want rumours starting with so many press here.'

William gave his talk, Victoria listening. She had insisted she was fine, perfectly well enough, and stayed for the dinner. Sitting next to William, her colour was back, the glow that he loved, but after the main course he tore himself away. He didn't want them to be seen leaving at the same time.

Driving back, he thought obsessively about the pregnancy remark. It was vital he talked to Victoria. There must be a way. Could they meet at Dinah's house? If Di picked her up, if he made his own way there? He drove on, refining the detail in his mind.

A new thought began pressing on his consciousness that caused his grip on the wheel to tighten, his knuckles showing white. She wouldn't have had instant cover from the pill; it could just as easily be Barney's baby as his own.

She might not be pregnant – but he knew in his heart she was. Establishing the paternity would be a messy business – and what if the worst happened and it wasn't his? If she wanted to keep it, as he thought she would – what then?

CHAPTER 35

Victoria dressed in the bathroom as quietly as she could; she was feeling sick and wanted to get downstairs without waking Barney. It wouldn't do if he heard her throwing up and then word of her faint got back to him from the village.

It would hurt him unbearably, she thought. He would insist the baby was his, not William's. She wasn't even certain she was pregnant; her first priority was to find out.

Barney appeared at the bathroom door. 'You had a successful evening? A jolly time?'

'Yes, it all went fine, very hot and crowded. And you? I didn't hear you come in. 'Were you very late?'

'I drank myself into a stupor at the golf-club dinner with old Dick, if that's what you mean. He's wretched about June – we had a great time.'

Victoria's nausea was hovering. 'I'll just get breakfast going,' she said, pushing past.

They read the Sunday papers, always an escape from talking. She said to Barney finally, 'I'm planning to stay down tonight; I've got one of those routine breast checks tomorrow. Will you stay too, darling?'

'You hardly said that with enthusiasm. I'll go tonight, I think. Might stay for supper.'

He left at ten that evening after an unbearably ill-at-ease day, and minutes later she had a nasty shock. The Press Office called. Angie said the *Courier* had a story about a Roland Chalfern, a client of Barney's, having Downsland connections and they were going to splash it. It was Victoria's worst fear. She told Angie that Roland Chalfern was indeed a client, but that she knew nothing of any links.

They worked on a statement to put out. She talked to Marty too, and told him she would be late in, but would immediately get to grips with the problem then.

With Barney professing unconvincingly to know nothing, she had a sleepless night. She couldn't talk to William, who was at home with Ursula, but felt sure he'd have told her anything he knew. It would all have to wait till morning. The feeling of crisis was unendurable. She might not even be pregnant and that would hurt far, far more.

She was at the doctor's surgery in Ferndale by eight, but there were still others ahead of her. She had time to slip out to the newsagents next door and buy the *Courier*. The front-page story alleged personal links with Roland Chalfern who stood to make a vast fortune if Downsland got the go-ahead. She was deeply embroiled, the paper said, and her position as Housing Minister was under serious question. She read on but the print began blurring and the walls closing in. Her new closeness to Nattie, the longed-for baby, all the joy was being wrung out of her, and reading the callously-worded story she still felt vulnerably in the dark, at a loss as to what it was all about.

'Twenty-two anywhere?' the receptionist called. Victoria saw it was the number on her tab-ring. She thrust the hateful paper in her bag and went in to see Dr Booth.

He was a kind, experienced country doctor and she felt able to explain that for personal and professional reasons she needed the result to be kept absolutely confidential. He promised to call with the result himself.

The drive from his surgery to London in the Monday traffic was a nightmare. The office, Angie, Barney, every media outlet, the Downing Street Press Unit, had all been trying to reach her. Her voicemail was full. She knew nothing of any links and waves of nausea were washing over her. She needed William.

When he called she said in a panic, 'For God's sake tell me what's going on!'

'It seems Chalfern's Company Secretary let slip something at a Rotary dinner,' he explained, 'and the councillor he spoke to smartly passed it to your crafty Shadow Rufus. He in turn has given it exclusive to the *Courier* – but nobody knows what. They're wetting themselves with excitement having such a scoop. We're working on it, I'm doing all I can.' William paused. 'Are you feeling better? Are you managing all right?'

'I'll have a result very soon.' She knew William must be incredibly tense to be asking so obliquely; she understood him completely.

'We've got to meet, we must talk,' he said urgently.

'How can we possibly do that? I'm in the biggest crisis of my whole career and it's going to get worse. There'll be a debate.'

'I've thought of a way; I've enlisted Di's help. You'll see off Rufus in any debate, you've got right on your side and you can honestly say you had no idea.'

'And since when has a politician ever been believed? Don't be funny.'

It was the worst day of her working life. And at home Barney compounded it. He confessed to Chalfern's having shares in the biggest consortium. She couldn't believe he had kept it from her, even lied, telling her at the very outset there were no links. She stormed at him and then burst into bitter tears. The feeling preyed on her though, that much more than a hefty share-holding must be involved – bad as that was. The *Courier* was far too juiced-up, and seeing Rufus at the Commons that afternoon, he had been looking very bushy-tailed.

That night at home she tore into Barney. 'You must know things you're not telling!'

'I don't, I promise. He's a comparatively new client, he's given us most of his business but there could be hangovers, past deals I don't know about . . .' Barney tailed off.

'Find out!' she screamed.

On Thursday, the Chief Whip confirmed there would be an Opposition debate. 'It won't be a vicar's picnic,' he said heartlessly. 'They're cocky – it's next Wednesday.'

A debate on a Wednesday would be right after Prime Minister's Questions, the Chamber packed, maximum press exposure. How could she possibly clear her name?

Dr Booth called with a positive result. William wouldn't want a disgraced ex-Minister as the mother of his baby, she thought bitterly. She told him about the call, the confirmation she was pregnant, saying quickly afterwards it was best talked about when they met.

Nothing had been said since, but she could sense his reserve and unhappiness; the tension between them was growing. His feelings for her were strong and passionate, but was her very success in part the attraction? She was a Minister, thought to be showing great promise, but what if she were written off as a grasping, greedy failure? No matter that there wasn't a grain of truth in all the allegations, mightn't it make him want to back away?

Could she blame him? He was married, an upholder of justice on *The Firing Line*. To be coupled with a failed Minister whose behaviour was thought reprehensible would make his life impossibly hard. She wanted to believe his feelings went deeper. Hers did. She loved him as he was, certainly not perfect. If he walked away, it would break her heart.

On Monday night, two days before the debate, she tried to slip out of the Commons for her planned meeting with William, but Simon Elliot, the Deputy Chief Whip, was watching her movements very closely. It was vital for her to get away and she led Simon a song and dance, into a bar, then the library. He could lick his chops over her downfall, she thought toughly, but he wasn't stopping her seeing the father of her unborn child.

Eventually, a persistent backbencher cornered Simon and she fled to the underpass, grateful. Hurrying through it, she thought of Chalfern being away in Spain. He was due back the day before the debate and had agreed to see Barney. It was an eleventh-hour ray of hope for possible enlightenment, if not for skin-saving. She felt powerless as a piece of thistledown.

Di was waiting in her car on the Embankment just as planned.

'Cheer up, you old prude,' she said as they shot off in the direction of Chelsea.

'Would you be shouting for joy if every national newspaper was writing you off as dishonest and done-for?'

'It'll be fine on the night,' Di assured with less than her usual conviction. 'Gerald and I are going out,' she said, parking her Fiat in a residents' bay.

William was there, standing with Gerald in the sitting room. Victoria thought of having a son with his looks, his good straight nose, those steady eyes that had been watching the door and trained on her as she walked in.

'Hurry up, Gerald,' Di nagged. 'We'll miss our table.'

It felt strange being alone together, the first time since the church car park. William was still staring at her. 'You'll manage the debate,' he said gravely.

'Bugger the debate, I can't think about that. I can't stand the way you've been so distant. I want this baby, it's the greatest joy imaginable. It's an extension of you; it's us, ours.' She was in this now, she thought, pouring out her feelings, laying herself bare. 'I need you to be sharing the thrill – sorry, but that's how I feel. I have to say it, I . . .' She faltered, in danger of letting out tears.

He took hold of her shoulders and touched her lips. 'Come and sit down,' he said. They went to the sofa. He was framing difficult words, she thought in panic, as he picked up her hand. 'It's not that I don't want you to have it, it's not knowing it's mine.'

She stared. With all that was going on, his most obvious fear simply hadn't crossed her mind. 'Of course it's yours!' she exclaimed. 'That's the least of our worries. After Milan with the chance I was pregnant, I didn't have sex with Barney. The baby's yours. But you mustn't feel tied or responsible in any way. If you don't think you can leave Ursula, you needn't be at all involved.'

It was a desperate thing to have to say but she couldn't let there be any doubt.

William looked angrier than she had ever seen him. 'You mean you'd pass it off as Barney's?'

'I'd rather that than be told to get rid of it.' He got up and crossed the floor in his fury, but she stayed sitting and went on, 'It's yours; the problems are huge but can't you feel any joy? You must feel something.' She wondered if he was even listening, he was still so white with rage.

He stared back at her from the fireplace. 'And when Barney gets to know, will you tell him it's mine?'

'I won't need to, he'll be under no illusions. It'll hurt him terribly, as for so long he's wanted another. But what he'd hate above all is people speculating that it's yours. If he discovers I'm pregnant before I leave, then he'll want to keep up the façade and be a proud father. He wants to stay married. He could love a baby that was yours, you see?'

'You'd love my children. I already feel love for Nattie, that's a non-point.'

'What *is* the point, then?'

'I think half of you still wants to go on living with him and you'll never leave.'

'It hasn't been the right time – though of course,' she smiled wryly, 'since every paper says my days as a Minister are numbered, the right time might be any day now.'

He was back at her side. 'Have you given the slightest thought to how you're going to manage in your condition? You might faint in the middle of your debate.'

'That wouldn't help my chances. But I'm made of tough stuff.'

'I can't quite feel all the joy yet,' he said, pulling her into his arms. 'There are so many problems,' he leaned back, taking her with him and kissed her, 'like you not being able to lie on top of me like this when you get too big a lump.'

'I didn't get very big the first time round.'

'If he's a son he's called Charlie,' William said.

'Don't I get a say in this?'

'No, you've done quite enough talking. It's my turn now.'

CHAPTER 36

After Victoria left in a taxi William walked on a while down the King's Road. The heatwave had arrived; it was muggy. The air felt tropical. How long would it take for the press to get the story? He desperately wanted not to have to tell Ursula sooner than planned, knowing he could sort out his life much better when he had time off in August. And he had a more pressing priority, to get Victoria away from Barney.

The bastard must have known about Chalfern. Barney would have arse-licked and promised delivery: 'I'll fix it, I'll see she's sound; no worries there.' It wasn't so much for the pay-off, William thought, as Barney's need to impress. He wanted people to love him.

Thinking of the baby, William believed now that it was truly his and the certainty was bringing an extraordinary feeling, making him light as air one minute, and bowed down with the weight of reality the next.

He thought of her debate. She was in a hole and the press were throwing bricks; they were convinced Rufus would make mincemeat of her in Wednesday's debate. The entire media pack, that was, except the *Post*. William was taking a different line and giving her the benefit, but being a lone voice and out of kilter was losing him a lot of ground.

The office certainly thought he was letting his affair influence his judgment. Jim had said as much in conference. 'Chalfern's a close personal friend of hers, Bill, and we're the only ones not saying so. It's relevant and I've had it confirmed. Guy Harcourt told me it's true last night. It's solid fact.'

'Solid as a smoke-ring,' he had muttered with his inside knowledge of her single meeting with Chalfern. 'You're slipping, Jim, if you believe a word Harcourt says.'

'They've got something big and they'll make it stick. They say she's neck-high in shit. We'll lose out. She's history after that debate, hung out to dry.'

'What if she comes out of that debate smelling of roses? Her career's on the line and *that's* the story. We're having no fucking hearsay about "close friends".'

He flagged down a cab and told it to go to the office. It would be bad for his authority if she didn't clear her name. If he was to be vindicated in his stance, she had to cut them right down to stubble. Hard to see how she could. The media had the scent of the kill; a glamorous Minister sacked for corruption was good, hot, easy copy.

Paying off his cab, William thought the Harold Reid story could get buried with all the attention focused elsewhere. He might need it to salvage some pride, so he decided it was best held over until Victoria's fate was known.

Calling on the morning of the debate, he felt unsure whether to sound confident or commiserating, the papers were so bad. He worried about her stamina in her condition.

She didn't sound low and she had some news. 'I've found out more. I'm not sure how much knowing will help though. I can't plead ignorance now.'

'Can you tell me?' His journalist's blood was up instantly.

'Barney's been amazing – he got it out of Chalfern late last night.' William seethed. That shit kicked away her precarious foothold and then got the kudos for throwing a rope. 'He really had no idea,' she said defensively, sensing his thoughts, 'but you see, Chalfern owns *all* the land earmarked for Downsland – the fields, farm cottages, the lot. The winning consortium would have to buy it all from him before they can lay a brick – and at what premium! He's had the landholdings for years, long before he came to Simmonds and Key. I'm quite sure Barney didn't know. Look – I've worked out a strategy. I'm about to go and discuss it with Ned. I just hope it comes off!'

Having failed to break in on the *Courier*'s story, William felt spare, soured-up; he didn't even ask her plan. He bitterly resented her warmth and gratitude to Barney. 'Good luck,' he said stiffly. 'Keep strong, it'll be fine.' Then he clicked off.

He felt as low as could be. Inside knowledge so late in the day couldn't help much in the debate. The mud would stick; Barney had a lot to answer for. Half-listening to some political commentary on his office television, William was thinking how GD's file was building. There were ways of getting Barney, of sorting out Victoria's life and settling a fistful of scores.

William heard the commentator saying the Housing Minister was expected to have resigned by the day's end, and suddenly burned to have been more supportive. He rang back in a frenzy; she would have left, she'd be with Ned. 'Thank God you're still there!' he said when she answered. 'You'll do it; you'll see 'em off. Remember I love you and I'm holding you tight.'

'I never thanked you for playing it straight in the paper; that meant a lot.'

'Don't stick to any speech, say it from the heart. Do it for Charlie.'

'Or Charlotte or Charlene?'

'Not Charlene,' he said.

He had got Margie to clear the lunch-hour; he felt justified in watching the debate. It was news, tomorrow's headlines.

They'd been having a team meeting and those in his office stayed. Prime Minister's Questions had been on and they'd had half an ear if not an eye to the television but a hot news debate had all their attention. George brought up a chair and the others gathered round.

William left his desk and stood behind them. The Prime Minister had taken his last question but he hadn't left the Chamber. They all knew what that meant and there was fresh interest, a strong frisson. If Victoria James was thought to be toast, the PM would have gone straight off and offered no supportive presence. The business of politics was rough.

Victoria was seated beside him on the bench with Ned on her other side; she was looking very slim in her light-grey suit – too pale, though.

Jim was over in the Press Gallery, pen poised. And Marty would be there too, William thought, in the little box reserved for officials.

The Chamber was packed, the buzz was leaping off the screen. He could understand the lure of politics, what it must be like to triumph in that close intimate atmosphere, to win hearts and face down a hostile opposition.

The Speaker nodded. 'Mr Rufus Coram.'

Rufus got to his feet. He spread his fingers down the sides of the despatch box; this was his big chance to shine. He lacked some indefinable quality, William thought, and decided it was dignity; Rufus was no great statesman-in-waiting. Victoria was looking very white but fainting would send all the wrong signals. It would be a disaster, she had to last out.

'The Honourable Lady, the Minister for Housing, has some awkward questions to answer,' Rufus began. 'It seems her delicate snout has been sniffing out some tasty truffles; they're buried in the country, in a very choice piece of land.' The benches behind him egged him on and he got into his stride. He spoke of her concealment of the considerable fortune her husband's client – a close family friend – stood to make from the sale of that land; he suggested that friend would feel quite a debt of gratitude.

Opposition fingers jabbed. Rufus concluded by saying the Government had plumbed new lows and then sat down looking well pleased with himself, sleekly coated in complacency. William thought it an ill-crafted speech, but knew Rufus was banking on substance and killer darts. The Government benches were totally silenced, looking glum. The group in his office were silent too; they well understood the deadliness of Rufus's darts.

'Looks bad for her,' the Picture Editor said awkwardly. They were all itching to say she was done for, William thought, longing to turn and see how he was taking it.

'Dynamite stuff, this,' George said, unable to stop looking round.

William ignored them all; Victoria was on her feet at the despatch box. The tension was getting to him and he brought up a chair, crossing his fingers under its seat.

She tidied her papers, took a sip of water and began. 'I have been given the immense privilege of this job, but the Honourable Gentleman seems to think I might have acted less than honourably.' She was so white, William willed her to find reserves. 'But has he, I wonder, while he's been so busily scraping barrels, lost sight of the heart of the matter, the true concerns – how Downsland would affect people's lives? Young families are living with no space for a buggy; children are skateboarding beside juggernauts. Yet we have a vital responsibility, a debt to future generations to conserve our glorious countryside and its precious wildlife. The Honourable Gentleman opposite has been having fun but the things that really matter – air free of diesel fumes, hedgerows, bluebell woods – and the need for decent homes – these things have simply passed him by.'

She was sounding confident but moral indignation alone wouldn't do it.

George said, 'Fighting talk. Rufus is looking a bit set-faced but she'll have to come up with more than that.' He never knew when to fucking shut up, William thought.

Victoria carried on, her voice sounding clear and confident. 'I had no idea until last night – and nor did my husband – that his client had landholdings in the area. They were bought prior to any involvement with my husband's firm. I give this House my word on—' She was interrupted as an Opposition Member sprang up and intervened.

'Can the Housing Minister tell us the extent of her relationship with Roland Chalfern?' Rufus looked intensely irritated. It was an unhelpful question from his own side. He knew Chalfern was no close family friend all right, William thought.

'I have met him *once*,' she responded. All the glum faces were now on the other side, and William saw each of his executives sit or lean forward. The dynamics were changing.

The Prime Minister, he noted, was sitting straight, looking serene. 'But of course I know that more than my word is required to satisfy the Honourable Members opposite,' Victoria said, 'and I have therefore taken the necessary action.' William, too, sat forward now, feeling frustrated and in the dark. If he hadn't been privately cursing Barney so bitterly, he would have certainly asked the plan.

Victoria continued, 'As I have said, the landholdings were unknown to my husband and his firm. Today, I can announce that Simmonds and Key have undertaken not to act in any single transaction involving Downsland.' There was an audible intake of breath. 'And in the light of this,' she said with a smile, 'my Right Honourable Friend, the Secretary of State, has asked me to continue to play my full part in the Downsland process. I am, of course, delighted to do so.'

The Opposition benches looked disbelieving, like vultures whose apparently dead prey had soared into flight. On her side there were loud cheers and the waving of order papers.

William felt an exquisite blend of pride and relief. But he had two disparate thoughts: one, that he hadn't a hope now of getting Victoria away from Barney before Downsland, and two, that the appalling monstrous Chalfern was just as likely to win his vast fortune as not.

Victoria was rounding off her speech, saying that a development that would so profoundly affect people's lives was a decision the Government would never take lightly. William forgot his executives and openly smiled; she was sounding so sweetly pompous.

She sat down to a rowdy House and the BBC's commentator said over the din, 'Well, the Housing Minister has just completely confounded her critics! That's the Secretary of State, Ned Markham, giving her a steadying hand; she is looking a little white and wobbly, but for all the difficult ordeal, she's come through with honour restored.'

She was looking as faint as she had at the literary festival. William went to his desk and, using his mobile, quickly sent her a text: *Hang on in there, not around to catch you. Charlie very proud.*

Headlines were tossed around at the evening conference.

George suggested, 'Victoria Victorious!' It was met with justified groans.

Jim was just back from the Commons and offered a contribution. 'Rufus the Rueful? It's how I feel – you were right about her smelling of roses, Bill. She surprised us all!'

It was a graceful concession. William thought it was generally assumed he'd had inside knowledge, but far from that, he had feared being loyal was putting his professional head on the block. He looked confidently round the table and enjoyed claiming the last word. 'Rufus Rues the Day,' he said. 'We'll go with that.'

CHAPTER 37

The morning after her big triumph Victoria was reading the Inspector's report on Downsland, ignoring the headlines and sketch-writers' of praise. No basking, she was straight back in the working groove. Bending over the report concentrating though, the familiar wave of nausea overtook her and she sat up to let the moment pass. It had been leaning over her notes that had so nearly done for her in the debate. William's message had come just in time.

She had found the extra reserves. It had been that inbuilt instinct for survival, she thought, giving her the last-minute career-saving idea of going over Barney's head and appealing directly to Hugh. The hope and prayer that he would rise to the occasion, that there was more to Hugh than blandness and ultra-conventionality.

He had risen like a stallion, taken an instant decision and been truly decent and unselfish. Barney's hurt pride and anger at her action was the only sadness.

Marty must have come in silently; he was standing in front of her desk. 'You're a little pale, Minister, are you all right? Can I get you a glass of water or anything?'

'I'm fine, just a tiny turn.' She indicated the Inspector's report. 'And it's not to do with this, I promise. He makes a convincing case for allowing the development, Marty, but I'm not entirely happy. I'd really like to go and see the site for myself. Would it be a real headache if I made a low-key private visit?'

'It would be unusual, but I think it could be arranged. Tim or I would come, of course, and there would have to be an official along – someone who knows the site. Colin Smith, perhaps, he's very reliable; he could take you round in a Land Rover.' Marty's weight shifted. 'I really would advise against it, but of course, the decision is yours. If you do go, it would be very important to avoid any word getting out in advance. You'd be spotted immediately you were there, of course, but it would give the rent-a-mobs and deputations little time to gather forces.' He gave one of his distracted White Rabbit smiles.

Marty's strong stand was unusual, his misgivings clear. He was a natural worrier though, and she needed to go; it was important to her. He would come round.

She was still feeling quite sick and the heatwave wasn't helping. At nearly twelve weeks the nausea should soon be over, she thought.

William had reported that morning that the watch on the flat was being reduced. It was to be Tuesday to Thursday – on the basis that Monday was late voting and her weekends were spent in Hampshire. Whether it was her new shining-virtue image, whatever the reason, somehow they had worn the *Courier* down. She was worried about seeing him. Were they tempting providence, with the Downsland decision so close?

He was splashing the Harold Reid story on Monday and citing all the evidence. It was a great coup he'd be making as well as breaking the news. Guy Harcourt would know how long such damaging stuff must have taken to collect; he would feel certain of her prior knowledge of Reid's unsuitability and aware that she could have warned him. Guy's ruthless desire to get even, Victoria thought, would be untrammelled.

She went to the constituency next day in the continuing heatwave. Feeling too hot for comfort she was also nervous about the weekend. Her stomach might still be flat, but her breasts were impressively larger. Barney might start asking questions, and any answers she gave could only cause him real pain. How she handled it was vitally important. The timing, too, was terrible; he was feeling so wounded that she had gone over his head to Hugh. It had been the only way, but in normal circumstances *he* should have been the one discussing such things with his senior partner. It was the worst thing for Barney's highly developed sense of inadequacy.

The little constituency office was stiflingly airless. Jason had great moon-shaped patches of damp under his arms. He was in exhaustingly good spirits; his relief, she thought, at her coming out like the baking sun from behind the stormy clouds of imminent political wilderness. He chivvied her along as usual, anxious that she wasn't late for her lunch with the Editor of the local paper.

Dermot was already at Betty's Fish Plaice. It was his turn to buy lunch and he had reserved a shady garden-table, for which in the extreme heat she felt undyingly grateful.

He was a big bearded bear of a man; well disposed, though most of his reporters were politically less so. They talked about the literary festival and she plugged their fundraising summer fête. 'It's being opened by Fred Buckley,' she pressed hopefully.

'Great Home Secretary in his day,' her bearded host commented. He looked at his monkfish kebabs and then up at her. 'I thought perhaps you should know there's a girl from the *Sunday Courier* down here. She's badgered us no end about William Osborne being seen in the area – *not* just at the festival. We've had no word of sightings and told her so, but she's still going round knocking on doors and asking questions.'

'Thanks, good of you to tell me,' Victoria said, wondering what the odds were on the girl encountering young Luke's mother. There was no proof, with luck, and nothing to be done about it anyway. But it could get the press more actively on their tails again.

When Barney arrived at the cottage he made straight for a cold beer. He downed it in seconds and crunching the can, lobbed it successfully into a distant swing-bin. He had a disproportionate look of satisfaction and pride and it brought back memories of her brother and his friends showing off such skills. She thought of Nattie being brotherless. Charlie wouldn't quite fill the role; Nattie would be more of an aunt than a sister.

Nattie was hating school. Seb had taken up with a girl in her year, an easy lay, and he was cruelly spreading stories making comparisons. It was as bad as Nattie had feared. William said there was no practical action she could take, just love and support, but Victoria wished Seb could get a bit of what she thought he deserved. She decided it was too soon to tell Nattie about the baby; she just hoped the press wouldn't sensationally do it for her.

Barney took a bottle of Sauvignon out of the fridge and uncorked it. He poured two glasses and went with his to stand in the open door out to the back garden. He stared across at her. 'You're pregnant, aren't you?'

Even anticipating it, she felt nakedly unprepared. 'Yes. I've seen Doctor Booth.'

'But you didn't think of passing on your news? Perhaps you told Hugh Simmonds – or one of your other friends. What are you, let me see, about twelve weeks?' He was taking it back to Milan. The hurt look in his eyes was that of a thrashed dog's, but he could be so menacing when he chose. 'Tell me,' he said icily, 'do you get maternity leave? Does a Minister temp for a Minister? Or do they give you the sack?'

'I haven't thought about any of that,' she said truthfully.

Barney left his position and came to lean against the fridge. Emotion was slowly seeping out of him like blood from a cut finger. 'Well, well, baby-buggies in the hall! Dick will be amazed when I tell him.' His eyes were hard as he falsely smiled.

Was he thinking that talking about it was a way of establishing claim? She wasn't sure if he could yet have focused on the media's voracious appetite for gory detail. They, too, could count the weeks back to Milan.

She gave him a rueful smile. 'It might be best not telling anyone till after my Downsland decision. I'll be right back in the news and you can't, I'm afraid, discount any press speculation. All that attention they gave my Milan visit – and the press with an idea in their heads are like ants on a path. There's no stopping them!' She had to warn him, though it was cruelly making him face the facts and salt his own wounds.

The back door was about to bang; he went to prop it or close it but he stood holding it open and looking out, keeping his back to her. She stared past him into the small garden with his herbs and potato patch, out to the dusky purple fields beyond. It was still light, nine o'clock on a summer evening. Would he swing round with some violent reaction that might harm the baby? She froze and fastened her eyes on the small pile of strawberry tops on the chopping board in front of her.

'When are you going to tell Nattie?' he asked. 'Or have you already done so?'

It was unexpected. 'No. Possibly after her exams — what do you think?'

'She was very knocked by the Seb break-up, she's got quite enough on her plate.'

He was implying it would be another bad knock, his daughter made to suffer too. His tone was reproachful, hangdog even, and Victoria's state of fear turned full circle to one of resentful frustration. He wasn't blameless, he played around, he was exploitative whenever it suited; even without William filling her life she couldn't have gone on.

He said, 'You want to keep it?'

'Yes.' She felt cruel, saying it and longed to lessen the pain. 'Can we, perhaps, just get through the next weeks and think more about things later on?'

He would agree to that, she thought. He would want to postpone the life-changing agonising upheaval ahead.

He went back to the fridge for the wine bottle. 'It's late,' he said. 'We'd better have supper. I brought down the rest of that salmon — there's enough for tonight.'

She got up and went to the fridge; he was beside it and she touched his arm. He seemed transfixed and stared down at her hand. Letting it rest there and looking at him, forcing some eye-contact, she smiled. 'We'll face all the problems in time, darling – shall we have a little hug now?' He held her a moment, stiffly, then turned away and poured himself another glass of wine.

CHAPTER 38

William felt confident of GD's intelligence about the times the flat was being watched. He had sussed it out for himself, anyway – seen someone on midweek days but not on a Monday – and had finally persuaded Victoria to come there again. He decided to use Dave for cover when he was leaving the office that evening and ask to be dropped at the Travellers' Club. Then he could double back on foot to his flat.

He felt ablaze all day at the thought of seeing her, completely distracted. The Harold Reid story was finally out – in big black headlines, front-page news. It was a massive scoop, a huge triumph for the *Post* and he planned for it to fill the paper all week.

His need of Victoria was empowering, a spur that made him feel driven to achieve all his ends. Never lacking in strong conviction, he was now coming to value, even to rely on, her take on things. It gave him a moment's pause before leaping in.

Dave dropped him at the Travellers', he went in to the bar, sat down, studied his diary with a frown, stood up again and left. He walked fast, keeping an eye out for Dave or anyone else, and resisted an urge to buy flowers to avoid drawing attention to himself.

Waiting for Victoria – before hearing the lift-shaft cranking up so slowly, so creakily he wanted to erupt with impatience – he thought how much easier life would have been, his distress over the debate and the baby, had he only been able to see her.

And now he was doing just that. He gave a momentary thought to her condition but he was beyond any restraining influences as they reunited, and leaving a trail of tie, jacket and kicked-off shoes, he just had to get her to the bedroom. The scent of her, the feel, her exquisite softness . . . he was living the intoxicating moments. The feeling reached into his very fibres: it reverberated. As he lay recovering fatherhood was in the jumble of his thoughts.

She was tucked in against him, his arm resting comfortably across her. Her breath was light and even on his chest – his own was still shaky. He felt a huge outflow of tenderness and he even had a spark of genuine sympathy for Barney, thinking of the pain of knowing the baby wasn't his.

Victoria hitched up on an elbow. 'I'm going to Downsland,' she said carefully.

That shook him out of his luxuriant torpor. 'For God's sake! It would be madness.' He hitched up too, sharply brought back, having instant thoughts of a confrontation with Ursula. 'The media out in force, deputations, the Vicar and the DAG turning up it would be bedlam. And you're pregnant,' he reminded her, 'you can't possibly take the risk.'

'I need to go. I'll make sure it isn't leaked.'

'Don't be mad. Of course it will get out – you know how these things work.'

'You're the only one who knows – and Marty.'

'And? And?' He made an impatient beckoning gesture. 'Come on, think of some more!'

'Well, Tim and one very reliable official, I suppose.' She looked peeved. 'And before you start off again, the only possible day is on our joint birthday.'

He sat up, completely infuriated. 'How can I possibly see you if you've just been to Downsland? The whole media circus would be jumping though hoops. It's our fucking birthday! I can't not see you, it means so much.'

'You can't be this sentimental! And the very fact of us sharing the same day will have the press even more on the lookout.' She had a point there. 'We'll have our private party another day. I do want to go to Downsland, please, don't be difficult.'

'You do realize Ursula might come,' he said defiantly, and earned himself a rather touching, sad look.

Victoria got up. 'I know,' she said, starting to dress. 'But it's still something I feel I must do. It's late – I've got to vote. Harold Reid's been all the talk – everyone's agog,' she added, 'it's really shaken them all up. But think of me tomorrow when Guy Harcourt has slept on it and worked out that I must have known. He will be much criticized for appointing Reid, by Parliament and the press – by the *Post* too, I expect. I dread to think what he'll do.'

They had a last kiss at the door. William hoped GD had his ducks in a row and the flat *wasn't* being watched. Thinking he'd heard the clunk of the main door, he opened his own and keenly listened. He kept his arm round Victoria; it was hard letting go. The lift hadn't started up though, so it must have been for a down-stairs flat, or more likely he had just been mistaken.

He heard bounding steps, to his horror and alarm. Then, even before he had time to think, he found himself face-to-face with his own, similarly shocked and startled, son. 'Bit of a surprise this, Tom,' he said, pulling himself together, thinking the boy must have sprinted up five carpeted flights of stairs in a flash.

Tom was full of apologies, 'I tried getting you on the mobile, Dad. I knew it was a long shot coming, but I've just had my wallet nicked, you see, and I was very near.' He was falling over his words, trying to keep his eyes on his father but letting them stray and turning bright pillar-box red.

William had dropped his arm, but he was so embarrassed and slow in making introductions that Victoria had to do it for herself.

'It's good to meet you, Tom.' She held out her hand with her lit-up smile and he took it. 'I should go, though,' she said, 'you'll both have things to talk about and I'm very late for a vote.'

William went to press the lift button for her. 'Go on in, Tom, ' he urged, 'I'll just see Victoria off.' His son stared, but then said goodbye to her with another blushingly shy smile, and went in as told.

Giving her cheek a quick brush, William whispered, 'Sorry. You're OK though – sure?' She nodded. Her eyes went to his socked feet and she gave a whimsical grin. 'I am in a bit of a hole,' he admitted, grinning too, but feeling really bad. 'Call you.'

It can't have come as much of a surprise to Tom, he thought, going in to face his son. Did he apologize, ignore it, say nothing – what the hell was best?

Tom was hovering in the hall. 'I'd been to the National Gallery with two friends, Dad, but I'd got the message they wanted to be alone – I do seem a bit in the wrong places tonight – and then there was my wallet . . . I'm really sorry.'

'No need to say that,' William smiled, trying unobtrusively to upturn his shoes with a foot and put them on. He managed it. His tie was still lying strewn, pointing the way like directional floor lighting towards an open bedroom door and a very mucked-up bed. He wished it wasn't quite so in Tom's face.

'Dad,' his son began awkwardly, 'mightn't someone have been watching the flat?'

William had been prepared, braced, for him to say something about his mother, but Tom was jumping ahead, imagining the head-lines.

'They have been for weeks,' he answered, 'but I'd heard on the grapevine that the tail had just come off. She hasn't been here in so long, you see? It's sort of sod's law.' He picked up his tie and then with an embarrassing worse-than-just-leaving-it backwards shove, got the bedroom door closed. 'Like a beer, whisky?' he offered.

'I'll stick with water, thanks.'

Tom was in a plain US Marine's green T-shirt and beige cargos. He was trying not to say the wrong thing, his open young face anxious. William felt bursting with love, incapable of excuses or apology, but almost needing recriminations and his son's wrath. Telling him to get a bottle of water from the kitchen, he went into the sitting room and poured himself a much needed whisky.

Tom soon seemed more relaxed. With his arms along the back of the sofa and the water bottle tilted loosely, he enthused about iPods. 'Twenty thousand tracks, Dad, and think of all the CD space saved!' He was nineteen and an adult, but he had just virtu-ally seen them in bed together. William longed for some clue to his feelings.

He must have transmitted his need; for Tom brought his arms down from the sofa-back and sat fingering his water-bottle. 'She's very nice, Dad. I thought she'd be more sort of cool and distant. I suppose I got that impression from Mum. What with Downsland and everything, she's – well, not too keen, you might say.'

The 'and everything' stuck out. 'But Mum doesn't actually know,' William said. 'And there's the press – you won't mention meeting Victoria?'

'Of course not, but I don't think Mum's under any illusions.'

'But she hasn't heard it from me, you see?'

Tom looked about to comment but changed his mind. He talked of Harold Reid being a coup. They were both as bad, William thought, skirting round questions and explanations with typically British coyness. It felt wrong though, to leave loose ends to fray.

'It's not some sort of midlife crisis, Tom, it wasn't looked-for. Victoria fought hard against it. I couldn't though, and nor could she in the end. You can be strong-willed, deny yourself, live blamelessly but you can't shut off love if, extraordinarily, it happens. I'm afraid I failed in the strong-will department. Love can be a very selfish emotion.'

Tom stared. Love was a powerful word. Would it clarify things a bit for him and part-condone, even help take some of the sordidness out of the scene in the flat? 'And Mum?' he said, still looking stunned.

'Of course I love Mum, but we've been growing apart for some time now, you must know that?' He nodded. But had love sounded a low demeaning excuse instead of genuine and heartfelt as it was? Tom loved both his parents, but he and William had always been especially close. He passionately hoped his son wouldn't think it an apologist's over-protesting.

They made the calls and cancelled the cards in the nicked wallet. William gave his son some money and saw him off, telling him to take care on the Tube going back to college so late.

Alone, he suddenly felt absolutely shattered, with barely the energy to get to bed. He stretched out, thinking of being in it with Victoria and of love transcending all his many and varied sins.

CHAPTER 39

The day before Downsland Victoria had an ultrasound scan. It indicated that the baby was indeed a boy, but she wanted to tell William face to face.

She woke on her birthday morning feeling wound-up and wistful. Di had done a painting, at a special rate, of the pretty Ferndale church and car park for her to give William, but presents and news of the scan would have to wait for another day.

Leaving early for Downsland, Victoria's nerves were in bad shape. Bob was to drive her to a country pub a few miles from the site. There they would meet up with Tim and Colin, the official whom Marty had thought so reliable, and swap over to the Land Rover. She wished Marty were coming, but he had felt Downsland was really Tim's area.

In the car, Bob handed her a present and card. 'Happy Birthday! Little box of chocs from the missus and me.' Victoria had met his wife at the Christmas party.

'Thanks to both of you,' she said happily.

She would rather a small box of chocolates from Barney than the armfuls of flowers and beautiful gold skein necklace he had given her. A fortieth was special, he'd said, beaming – succeeding resoundingly, as had been the idea, in making her want to crawl into a hole. He really believed if he just persevered, she thought despairingly, they still had the chance of a future together, baby and all.

William called on her mobile. She had half-expected he would, in spite of being in the car with Bob. But it came as a cruel shock that it wasn't about their birthday.

'Your visit is in the *Courier*'s final edition – just a paragraph, they must have got it very late. It's serious. The entire media, the *Post* included, will be hotfooting it to Downsland now. They'll tip off the Reverend Jeremy, Sam Swayne and the rent-a-mobs. There's a real risk of trouble, you've got to turn home.'

It was like an icepack on her skin; she shrank from his news, but said firmly, 'I can't possibly *not* go now – you must see that?'

She got the same news, the same advice from Marty, and argued just as strongly. 'For me not to go now would be the worst of all worlds. I'd be torn apart by the press, and rightly so.'

'We thought that would be your reaction,' Marty said wryly. 'Angie's coming to help with the press and I'm making sure the police are fully informed.'

She imagined meeting Ursula while surrounded by a goading press, and felt shivery in the car's air-conditioning. There was no way out, her professional head told her, but in her private heart she felt terribly fearful and low.

Nick Bates called on her mobile. 'You free to talk? It's possibly urgent, Downsland connected – something it's better you know.'

'I'm in the car,' she said guardedly, thinking it unlikely he had yet seen the *Courier*.

'I was in the Tea Room last night, queuing for a snack. Guy came and stood with me, but I'm sure it was only because Rufus Coram was right behind me and he wanted him to overhear. You know my views on Guy! Anyway, he said, pretending to make a joke of it, the slimy bastard, that from the mysterious blank space in your diary he thought you must be off to Downsland today. Rufus heard him all right; he immediately dropped out of the queue.'

'Thanks, Nick. At least I know now how they got it – it's in this morning's *Courier*, you see. I am on my way there, but so will everyone else be, too. Guy's certainly achieved his ends.'

She called William back, feeling, even with Bob there, in too fuming a white rage not to pass on the intelligence. He indicated that the *Post* might be less than glowing about Guy.

He continued begging her not to go. It was just the sort of hot muggy weather for fraying tempers; it wasn't safe. And he would be out of contact mid-morning, giving the tribute at a journalist friend's memorial service, unable to be reached.

His concern was sobering but she felt obstinately committed and tried hard to focus on Downsland. Out of the car window, South London looked drab and depressingly built-up. She wondered if the clusters of work-bound people waiting at bus stops, all so uninvolved in each other, would sooner live in a flat over the launderette or kebab-shop than a country starter home and commuting?

People had babies, singly or as couples; they divorced. New-build estates were desperately needed.

William had said Ursula's outbursts of temper were rare and she hated making scenes. Would she stay home? In her photograph she was very fair and her serene face gave little away – unlike her own.

Victoria felt a wave of dread, thinking of seeing that face in the crowd.

Leaving Bob's car at the pub felt like letting go of her mother's hand on the first day of school. Victoria sat in the front of the Land Rover with Colin, Tim and Angie in the back, and thought of the barrage of hostility awaiting her. If Guy knew – as he might from all his cosying up to Jim at the *Post* – that Ursula was active in the DAG, he'd soon work out the potential for an explosive scene. She hated to think of him having that added satisfaction.

Colin turned with a smile. 'You're looking glum, Minister. Don't worry; I'm sure we can get a quick look-see before anyone twigs we're here.' She doubted that. 'I've been to the site,' he went on. 'There's a sizable field this side of the ridge that we can drive into – if you can picture the plans. I've cleared it with the farmer. I'll park just below the brow, then you can walk up and get a good view of the whole proposed area. The far side slopes down to the River Traithe. With Sam Swayne's camp sprawled all along the river-bank, and all the dogs, goats and general commotion, the farmer's had to take out his sheep. He's not too pleased about it.'

'He's certainly let me know that,' Victoria said, 'almost daily!'

'They'll be expecting us to come via the main road,' Colin said with confidence.

'Surely the press will be watching all roads?' she suggested dubiously.

'Too right, they will,' Angie chipped in.

'The gate to the field is just coming up now,' Colin said unperturbed, rounding a bend. 'Oops!' he exclaimed, seeing a posse of cameramen leaning on it. He turned with a sheepish grin and slowed to a stop, some distance short.

'We'll give them a photo-op, that should get 'em off our backs,' Angie declared. She strode up, formidably large in a long black cotton shift, waving her arms like a great windmill. 'Cool it you lot, will you?'

Returning with a satisfied look on her face, she said, 'Done! We give them their pics and they'll keep their distance in the field.'

Victoria wasn't convinced. 'I'm not keen, Angie. If I'm gazing out at a nice green field it just invites people to imagine it concreted over.'

'The cameras will be pointing at you, not the effing field.'

Victoria got out, knowing the field would be pictured too, but giving up the fight. She felt quite shaken-up and worried about the baby; the lane had been full of potholes. It was oppressively humid, too. She smoothed down the skirt of her khaki short-sleeved suit; the white T-shirt underneath was sticking to her and she hoped her new cup-size wouldn't cause any comment.

The shouted questions were as provoking as buzzing flies. What message had she for the DAG? Would she be overturning the Inspector's report? She ducked and evaded until Angie finally interposed herself and they could get going. Colin drove in through the gate. The press jumped in their vehicles and followed.

A terrace of farm cottages took up a corner of the field. The farms were all tenanted, the cottages too, probably owned by Chalfern. On the other side of the gate was a Georgian house whose owner insisted he would never move; he'd lie down in front of the bulldozers first, he said. The field had a crop of beet but there was a tractor track round the edge and keeping to it carefully, Colin set off up the hilly field.

Further along the hillside from the field was some ancient

woodland. If the developers had their way, it would disappear. The protestors had complained that if the destruction of rain-forests was condemned, why not the felling of our own fine trees? On paper Victoria had thought it insignificant and had been impatient at all the fuss. Now she felt quite humble, seeing the fine tall ash trees, the beeches, oak, maple and alder. There were the dark shapes of rooks' nests in the top branches and she pictured the rooks circling and cawing at dusk. Where would all the wildlife go?

They bounced on up the drought-hardened field; overtaking the woodland. Distant fields in either direction looked pinky-gold in the hazy sunlight. Downsland would cover many fields. Over the approaching brow, on a rise the far side of the Traithe, was the village of Hemble Benton. Its dominant church spire was just coming into view. William's local town of Brearfield was two miles further on. Near enough, though.

Angie said, 'The coaches are pouring in, I'm told; protesting is so well-organized now, and of course the locals will be out in force.'

'I must have a proper look,' Victoria said, moving to open her door. 'It is helpful coming here; it couldn't be more frustrating about the media, the coaches and crowds, and I know I might have to meet delegations, but there it is.'

Tim leaned forward from the back. 'Marty was very anxious you stay in the car.'

'Marty's always anxious!'

'But there could be trouble and disturbances. He was most insist-ent.'

'I can't refuse to talk to people, Tim. The police have been told.' She got out and he scrambled out too. They walked to the top.

She tried to picture rows of redbrick houses, rectangles of garden, pavements, streetlights. The houses would look out on more soft pink hills, she thought, and children would hear song thrushes in spring – maybe not nightingales – and find frogspawn in the Traithe. Was that a fair exchange for the influx and strains on the infrastructure, the destruction of nesting habitat, the residents of Hemple Benton and Brearfield losing their long-preserved rural idyll?

Glancing behind, she saw Angie was out waving the press back and Colin was turning the Land Rover round. She and Tim were by an open gate; the brow of the hill had been an acoustical brake, but now she was horribly aware of the cacophony of sound. It was the noise of people, vehicles, amplified belted-out rock, hooting horns, belly-yells, children's wails.

The scene spread out below had something about it of Epsom Downs on Derby Day; the sultry heat, the extensive grassy field, lined-up coaches – the smell of frying onions from burger stalls.

There was nothing sunny and race-day-like though, about the disorderly approaching crowd. The protestors fanning out up the hill were like a tanker's spilled load, unstoppable, out of control. Mothers dragged screaming toddlers, there were older children who should have been in school, dogs and goats. And cars were arriving, four-by-fours bumping over the field, local women in flowered frocks climbing out and setting off at a trot.

It was odd how suddenly fear can invade; the body's thudding a warning sound as it garners its reserves; ready for flight, for speed of action. Until that moment Victoria had been feeling confident, almost complacent, but Colin had been reversing for a speedy exit and she knew they had to go.

'I really think, Minister,' Tim was sounding painfully anxious, 'that this isn't wise.' She nodded, but they had missed their chance. The Reverend Jeremy was closing in, trailed by his delegation, all the locals trying to keep up. 'I must get you away, Minister,' Tim pressed urgently. 'There are so few police, I can only see two right down the hill.' He was peering, his eyes watering in the glare.

'Here's more,' she said. A Panda car had been bumping over the grass in their direction. The two officers had got out and, along with the Reverend Jeremy, were almost upon them. The Vicar's chin was well forward, his face set; his wavy brown hair had been flowing out with every step and it lifted once more as he turned to speed his delegation.

There was a rapidly building mass of people, a surreal farrago of angry residents and rabble-rousers. The threatened householders seemed oblivious, prepared to stand scrubbed shoulder to tattooed biceps in the desperate fight for their cause.

Victoria was becoming surrounded. The two Panda policemen, one young, one more solid, spoke rapidly into their talkies then started yelling and ordering people to stand back. Jeremy's mouth was open, but he held his fire as Tim shouted hysterically at the policemen, 'Just you two? What's happened? We were promised more cover than this.'

'Carriers on the way, sir,' said the younger officer with a neck skinny as a tortoise. 'They'll be here any second, grills and all the riot gear, but you'd be wise to leave. There's a very disruptive element, we hadn't expected it to be quite like this.' Why hadn't they? Marty had told them. 'We're from the local station, you see,' he said, turning to Victoria as if in answer. 'Any riot info goes through C-squad, it's different channels.'

The Reverend Jeremy could hold his tongue no longer; he had an angular inquisitive face, a long nose, the glinting eyes of a zealot. 'Just picture the destruction and havoc! Nature's rhythm and all its harmony, the balance and beauty.' He seemed oblivious to the mounting mayhem. 'This is a quiet peaceful community.' Not today, she thought. Scuffles were breaking out and the crowd was swelling as more and more people caught up.

Tim asserted himself. 'I really must insist, Vicar, the Minister has to leave. And I think you and your group would be well advised to do so, too.' Some of Jeremy's troops were already edging clear; there were missiles being thrown.

He wasn't to be silenced. Turning fervid eyes on Tim, he snapped, 'It's only a skirmish, a small rebellious element – newcomers – it's hardly surprising that strong passions are being aroused. Sam Swayne's people will soon have things under control.'

A scream rang out, so piercing that the older officer hurried away. A face-pulling lout thrust two fingers close to Victoria's face. Sheer panic took over. Her thoughts were for the baby. Angie had just forced a way through and Victoria turned and clutched her for protection. 'You hang on, soon get you clear,' Angie spoke soothingly. She was a strong, dominant woman and Victoria had never needed her more.

Angie was her shield. Solid and fearless, she was pulling, practically lifting Victoria along. 'Keep your head down,' she ordered. 'Leave the rest to me.' Tim was pleading for space to be made.

'You've got a lot to answer for!' a woman shouted. The voice was so loud and clear Victoria froze, but she instinctively looked up and turned to where it had seemed to come from.

It was only a split second of time, a single framed moment. Then something came hurtling through the air from another direction, quite unconnected, and hit her on the side of her head. It hurt; it made the dull sound of a heavy object, hitting the ground with a thud.

Everything was sounding muffled. She felt pain, dizziness; there must be a sudden storm, the light had all gone. Why weren't her legs supporting her? Why did she feel so limp?

Was it Angie shouting? 'DO something, Tim, for fuck's sake! Call 999. Get an ambulance. Get out of the way, can't you all? Get the hell out of the way.'

'She's coming round.'

Tim and Angie's faces were peering at her. 'What happened?' Victoria said, focusing on them. 'Did I faint? I'm really sorry.'

Someone was propping her up, a navy arm: a policeman. 'You were hit by a stone, we think,' he said. 'It was a very bad scene.'

'Thank God you're all right!' Tim exclaimed.

'An ambulance is just arriving,' Colin said. 'We need to get you to hospital. Can you stand? Tim, can you take her other arm?'

'There's no need for an ambulance. If you can just help me to the car – Bob's car, I want Bob.' A feeling of hysteria was building. Where was William? She needed him. 'I want my mobile, where's my bag? I must have my bag. I need to make a call.'

Colin had tight hold of her. 'We have to get you to hospital urgently; you might go unconscious again, any minute. It happened to a friend of mine – a cricket ball that time – but I'm sure in your case it could be the same.'

She wasn't listening, she was distraught. 'I want to call, it's urgent. I need to call . . .' It had gone so black again; she was feeling awful, so ill, unable to see, terribly sleepy.

CHAPTER 40

William was waiting to give the tribute at his friend's memorial service. He loved St Bride's Church. Built by Wren, the media's spiritual home for over five hundred years, its rebuilt interior was light and fresh, helping him regain perspective. His anxiety over Downsland was dissolving and dispersing like a pill. He had hoped for a text from Victoria before having to switch off his mobile in church, but perhaps his slight lingering feeling of unease was fanciful. The police would be out in force; she had responsible people with her.

There was one more hymn before his address. The front pews were facing and his friend's widow and two sons were opposite. They looked very drawn, close to breaking down. It had been a brain tumour and William felt for them. He would make enquiries, he thought, and see they were financially cared for.

It was probably some instinct, but he had another quick look at his mobile before they stood for the hymn. There was a text, from Margie, and it came as a ghastly shock.

Terrible accident at Downsland. He stared, it couldn't be. His chest tautened, his breathing became short; he could feel the shock in his very sinews. His thoughts became more concentrated; he had to let down his friend's poor family and go, just get there.

He had to call Margie. No one had that number – it was his mobile kept exclusively for Victoria. He remembered Margie had bought it for him, she must have retained the number and been trying to reach him by any and every means.

The congregation stood and began singing 'Dear Lord and Father of mankind.' The vicar looked over with a reminding glance. Avoiding his eye, William slid out of his pew and went up the aisle to the back of the church. He had seen Carl Hancock there, earlier. 'O calm of hills above . . .' How many verses left? He could feel the vicar's eyes on his back, 'Interpreted by love . . .'

Reaching Carl, gripping his arm, he said, 'You've got to do this for me. Just get down to that pulpit and give the poor blighter a rousing good send-off. Say he was unique, a helluva guy; say any fucking thing. Tell them I had a crisis. There's been an accident, I've got to go.'

Carl was looking astounded. William let go of his arm, shoved useless scribbled notes in his hand and ran. The hymn was ending as he pushed on the heavy door. '. . . O still small voice of calm.'

Bringing up Margie's number he sprinted to where he hoped Dave would be waiting. He was, and he had the engine running. Dave was gesticulating at the car-phone. 'Margie keeps trying for you,' he said, pulling away from the kerb.

William grabbed the phone. 'For Christ's sake tell me what's happened, Margie.'

'Victoria's unconscious, Bill. There was a riot and she's been rushed to hospital.'

'But she's come round, surely? She must have. Tell me she's all right!'

'Not conscious yet, Bill. I'm dreadfully sorry. Here's George, he wants a word . . .'

It wasn't true, it wasn't happening. 'They think it was a stone,' George said. 'Big story. The riot didn't last that long, she was dead unlucky – sorry, wrong word. Sorry.'

William listened in frozen disbelief. He punched on the radio but a news bulletin told him nothing further. 'You still there, George?' he said. 'Can you get everything downloaded – every pic, every word? I'm almost back at the office, but going out again in a hurry. You OK to take over?'

George wittered on. William couldn't listen, couldn't stand it. He suddenly thought of Victoria's brother. He was a neurologist – he'd know. Would he be prepared to help?

'Give me back Margie,' he said abruptly. She cared; she had genuine feelings. Fucking George couldn't begin to understand. 'I want a doctor paged,' he told her. 'His name is Robert Winchwood, at St Mary's Hospital, Paddington. Give him that mobile number, the one you just texted, Margie. And cancel the day. Personal reasons – got that?'

'Yes,' she said. 'I've got that.'

William clicked off his phone. 'Dave, when we get to the office I need the car,' he said. 'I really want to drive myself.'

'Sure I can't help?'

'No, no. But thanks – you've been great. Can you shift it any more? I must get back.'

William shot into his office and grabbed everything Margie had ready. George was with her. 'You do know, Bill,' he said, 'just going there is all the proof anyone needs?'

'It's her life, George – *her life*. All that matters, everything there is.'

He had to get there. Every light was red, everything a disaster. Every street was clogged; he jumped lights, screeched his brakes. Better get to Wandsworth and make for the A3. He saw a newspaper billboard, *Victoria Critical*, and pressed his foot down harder.

Tim had been there and an official, probably Angie, too. Where the fuck had any protection been? Who had thrown the stone – a stone at his Victoria? He felt blinded by rage.

The doctors wouldn't know she was pregnant. That might really matter. Her brother could tell them. Robert could help get him in – would he even call?

Barney would be on his way, travelling the same roads. He wouldn't know them so well, not the back way to the Brearfield, to the hospital where Emma and Jessie had been born. Victoria *had* to make it, she had come through. William drove like a maniac, seized with an absolute need to get there before Barney.

Why wasn't Robert calling? Wouldn't a doctor, her brother, respond? Especially knowing the particular circumstances, as he must.

His mobile rang.

'It's Martin Whiting – Marty. Your PA gave me this number. I just wondered if there's any way I can help; anything I can do. I feel so responsible. If only I'd gone myself.'

'It's not your fault. Has she come round?'

'No, she's still unconscious. They think it's an extradural haemorrhage; she's about to have an emergency operation. The Brearfield has the only neuro-surgical unit in the area or she'd have had to be helicoptered to Southampton or London. So that's a huge relief.'

'And her parents, family – are they on the way?'

'Her husband is. Her parents are coming from Worcester and going to get Natalia.'

'And her brother?' William said it more to himself than Marty. He went on, 'Is Tim at the hospital? Would you feel able to tell him that I'm on the way there?'

'I've already told him to give you all the help he possibly can.'

'I owe you a lot,' William said. 'Victoria – we both do.'

He drove on. 'Death is only a new horizon,' the vicar had said in the memorial service only half an hour ago. He couldn't lose her.

Ursula had called earlier with birthday wishes. She was back from the school run and he'd been sure she would have heard about Victoria's site visit. When he advised against her going and warned of possible trouble, she had put the phone down on him.

It hadn't been entirely self-interested, he thought agitatedly; it had genuinely been for her safety, too. At least she would see that now – would she feel bad about it?

Shouldn't he call and check that she was all right? He would have been told of anything untoward. And he couldn't: not now, not possibly. Ursula was going to have to live through a media hell, her worst nightmare, but he wasn't moving from the hospital till he knew all was well. Shouldn't he call though, and try to explain? It was weak and dreadful, still not being able to face it.

His mobile rang and it was Robert at last. Not knowing him, it was hard to start. 'It's difficult, this,' William said, 'very personal, but I badly need your help.'

'I'll do my best,' Robert said. 'My sister hasn't put me much in the picture though.'

'She's pregnant and it's mine, not Barney's. I'm worried the doctors won't know her condition and should be told. Can you somehow get it through to them in confidence? Is that possible? I'm driving to the hospital. Victoria *is* going to be all right?'

'I know the doctor who's doing the operation, Gordon Bryant, he's first rate. I'm on the way too, almost there. You'll want to get into the Unit. When you get there, go to Intensive Therapy and ask for me and I'll see what I can do.'

William poured out his thanks. 'And the baby?'

'Trauma can sometimes bring on a miscarriage, not always.'

'Can you explain a bit about extradural haemorrhage?'

'There's a point on the side of the head where the skull's very thin, and if it's hit by a heavy object, a stone say, the build-up of blood puts intense pressure on the brain. It's life-threatening if it's not operated on quickly. We're lucky she was so close to a neuro-unit.'

Driving on, he felt a little better. Robert had accepted what he'd said and would do what he could. Was he right to be feeling some hope, or was it just Robert's professional calm? Would the operation be in time?

Robert was almost there but was Barney? It was so vital to be ahead of him; William hit the short stretch of the M25, single-mindedly concentrating on speed. He had the memory of not being in time to see his father, feeling he could have driven faster.

The needle was on 110 when he first heard the siren. The police car forced him to slow to a standstill. He gripped the wheel. A shadow appeared at his window. He slid it down.

'Have you any idea, sir, what speed you were doing?'

'No – I need to get to a hospital, it's a matter of life and death. Can you let me go?'

'Would you just step out of your car, sir?'

William banged his head in his hands on the wheel, then forced some control and got out. There were two of them and the other said with a fascinated air, 'It's Mr Osborne, isn't it? Would it be the Brearfield Hospital you're headed for, sir?'

They knew; they'd got the message. William tried to transmit his desperate urgency. 'I must get there, you must understand. Take me to court, do anything, just let me go now.'

They were exchanging looks. The first one said, 'I think we'd best give you an escort, get you there in one piece.'

William stared disbelievingly. But it would be a mixed blessing, turning up with an escort. He pushed his luck. 'That's fantastic, but you see, there'll be cameras, television. Could you perhaps, I know it's asking a lot, help me get in round the back?'

'We'll see what we can do, sir.'

They carved up the traffic with ringing sirens and got him in through the kitchens. They left him with fervent hopes she would make it and warm wishes of good luck.

He had avoided the television cameras but the hospital was swarming with reporters and once seen, he was done for. Photographed, chased, followed down corridors, he got to the Intensive Therapy Unit with a whole new and much less helpful escort in tow.

He rang the bell and a nurse came to the door with exasperation written all over her face. 'I've repeatedly asked for this passage to be kept clear.' She glared at him. 'Yes – what is it?'

'Robert Winchwood is expecting me.' Was she going to let him in? The reporters must be so frustrated in a mobile-free zone, William thought distractedly, desperate to pass on the extraordinary event of him there at the unit and appearing to have a genuine in.

A man with a slight look of Victoria – he must surely be Robert – came up beside the nurse. She glanced at him for confirmation then nodded at William to come in. She shot a look of fury at all the reporters. The relief at shaking off a heartless press was immense.

The Unit was hushed; nurses moved about silently, their shoes making slight squeaks on the shiny floor. 'I've negotiated a side-room for you,' Robert said, leading on. He was slim, dark-haired. William tried to gauge the degree of worry evident in his face. Robert appeared outwardly calm, but what was going on inside? Would he, as a professional, try to sound reassuring? Was it to be believed? Would he be straight talking? Could he really know? Oh, God, she had to pull through.

They reached a door. A nurse came and had a quick word with Robert then hurried away. 'Barney's just got here,' he explained a little wryly, 'I'd better go, but you'll be all right in this room. The nurses will look after you. I'll be back as soon as I can.'

'Have they started operating?'

'Yes, she's in theatre. You mustn't worry, all will be fine I'm sure.'

Alone William stared round the room. It was more of a cubicle. It had a grey plastic-leather chair with wooden arms, a bed stripped of all bedding. Without pillows the iron-poled headrest looked like prison bars.

They'd never find who threw the stone. A few people would be rounded up, charged with affray, released on bail, given a community sentence. William felt galvanic rage; he wanted justice, tougher laws, to fight woolly sentencing in the paper. He could if he kept his job, if all the media coverage hadn't already put the shits up Oscar. But the frenzy of press interest was only beginning, his dealings with Barney would certainly see to that.

Tim came and introduced himself, looking abjectly concerned. Victoria had painted him as a cold condescending fish; rather unfairly, William thought, but he knew they didn't get on.

Tim was unassertive, the wrong person to have around in the black hole of a Downsland riot. And his embarrassment at the peculiarly inappropriate situation, having to attend to a Minister's lover was palpable. It didn't fit the rulebook. But nor did letting down your Minister in a riot – and that, William thought, was the real cause of his distress.

The man had brought him coffee and a sandwich, but he was slow in leaving and seemed to want to talk. 'We were trying to get her away, but a woman shouted something accusing and it made Victoria raise her head and look round. The stone wasn't connected, not specifically aimed, we think, just part of the rioting and general fracas.'

'Thanks for telling me,' William said. When Tim had left and he was alone again, he worried about who the woman might be – but he didn't even know if Ursula had gone to Downsland.

A nurse came to say his office had called and he bought a phone card from her, to use in the room. He spoke to Margie. She said Oscar was after him, calling from New York, and that William's son was also anxious for a call.

William got through to New York with ease. 'I'm on a payphone that might run out, Oscar. Sorry to be causing a storm and making the news – it will go on a while, I'm afraid. But I had to come,' he said, and then added emotionally, 'I love her.'

'Jeez, Bill, I'm sorry. You stay right there. She gonna be OK?'

'They're operating now.'

'She's gonna make it, I know it. Take a few days – I'll see you right. I've told George—' The card ran out but William felt quite moved and heartened by Oscar's reaction. He called a nurse, bought more cards and phoned Tom.

'She will be all right, Dad? I feel so desperate; I can't bear to think what you're going through. It's all on the news though, I saw it at lunch, and Mum's going to take it so badly. The very fact of you caring so much as to be there will make it all the harder.'

'I'm having a few days off work, Tom, and if she'll have me there I'll be at home and doing all I can to try and explain. I feel completely distraught at hurting her. Perhaps it was funking it, not telling her before, but it's so hard to know what's best. I had to be here but it means the end of Mum's privacy – and yours. We're public property now. We'll be offered up like a bag of sweets for the nation to pick'n'mix from. I'm truly sorry, Tom.'

'I do understand,' his son said. 'You'll call when you know anything?'

William sat in the plastic leather chair. He drank Tim's cold coffee. The sandwich stayed in its wrapping. He thought about Victoria on the operating table. Were there complications? Wasn't it taking longer than it should? Robert had come and explained about drilling a hole to release the pressure of blood.

He saw a shadow; a nurse had come in. He rose to his feet but she waved him down and sat on the bed opposite. 'Don't you fret now. And you must eat that sandwich.' She came and touched his arm. 'I'll be away now and be bringing you fresh tea.' She had a soft Irish accent, a gently full face, and he fought an impulse to hold on to her hand.

Barney was in the Unit. The reporters would have told him exactly who else was, too, William thought, and he was no fool; he would have played to the cameras and put his own spin on things. He would go to any lengths, tell any lies. All being well with the operation it would be best to go back to the flat, call Ursula and then carry out the plan with Barney. There was nothing now to lose and it had to be done before trying to make amends at home.

He got up and walked to the window; it looked out on to another hospital wing. Directly below was a small dank square of grass and a few benches. There were people in dressing-gowns and student nurses having a smoke. Some of the reporters were there, too, busy on their mobiles. If he did it the way he planned, William thought, it would be giving the story new legs and energy, a whole new extra dimension.

There was a knock on the door and opening it, he knew instantly that the man facing him was Victoria's father. Nattie was there, too. She came in shyly, holding back a bit and blushing. William wanted to put her at her ease but he couldn't, for a moment, think of a thing to say. He had been right, she'd been the girl in the lane, but he hadn't seen her face and hadn't imagined it so lovely; it was so trusting and open. Amber brown eyes, wide as her mother's, and a mouth that turned up at the corners; he knew all her problems, so much about her, but words just wouldn't come.

She smiled hesitantly. 'Not much longer, my uncle says.'

William nodded and then did what he'd been fighting all this time, what was quite unforgivably awful; he covered his face with his hands and broke down.

Pulling himself together quickly and blowing his nose into a hankie, he looked up with a weak grin. 'Sorry about that,'

'It's all the waiting,' John said. 'We haven't been here long. But I think the operation has gone fine. She should be back from theatre any time now.'

'I'm afraid I've made things harder for her by coming. I'm sorry, I hope you understand.' He turned and said to Nattie, 'Sorry about cracking up like that.'

'I'm sure it's a good thing to do,' she said. 'Did you have to get through all those cameras?'

He told them about being stopped for speeding and coming in via the kitchens with the policemen. They smiled through their worry, and John said they'd better get back to the others – that they had just slipped away on the pretext of getting tea.

Robert returned and said the operation had been successful. Victoria was in another side-room and William could come and see her, but it would be a while before she came round.

Looking down at the slim mound of her body under a neat tight sheet and grey blanket, he dared to dwell on what might have been, had she died. He would have become desensitized, he thought, more cynical and brittle – the way he had been going before they met. Victoria knew how to soften his hard edges. And he knew how to stiffen her backbone over Barney, but that had to be without her knowing.

A crisp white dressing covered most of her head; her eyes were closed and her face had no colour, even her lips were blanched. Her arms were outside the sheet, palms down; he rested two of his fingers on the back of her hand. Robert was still with him and the Irish nurse was in the room too; they both noticed. Victoria's eyes stayed closed but he fancied her lips had the hint of a smile.

William parked the office Jaguar on a meter in Northumberland Avenue; it was after nine, still light and very humid. And still his birthday – he had forgotten that entirely. Driving to London, he had been raging about Guy Harcourt leaking Victoria's Downsland visit to the press, but foremost in his thoughts were his plans for Barney. He arranged for GD to come to the flat at eleven.

First thing of all was to call Ursula. Exhaustion was setting in and he hadn't eaten. William knew there were no right words, no excuses. With Victoria out of danger he could feel the shame; like rain trickling down his neck, steadily soaking in, making him utterly wretched. He should have called to warn her. The media would have been plaguing her; she'd had the afternoon school run and couldn't have escaped them. He hoped his daughters were all right.

He had a mission though, and it was such a dramatic high-risk strategy, so all-consuming, he postponed even the shame. He was suddenly very hungry and went into a brightly lit fast-food café and bought a baguette with salad and ham spilling out. People were looking at him; he was in the news. The press would be waiting outside the flat.

They were there in their numbers. 'Why London, Bill? You were so close to home.'

'Mr James says his marriage is rock-solid, Mr Osborne. Mr James says . . .'

Resisting a strong temptation to press his baguette in the face of the Mr James parroting reporter, William punched in his entry code instead. Inside his flat he poured a glass of whisky. It seemed sensible to see the news headlines before his call to Ursula. They led with Victoria, the operation and the riot. There were flashes of Barney and her parents arriving, detailed medical explanations. And then there was Barney, in the studio, being interviewed by a political commentator.

'You must be a relieved man tonight, Mr James.'

Barney affectedly pushed back his hair. 'It's too awful to contemplate what might have been. Can you believe it's my wife's fortieth birthday? I had a special dinner planned.'

'We understand that the Editor of the *Post*, William Osborne, was at the hospital all afternoon. Did you see him? Why do you think he was there?'

'I didn't see him – and I think you'd better ask *him* that question, not me.'

'But you must be aware of all the rumours about Mr Osborne and your wife?'

'Victoria and I couldn't be closer,' Barney smiled. 'Our marriage is very strong.'

The interviewer left it at that and didn't press him and William, in a burst of furious frustration, violently pinged off the set.

The phone was ringing and the answer machine picked up. He listened as Ursula said bitterly, *I'm assuming you won't actually be sleeping at the hospital and I'm sure you haven't considered coming home. I'd like to think you owed me the decency of a single call after what you've been doing all day, but perhaps that was expecting a little too—'*

He grabbed the phone. 'I'm here now, sweetheart, and I'm so very sorry. And tomorrow I'm coming home.'

CHAPTER 41

William stared at his half-eaten baguette. Ursula's hurt had been there, fresh and acute, but it was her icy control, her barrier of composure, that was leaving him feeling so flailed.

She had asked after Victoria but with an edge. 'She's going to be all right now, your Minister? And you said you were coming home tomorrow – why's that?' He had spluttered about his need to explain, to beg forgiveness. 'No, I didn't mean that. It's a working day, you're not going to the office?'

'Oscar suggested a few days off. I'm not sacked, as far as I know.' That could change, he thought, if things got out of hand with Barney.

'Why did you go to London tonight then?'

'There's one thing I still need to do. Do you not want me home tomorrow?'

'Is that one thing going back to the hospital – she wants you there, holding her hand? Can't you see through it?' Ursula cried, the cracks beginning to show. 'She's a politician; she's using you, wanting good write-ups, wanting to shut you up over Downsland.

She's a ruthless career woman – not much of a mother! And she's got a loving husband. He was just on television and you could tell how much he cares.'

God, Barney could turn it on. William cursed. Ursula seemed determined to blame Victoria entirely, but with people's hearts going out to her at such a critical time, perhaps it wasn't surprising. He had minded the unfairness though. 'It's me you should be getting at – I'm the one to blame,' he proteseted, adding, 'Did you go to Downsland? You weren't caught up in any of the trouble, I hope?'

'No. I had no wish to see her. I'm sorry about what happened.'

The call had ended flatly with no further hint of her feelings, and it had been hard to fix a time of arrival the next day.

He felt an aching need of Victoria, alone in the flat with all its memories, it was a physical longing, too. He wanted to drive to the hospital, kiss her blanched lips, her bandaged head and rest his own on the pillows beside her. But now Ursula's needs had to come before his. He owed her support and loyalty, everything he could possibly do.

First there was Barney. It was nearly eleven and GD was due. He would have to get past the press and they'd know something was up. They would soon enough anyway, William thought when he went to Hartley Street early next morning and carried out his plan.

Surely there were other ways than a public confrontation? Barney might agree to a private meeting; he was a lawyer, certainly no fool, but it would give him the advantage of time and he'd be more likely to try and bluff it out. Doing it out in the open was risky as hell, but the only way. It meant more intense press interest, more agony for Ursula, a greater chance of losing his job. And it might not even achieve its objective. But it was vital he tried.

Suppose Barney refused to take delivery? At least, William thought, he would have been able to threaten him with the evidence and state the terms. He felt obsessed; Barney was a leech and he had to break the hold.

He took one of the Polaroid blow-ups out of his safe and found a suitable envelope. Then, full of adrenaline, he paced round like a sentry waiting for GD and war.

GD came in wearing his predictable anorak and carrying a small navy kitbag. Taking him into the sitting room, William demanded, 'You said nothing to anyone, coming in?'

'Nope – they wanted to know plenty though.' GD made for the sofa and sat down. He took out two black files from the bag and put them on the coffee-table in front of him.

William poured him a whisky. 'You've brought all the tapes, negs, everything?' GD got out a package and put it beside the files. 'You know none of this is for publication and you're never to breathe a word?'

'More than my life's worth,' GD grinned. 'You've made that clear enough.'

'And meant it,' William muttered, getting out his chequebook.

Taking his payment, pocketing the cheque without a glance, GD said, 'You look dead bushed, Bill. I'd have some shut-eye and a shave before you go round with that file.'

'That bit of advice comes free, I take it?' William enquired, impressed at GD's percipient working-out of the plan. Life under a stone hadn't seemed to dim his wits.

GD finished his drink and stood up. 'I prayed for her today,' he said. 'She had to make it. Good luck with it all.' William saw him out feeling touched and surprised that his lowlife snout had a human side and was even given to prayer.

Alone, he went into the bedroom and kicked off his shoes. He was aching in every limb; GD's advice of some shut-eye seemed like a good idea. He wondered how early Barney might leave and decided he should get there about half-past five to be sure.

He woke at four, well before the alarm. Feeling instantly alert and in the grip of a powerful sense of unease, he called the hospital. He wasn't a member of the family, he was told. Hell no, he was only the father of her baby. Clearly four-in-the-morning callers were potential hoaxers and the staff wouldn't relent. Their guardedness made him feel even more pent-up and concerned, and he asked if all was well with the baby. No one knew; he wasn't even sure the nursing staff would themselves know.

There was a long pause. 'I'm sorry, it's really best if you ring at eight when Staff Nurse is here.'

How early could he call Robert? Not at four in the morning. Feeling intensely frustrated and anxious, William showered and shaved and decided on a suit and open-neck shirt. He wasn't going to the office, but Barney would be dressed for work and the cameras would be trained. He made coffee so strong it tasted bitter, but it was a fast-acting fix of caffeine. With a refilled mug beside him, he sifted through GD's material and chose what to include with the Polaroid blow-up. Looking at it again and seeing the bruises, it shocked him afresh.

He printed off emails of all the papers' first editions to take with him to read while he waited. They were pared-down versions but sent every night without fail. Whether or not he was on holiday or taking a few days off, the Editor was always assumed to be around, never known to be away. It would be bad for discipline, an open invitation to slacking.

No press had arrived yet at that early hour. As he set off in the Jaguar, William thought he should call Dave about collecting it and get him to book a car for going home. In Hartley Street he parked far enough away to be sure of being out of sight from any window, and switching off the engine, he heard the birds in full-throated song.

One pressman was already there and others were arriving – the *Post*'s reporter, Sadie, and a cameraman among them. William was soon spotted and Sadie came over. He slid down the window and she gave a cautious grin. 'You about to challenge him to a duel then, Mr Osborne?'

'I've got something to give him. I'll come and wait with you all soon.'

He read the printouts of the papers. The dramatic events, the exposing of a great love affair, it was all there and played for all it was worth. But the press had been responsive to the public mood. After so nearly a fatal accident, the sense of outrage and sympathy for Victoria had been huge. No paper, not even the *Courier*, had dared to moralize. True, the *Courier* called him a 'family values' Editor and had used an unfortunate, down-at-the-mouth-looking photograph of Ursula, but that was about all.

He tried the hospital again but was told no more than was on the radio news. It struck him suddenly, with great alarm, that in all the numbing worry he hadn't taken Robert's numbers. There was nothing to be done but leave word for Margie to ask him to call.

At the gate the press were milling and crowding round, all with their eyes fastened on number sixteen, as though watching a key match on a pub television. There were more of them than usual; word must have got round he was there. William went to join them. Keeping right at the back, he tried to persuade them not to swarm into the garden, trespassing, when he approached Barney; that they'd get a much better picture if they let the meeting happen.

Barney came out of the house at eight. He hesitated – slightly preening for the photographers in his immaculate beige summer-weight suit – but it was probably more the sight of all the press. There was a wary look on his face; after the previous night's patsy television interview, the morning papers must have been hard to take.

He looked strangely sad and lonely, standing on his doorstep like a pop idol who'd lost his crown. William felt less active hatred; it would be easier to stay calm. Then he thought of Victoria's picture again and setting his face, he pushed through all the reporters – who were yelling questions – and opened the gate.

As it clicked shut behind him, Barney began shouting hysterically, 'What the hell are you doing, coming here, you great prick? Fuck off, get off my property!'

He came down from the step, waving away his intruder, but William went close and held out his envelope. 'This is for you. I'd advise you to take it, and I've also got a few things to say.'

A glimmer of panic showed in Barney's eyes, a slip quickly corrected. Conscious of his audience, he shouted out, 'Get out this instant, you jerk, you're trespassing – or do I have to call the police?'

'You might not want to, if you have a look at what's in here.'

William held out the envelope at a sideways angle trying to give the press their shot, then, since he reckoned he had about a minute to get his message across before they poured in, he began speaking urgently under his breath to Barney. 'There's a picture of Victoria's bruised body after you caused her fall, and plenty of proof of your other women – not great for your innocent-party image. I've got duplicates of everything, but if you give her a divorce and you're out of this house within two weeks, I'll never use any of it, ever. The alternative is that I throw the book.'

'Don't you come trying to threaten and blackmail me, you cunt,' Barney hissed.

The glimmer of panic in his eyes had become an unhinged glint, as though some part of him was uncoupling and freeing itself of any lawyerly constraints. William took a step back, more aware, having said his piece, of the press's shouted questions that had made it easier not to be overheard. 'You owe it to Victoria to treat her decently,' he added.

'What's he saying to you, Mr James?'

'Will you be seeking a divorce?'

Barney seemed oblivious to all the noise. And the glint was still there. He suddenly lashed out but with his foot, not his fists; his polished black shoe-cap shot up and caught William in the balls.

William doubled over in excruciating pain, gagging, his whole body instantly bathed in sweat. He let go the envelope and blindly, unthinkingly, swung up with his fist. It was more by luck than aim that he made contact; Barney reeled and a trickle of blood started from the corner of his mouth. He toppled backwards into a hydrangea bush but it was so sturdy it helped prop him up and prevent a fall.

As the press surrounded them, William was on his knees on the paving stones, scrabbling back the envelope and desperately trying not to be sick. People gave him a hand up. 'You OK, Bill? Christ, that must have hurt!'

He couldn't speak but he could think fast; he staggered on to the doorstep. Barney was too surrounded to stop him, and to his immense relief, got the muddied envelope in through the letterbox. It landed with a thud. He was swaying, about to be sick. The pain was unbearable; he was half-blinded by the sweat.

'Car's right close, can you make it?' Someone was supporting him; he focused and saw it was Dave. 'Word got round pretty fast,' he said. 'I sort of guessed you might need help getting away. Had me own key – I've moved the car up.'

'Thanks.' William's jelly legs began functioning and he reached the gate. Feeling more in control despite being shoved and showered with questions – everyone burning to know what he had on Barney – he looked back to see what was happening.

Barney was encircled too, being questioned and photographed. An elderly woman leaning over the party wall called to him shrilly, 'You should press charges, Barney, being invaded like this. Shall I get the police?'

'No need, Cynthia.' He sounded supremely irritated. 'No point. I'm sure this lot will remove themselves soon.' He was being bombarded though, and looking desperate.

William felt Dave tugging at him. 'Best if we get out of here,' he was murmuring in his ear, which seemed on the whole to be extremely sound advice.

*   *   *

Barney was frantic to get back inside the house. 'I'm making no comment at all so will you kindly stop trespassing and get the fuck out of my front garden. I'm going in now.'

'I'll bring you some tea, Barney.' God save him from Cynthia, he thought.

'Thanks, but I'm just fine,' he called cheerily, thrusting his key in the lock.

'What was Mr Osborne saying, Mr James? What's in the envelope?'

He got the door open and saw the wretched thing on the mat. He kicked it further in; he didn't want a long-armed reporter suddenly grabbing it. Then, finally, he was able to slam the door in their snivelling faces and have some privacy at last in his own home.

He touched his throbbing jaw and his eyes began to smart. The telephone was ringing and the envelope was at his feet. He bent down stiffly to pick it up.

The answer machine should be adjusted to have fewer rings, he thought distractedly, as the phone was persistent. He heard the message being left then. *'Would Mr James please call the IT Unit at the Brearfield? It's about his wife.'*

He hadn't phoned. He'd heard on the news she was fine and the sight of all the press at the gate had so shocked him he had wanted to get straight off to the hospital.

He instantly called the Unit. 'I was just on my way – nothing wrong, is there?'

'I'm sorry to tell you but Mrs James is bleeding; she may be losing the baby. She's very upset and doesn't want to see anyone, but do you feel you should still come?'

The nurses would soon have heard all about the fight, everyone would. 'That's the most terrible news,' Barney said with a catch in his voice. 'There's surely still some hope?' The nurse tried to be re-assuring. 'I've just had a bit of an incident,' he went on, 'or I'd have been there by now. Perhaps, in the circumstances, it's best if she rests and I come a little later. I'll ring her directly and tell her that.'

He was past caring what the nurses thought and he couldn't have faced the press again. All he wanted was to be alone, indoors and out of sight. He had to find a way out, some solution to the ghast-liness of it all and how to recover some ground.

She was losing the baby. Did Osborne know? He wouldn't be so tied any more – might he even be half-relieved? Might he end up staying put with his wife?

The envelope was still in his hand. He tore it open.

She'd never have agreed to that photograph, she couldn't have. Had Osborne taken it without her knowing? How could she have gone to see him so soon after that fall? Naked on his bed, encour-aging him to think the worst – it was so foully, cruelly disloyal.

Barney tore up the photograph; he tore everything up in a frenzy of rage – photographs of himself, of Mary and June; transcripts of tapes. He had been bugged and buggered, he thought; no doing-over could have been more systematic and comprehensive. How could Victoria have fallen for a man capable of that? He was a cunt, a runt – the scum of the earth. He should be exposed for what he was.

If he showed her the picture, Barney thought, he might see from her reaction if he was right and she hadn't known it was being taken. Might it shock her into seeing through Osborne and turning against him? But the photograph was ripped to bits. Shit, shit. Could it be pieced back together?

Suppose she did finish with Osborne though, would they be able to rebuild something? It would be easier without the baby. He stared down at the mess of torn-up celluloid and paper at his feet. But just suppose they did, wouldn't Osborne with all his vindictiveness want to get at them? He had duplicates of all those pictures; he could use or sell them. He had all the power of the mighty press at his disposal, every fucking trump card in the pack.

Barney drank some brandy then began clearing up the mess on the floor. The telephone never stopped ringing; he got fed up listening to the calls, and eventually pulled it out at the socket.

He thought about the alternative, acceding to Osborne's black-mail. In the circumstances he could hardly be blamed for ending his marriage. And if he was dignified and forgiving about every-thing, Hugh would certainly approve: his job shouldn't be affected. No one had known Victoria was pregnant. If she lost the baby, there wouldn't be that added humiliation.

Mary was keen enough and her father was even some sort of tycoon. He could take up with her after a decent interval and she might possibly be persuaded to join the firm and bring in new busi-ness. That would show them all.

But he wanted Victoria, he loved and needed her; she was the only one who understood. And he had his pride. The thought of giving in to Osborne made him feel as though he had maggots crawling all over his skin. Leaving without blame or recrimination would make Victoria feel really bad, given her nature, he thought, stricken with guilt; she would have to live with that, at least.

He felt more able to cope and took the carrier full of the torn fragments and put a match to it in the sink. When it was burned enough he turned on the tap, reduced it to a sodden pulp and chucked it all in the swing-bin.

If Osborne stayed with his wife Barney thought, he might still get his second chance, like Napoleon. That was the brandy talking, but such things did happen. The brandy was giving him strength enough to get through. He would call Victoria and say it was better if he came in the evening.

He looked round the kitchen. They had built it up together and he loved it, the little red Aga, the patio: the fig tree. The thought of leaving this home – even Cynthia next door – he couldn't bear it. Even the awful old sofa: he went back to it and sat down again. Bending his head, he tried to hold back the tears but then he bent it even lower and his shoulders began to shake.

CHAPTER 42

It was after nine. Victoria tried again but William's mobile still wasn't answering. She left a message with her bedside phone number. Could he have gone home already? It was all over the papers, unbearable reading for Ursula. Had he rushed there to try and make amends for the dreadful hurt, just as he had rushed to the hospital? Wouldn't he have called first and said so?

He had been there, in the Unit, all through the operation. Victoria's new friend, the Irish nurse who had come on duty at eight, had been wonderful, telling her everything. It had been something to cling to, succour through the shattering misery of the bleeding, comfort in her desolate state.

Could he have called and they hadn't told her? She pressed her bell hoping for the Irish friend but an unfamiliar nurse came – brisk, with tinted brown hair.

'Two of your family have left messages,' she said. 'Your husband's coming in the evening now, he's going to call you, and your parents will be here in half an hour.'

'Mr Osborne hasn't rung?'

'I believe he did in the early hours, but the night staff were anxious; you were very stressed.' Victoria tried not to cry. The tears hadn't stopped, her body felt racked.

All the pleading, 'Do something, help me, you can't let it happen, it's my baby,' and they hadn't even told her the one thing to have given her the will and the strength.

She felt another outflow of blood; it was the seeping away of hope, and her face contorted. She was losing Charlie, her baby; she wanted to die. She couldn't lose him.

A young registrar in a white coat had come from Gynae and stood at the end of her bed. Lanky-limbed, he had looked more like a sprinter than a doctor but he had been straight talking, which had helped. 'You could spontaneously miscarry or partially abort it. In that case, we'd need to do a uterus evacuation. I'm very sorry, there's no easy way to tell you this.' He must have seen so many women in tears, she thought. But many more, crying with joy, and she had wanted to be one of those. She couldn't lose Charlie.

He had said it was best she stayed in Intensive Therapy, in her little side-room. She was glad to be in the same place, just in case William came. Why didn't he call?

Her head ached so badly. The seeping blood needed seeing to and nurses attended to her. They warned about stress and said staying calm was the best possible thing. They gave her painkillers and promised there was always hope. Then they left her alone. Victoria lay still with her head turned to the glass porthole in the door. She needed so badly to see William there.

Her father and mother arrived and they had Nattie with them, too. She came with kisses and anxious smiles and sat on the bed.

'You could have told me, Mum, and trusted me. I feel quite hurt. Don't lose it – you can't, I can't bear to think of it.'

Victoria squeezed her hand; she had her wonderful daughter, her loving Nattie.

'I'm so very sorry, darling,' Bridget said, coming round the other side of the bed. 'I had two miscarriages, you know, but then I had you. I do wish you had told us though.'

'I couldn't; please understand. How was the hotel? Hemple Benton's a pretty place.'

'You don't have to try with us,' her father said.

'It was too olde-worlde,' Nattie observed, 'so dark with the leaded windows. People gave us funny looks at breakfast. There's a picture of us arriving at the hospital. But at least this fight of Dad and William's hadn't happened! It was just on the news.' Victoria stared, stunned. 'You haven't heard about it yet then, Mum?' Nattie said awkwardly.

'What fight? Was either of them hurt? Who started it?'

'Barney kicked him in the balls, it seems,' her father said, 'but William punched back. Not many details – it was early this morning, I believe. In the garden outside your house.'

'For God's sake!' Bridget exclaimed. 'Don't start worrying her with that at this time.'

She would be so hating the idea of a fight, Victoria thought, sensing her mother's discomfort. 'It's OK,' she smiled, 'I've got worries of my own. But did it sound very serious? You see, William hasn't rung.' Her eyes were filling and she turned away.

'A kick there is no joke,' her father explained. 'He's probably been vomiting and he could well have passed out. That might be why. I'm surprised he managed to punch back.'

Nattie was looking quite horrified and Bridget gave a furious frown.

Victoria couldn't think why William might have sought out Barney, but it sounded as though he hadn't gone home to Ursula yet; she would almost rather he was out cold than that.

Her mother tried to be reassuring. 'Darling, you've had a major operation. It's the trauma of that which is probably causing the bleeding. Try not to be too upset if it happens. You've got such a difficult time ahead – possibly a divorce to get through and not forgetting William is still married.'

That did it. 'My baby means nothing!' Victoria screamed. 'You don't care! It's tidier all round if I lose it, all the better since no one will have ever known.' She was distraught. 'My baby's not a blob, he's fifteen weeks; he's a boy. I can't lose him.'

Fresh blood was trickling; she could feel it. She couldn't stop sobbing. She wanted her parents, even her daughter, to go – to leave her alone to her utter desolation.

Her father understood. They had to get Nattie back to school, he said, but they were staying that night with Robert and would come next day. Rest was what mattered now. They wished her luck and prayed all would be well. She hugged them, telling them how much she loved them, saying she was sorry. And then the door closed behind them.

She felt her world and all her longings sinking like the evening sun, slipping into a black horizon. She couldn't lose Charlie; he was everything.

William would feel crippling guilt about Ursula. He would go home, re-establish his family ties, be with his children. She would be bearing her grief alone.

Flowers kept arriving and she ordered them away. She wanted her tiny side-room whose grey curtains didn't meet to be cold and impersonal. She wanted no one near, just to be alone with her thoughts of Charlie, to lie still, to cling to dimming hope.

She wanted William there, holding her; she needed him to be sharing the pain.

Why didn't he ring? Why had he gone to see Barney when she needed him? Had he passed out? Was he lying unconscious, with no one knowing? She reached for the phone in sudden panic but had to lie back again, gripped by a pain like a tightening tourniquet. Was it a contraction? Please not yet. Let it not be the end.

The Irish nurse answered her call and immediately came to her side. 'Don't you fret now,' she said in her tender-soft voice. The pain calmed down.

The telephone rang. 'It's Mr Osborne,' she whispered, smiling. 'I'll be leaving you just now. Your bell's right there.'

'Darling, I'm so sorry, I'm desperate – on my way there, fast as I can. I can't bear to think what you're going through, and no word from me. I called in the night but I met a brick wall. I couldn't even get Robert. And then there was a bit of bother with Barney.'

He was calling her 'darling'; he never had before. 'But you're all right?' she demanded. 'Why were you seeing Barney? I don't want to lose the baby. Help me, I need you.' She was sobbing, choking on the words.

'Charlie will hold on if he can, he'll do his best. I'll be there very soon. If only I'd known, if only I hadn't had this problem.'

'Like passing out, you mean?' There was a silence that made her almost smile.

'How the hell can you possibly know that!'

'My father was here. He'd heard the news and knew how it might take you.'

'I'm so livid with myself — only just made it back to the flat. Robert returning my call brought me round or I might still be conked out. I'm off work for a few days — if not for rather longer, now. And then I had to get hold of a car but Dave's sorted me out with his friend, Sid. I'm with him now. We're going great guns, nearly there. Love you.'

She felt his transmitted energy, his back-in-charge support, but he could do nothing to help. She let the phone droop in her hand and lay listening to the dialling tone. When she eventually put back the receiver it was with a sense of finality. The tourniquet pains were gripping again. Would it all be over before he came? Wasn't that for the best? He was known; his home was up the road, the Staff Nurse's sister probably taught his children at school. No one would feel comfortable with William there holding her hand.

The pains were increasing, coming faster, just like giving birth; it was what she was doing. The doctor came from Gynae. The Irish nurse held her hand. 'Don't you fret, you've someone who loves you; he'll surely be helping you grieve.'

He was going home. She would lose him, just like her baby. Her world and her womb would be empty, her heart broken twice in a day.

More pain. Another contraction. They kept coming, oh God. She was losing her baby, her joy, her future. No future for Charlie. He'd had no chance against the mindless violence of a thrown stone. She had caused his death; she had gone there. It was something she would have to live with all her life. People said kindly things that she couldn't absorb. He was lost, her longed-for baby; he was gone.

She felt suspended halfway down a well and the light at the top seemed more distant. Her eyes were dry. The nurses were kind, the doctors, too. She just wanted to be alone.

William came then. He was suddenly in the room. She had done with looking at the glass porthole and was lying thinking of nothing, just dark blank thoughts of emptiness, of loss and loneliness. Her body felt a carcass, barren, all the innards out. She had the back of her hand to her eyes.

'Darling,' he said, needing her attention and she took her hand away and stared. 'He'll always be in our hearts, always be loved.' William looked grey with fatigue, his eyes sunk in their sockets. He was talking almost as if she was free of her ties. But he was going home and it would be hard and effortful, trying to leave Barney and all the while living with loss.

He stood looking at her, but she turned her head to the window, her heart unable to cope. 'Let me in,' he said. 'I need you to, he was as much mine as yours. Must we have separate grief?'

'But you're going to Ursula now, you have to. I've got to manage on my own.'

He sat on the bed. She couldn't turn and look at him; she lay propped up on the pillows. Her body had no energy, it was limp and inert. He picked up the hand nearest to him and brushed it with his lips. Then he pressed it to his cheek and she felt it was wet.

She turned back to look at him and he smiled. He moved closer, and lifting her off the pillows, he wrapped her up in his arms. His cheek was wet but hers was dry; she hadn't cried since before giving birth to a baby who'd had to die. Their two hearts were beating but not her baby's, not Charlie's.

'Don't let go, hold me tight,' she said. 'I'm so empty, I feel so helpless.' She couldn't explain about losing him as well. Whatever happened, if he stayed with Ursula, he would have been there in a growing child. 'When you go I'll have only this moment to remember, this feeling of closeness.'

'I'm here for you, always — I will be when I'm at home. Don't be bitter.'

But she had to live with a death that she had caused. And Barney would feel there was hope; it would be harder than ever, leaving. 'Why did you go there and have the fight?'

'I didn't go to fight — but I did want to even the score. We've got some stuff on his women and I wanted him to know that. I thought it might be a way of encouraging him to do the right thing.' But Barney wouldn't be easily scared off by dirt on his women, Victoria thought. It might even help with salvaging his pride.

William laid her back on the pillows and studied her. 'I've got to go soon,' he said gently. 'I've had strict instructions not to tire you and not to be long.'

'And you've got to go anyway?'

'I have to be at home now and I don't know for how long. Nattie's holidays start in a couple of weeks — she'll look after you. Could you go and convalesce with your parents till then? You're as white as that dressing; you need loving care and Barney might have moved out in that time-frame.' He kissed her eyes. 'Keep Charlie close.'

'I went to Downsland against all the advice. I killed him.'

'I could have stopped you going, I think of nothing else — can't we share the blame?'

A nurse looked in to say she was sorry but the doctor was coming in a couple of minutes.

Victoria kept her eyes on William's exhausted face. 'Once you're home, you know you can't get in touch? I've thought about it hard and it won't work. We must be completely separate; no contact while you decide what's best for you and Ursula and your children. You're not beholden to me in any way, you have to think and act freely and be whole-hearted.' She thought William could see the sense, but she longed for him to argue and fight it.

'It's going to be hard,' he said. 'I needed to feel I could call. Oscar told me to take a few days, but we talked just now and he wants that stretched to include my summer holiday at the beginning of August. He thinks I need to get my life in order, which is patently self-evident. Oscar's been great, he's got a real heart bobbing around in that funny little frame – it really showed when I was so desperate yesterday.'

William kissed her and held her close. But then it was time. He stood up. 'I'm not having you getting your way completely. I'm going to email.'

'Don't – I won't email in return.'

He said from the door, 'You won't be laying down the law in future; you'd better be prepared for that.' He was hesitating, not leaving. 'Can you wait for me and have faith?' And then he came and gave her the kiss that would sustain her. Her tears streamed. 'Keep crying,' he whispered. 'Do it for me, too; I won't be able to at home. Keep strong and be patient,' and then he was gone.

She lay in a comatose state all afternoon, but as the time drew near for Barney's arrival, her senses sharply returned. She dreaded him coming. Trying to distract herself, she read a few of the cards from all the flowers, although still refusing to have any in the room.

There were so many: Marty and the office, Di and Gerald, Ned and Claire. Giulio Tourellini had sent flowers, surprisingly, and the Downsland Action Group had too. That hurt. Did Ursula know they had? Had she been there – was she the woman who'd called out so piercingly? There were flowers from the Prime Minister and Bob.

The Irish nurse came in with a bunch of blue cornflowers in a hospital vase. She was beaming. 'Mr Osborne says you're not to send them away, they're for Charlie.'

Barney looked through the porthole before he came in. She guessed he had taken a lot of trouble with his appearance; he was in light trousers and a linen jacket and was probably freshly showered and shaved. His jaw looked slightly swollen. He leaned towards her as though he might kiss her, but changed his mind and pulled up the visitor's chair.

'Is your head bad?' he asked, his eyes on the dressing. 'Sorry I didn't come sooner, but it was better not to. I'm sure you know why.' He picked at a loose thread in his cuff.

'Yes, it was understanding of you.' His well-pressed look was a protective front; she knew from the slight shake of his fingers that he had been drinking. She worried about him driving home.

He glanced round in a rather awkward way like a bystander, then looked at her. 'I suppose you've heard it all from his side?'

'I don't know what was said, only that it ended in a fight.'

He had a doubtful expression as though gauging whether to believe that. The light was hurting his eyes, she thought; he rubbed them and sat straighter. 'I had already come to some pretty fundamental decisions,' he began, 'which I'd thought should wait till you were better, but having it all out with him this morning, it seems I have to tell you now. Thinking he could order me around, trying to blackmail me with some underhand gutter-level newspaper smut. I mean, I ask you!' Barney attempted a lip-curling sneer, but it petered out.

'I told him he was wasting his time,' he muttered. 'Whatever the rights and wrongs, it's probably best I move out and give you a divorce and I told him that.'

She stared in complete amazement. 'But why did you start fighting him, then?'

Barney looked impatient, more his old self. 'It's hardly surprising, is it, that I lost it! The press were all there, he was bugging me; what do you expect? I'm planning to leave right away, within two weeks – if that's what you want?'

'Have you somewhere to go?' She thought he was longing for her to ask him to stay; his face was cloudy, as though his feelings had been shaken and hadn't settled again.

'I'm moving in with Dick, short term. He's on his own in that huge Holland Park flat.' Barney was sounding so spiritless, speaking almost mechanically.

'Dick will be glad of your company – and cooking was hardly June's thing.' Barney's dismissive shrug made her think June was out of favour. 'Have you told Hugh your decision yet?' she asked.

'Yes, I rang him. He's understandably upset but he thought I was acting decently. He's got an idea the firm should move, he was very full of that.' Victoria showed her surprise. 'It's Mandy's doing,' Barney went on. 'She thinks our offices have bad Feng Shui!'

'Don't knock it; it's a good idea. And you should take on one or two bright young female associates too, the firm is too male and middle-aged.'

There was a silence between them. Barney had become self-absorbed. He was being reasonable, dignified, an incomprehensible transformation.

He looked at her. 'You know I don't want our marriage to end, don't you?'

Had William really held a gun to his head? Surely Barney would have toughed it out about his women? She would never really know the truth of it.

'We couldn't have gone on,' she said, but she was beginning to see the anguish behind his eyes, the quivering within; he was close to breaking down. She put out her hand. 'We'll stay friends, won't we? I'll see you with Nattie?'

He dropped his eyes to her outstretched hand. Taking it, he rubbed at her knuckles with his fingers. 'What about convalescing? Won't you need some help?'

'I'm planning to go to Mum and Dad's. The doctors say I might be back at my desk in a couple of weeks – that's if I still have one.'

'I'll take my personal things, but at some stage we'll need to sort out furniture and finances and things.' She nodded; they'd manage that side. He had put down a small carrier that she'd thought was chocolates or a duty gift. He reached for it and handed it over. 'I think this belongs to you.' He couldn't look at her: his eyes went to the floor.

Feeling the weight, she knew it was the silver mermaid. 'Oh Barney,' she cried and let out the tears; her heart couldn't take it, the goodness he was finding, the sadness.

She thought of him driving back from the hospital, having to pack up and leave. She thought of the kitchen he loved that wouldn't be the same without his wonderful cooking. He would put on a confident show though. And Nattie would sense his need and be sweet. But would he be all right?

Wiping her eyes on her nightdress sleeve, Victoria reached out again and took his hand. 'I'll see you Saturday – you're coming with Nattie, aren't you?' she asked anxiously. 'But this is our private goodbye. We'll remember our good times, won't we? We've been through so much together.'

CHAPTER 43

The nights were the worst; long hours of steady misery.

Di came to visit. She looked disgustingly tanned and had on a pair of tight white jeans and a clingy pink top. Victoria sat up, smiling. 'Are you trying to show me up?'

'It's a hot summer out there and painting façades is an outdoor job. I wouldn't mind a bit of indoors – this new client of mine is as dishy as they come!' She looked round. 'Those cornflowers are dead – don't be too morbid. There's an appalling OTT arrangement arrived for you, you could always have that to replace them.'

'It's from Roland Chalfern, but it won't help him,' Victoria said, feeling confused at the remark about the cornflowers; not even Di knew of the pregnancy. 'Ned will deal with Downsland himself now,' she went on, 'he certainly won't give Guy Harcourt the responsibility. I saw in the papers that Guy's been fingered for leaking my visit and he's getting a rough ride. He's certainly owed one.'

'I suppose you won't let on what you would have done?'

'Going there had made my mind up for me – whatever else it did.'

Di gave her a look. 'Don't be too cross or shocked,' she said, 'but I do know about the baby. William told me, he needed to let it out. I'm very sorry. But I think you should take on board the glaring fact that he loves you. He's hardly acting like a man who's looking to stay with his wife. He rings me – it'll be fine.'

Victoria thought it wouldn't be fine for long. He would be with Ursula night and day, something he'd never done in all his busy newspaper-world life. His children would soon be on holiday, it would be proper family time and the ties could prove too strong.

When Di had gone she sank low again and felt she was deeper down in the well.

She had other visitors, but it was a struggle to smile, even for her Chairman Giles and Margaret when they came with a bag of cherries and homemade gooseberry jam. Apologizing for all the trouble she'd caused, she asked if there were many 'Disgusteds of Ferndale'.

'Hardly one,' Giles assured her. 'There's plenty of speculation though.'

'I should tell you, Barney and I are getting divorced,' she said. 'It's very amicable. Will it be accepted in the constituency, do you think?'

'Taken as read, I'd say. Even Jason's sanguine. He's had his work cut out with all the excitement. I told him to be thankful we're nowhere near an election.'

'Will you and William eventually get together?' Margaret enquired.

'Now, dearest,' Giles said, 'you know how much your daughters hate those sort of questions!'

They soon left. She was glad to be alone but the Irish nurse came to say she had another visitor. 'It's good to see people,' she said chirpily. 'I'll be away now and bringing you some tea.'

She was gone before Victoria thought to ask who her visitor was, but it turned out to be the one person she longed to see. 'Marty! You shouldn't have come. And in all the Friday traffic.'

He made a smiling, deprecating gesture. 'It's wonderful to see you're really on the mend. I can never forgive myself for what happened.'

'Stop it, Marty – not another word! I'm the one who caused it all, not you. Come and tell me all about the office.' She patted the bed near the visitor's chair.

He gave her the Department gossip and talked of her direct concerns. 'I believe the Secretary of State intends to overturn the Inspector's report and find against Downsland. He thinks more weight should be given to the environmental objections and that the absence of sustainable transport infrastructure is of critical importance.'

'It'll be a popular decision.' It would have been hers, too, she thought. Going there, seeing for herself had changed her mind at the eleventh hour. For all the crying need for more housing it hadn't been the place for a Downsland. Balancing needs was the hardest thing of all.

'And MDF, Marty?' she queried. 'Weren't we due some feedback?'

Depressingly she was still getting a bad press over the issue; all the carping and sniping had never really stopped. Opinion columns talking of interference, nannying: kow-towing to the unions. That decision, too, had been a tight call. Had it really been the right one? It wasn't a thought she could ever share.

'The manufacturers are producing alternative fibre boards,' Marty was saying, 'and we do believe that the larger DIY stores at least, will absorb much of the extra cost. I think it's safe to say no one's in open revolt!' He re-crossed his legs and his eyebrows jumped. 'There's something I'd like to tell you if you'll forgive me. I had a call from Mr Osborne – please don't look so alarmed! It's just that he and I have communicated once or twice in the past months. I thought he probably wouldn't have told you though, and he's confirmed that. I'd – well, known about the relationship for so long and it was helpful to make contact.'

She felt overwhelmed and bemused. What he was saying was impossible to absorb, 'You shouldn't have had that burden,' she found herself saying. 'I feel quite overcome.' But it was making her think of William and her wounds were too raw. She changed the subject. 'I can be back at my desk in two weeks, they say, but with this reshuffle I'm sure to be moved or removed.'

'I very much doubt the latter. But I see a move is possible; we'd be so sad to lose you.'

'Perhaps we might have lunch from time to time?' she asked.

'Yes, I really do hope so.' He stood up. It was time for him to go. Another loss. It was a near-certainty she would be given a different job, if one at all. Another person who had meant so much to her was walking out of her life.

'Thanks for everything, Marty – and for more than I ever knew. I'm sure though, your next Minister will give you a far easier ride.'

'I shall miss all the excitement,' he said, 'all the bumps and thrills. I might have to take up hang-gliding or jet-skiing.' He gave her his gentle, alarmed-looking smile. 'I'm sure things will turn out well; the future holds so much for you.'

It would hold nothing, she thought. Nothing at all.

CHAPTER 44

Faced with the prospect of an enforced sabbatical, six long mind-stifling weeks, William had impulsively decided to try and pack in a book. He was working on it in his study and thinking of titles. *The Freedom of the Press: Liberty or License?* Too long, *Press Liberties* might be snappier. As both poacher and gamekeeper, he had a unique slant, but finishing it in the time would be a test, especially with the two-week Algarve holiday Ursula had booked. It helped that *The Firing Line* was on its summer break, and working late suited him – especially in the present circumstances.

He was glad of his study, a small room beyond the kitchen and laundry area that had two big windows; he could live with the washing-machine's rumbling crescendos, he had his music and also the television that Ursula had thought anti-social. He'd persuaded her, though, that he had to see Sky News; it went with the territory.

His desk overlooked the garden, but staring out at Jessie lying on her tummy on the grass reading a book, he thought it should be facing a blank wall; it was hard to concentrate. Books were his younger daughter's great love. They were also her refuge and escape, and he worried how hard it would be to know if she was feeling badly hurt and left out.

Emma had more bounce-back capacity; she was much the more talkative and outgoing child. When they'd got home from school the day of his return and found him in the kitchen, she had raced over with a big hug and kiss for him. 'All those press people said you were here, Dad. I didn't know whether to believe them!'

Jessie had hung back, scuffing the skirting board with her heel. He'd smiled encouragingly. 'Come for a hug-a-rug, Jess?' They often had a three-way hug. But she'd turned and rushed through the open kitchen door and out into the garden, leaving him with a sinking sense of panic that he might have irrevocably harmed a close, precious bond.

Emma had needed reassuring that all the press attention would be over when she started at her new school in September, but she was soon off phoning her friends. William had gone after Jessie then, knowing she would be with her guinea pig, Elton. No little bundle of shaggy black fur could have had more love heaped on its ginger-streaked head.

She had slipped her pet back in his cage as her father approached, and sat hugging her knees. He dropped down on the grass beside her. 'Sorry, Jess, about all that's gone on. I love you so much and it really hurts if you're upset. Can I try and explain a little?' She had shaken her head, turning it away, but then nodded.

Had he said the right things? He could never know. At some point she had edged closer and crept her hot little hand into his.

'I shouldn't have got involved, Jess, and let Mum down but there's no going back. You'd like Victoria; she's kind, she's got deep feelings just like you.'

'Will you go away and leave us now?' she mumbled.

'If I did, Jess, I'd see you lots and love you more than ever.'

She looked up with her limpid brown eyes. 'They said she could have died. It would have been a murder if she had; I hate thinking of that. I've got you a birthday present, but Mum says it's best to have them at supper. I want to go and wrap it up now.'

She had rushed off, almost bumping into Ursula, coming across the lawn.

'Is Jessie still upset?' she asked, looking very slightly complacent as he got to his feet.

'She's gone to wrap up a present,' William said tiredly. 'Not that I deserve one.'

That first supper with the embarrassing present-giving felt like weeks ago, but it was only days. Ursula had let nothing ruffle her composure: not an entire media camped at the gate, nor all the humiliating extra publicity over the fight and a second trip to the hospital – not even his unslept haggardly condition. All the grief and stress and barely any food in two days had left him shatteringly exhausted.

Jessie had made him a fat candle with her candle-making kit and stuck it in a small round leather box. 'It's for your desk, Dad.' He'd told her all about the book he was planning to write that would mean working late into the night. Emma had bought him a smart slim wine guide and he promised that, too, would come in incredibly useful.

Ursula's present had been neat; he had to admire her style. She'd found an early edition of Evelyn Waugh's *Scoop* – an irreverent satire of Fleet Street. The mad hunt for hot news seemed just the right touch of sarcasm. The Brearfield antiquarian bookshop was Jessie's great love; she really seemed to feel the romance of rare old books, even at ten, and could spend hours in there.

They had got through another two weeks. Tom was home for the summer; he had a holiday job in a local bio-chemical lab and William was glad of his company at weekends. His top A-levels had got him the job but he was dead-set on art as his career. He would be doing something he loved, William thought, looking at his watch and flicking on the lunchtime news. Ursula shouldn't worry, he'd do fine.

The news was full of the imminent Government reshuffle. There was talk of Victoria's excellent recovery and her expected return to work next day, speculation about possible jobs she might get. It seemed taken as read she wouldn't be sacked.

Their relationship came up. She was said to be separating while he had gone home to his wife. There was a shot of her leaving the hospital, though it had been two weeks ago. She was wearing a beret as her head had been shaved for the operation.

He got up and put on Albinoni's *Adagio* and stood listening to the music for a few minutes. Then he went to his other window and stared out at an apple tree. Thoughts of Victoria's intense grief and their last kiss never left him. His own grief grew steadily and was causing tumultuous rage. It was the riot; he felt so utterly impotent about it.

He craved Victoria with a yearning that pressed like lead weights. It was such bleak heaviness, his smiles and grins were as a clown's mask and he padded about, an intruder in the house, trying not to expose his feelings or cause cracks in the façade.

The nearness of loss, staring into the abyss the day of the riot, it was as sharp as yesterday, but he had gone away and left her in her hour of greatest need. Why? He could have come home, told Ursula it was all over, talked to the girls and packed a bag. What was the unfinished business keeping him here, play-acting and pitting his wits against Ursula who was in any case the more skilled at it?

It was in part insecurity about Victoria's feelings for Barney, he thought. Even Di, his lifeline to the outside world, who he talked to often, hadn't managed to be especially reassuring. He'd asked casually, 'Am I right still to feel worried about Barney's hold?'

'Good God, I hope not! I'd like to think she had more sense than that.'

But he had forced Barney out, sure that Victoria would never do it by herself, and now his own actions bothered him. Doubts were creeping in. Had it been the right thing to do? Could the bizarre hold he'd had on her, so distressing and incomprehensible, still be there, however tenuously? He imagined Barney worming his way back into her sympathies when they met with Nattie, like the true conman he was. No, it was right to have walked away and given Victoria space, William thought. He'd needed to feel certain it was truly over with Barney.

There was his life to be sorted out, too. What was the blockage in *his* system that made him so incapable of looking Ursula squarely in the eye? Was there a hidden inner-self that saw the practical benefits, the creature comforts, of a large country home and life of minimal complications? Battery-charging weekends, easy relationships with his children, everything done for him – the weekdays his own for unsociable living or falling in love as he pleased. Was he subconsciously clinging to a selfish possibility of just seeing Victoria in the week? Was it as shaming and simple as that? Surely not.

He realized with intense relief that the idea was anathema to him. Victoria was everything. That was the whole problem and it was directing him back to his guilt.

Ursula's hurt was bitter and apparent – but where was the heartache, the agony and fury, the passionate fighting against rejection? In the eighteen days he'd been home he hadn't once found her wet-eyed. He couldn't imagine that she still felt any love for him, so why then did she want him around? If it was to punish him, William thought, by making it harder to leave, then where was the glint in her eyes, of satisfaction and revenge?

Did she have a sophisticated awareness of how much better off she was as the wife who'd won through than a forgotten, cast-aside divorcée? Or was it just a basic human need to hold on to what was hers, and for the children's sake?

Before his heartrending departure from the hospital he'd had hardly a thought for what went on inside Ursula's head. He'd certainly never considered asking. Now his guilt wouldn't let him alone; he wanted to feel clean and clear, free of the past. The future was holding out her hand.

He went back to his desk with a sense of losing his footing on a sheer mountain face. Emailing Victoria was his life-saving rope and he sent another, deleting it afterwards as a precaution. He had tried to keep all the emails light but this time he poured out all his feelings with greater intensity.

The Government reshuffle next day was in his thoughts; he missed the office acutely. As he sat nursing his frustration, a couple of emails came through and he saw there was one from Victoria. It was her first. No reference to his, no matching of passion, but it was a chink. *Just back at Hartley Street and couldn't eat for a week after all Mum's cooking! Barney's left neat notes everywhere – all about trip-switches, mains taps and plant watering. Very sad. Nattie's off to stay at a villa in Italy with her friend Maudie soon. I'm glad but I'll miss her lots. Waiting on reshuffle, bad for nerves! All love. No reply.*

He couldn't delete it. He sat back feeling quite shaky. *Very sad.* Why had she put that? Fuck Barney. She was everywhere in the room. Thinking of her made him think of Charlie, too, and with such a lump in his throat he could hardly swallow.

The telephone rang and he sprang to it like a nervous gangster, but Victoria would have called the mobile.

It was Jim at the office. 'This reshuffle,' he said, 'I'd love a word of advice. I know we've always shoved the boot in and George is a bit iffy, but I think Chris Hartstone's doing OK now. I want to press for him staying in place and just wondered what you had against him, if you knew something I didn't – anything I'm missing?'

'No, and I think you're right; he's an original thinker – just one who gets up my nose! But that's entirely personal. You could turn it to advantage, say we were his sternest critics but we've been persuaded, that sort of stuff. What do you reckon for Victoria, Jim, what's the talk?' No reason not to ask now, he thought.

'Culture's a strong contender or Social Security. George thinks Education.'

'Unlikely that, with a daughter at boarding school. Tell George plugging Hartstone will give me quite a surprise – he'd like to feel he was chalking one up on me.'

'He should be so lucky!' Jim gave a congenial snort.

Jim was working there on a Sunday. It felt like being outside a bakery, looking in. William could smell the office and it was painfully luring. Putting back the phone he sensed he wasn't alone. Ursula had come in and stayed near the door. 'Lunch is ready,' she said. 'Who was on the phone? What was all that about boarding school?'

'It was Jim Wimple, about the reshuffle – and whether Victoria might get Education.'

'I can see day-school for her daughter might have been inhibiting for her,' Ursula said sharply. 'Well, I expect you can pass on Jim's views.'

'I haven't spoken to her since I've been home,' he said truthfully, and added when Ursula made no comment, 'I'll be there in a tick for lunch.'

It had been a small chink in her impregnable front. He thought he would tell her at supper that he couldn't possibly go on holiday with them all, he'd never get the book done. It might prompt some sort of reaction, more dropping of her guard.

He worked hard all afternoon. Tom came in towards evening. 'You up for tennis, Dad?'

'It'll be bad for my morale,' he said, glad of a break. 'I'm so short of sleep!'

'Getting your excuses in early?'

It was the hottest summer for years, still sticky and humid. The sun was low and drowsy and the garden's one magisterial oak was casting long shadows over the lawn. The pink-gold evening light was exquisite.

They played two sets. Tom won both. He said grinning, 'I'll get the drinks, Dad; you sit there quietly and recover.' He came back with cans of Perrier and sat beside his father on the garden bench. Leaning forward on his knees, he turned to look at him. 'What are you going to do, Dad? Life's quite tense around here, you know. Something's got to give.'

'I'm not going to go to the Algarve, I'll never finish the book on time.'

'Couldn't you work on it out there? It is Em's and Jessie's hols. And Mum's been through so much – couldn't you just manage to go somehow and give her a nice time?'

Surely Tom could see that a sexless holiday in the sun would hardly do that? He must so hate the strained, wrought-up atmosphere though. William smiled at him. 'In answer to your first question, I do know what I'm going to do – but all in good time.' Tom's raised eyebrow was a look of quizzical resignation at that.

They went in to clean up and were soon having supper, all the family together.

William said his piece as the girls doled out ice cream from plastic tubs; he had thought it best they were there. '. . . So I'm truly sorry I can't come. Perhaps your mother could take my place, darling?' Ursula's violety-blue eyes flashed. Her mother coming on holiday with them had been an early bone of contention, but he'd felt he was owed a little marital privacy. Relations with his mother-in-law, never easy, had been on an accelerating downward trend. Hardly surprising, but it pre-dated Victoria.

Emma was looking at him in consternation. 'You can't not come, it would be awful!'

'Dad's got a deadline, it's not easy for him,' Ursula said smoothly, taking over, 'and it'll be so nice for Gran. Family holidays mean so much when you live alone.'

Jessie kept pushing at her cuticles with her little thumbnail.

'Well, I'm stuck at home with my lab job,' Tom said, 'and Dad

around is really going to cramp my style!' Emma enjoyed that. He
was so good-hearted, his father thought.

'At least I can help Tom with looking after Misty and Elton,' he
said. Jessie's head shot up and he regarded her gravely. 'You'll leave
me lots of instructions, Jess, about what Elton likes?'

'Lettuce,' she said, 'and carrots. Not cabbage, much.'

In the early morning he was shaving with the radio on and heard
his liaison with Victoria being discussed yet again, its effect on her
reshuffle chances. Ursula left the bathroom. Reading Jim's copy at
breakfast she was watching him and he minded.

It was a relief to escape to his study, but hard not to feel distracted
and in a mood to prowl. He sent Victoria an email and then set
about researching anecdotes for his book.

The reshuffle appointments came through at noon. There was a
Cabinet change at Defence. Many people had been expecting
Harcourt to be promoted, not least Guy himself. Instead he went
to be number two at Social Security.

Victoria went to Health. It was praised as a sound move. She
and the Health Secretary dovetailed together nicely, the commentator declared. Nick Bates was to take over from Victoria at Housing,
a good promotion: sensible continuity.

She was interviewed. Seeing her cropped hair for the first time,
William thought she looked irresistible, absurdly young. Ursula came
in. She stood watching over his shoulder with her hand on his chair;
if it was to shame and frustrate him, it was succeeding only in the
latter. She left as quietly as she'd come in though, with no flouncing
or sarky parting shots, and her silent dignity made it hard to evade
any feelings of guilt.

Victoria talked of being sad at leaving her old job, but delighted to be working with Chris again. William cursed. She confirmed divorce plans, said it was amicable but then cleverly blocked all other personal questions. And then she was gone.

He jumped channels. He wanted more of her, he needed to hold her; he wanted his hands in her short spiky hair. He didn't want her anywhere near Chris Hartstone.

Then he went to the kitchen where he and Ursula had a bite of lunch, just the two of them – some pâté, salad and cheese. The girls were off swimming with friends.

'Not what was thought for her, then?' Ursula remarked, watching the lunchtime news.

'No,' he agreed. It was a big job, a restoration of faith, but he didn't say so.

The Algarve holiday was in days. The girls would love it; five villas round a pool and two other families they knew. He would have loathed the lack of privacy but had clearly forfeited any say. It seemed odd though, and hurt him slightly, that since Ursula appeared to want the marriage to survive she should have chosen a holiday he would absolutely hate. It was a selfish thought; the girls' needs had to come first.

When they got back he suggested a game of croquet. 'We haven't played that in ages!' Emma said. 'Singles or pairs?'

'Mum's got research work to finish.' He glanced enquiringly at Ursula who nodded. 'Singles, every man for himself.'

'Dad! Person, woman – per-lease!' They hammered the hoops into the striped lawn; he had mown it at the weekend. 'Will you see Victoria when we're away?' Emma asked.

'Only if Mum and I were splitting up, Ems.'

'Are you?' She stood staring at him in her shorts and sockless trainers, mallet in hand.

'Mum and I haven't talked it all through yet,' he said without flinching.

'She thinks you'll get over it. When I asked if you were splitting she just said marriages went through bumpy patches. When Zoe's parents split they told her everything that was going on, we heard all about it at school.' William shuddered at the thought. 'You'll have to talk to her,' Emma said as though it were as easy as pie. 'You're being so polite and avoiding.'

'I'm not playing this stupid game.' Jessie threw down her mallet and ran towards the house. He and Emma decided, a bit half-heartedly, to carry on playing.

He didn't work late on his book that night, but went up to bed at the same time as Ursula and into the bedroom. He had been sleeping in the spare room, saying it wasn't fair to come in crashing around and disturbing her at three in the morning.

With the holiday in two days she had a half-packed case open on the floor. She had on cotton cut-offs and a man's-style shirt and he stood watching her undress. She had a good body though she would never show it off; he had long given up on any attempts to influence her choice of clothes. He thought her crippling conventionality was the product of a straight-laced upbringing, the conforming diplomatic circles of her parents' world.

'Why are you staring?' She had turned to face him.

'I was admiring you.'

'Are you warming up to saying something?'

'We have to talk. I know you don't want to. You needn't say

anything, but can you at least listen? I'm sorry, but I'm leaving you. I'll see you're not short of money or expect you to move.'

'You're saying you want a divorce?'

'Yes.'

'And if I refuse?' She sat down on the bed in her bra and pants and stared up.

'It would just take longer and be harder on Emma and Jess. I'm desperately sorry, darling, but we can't go on.' She went on staring, white-faced, expressionless.

It seemed more of a shock to her than he'd expected. He had been so unutterably wet, he thought, funking it at every turn, making her feel, for all the passionate dash to his paramour's bedside, for all his abandonment of appearances, that in the end, like so many others before him, he might just possibly have stayed. 'I'm sorry,' he said, 'so sorry.'

'Have you given a single solitary thought to your children? Don't they come first? Do you have to be so thoroughly selfish as well as lying, cheating and breaking my trust?'

'At least you're blaming the right person at last,' he said, relieved at a sign of her temper.

'She's such a paragon, isn't she, your Minister? Isn't a tame newspaper editor really quite handy? Is it your age, your vanity, not seeing through someone like her? And how can you ever trust her when she's done it to her husband with you? Some example you're giving to Tom – he'll think it's perfectly fine now, to move on if ever the fancy takes him. I've brought up your children virtually single-handedly and now you throw it all back in my face.'

'That's not fair – you could have stayed living in London, but you chose the move to the country. I had to be near my work.'

'Does it always have to be the woman who bends, who gets carried along, making sacrifices, and then gets carelessly dumped? Does it?' Her eyes were steely.

'No, and I tried hard to commute,' he said, 'and when I got the flat, I wanted you with me but you so seldom came. We could have got live-in help, your mother offered to come more often. Leaving me alone so much almost encouraged me to fail you.'

'It always ends up my fault,' she said bitterly. 'Being so obsessively wrapped up in your pointless, ruthless newspaper world had nothing to do with it, I suppose? Silly of me, imagining that at least I could trust you.'

He resisted an urge to defend his profession. 'You stayed loyal, I didn't,' he said. 'The blame is entirely mine.'

She bent her head, her hands covering her face; it was painfully hard.

He dropped down beside her. 'Darling, you must see we can't go on? Ems and Jessie will be OK. They have eyes, they're not fools, they know it's not just a bumpy patch.' She didn't answer, she was openly crying. 'We'd reached a fork in the road, years ago,' he said. 'Your mother saw it, she's always blamed me for our separate paths.' Ursula had brought her hands to her face again and he touched one gently. 'Try and see things positively. There's so much life out there.'

She twisted away in a furious gesture. 'Don't you go patronizing me!' she shouted. 'Don't you dare use that superior tone! And her divorce might be "very amicable" but yours won't be. I won't let her anywhere near my children.'

'They'll have to meet her in time and she isn't at all as you'd have her. Try not to be bitter, sweetheart, for their sakes – I know it's a lot to ask.'

He stood up, he ached for her not to hate Victoria. 'I'll talk to the girls in the morning. I'm so very sorry, but can we be OK together when I come and see them?'

'"How should I greet thee? – With silence and tears",' Ursula said tightly.

As he went to the spare room, William wondered whether Ursula spouting Byron was a good or bad sign. Either way, the tensions and resentment, the difficulties over seeing the children were going to be huge.

He took them all to Gatwick in the morning; Ursula's mother was coming by train from Hove where she lived. Emma clung to him saying goodbye but not Jessie.

They had gone out alone together the day before, he and Jess. They'd taken Misty for a walk and he had talked as his heart dictated. He'd told her that if people grew apart they developed new lives like plants divided in the garden, but that his love for his children was indivisible. They were his very being. He would write special letters and send special books, see her really lots. She hadn't said a word but her arms had been tight round his neck as he kissed her good night on the last night of his marriage.

Back home from the airport he walked round the empty house. He packed and loaded up the car. He wanted to leave immediately. Tom was at work but he would persuade him to come to London, he thought. They could talk then and Tom could drive the car home.

William looked up the number of the Department of Health, put it in his mobile and went out in to the garden, to the bottom of the lawn. He sat on Elton's solid wooden hutch. Jessie had taped a set of back-up instructions to the door. Tom had just better take good care of the little thing, he thought. He looked back at the house. His eyes were pricking and he rubbed at them. Then, with a feeling of held-back elation that was surging and straining at the leash, he pressed the green button on his mobile and got through.

Victoria had felt incredibly lucky at being given a serious job. No sacking or sidelining – unlike Guy, who wouldn't be pleased with his backroom slot at Social Security. From her new desk she had an impressive view, though nothing to match William's at the *Post*. He must be badly missing the office, she thought, collecting papers, preparing to go up to her new Secretary of State.

It was time for Prayers. Minister's meetings were very different now, Chris Hartstone so much more hands-on than Ned. It was getting late but she was distracted for a moment, thinking about her previous day's working lunch with Jim. He had mentioned a call to William who, he said, was expected back in the office in days. That had surprised her, but she thought Jim must have been talking in vague terms.

No email from William that morning. Had he gone off on his family holiday – had he decided to make that the cut-off point? His emails had talked of love, very emotionally, but had he finally known in his heart that his loyalties lay with a wife of twenty years?

It was five weeks since his sustaining goodbye kiss at the hospital when his support had stopped her from going completely under. The pain of losing the baby was still all-encompassing: her life would have been so joyous, and a part of William would have been hers for ever, whatever happened.

Her new Marty came into the room. Avril was in her late forties but ageless; she had a completely unlined face and sprinkled-grey hair. 'Just a reminder,' she said. 'It is ten o'clock.'

Victoria sprang up. 'Christ, it's not! Thanks for chasing me.'

After the meeting Chris kept her back for a quick word. 'Can we get you over for supper tonight? It's very short notice, I know, but my new young special adviser's coming.'

'Love to,' she said a bit tiredly. It wasn't a thrilling prospect.

She went back to her office and had just sat down at her desk when Avril buzzed. 'There's a call for you, William Osborne. Shall I put him through?'

'Yes, fine,' she said, trying to keep the tremor out of her voice and control her heart's thudding. What on earth was he doing, ringing the office? Why not her mobile? He must surely know calls to the office were always monitored?

'Sorry if you're busy,' he said, 'as I'm sure you are, but it's quite important.'

'I'll get back to you,' she said, desperate to get him off the office line.

'I just need to know if you're free tonight – well, every night actually?'

The office was hearing every word; she couldn't think straight. 'I'll call back,' she said coolly. 'I might be a couple of minutes.'

She got through to Chris's office with fumbling fingers and asked to speak to him if it was convenient. He came on the line. 'I've had an unexpected call,' she said. 'I won't bother you with it now though I may need to later. But I'm really sorry, I can't come tonight.'

'Don't give it a thought, it was just if you were free.'

She *was* free, Victoria thought, free as air with no ties. Was it right to be blithely thinking of taking on new ones? William was a tough man in a hard world. However much she loved him, sanity told her his tactics weren't always to be trusted. He might do things she disapproved of, things that shocked and affronted her. 'Have faith,' he had said, and he hadn't let her down. He had his faults, she thought smiling. No one was perfect . . .

She called back. 'You do know the entire Private Office was hearing that call?'

'Of course. But they need to know what's happening in your life, things that particularly affect them.'

'Such as?'

'That if you'll have me, it'll mean another burst of press, ongoing coverage, clashes of interest, and the *Post* might be no less a thorn in your new boss's side. How soon can you get away?'

'I'm supposed to be having dinner tonight with my new boss and his wife.'

'But you've just chucked him and I desperately need to talk to you. I have to know you're really sure. How soon?'

'I do have to work a full day.'

'It's August, for God's sake!'

'You could spend the afternoon booking two flights to Milan this weekend, and a particular hotel room if possible. From memory it was 507. You asked me a long-term question last time we were there and I said I'd answer it in the future. I think the future's here at last.'